He was

He observed her over his glass, a hint of amusement in his eyes, and the part of her that relished the freedom of her anonymity wanted to test her boldness against his arrogance. But the wiser part dared not, and she returned to her card game, aware that they were sitting too close. Not that body contact could be avoided in the tight space between his chair and hers—it was inevitable that part of her would touch part of him—but he could have moved his legs.

"No doubt you were raised by Gypsies," she said. "If I want a cow stolen or a man's throat cut, I'll be sure and contact you."

His eyes glowed warm in the candlelight as he gave her a lazy smile. "Why? Do I look like a murderous Gypsy cow thief?"

She looked at him sharply, wondering at that very possibility. With his black woolen cloak and floppy hat worn low over his eyes, shadowing his bearded jaw, he could certainly pass for a highwayman. She remembered the gun she'd seen him wearing earlier, and knew he kept it in a sheath against his chest.

"Are you?"

Other **AVON ROMANCES**

Coming Soon

And Don't Miss These
ROMANTIC TREASURES
from Avon Books

Melody Thomas

Wild And Wicked
In Scotland

AVON BOOKS
An Imprint of HarperCollinsPublishers

AVON BOOKS
An Imprint of HarperCollins*Publishers*
10 East 53rd Street
New York, New York 10022-5299

Copyright © 2007 by Laura Renken
ISBN: 978-0-06-112959-9
ISBN-10: 0-06-112959-3
www.avonromance.com

First Avon Books paperback printing: January 2007

Avon Trademark Reg. U.S. Pat. Off. and in Other Countries, Marca Registrada, Hecho en U.S.A.
HarperCollins® is a registered trademark of HarperCollins Publishers.

Printed in the U.S.A.

10 9 8 7 6 5 4 3 2 1

For Debbie Pfeiffer, Anna Jeffrey and Linda Kampshroeder, my critique taskmasters, for burning the midnight oil to help me shape this manuscript into a wonderful story. I owe you for your support and your magnificent wealth of knowledge about grammar, Scotland and life in general.

To my agents, Annelise Robey and Kelly Harms. Thank you for your intelligent insight and encouragement in an industry that can be chaotic at times.

And finally for my son Ross across the world. I am so proud of all that you do. I love you.

Prologue

Hampshire, England
Spring 1874

Cassandra Sheridan's finest hour had turned sour as a lemon. A tart one fresh off the tree. The shivery bitterness hurt more than she'd imagined possible. She would not display emotion, certainly not in public on a night when all of England seemed to be watching her every move.

A tall clock at the far end of the glittering ballroom marked the midnight hour, the official end to the night. Dressed in a shimmering Worth gown of the finest glazed amber satin, Adelaide Mary Cassandra Sheridan, sole heir to Magnus Steel and Shipping and future bride to the heir of the Hastings ducal dynasty, looked away from the clock's opalescent face. She found the resources to keep her features blank, refusing to allow anyone to see that she was anything less than the Yankee Ice Princess the

British rags had anointed her upon her arrival in England a week ago. The stories had continued to follow her trek north.

Amazon. American.

She'd heard those words, accompanied by snickers, less than an hour ago in the ladies' drawing room.

"Dear," her mother whispered. In gentle reassurance, she leaned over and grasped Cassie's hand, holding it between the press of their skirts. "You have not danced."

Cassie had no interest in dancing. At ten inches over five feet, towering to six feet when standing tipped on her toes, she could look down on most every man present. "Really, Mother." She worried a speck of flint from her white glove. "Don't embarrass me more than I already have been."

"It's important that we show a brave face, Adelaide."

Cassie disliked the name Adelaide, though she'd once been told she'd been named for Queen Victoria's oldest daughter. She preferred Cassandra. It was her beloved grandmother's name. Cassandra was also the mythical love interest of the god Apollo, purveyor of music, poetry and all things exemplifying manly youth and beauty. Only her mother called her Adelaide. Her closest friends and her father called her Cassie.

But here in this cold part of England, instead of friends, she had three hundred acquaintances who wanted nothing to do with her. Curious onlookers who had come to Sinclair Hall to glimpse the American bride of one of England's most sought-after bachelors, the Earl of Hampstead and future Duke of Hastings, Devlyn St. Clair. No friends hovered among the flock of snobs who considered her, with her height and uncultured accent, an oddity. "It is no wonder his lordship chose not to make an appearance," she'd overheard more than once over the course of the evening.

Lord Hampstead had made her the butt of every joke among England's elite at her own betrothal ball. The seat of honor beside her sat empty because her fiancé had not made an appearance. She'd been horrified to learn the crowd had wagered on whether or not he would appear. Especially after he'd failed to show at the docks in Liverpool to meet her for the first time.

Ignoring the drone of whispers gathering in force behind the colorful array of fans pressed close to lips and hiding snide glances, Cassie remained with her hands folded, her features calm as if she wouldn't rather dry up into a dust ball at her feet or be anywhere but England. Anywhere but talking gardening with her betrothed's beautiful mother, the duchess, an Italian countess in her own right, her foreign accent more aristocratic-sounding than her mother's slight Virginia drawl.

"You must come to our home in New York in the spring," Cassie's mother said. "If you love roses, I must give you cuttings of ours to add to your collection."

The tart-faced woman next to Lady Hastings pursed her lips at the mere suggestion of mingling the flower varieties. Her mother attempted to enlighten the dialogue with additional talk of flora and fauna, which was promptly dismissed. "Our roses have been bred and groomed on this land for five generations," the duchess politely explained, expanding on the beautiful gardens surrounding Sinclair Hall.

"So have ours," Cassie said. "They are bred from sturdy stock. Enough to last another five generations if properly nurtured."

The duchess turned to Cassie. "Have you knowledge of roses, Miss Sheridan?"

Having offered little to the conversation tonight, she felt herself redden as Lady Hastings stopped talking to observe her, the diamonds in her dark upswept hair glimmering softly in the light. Cassie had finally drawn the interest of the one woman in the room whose attention she did not want. "I understand color is only part of the many elements that make a perfect rose, Your Grace. Every petal brings to the flower a diversity that makes each bloom unique. Variety brings strength."

"Perhaps to some it is less important to be unique, Miss Sheridan, than it is *not* to be different," she quietly offered. "A lesson some of us must learn, *sì*, Signorina Sheridan?"

"Naturalmente," Cassie replied, having studied Italian in the desire to impress the duchess, though the language was also part of the music she loved. "But neither should one underestimate the power of diversity, Your Grace."

Lady Hastings raised the silver-stemmed quizzing glass to her eye. "No." Her mouth turned up gently at the corners. "I believe one should not."

"Have you perhaps seen the newest genus of lily, Your Grace?" her mother asked, only to have her query interrupted as someone turned to Lady Hastings with another question about roses, essentially excluding the "foreign element" in their circle.

Their loss, Cassie thought as she returned her gaze to the ballroom floor. Her mother's knowledge of flora was extensive. Gardening was her passion. Give Samantha Ambrose Magnus a weed to nurture and she would create a flower. It was her special gift. Securing a flawless blossom for the Magnus Sheridan family tree—the title Duchess of Hastings—was, after all, why Cassie was here in England. Wealth might not buy entry into society, but it could purchase a dukedom. As if that would bring her mother the deference she so desperately sought among the Knickerbocker matrons in New York.

As Cassie watched the colorful swirl of dancers on the ballroom floor in the way an artist studies an all-too-familiar portrait, she realized not for the first time in her life the hypocrisy the cheerful tableau presented. There was a sameness to it all, and something so beautiful on the outside should not be capable of hiding the ugliness inside. She would never understand her mother's need to be accepted by such people.

With a subtle shift of her chin, Cassie looked through crystalline windows to the outside. Low hills clustered against the pale misty moonlight. Doors to her left opened onto a marble terrace that stretched into the darkness of the surrounding woods. The stars beckoned as they had all night. Before her mother could stop her, she bobbed a curtsy to the duchess and made her exit onto the terrace. She loved her mother, but if Cassie heard her say one more time that Sheridans did not admit defeat, she would rip the diamond tiara out of her hair and feed it to the many sheep that dotted the parkland.

Once she was outside, her satin-slippered feet carried her past an ivy-covered wall and down the stairs into the gardens, her train dragging behind her like a carpet. She took the gravel path around the back of the palace-like hall. Every window blazed a brilliant gold in the thickening mist. She could hear muted laughter as a couple sought privacy beyond the tall box hedge. Another couple stood near the gazebo, but she ducked away before they spied her.

Yanking her snagged train off the prickly rose-bushes, she hurried her pace and walked toward the side of the house where she hoped to find a servants' entrance and secretly escape to her chambers. She didn't know where her father was. He had been livid earlier, and he and Lord Hampstead's father had disappeared behind closed doors to discuss their respective off-springs' future.

People were laughing at him as they were laughing at her, and she was indignant on his behalf. She wanted to reassure him that it was not in her heart to shame her family as Lord Hampstead had shamed his tonight by failing to attend his own ball. So how could she tell him that, from her perspective, there couldn't possibly be any worse fate than marrying the duke's scapegrace son?

During supper, she had heard rumors that her future husband was not a willing participant in this betrothal. That he might not even be in England. She had heard other gossip as well about Lord Hampstead's character and nefarious past. The little she'd gleaned was not reas-suring to a young future bride who knew little about men on any level and nothing at all about Devlyn St. Clair, an obvious blackguard who was rumored to dally in shady activities and who kept a mistress. As far as Cassie was concerned, he'd lost all status as the romantic figure who had received the British War Medal while serving under Charles Gordon in Peking, and who had worked as a dignitary in Russia three years ago.

She only knew that Lord Hampstead was old, at least nine and twenty, maybe even thirty. The only image she had of him had been taken before he'd joined Gordon's services years ago, an image produced when he was closer to her current age.

She'd carried the silly portraiture with her for a year. She pulled it out of her bodice and gazed down at the dark eyes of the man to whom she was betrothed, yet had never met. A man her young mind had framed into a shining knight of impeccable character.

Love was truly an illusion. A fraud perpetrated on foolish girls by romantic troubadours who had nothing better to do than stare at moonlight and create fantasy.

Until tonight, she'd believed she would find pleasure in her future through fulfillment of her family obligations. Now, as she stood alone on the gravel drive that stretched miles into the mists, listening to the fading chords of a waltz behind her, she was no longer sure of anything but an acute sense of loneliness and a desire to escape into a life of anonymity.

How would it feel to dress in simple clothes that did not fit someone's social standard for decorum? Or to be able to leave the house without an entourage, sometimes armed, anywhere she went?

Indeed, how did one run away from a privileged life and become a nobody? Or, at the very least, someone people wouldn't ridicule?

Where did one go to truly experience life? Suddenly her heart raced. Her closest childhood friend, Sally Ann Maxwell, the daughter of the American ambassador to England, was vacationing in Scotland until summer's end. Cassie had not seen her friend in almost a year, since her betrothal.

But her parents would never allow her to make the trip to Scotland, certainly not alone, she thought dismally.

Yet, her heart lifted at the prospect of seeing Sally Ann again and maybe even her older brother. Closing her eyes, Cassie let the hush of the late night air fan against her upswept hair and wondered what would happen if she carried out just one defiant, daring act in her life.

Chapter 1

⁓⌯⁓

Naked blades flashed silvery blue in the moonlight. The sound of clashing steel grew louder as Devlyn St. Clair drove his opponent out of the shadows and into the moonlit clearing, the eerie tableau surrounding the deadly duel framed by the nearby family cemetery. Holding a saber in his black-gloved hand and a short-bladed Kinjal in the other, he circled his opponent, his tall boots soundless in the grass. He could hear distant shouts coming from the sprawling stone manor house.

"I will see you flayed alive this night, Hampstead," his foe boasted. "My father will hunt you down himself, then he will find my slut of a wife and slit her throat."

A faintly mocking smile curving the corner of his mouth, Devlyn broke away from the attack. "And you are a man of your word, Stefan. I have witnessed just how committed you are to carrying out your father's orders. Count yourself fortunate I need you alive."

Devlyn Holt St. Clair had gone by many names in his

lifetime, most not real. Personas he donned like an actor on the stage. But tonight's performance with Ivanov was real, though executed prematurely, an unfortunate circumstance precipitated by the man's wife's untimely visit to Devlyn's bedroom last night.

He knew Ivanov's intent was to anger him and make him careless. Devlyn's intent, on the other hand, was to get Ivanov away from the house so Devlyn's men could grab him. But he felt the bloodlust burning past the walls of his restraint. Stefan Ivanov was a vicious, murdering bastard who had brutalized his own wife tonight. Devlyn had found her barely alive.

Stefan attacked with a roar. Devlyn stepped behind the riposte and slashed his saber across the other man's blade. They'd leapt off the terrace earlier, and the battle now carried the two men across the back stretch of the yard. People began spilling out of the house. Without pause, Devlyn ducked, whirled and faced his opponent, slamming the saber against his opponent's blade. The sound of sliding steel hissed, until they stood nose to nose. "Your father killed the wrong bloody brother, Stefan," he rasped in a cutting whisper. "He should have come after me."

"Dominick was a traitor, Hampstead. Your brother was a—"

Devlyn swung his fist, hitting the Russian across the jaw and felling him. Ivanov rolled and, barely evading a fatal blow, slashed with force at Devlyn's shoulder, tearing through his cloak and shirt into flesh and sending a riptide reaction through his body. The saber flew from his hand. He stumbled backward. Stefan pursued him. Devlyn brought the Kinjal up to counter the attack, struck out with his leg and knocked his opponent off his feet. Utter fury filled him.

He launched himself toward the prone man, only to be dragged away. "Stefan is down," his partner rasped. "He's no good to us dead."

Devlyn braced a hand on his legs. His chest heaving, his breath coming in gasps, he struggled to think. "Get him in irons, Rockwell." He felt a warm stream of blood down his arm. "Now."

But with a roar, his black hair wet with sweat, Stefan rolled back to his feet. Devlyn shoved away the hands holding him. The man just would *not* bloody go down. Promising retribution, the Russian raised the saber high above his head, a Cossack aiming for the final lethal thrust.

Devlyn reached behind his back and caught more of his cloak around his forearm, hoping to deflect the attack, the pain in his shoulder forgotten. Stefan was skilled and very dangerous, a cold-blooded killer. Unfortunately for the Russian, so was Devlyn. At the last possible second, he deflected the sword with his remaining strength. As Ivanov spun to attack again, Devlyn impaled him through the chest. For a moment, they swayed together like dancing lovers, and Devlyn feared he might go down beneath Stefan's heavier weight.

"Enjoy hell, you bastard," Devlyn rasped. He yanked his Kinjal free. "And know that your father is next."

Blood stained Stefan's teeth. "You're a fool, Hampstead." His laughter caught on a sputtering cough. "You still do not know who betrayed you."

He dropped to his knees, then fell sideways into the grass. "Good God, Hampstead." Devlyn's partner was suddenly beside him, dragging him away. "You've killed Nicholas Ivanov's *son*." A cloaked hood covered Ian Rockwell's dark blond hair, but did not hide the look of disbelief in his eyes. "Bloody damn hell, Hampstead, the Americans wanted Stefan alive. Lord Ware guaranteed him alive."

Devlyn tossed the Kinjal to the ground. "Where is Maria?"

"She is safe," Rockwell answered. "For the moment. I got her out of the house."

Blood streamed from the wound in Devlyn's arm into his glove. He turned on his heel, his cloak swirling around his calves as he strode toward a horse trailing its reins near the cemetery entrance. "If Stefan's father finds her, he'll kill her. Take her west to Whitehaven. It will take you three days to get there. The local innkeeper works for us. I've already arranged to get her out of England. Stay there until Jameson contacts you."

Rockwell's long stride brought him to Devlyn's side. "What will you tell the Americans?"

Devlyn, while having no desire to be castrated in the cesspit of international politics, couldn't care less who wanted jurisdiction over a murderer. Stefan's powerful father would now be hunting the breadth of England for him and he had to reach his superior. Devlyn bent with difficulty and procured the reins of his horse with his good arm. "Lord Ware left for Edinburgh a week ago on his way to Balmoral," he said. "I believe he is stopping to meet with the American ambassador, who is in Scotland for the summer." He faced Rockwell. "Did Maria retrieve the papers from the safe?"

Rockwell hesitated. Beneath his long cloak, he still wore his formal dinner attire, a jacket and silver waistcoat and a neatly turned tie. They had both left the night's diplomatic dinner hosted by the Earl of Woodhall after Devlyn had received a note from one of Maria Ivanov's servants that Stefan had beaten her nearly unconscious.

Devlyn had ridden to Ivanov's estate, thinking only of Maria's safety.

After a moment, Rockwell reached inside his jacket and withdrew a packet of papers, a leather casing and something that looked like a journal, something Devlyn had not known existed until last night. "Have you read it?" Devlyn quietly asked.

"Maria was adamant only you should see the journal."

Taking the packet, Devlyn couldn't explain to himself why he had broken protocol to secure that journal, nor could he worry that his act bordered on treason. He only knew he couldn't allow the journal out of his hands.

"We have enough to break the consortium," Rockwell said. As he talked, he traded cloaks with Devlyn like a doting mother bent on dressing him up to standard, knowing Devlyn didn't have time to stop and change his bloodstained clothing until he reached Carlisle some-time tomorrow night. "Everything else is in order should you be stopped. Can you rid yourself of that upper-crust accent?"

"Which one?"

"The one you don't like."

Devlyn felt the bond of long friendship. He and Rock-well had attended Eaton together, joined the service at the same time. Rockwell became a member of this case a year ago after Devlyn's partner was killed in St. Peters-burg. "There is also something in the packet about you. A broadsheet piece I tore out of the *London Scandal*. I be-lieve you missed your betrothal ball last night." Rockwell managed with a slight grin. "Mind you, it is only conjec-ture, but didn't your father threaten to disinherit you?"

In no mood to brood over his precarious relation-ship with his sire, Devlyn stepped into the stirrup and laboriously swung into his saddle. The sorrel stallion tossed his head and sidestepped. Devlyn gripped the reins, bringing him around. "I doubt it is conjecture."

The sound of approaching horses drew Rockwell's attention. "Maria will not understand why it is me and not you taking her to Whitehaven."

Before Devlyn could reply, a row of mounted uniformed men crested the drive two hundred yards away. Ivanov's guard. Their horses stomping restlessly, they fanned out and continued toward the estate. "Captain Valerik," Rockwell hissed.

"Get Maria out of here before Ivanov's butchers realize she is gone," Devlyn said.

Holding tightly to the reins, he watched Rockwell's tall form vanish in the shadows. They were each on their own.

Voices and shouts followed as someone pointed in Rockwell's direction. Devlyn's horse sidestepped in an agitated dance. Whatever happened, he could not allow Maria and Rockwell to be captured by the Cossack guards.

He held tight to the reins, looking over his shoulder as he brought his mount back under control. He pulled a rifle from the scabbard, raised it with some difficulty to his good shoulder and fired into the trees. The shot sent the troop of men flying off their horses and scattering for cover. Panic ensued. Horses bolted. For good measure, Devlyn shot out a lantern sitting atop a fence post, spattering oil and starting a fire in the grass. Then he meticulously aimed and shot out three more lanterns, a move that sent the terraced parkland descending into darkness.

Swinging his mount around, he galloped down the path that skirted a nearby hunting cottage. A bullet splintered the tree closest to him. A felled tree lay across his path and he kicked his horse hard and leapt the obstruction before disappearing into the woods. A moment later, a sudden, louder crash followed him and he knew a few of the braver guards had remounted and now pursued him through the underbrush. Fortunately, the horses following him had just ridden a long distance from the city and lacked the stamina to keep pace with the sorrel stallion. Soon Devlyn outrode them all.

Finally, he stopped at the edge of the woods. The backside of his cloak draped the sorrel and shielded him in darkness. Devlin looked at the black sky. No wind touched his face. The mist hovering over the uneven landscape prevented him from seeing very far. He wiped a gloved finger across his swollen bottom lip where Stefan had struck him earlier, worked his jaw and felt a deep ache. A bruise would form, but his cropped beard would hide it.

He pulled a kerchief from his pocket and struggled to bind his wounded arm, flinching from a wave of intense pain. He would have to find a physician and get the wound stitched. Find a place to lie low for a few days. Whirling the horse, he pushed on, turning north toward Scotland.

Devlyn had first noticed the woman from his place next to the window. He sat sideways, buttressed against the wooden bench, one boot propped on the seat as he awaited the mail coach to Edinburgh. Wearing a large floppy hat low over his eyes, he felt like something between a criminal and a half-eaten rodent the cat had dragged inside the noisy inn. He'd managed to change into laborer's attire, clothing he'd stolen from a farmhouse before he crossed over into Scotland last night, but he had not shaved in days.

A bout of heavy rain had brought the women and children who had been waiting outside to the fire inside the common room. The sound of a carriage rolling into town had been what had awoken him, as he realized he'd fallen asleep. He didn't know how long he had slumbered. Minutes, maybe. Perhaps an hour. It was more than he'd slept since a doctor in Carlisle had sewn up his shoulder.

Pulling his hat low, he watched the new arrivals as one who observed people for a living, and found himself unable to look away as a woman entered through the heavy oaken door. There was nothing immodest about her long-sleeved jacket. She was bandbox-polished right down to her buttery-soft gloves. Spine ramrod-straight, she handed her cloak to the red-haired girl beside her to hang on a peg. Yards of plush blue velvet gathered in a bustle fell like a layered waterfall down her backside. He might not have stared at all if she had been dressed like the other women present or had not been so tall. Or if the younger man standing beside her were not carrying a huge wooden case that looked to be holding, of all things, a cello. That alone was worthy of a second glance as the trio entered the common room.

But her height kept him staring when he would have otherwise dismissed the slightly anomalous scene. His gaze followed her movement across the crowded room. At two inches over six feet, *he* was considered tall. The top of her head would reach his nose, which made her quite statuesque for a woman.

And everything about her radiated sensuality, though he could see not an inch of flesh beneath the copious layers of fabric. It poured from her in the flare of her hips, the curve of her breasts, the way she spoke to the man sitting behind the lattice cage selling seats for the next coach to Edinburgh. Watching her from beneath his floppy hat brim, he let his eyes follow the march of tiny pearl buttons up her bodice to where the carnal trail ended beneath a tiny bow at her throat. He frowned when his perusal was halted by a wide-brimmed hat and black veil over her face.

With a quiet oath that reflected his self-disgust, Devlyn pulled a timepiece from his pocket. The coach was already two hours late.

He returned the watch to his pocket, shoved his hat lower, rested his head on the back of the bench and closed his eyes. The velvet woman's presence remained at the periphery of his awareness as his consciousness picked out her voice over the din humming around him. She was speaking in French, her melodious tone perfect for the lilt of the language, but it was not her native tongue. Nor was she British.

His eyes still closed, Devlyn noted his beard itched as he tried to think about something other than inviting her upstairs for a quick go-around on a soft, comfortable bed.

The room was suddenly too hot. His shoulder ached like blazes, and he knew he was feverish, which could account for his sudden delirium. He thought about going outside away from the noise. Or getting a room and sleeping for the night. But each thing he thought of doing canceled out the thought before and he ended up doing nothing, except opening his eyes. His hooded glance took in Miss Prim's veiled profile, even as her head turned and he suddenly found himself trapped within her gaze.

Cassie abruptly returned her attention to the man sitting behind the ticket-teller cage. A shudder ran through her. Her heart racing, she lowered her voice in alarm. "Surely you are mistaken," she whispered in English, because the obtuse man behind the cage could not understand French. She didn't like speaking English. Everyone picked out her accent from the first syllable, and a woman on the run did not betray her identity if she could help it. "There must be someone else in this room with whom I may speak. I *need* one more seat."

"If you want another seat, Mr. Holt be the only *single* seat I have sold on the coach, lass," he said in a slight Scottish burr, then politely pointed to the woman sitting near the warmth of the fireplace. "Perhaps ye'd rather ask that mother and her three wee bairns or the elderly couple eating lunch to give up their seats to ye, instead."

The room smelled of unwashed bodies and the boar roasting in the next room. The combination made her queasy, and she dabbed a floral-scented handkerchief beneath her nose. No doubt somewhere in the world the sun shone brightly on happy, smiling people, but not here in this part of the border country. The rains caused havoc on the roads. The bridge had been closed ten miles back, forcing the coach in which she'd been riding to take a detour just as they'd crossed into Scotland. A little dirt and grit never hurt anyone, her grandmother used to tell her, but her grandmother had never visited the borderlands during a spring deluge.

Reluctantly, Cassie turned her head and found Mr. Holt still sitting with one knee raised on the bench beside the window, one wrist propped on his upraised knee. A black cloak draped to the side revealed ragged homespun garments. The light streaming in from the window behind him cast his face in shadow beneath the brim of an unflattering hat, but she could feel his eyes on her. She was glad for the veil covering her face. At least it provided a slight barrier.

She'd found it easier to travel with her face veiled.

Her dress was so dark blue it looked nearly black in the shadows. People thought she was traveling as a widow, and she was not of a mind to correct that assumption. Men paid her more respect as a French widow than as a single American woman traveling with her two servants.

"When does the next public conveyance leave here?"

"Tomorrow, but it is also full, lass. I have one seat left."

That was not acceptable. "It's important I be on this coach," she explained, because he clearly did not understand she could not remain here. "I've already telegraphed my friend in Edinburgh to expect me by the end of the week."

"Then might I suggest if ye wish to go to Edinburgh ye ask Mr. Holt for his seat." With that haughty pronouncement, he shut his little window, as if she couldn't continue talking to him over the metal grate that wrapped around his cubicle of a desk.

Tugging nervously on the netting covering her face, Cassie groaned silently. She had not come this far to be stranded in some godforsaken village that lacked the simplest modern convenience. Not when she had defied her father and run away.

He'd understood nothing of her need to taste a little freedom. But she'd left anyway just before dawn a week ago and boarded the train to Manchester. Knowing her father had probably telegraphed ahead, she had switched trains in Northampton, then embarked on the vehicle of conveyance least likely to be followed. She'd been traveling for days over bumpy roads and overcrowded carriages, only to have her coach diverted to this town at the last moment.

But Cassie wanted to experience real life, even if it

meant suffering a little along the way, or facing the possibility that her father might choose never to speak to her again. She had no desire to add to the scandal the arrogant Lord Hampstead had already caused both families, but if she decided not to return by summer's end, then so be it. She wanted to travel, to see her friend, to experience the world in her own way without fear of some wretched calamity befalling her, and refused to allow anyone or any circumstance to end her adventure before she'd even managed to push beyond the suffering part.

Cassie held to her place a moment longer, but with renewed determination building a fire beneath her feet, she bravely approached Mr. Holt, moving toward him as one moved toward a stray hound. She'd learned well enough to exercise caution the first time she'd tried to pet a strange dog she had seen once in an alley while with her grandmother. At five years old, she'd learned her first lesson about the very real dangers of the world.

A subtle frown grew on his bearded countenance as she drew closer to where he sat near the window. Short of holding her hand out for this man to sniff, there was nothing she could do about it.

His hair, she noticed when she drew nearer, was nearly black and touched his nape from beneath his floppy hat, and was by no means thin. She gleaned from the shape of his jaw and mouth he might be handsome, if one had a penchant for scruffy, flea-bitten men. Her heartbeat fluttered as she stopped at the table and waited expectantly for him to rise. *No manners,* she added to her assessment.

He did not stand or pull out a chair for her as any gentleman would. "I would have but a moment of your time, sir." She didn't bother speaking in French, considering he looked barely capable of proper speech as it was. Kneading her reticule, she took a seat at his table without an invitation—since it was clear she wasn't going to receive one. "I was told that perhaps—"

"You're not French."

She felt a moment's alarm, but resisted informing him the pretext was meant as a disguise.

"Remove the veil," he said, not just in any English but in a smoothly spoken American dialect.

The last thing she wanted was to remove the barrier between this man's eyes and her face. "I'm an American, Mr. Holt," she answered without removing the veil. "The gentleman at the desk told me your name and said I should speak to you concerning my current dilemma."

He remained sitting sideways on the bench behind the table, one knee drawn up to his chest. "If you are going to sit here, I prefer to see your face," he said.

On any other occasion, Cassie would have been affronted by such boldness, but she needed his seat on the coach.

After a moment's hesitation, she reached a gloved hand to her hat and unfastened the pins, frustrated to feel her fingers tremble slightly. She lowered the veil, laid it on the table and raised her chin. If he wanted to look, let him look. Without the veil, she could better see the man's eyes anyway and, as they held hers, she gazed back.

His brown eyes were so dark they looked nearly black in the shadow of his hat brim. She saw nothing else in his expression, yet she'd never felt so undressed in her life. The sensation startled her, then angered her. For a moment she couldn't help her gaze traveling to his lips. Lips that were smiling slightly.

"What is your name?" he asked.

"I am Mrs. Ambrose," she said stiffly, using her mother's maiden name, but he must have sensed her hesitation and guessed she was lying because his eyes narrowed. No longer hooded, they held a spark of something she could not name for certain, but it touched her beneath her clothes and heightened her senses.

"What can I do for you, Mrs. Ambrose?"

"I wish to purchase your seat on the conveyance to Stow."

"It isn't for sale."

"As you might have noted, this village is somewhat isolated and crowded with stranded passengers. Unfortunately, the weather also diverted my coach or I would not be sitting here, Mr. Holt. There won't be another mail coach until tomorrow afternoon. There is one seat available and thus no room. I cannot go tomorrow, either. I need four seats today."

"Who else besides those two are traveling with you?" He nodded his chin toward Mary and Frank, her two faithful servants.

Realizing Mr. Holt had been watching her since she'd entered the common room, she turned to glance over her shoulder, and smiled briefly at the pair to reassure them.

"I see only three of you," he said as she returned her attention to his face. "And you do not look wide enough to take up two seats, Mrs. Ambrose."

"It isn't for us. I need a seat for my Lady Rose. I couldn't bear to see her tied on top of the coach where she would get wet. Or worse, fall off. I could never replace her."

The shocked man arched his brows. "Your traveling companion?"

"My cello."

His eyes widened. "You named your cello Lady Rose?"

"She isn't just a cello, Mr. Holt. She is a Stradivarius. One does not install a Stradivarius atop a mail coach, especially in the rain. She belonged to my grandmother."

"Let me understand this. You want me to give up my seat for a musical instrument?"

Everything was for sale and anyone could be swayed by money. Her father had taught her that much. Cassie opened her reticule, prepared to buy him off. "I need your seat. I will be glad to pay you more than the fare you paid."

To prove her point, she shoved a coin across the table, sure he would be pleased with the wealth she offered him for his one measly seat in a crowded public conveyance. "This should compensate you for your trouble, Mr. Holt."

"Are you sure you are not overpaying me, Mrs. Ambrose? I would not wish to take undue advantage of your generosity."

Cassie perched stiffly on the edge of her seat, aware of the subtle insult to her intelligence, much as she now realized she had been insulting him since she sat down. She was also aware that despite her family's massive wealth and her own extensive classical education, she knew very little about such practical matters as foreign currency or what a room in a run-down inn even cost. She lost some composure. She'd begun to fear maybe she had not brought enough currency to get everyone to Edinburgh where she was supposed to meet Sally Ann's brother.

But she was positive the coin she presented him was worth more than his seat on the coach. "I cannot give you more, Mr. Holt, or I would."

He angled his head to one side. "Do you want to explain to me why someone of your obvious station is riding a mail coach to anywhere?"

"I am on holiday."

"Just you and your Stradivarius?"

"And my two servants."

"And your Stradivarius."

Cassie took the insult with judiciousness. Most people thought her perpetually singular anyway. But for some reason, it bothered her this man did as well. "I have never gone anywhere without my cello, Mr. Holt."

Finally, he leaned on one elbow. "Are you insane, lady? Does Bedlam ring a bell? St. Mary of Bethlehem? Madhouse?"

She'd had enough of his humor at her expense, and it nettled her sorely that a man who smelled of brandy and horses had put her on the defensive. "If you were the least cultured, you would understand the value of that of which I am speaking. That coin will purchase you a bath and board for another night and a seat to Edinburgh later," she said. "From the looks of you, you could use the money."

"Is that right?"

He laughed outright. But his contemplation of her remained steady, if not amused. Leaning nearer, he lowered his voice as if they were sharing a secret. "Are you running from some irate lover?" he asked.

She gave him a level look when she actually wanted to hit him. Her hands knotting in her lap, she debated adding another coin to the first just to change the topic, but decided she had no more to spare. "Surely it would be no hardship for you to take another coach. There is one that leaves tomorrow." She leaned forward. "The cello means a lot to me. Lady Rose *will* ruin atop the carriage in the rain," she said, aware that she was now pleading, and hating that the grubby charlatan would reduce her to begging.

"Then maybe you should have thought of that before bringing the damned thing on a public coach, *Mrs.* Ambrose."

He came to his feet, his movement strangely graceful. His height drew her gaze up to his face, less concealed beneath the hat brim now that he was standing. Even with the closely cropped beard, he was more than handsome, she realized with shock—and vaguely familiar, though she was positive she would never have had an occasion to meet someone like him.

He wore no neckcloth and his homespun shirt was unbuttoned at his throat. A long cloak hid his shoulders, yet framed their width. Everything about him cried duplicity, for the man beneath the clothes did not match the image she'd first perceived. He did not possess a simple mind or background.

Her appraisal of the faint corded tendons of his neck came to a stuttering halt as she realized he was watching her study him. Dismayed to be caught gawking, she found herself speechless.

Moving around the table, he came to a stop beside her and she stood.

His amused eyes drifted over her features and touched her as tangibly as if he'd physically stroked her face. "Put the veil back on, Mrs. Ambrose." Scraping the coin from the table, he brushed his shoulder against her arm. "You might make me forget myself."

"You, sir, are presumptuous," she whispered.

It should have been possible to find an excuse for a

man who had clearly experienced such a laborious upbringing handicapped by moral poverty, but there was something indefensible about impertinence.

But he had taken her hand and, pressing the farthing into her palm, silenced her thoughts. Their gazes came together and held. "Your cello may ride dry, Mrs. Ambrose." He lifted her hand to his lips like a gentleman, but he smiled like a wolf. "And I can pay for my own bath, madam. Yours as well, if you wish to join me for the night."

Cassie yanked her hand away as if burned, but could not hide the rush of heat to her face. She glowered at him in stunned outrage. "I would not dignify that invitation with an answer."

"No?" he asked, humor glinting in his eyes. He seemed little concerned she had just rejected him. "You do not smell like a bouquet of roses, either, madam."

Then, sweeping into a brief bow like a man born to the court, he walked slowly around her and said close to her ear, "I bid you good day, Mrs. Ambrose."

Watching him weave a path through the crowded common room, his cloak flowing around him like wings, Cassie shivered, aware of him as she touched where his lips had pressed against her hand.

Tugging at the string on her reticule, she stopped a buxom chambermaid on her way upstairs. "I wish to have a bath sent up to Mr. Holt's room. Scented," she added, withdrawing three halfpennies and giving her the coin required.

The girl gave her an oblique look, her dark hair hugging her cheeks. "Will ye be wantin' me to join him, mum?" She batted her blue eyes. "This is enough for more than a bath."

Cassie removed two coins. "I only want him to have a

bath," she managed placidly, annoyed by the girl's indefensible eagerness.

"But then I'd be doin' it fer free, mum."

The girl sashayed away, dropping the coin down her blouse. She wore nothing beneath the flimsy garment. Cassie was surprised to see it didn't drop to the floor.

Chapter 2

⌒◯◯⌒

The coach did not arrive at the designated time. An hour later Cassie left the common room, found the innkeeper and obtained a room. There was no sense in everyone suffering the long wait.

"But you should be coming upstairs, too, ma'am."

"It's a small room, Mary," Cassie said, handing her cello to Frankie as she hustled them both upstairs. "I will rest on the coach."

Cassie didn't trust anyone to alert her if the carriage should arrive. Besides, she wasn't a newlywed in the blush of first love. Mary and Frankie had spent very little time alone since they had been married last month. This was Scotland, after all, with its wild landscape and stirring images of beauty, mystery and romance. "I'll come upstairs if the coach is delayed too much longer."

She walked out of the crowded, smoke-filled common room into the muted daylight outside. Heavy clouds hung low across the sky. The air seemed filled with electricity that had nothing to do with the worsening weather. For the first time in her entire life, she was alone. No servants. No guards. Nobody. Adelaide Mary Cassandra Sheridan, from one of the wealthiest families in New York, stood in complete anonymity in the middle of a crowded walk in a foreign country, hundreds of miles from anyone or anything familiar.

Cassie had wanted to come to Scotland from the time she was a little girl and she and Sally Ann had shared their childhood dreams over a tin of chocolate Sally Ann's brother would bring back from some faraway place in a world that she could only dream of seeing.

Wind stockings cracked sharply in the breeze. The streets were busy with buggies and carts. Accentuating the awe that filled her as her eyes roved the scene was the din around her—talking, laughing, a child crying. Even with the occasional grumble of thunder, the village was alive with color and noise. Having grown up in the bustle of a grand city, surrounded by servants and high stone walls to protect her, Cassie suddenly felt like Rapunzel let out of her tower, even if she was a little anxious. She would be a fool not to be.

An old trader wagon sat to the side of the walk, filled with an assortment of wares. Pots and pans dangled from the roof. A man stood hunched over a case, artfully arranging a row of cheap jewelry. He wore a tatty loose-fitting jacket and tweed trousers that had seen better days maybe two decades ago. A big beaver hat crowned his bushy red head.

He was a curiosity, and she found him interesting. Before she could discreetly turn her eyes away, he spoke. "May I be 'elping ye out, mum?"

She caught a glimpse of his quicksilver eyes before he

pulled the hat lower over his brow. "I haven't any money to purchase anything today," she said in apology.

"Don't need any." He pointed at the fox muff she carried on one hand. "I'll be givin' ye your choice of anything ye be wantin' for that pillow yer holdin'."

Cassie looked down at her hand and laughed. "It's hardly worth much," she said, though it was her favorite muff. She'd received it for her sixteenth birthday and it was well worn. But as she approached his wagon, her eyes fell on an old silver fob beside the brooches. Garnets embellished the name of a great clipper that had made one of the first transatlantic runs. Her grandfather had made models of all those famous clipper ships.

"Where did you get this?" she breathed reverently, and plucked it from its velvety bed among the feminine brooches. Consulting the dial, she watched the needle spin and settle, sure that such a beautiful piece must have been stolen. "It's perfect."

"Me old friend was a bosun's mate. Do ye know what it does?"

There were some skills Cassie knew well. Better than well. And some, like reading a compass, she had forgotten she possessed. "A compass is an instrument consisting of a magnetic needle swinging freely on a pivot and pointing to the magnetic north, which isn't necessarily to say the true geographical heading. North is the point on the compass at zero degrees. That storm is coming at us from the northeast." Smiling whimsically, she shut the lid. "I learned how to plot a course at sea before I was twelve. My grandfather considered it necessary training for my future."

Her thumb traced the crisscross engraving, then she carefully returned the piece to its place. She hadn't been back on a yacht or sailing vessel since her brother's death.

"I've not found a person worthy enough to sell it to," the peddler prattled on, holding the fob to the light so it would make the stones flash prettily.

Knowing its value, she should have walked away. But she didn't. "You want this old muff?"

"An even trade clean across the table, mum." Holding the compass between his index finger and thumb, he continued to hold it to the light.

"I'll take it," she said.

He lowered his hand and she was left looking at the second-floor window above the street. Mr. Holt had stepped to the glass.

Cassie caught her breath. He had not removed his hat or changed his clothes, but he no longer wore the cloak. Something that looked like a holster was attached to an odd-looking shoulder strap just beneath his arm. A gun? This was not the American Wild West. What manner of man carried a gun on his person in Scotland?

He looked briefly across the rooftops, then shut the curtains. He hadn't seen her. At least she didn't think so. The curtains abruptly parted again and he appeared, a shadow in the glass looking down at her. Compelled by the strange heat and energy seeping through her body, caught by the force of it, she held her breath. Her heart beat a strange tattoo against her ribs, almost as if she'd been running a great distance. There was nothing about him that was attractive to her, yet . . . she felt him anyway.

Catching herself staring, she gave him her back and returned her attention to the compass. The peddler was watching her curiously. A flush crept over her cheeks. Aware that her hands were shaking, she spoke quietly. "I'm sorry. You were saying?"

"Is Mr. Holt an acquaintance of yours?"

"No!" she blurted, and resisted the urge to place a cooling palm against her cheek, aware that this man was being somewhat intrusive. "I mean, I only just met him this morning. He was kind enough to sell me his seat on the coach."

"Kind?" The man lowered his voice to a conspiratorial whisper and she had to lean closer to hear his next words, surprised the peddler would know someone like Mr. Holt. "That man be a 'oly terror to anyone what be gettin' on his bad side. Be careful wit' yerself, mum. It's rumored he's a Gypsy." He intoned the word "Gypsy" in a rasp.

"Gypsy?"

Clearly sensing the romantic undertone beneath the query, he turned his head. "They travel through these hills. Especially when the fairs are about."

She frowned. "I thought he was an American."

"I've heard Yanks is just as bad a lot to tangle with. But if it's a cow ye need stolen or a man's throat cut, ye find a Gypsy what's roving these hills. They know every hidey-hole between here and Edinburgh."

Cassie pulled back, appalled. She certainly didn't want to steal or have anyone murdered. He tipped his beaver hat. "Ye can call me Hector, mum. Mr. Hector, if ye be indisposed to using me Christian name."

"Mr. Hector," she said, thinking it sounded very much like his Christian name nonetheless. "I'll take the compass." He took her fox muff in exchange and rubbed it against his stubbly face. "This will be soft beneath me head tonight, mum."

Distracted, Cassie closed her gloved hand around the compass. "At least you have a place to sleep. I'm awaiting the coach."

He shoved back his hat and stared up at the roiling sky. "This time of year it rains a lot in these parts."

Cassie looked toward the distant vale crowded with colorful cottages and thatched roofs, ending where the hills rose into the low-hanging angry sky, and wondered why nothing looked as charming as it had ten minutes ago. With her new purchase in hand, she turned and stole a glance at the window, moved by some force she didn't understand.

But the curtains were shut tight.

"If I made a list of supplies, do you have someone who can see it filled?" Devlyn asked the innkeeper, not caring if he reached Edinburgh by tomorrow night as much as he cared that he had the means to leave town.

"Do you need paper and pencil, Mr. Holt?"

"Please."

The innkeeper walked into the small room behind the bar. Braced on his elbow, Devlyn scanned the tables, the din surrounding him creating a hum. A fire burned in the stone hearth, and the veil of smoke it layered in the room hardly helped the ache in his head.

He'd stayed at the Crossroad's Inn twice before when he'd come this way in the last year. The remote stop served as a resting place for those brave souls who wanted a more scenic route to Edinburgh. He came here as much for the family that worked this inn as he did for the remote location. The place was never this crowded.

"What is afoot?" Devlyn asked when the innkeeper returned.

"The weather has delayed the coach. Most of the folks are in the dining room. Ye planning to ride out on horseback?"

Devlyn scrawled off a list of supplies he'd need to make it to Edinburgh. "It doesn't appear I'm going to get out any other way. I want these items delivered to the livery."

"I will send my son to see you get everything you need. It will take a few hours."

Devlyn knew it would. He needed sleep, so he would leave before sunrise and take his chances on the road. Someone bumped his shoulder and he grimaced as he moved to the side of those standing at the bar. "What do you have in the way of a hot meal that can be delivered to my room?" he asked.

The man smiled, revealing a missing front tooth. "If you have the coin, Mr. Holt, my wife will make you a feast."

Devlyn needed a decent meal. A physician, too, but that would have to wait. He finished writing out the list of supplies and turned it over to the innkeeper. "I've already sent a note to the hostler to expect a delivery sometime tonight."

He'd already sold his rifle that morning and paid the livery a month's boarding for the sorrel before the persuasive Mrs. Ambrose had talked him out of his seat and forced a change of plans. Going by coach would have allowed him to avoid the bridge toll collectors, not to mention the fact that on horseback he'd be in clear view of anyone who wanted to shoot him in the back.

He turned into the room. Through the wide archway separating the public house from the common room that was part of the inn, he glimpsed Mrs. Ambrose sitting alone at the table he'd vacated earlier. The sun had set behind her, leaving her in the shadows of the day's demise. A single candle burned on the table where she was flipping cards, her attention so focused she didn't seem aware that half the men in both rooms watched her. At once, he felt a strange undercurrent in his veins.

She still wore her blue velvet dress, the same she'd been wearing that morning and when he'd seen her on the street a few hours ago. The large hat remained on her head, a frilly monument to the foolishness of feminine apparel of the time.

There was nothing about her he should find tempting. She was too young, too peculiar and too much trouble for any one man to endure in patience. Yet he found himself intrigued.

"Can I get ye some ale, Mr. Holt?"

"Whiskey," he said in distraction. "Two glasses."

A stiff jolt of whiskey was the least he could offer someone who went to all the trouble to buy him a bath and the pretty maid who delivered it.

"If you move that card to the knave, you'll find your way out of the hole you're in."

Cassie's head snapped up to see Mr. Holt standing at the table.

"Where is your footman?" He spoke as one used to authority and issuing orders, who seemed to know his way around the servant pool of a large household.

"He is upstairs with Mary. They are . . ."

"Occupied?" he said unhelpfully. Clearly, by the sparkle in his eyes, he knew such things were not discussed in mixed company. "In bed?"

"Mary and Frankie are newly wed," she felt obligated to point out.

Mr. Holt set a whiskey glass in front of her and, without asking her leave, dropped his haversack next to the chair and made himself comfortable across from her. He leaned so that his weight rested on the back of the chair, causing it to creak. His long legs extended under the table and he crossed them casually at the ankles just at the hem of her skirt. He wore his cloak and that floppy hat she found so ghastly, both still possessing a similar dusty appearance.

The room lacked light and it wasn't until he leaned his elbows on the table and poured her a glass of whiskey that she glimpsed his eyes, dark as the night beneath the hat brim.

"I am not that kind of woman," she said.

"To drink? Or enjoy the marriage bed?"

"To cheat." She ignored the latter question as highly impertinent and returned to flipping the cards in her hand, but her hands were no longer steady. "The cards in that pile are dead at the moment. If I took them, I would be cheating."

"Who would know?"

"I would, and I find it unacceptable in the spirit of the game. It is against the rules."

"Why do you play a game?"

She slapped down an ace of hearts and slid it to the appropriate place in line. "To win, of course."

"What if winning entails breaking the rules?"

"There are no circumstances to justify cheating." She peered at him, as if to smugly dare him to deny her assertion. "None."

Beneath the dark brim of his hat, his gaze no longer remained expressionless, but held an unspoken challenge. "You don't drink, lie or cheat"—he leaned on his elbow— "but you had no problem procuring a young chambermaid for me. So fornicating is acceptable in your eyes?"

Cassie's jaw dropped. "Of course it isn't . . . acceptable." She went back to flipping each card, now having lost not only her train of thought, but also her place in the deck. "Besides, I did not procure her for you. I paid her to deliver a bath."

He sloshed whiskey in his snifter and brought it to his lips. "You have a complicated view of the world, Mrs. Ambrose."

Her mouth was set grimly. Clearly, he was entertained by her mien. "Your wisdom escapes me, Mr. Holt. How could you demean honor and integrity? Surely your mother—"

"Ran off with an actor shortly after I was born."

She glanced up but found him studying the glass dangling between his fingers. Feeling considerably less conciliatory than she had moments before, she said, "Then your father—"

"Wasn't married to my mother. I've had a tragic life, Mrs. Ambrose."

He was *such* a liar!

He observed her over his glass, a hint of amusement in his eyes, and the part of her that relished the freedom of her anonymity wanted to test her boldness against his arrogance. But the wiser part dared not, and she returned to her card game, aware that they were sitting too close. Not that body contact could be avoided in the tight space between his chair and hers—it was inevitable that part of her would touch part of him—but he could have moved his legs.

"No doubt you were raised by Gypsies," she said. "If I want a cow stolen or a man's throat cut, I'll be sure and contact you."

His eyes glowed warm in the candlelight as he gave her a lazy smile. "Why? Do I look like a murderous Gypsy cow thief?"

She looked at him sharply, wondering at that very possibility. With his black woolen cloak and floppy hat worn low over his eyes, shadowing his bearded jaw, he could certainly pass for a highwayman. She remembered the gun she'd seen him wearing earlier, and knew he kept it in a sheath against his chest.

"Are you?"

He regarded her steadily. "What if I were?"

"I already don't believe a thing you've told me, Mr. Holt."

"Maybe not, but there is some truth in everything." He stole a card from the pile to her left and laid it on a knave. "Now you have a chance to win."

Cassie brushed her hands over the table and gathered up her cards. Patience had always been her strongest suit, though she had just learned its reach with Mr. Holt. "Were you one of those boys who enjoyed picking the wings off flies, sir?"

"Not when I had a magnifying glass in my hands and an anthill at my feet."

Her eyes narrowed. Perhaps he believed her naïveté was a measure of something less flattering. "Do you know what I think?"

She awaited his response, but he merely set his glass down, awaiting hers.

"You are not at all what you seem, Mr. Holt. You carry a gun, which makes me think you are either a criminal or something else entirely. I go with the second theory. For instance"—she flicked her hand at the haversack at his feet—"you carry that thing everywhere as if it contained your life. No," she pondered another theory aloud, "it contains something to do with someone else's life, because if it were yours, you wouldn't protect it with the same precious care. Your conversation tonight has told me that much about you.

"But you *did* take a bath this afternoon, so that means you have a general respect for yourself, though I doubt your decision to bathe had anything to do with anyone else's sensibilities. You don't care a whit for what anyone else thinks of you or you would not wear that silly hat.

"I also know you didn't do anything with that chambermaid because I saw her five minutes after she filled your tub and left your room just before I sat down to tea, so you are not without some integrity, though you would have me believe otherwise."

"Is that right?"

"But more than that," she continued in a whisper, "you gave me your seat on the mail coach this afternoon and returned my coin when you didn't have to. That is not the action of a cold-blooded Gypsy cattle thief. It might even make you half a gentleman. Hence, my conclusion that you are more than you seem."

He stared at her incredulously, and Cassie was momentarily pleased with her coup.

Let no good deed go unpunished or create idle worshippers in its wake, Devlyn thought in agitation, having bent nearer to the candle flame as she'd spoken and without realizing he'd done so. "You base your opinion of my entire character on that one single act?" He couldn't keep a hint of astonishment from his dry tone.

"I do." Lifting her chin, she dared him to doubt her intuition.

Then his eyes moved of their on accord to the rebellious strand of blond hair that had fallen from her temple and down one shoulder, and he was suddenly distracted by the absurd desire to slide the hat off her head to see what was beneath.

Instead, he rose to leave and she followed him up, not to depart with him, but to await his exit on equal ground. They stood facing each other like two gladiators in the death arena, nearly eye to eye. And in some indistinct part of his mind, he realized he liked her height. It had been the first thing he'd noticed about her. But it was her mouth that finally plundered the last of his indifference and brought him into full carnal awareness, much as he had been when she'd removed her veil that afternoon. A dangerous place to be, even before he returned his focus to her face half hidden within the shadows of her wide hat.

In that glance and a dozen others since he'd met her, he had also figured out a few things about her.

She had never traveled from home on her own, which might have made him wonder why she did now if he'd not already told himself she was none of his concern. She was an eccentric who saw nothing wrong with hauling a cello across England, amusingly prim as she was priggish, and he remembered the way she'd reacted when he'd brushed against her that afternoon.

"Answer me this, love." A strange undercurrent of steel marked his tone, and something else he could not discern in his own voice. "Have you ever been with a man?"

Her perfect mouth opened, and he knew he'd finally shocked her. He was heartily glad of it, too. He was beginning to think she was made of ice.

"My personal life is none of your business, Mr. Holt."

"My point exactly," he offered in clipped politeness. "But you must admit, the answer poses a compelling question in itself, since you never lie, *Mrs.* Ambrose."

Outside, it had started to rain. Water sluiced against the window, drawing her attention and his to the coach that pulled into its place beside the inn, still rocking on its springs, having just come to a stop.

Devlyn grabbed the neck of the whiskey bottle and hesitated as he glanced again at her, feeling as if a drug were crawling through his veins, neither stark nor painful, but gradually warming his blood like the swallow of whiskey.

Hell, he should have been in bed two hours ago. With that thought, he dragged up the haversack and tipped his hat. "I acquit myself from your presence honorably, love."

Devlyn walked through a line of people crowding into the inn, their heads lowered against the rain. He stopped the innkeeper at the stairway. "If I'm not down here in six hours, pound on my door."

Upstairs, Devlyn jiggled the key in the door and stepped into the room, waiting until his eyes adjusted to the darkness before he locked the door and set a chair against the latch. His dinner tray was on the bed. The smell of roast beef permeated the room.

Without lighting a lamp, he walked to the window and edged aside the curtains. Lightning pulsed, allowing him to scan the silhouette of the buildings on each side of the street. The Gypsy peddler wagon was gone. The heavy downpour had chased away all but the most stalwart, and he momentarily thought of the girl downstairs. He could no longer pretend that she hadn't interested him. Dropping the curtain, he tightened his fist on the bottle of whiskey and carried it with him to bed.

Devlyn sat with his elbows braced on his knees and stared at the haversack on the floor beside the bed. He unlatched the flap and withdrew the journal, drawing it out into the light. It was not as big as the size of his palm and was thinner than the width of his index finger. He flipped open the flimsy leather cover and held it to the light. He recognized the encryption because he recognized the hand behind the script.

Dominick was a traitor, Hampstead.

Stefan Ivanov had condemned one of the few persons in this world Devlyn had truly loved. The favored son. The brother whose title Devlyn now held and whose shoes he'd been forced to fill this past year. Dominick, with all of his high ideals and passion to change the world, had only managed to get himself killed.

But for what?

Devlyn did not replace the journal in the haversack. Instead, he cut away part of the oilcloth beneath the haversack flap and wrapped it around the journal. Working away the felt lining in the crown of his floppy hat, Devlyn inserted the journal in the pouch that sometimes carried other valuables.

He lay back on the bed. Mrs. Ambrose had been correct when she said he protected the haversack as if it contained someone else's life—even if the secrets he protected were now his own.

Chapter 3

〜⌒◯◯⌒〜

Devlyn opened his eyes. Somewhere a door slammed. He pushed himself up on his elbow, letting his eyes adjust to the darkness of an unfamiliar room. Thunder drummed and a flash of lightning illuminated the room, revealing a nearly untouched bottle of whiskey on the dressing table. He gave up trying to remember why he was here, slid to the edge of the mattress and fumbled on the nightstand for his timepiece. Not finding it, he lit the lamp and sat on the bed, folding his palms around his head. He felt as if he'd tumbled off a cliff and hit every rock and tree on the way down. His right shoulder ached.

He saw the watch on the floor. Reaching over the discarded dinner tray, he picked it up and read the time. He'd slept more than six hours. "Bloody hell."

Someone was pounding on his door. The innkeeper's voice came through the door. "Mr. Holt."

Something was happening outside in the street. He could hear shouting. He reached behind himself and extinguished the lamp. Then, shrugging into his shirt, he walked to the window, lifting the edge of the curtain higher to look down at the street. Two coaches sat empty outside. Wagons and carts filled with people labored in the mud beneath a torrent of rain. He peered at the darkening sky and frowned. A moment later, working the cuffs on his sleeves, he opened the door.

"Ye asked to be awakened, Mr. Holt." The harried innkeeper adjusted the spectacles on his nose. "But ye might be wantin' to stay. The river flooded its banks last night. We lost the coach that left out of here. We are fortunate no one was killed."

Devlyn looked past him up the hallway, which was crowded with people. Children were running underfoot. Trunks were piled against the wall. Somehow he'd slept through the mayhem. "Is everyone back?"

"Some of the passengers made it across after the coach became trapped in the rising waters. Some did not. They returned a few hours ago. The others who have not returned remained behind to try and salvage what was left."

"There was a cello. . . ."

"I am told the cello made it across."

Devlyn rubbed his temple with the heel of his hand and looked back at the window. "Where is the next closest river crossing?"

"There be another crossing fourteen miles west if ye want to be takin' your chances with thieves living in those wild border forests. Ye best be keepin' your room for the night, lad, and wait for the rain to clear. You'll stay alive longer."

He doubted that. "Did my supplies get delivered to the livery?"

"Aye, Mr. Holt. Everything ye asked for."

Devlyn paid him with gold, then shut the door. He grabbed the whiskey bottle off the nightstand and padded to the small looking glass above the washbasin, his trousers hanging loosely at his hips. He lit the lamp and examined the purplish, puckered flesh on his shoulder. He swallowed a slug from the bottle, then leaned over a basin and poured the rest of the contents over the wound. Pain ripped through his upper body and took his breath.

Braced with one hand against the dresser, he shook off dizziness and focused on the room—the sparse furnishings, the blue peeling walls, the water tins still on the floor from yesterday's bath. Anything but pain. After a moment, he began searching for his clothes.

Devlyn found the haversack and checked to make sure its contents were intact. At least his life wasn't a lost cause yet.

Everything Cassie had brought with her was lost.

Gone.

All of her traveling papers in her trunk had been caught up with the river's monstrous flood and were probably miles downriver. Cassie had returned to the inn long after most of the other passengers had left the riverbank. Her head pounded. She heard herself make a whimper.

Oh, God. She couldn't breathe.

There was a hysterical edge to the sound of her voice. But it would do her no good to scream, even if she could.

Cassie had been one of the last out of the overcrowded coach last night. She'd been attempting to help the older couple sitting next to her escape. The poor woman had been terrified and had refused to move until the roiling river began to rise above the spoked wheels mired in the mud and finally into the coach itself.

Everything had happened so fast. One moment the carriage was stuck in the mud, the next it was on its side riding an icy torrent downstream, with trunks and valises floating away like so much loose ballast. Cassie and the elderly couple made it safely to the bank because the dray driver trapped behind them had a rope and Cassie knew how to tie a knot. She was heir to Magnus Shipping, after all. She knew her way around every ship her father had ever built and every knot ever invented.

The cart driver standing beside her gave her a blanket. They stood in front of the inn. "Och, lassie, the people with you made it across, did they?"

"Yes, they did."

Mary and Frankie made it with Lady Rose before the current had lifted the carriage and tossed it on its side. She would have worried about Mary had the girl been alone, but Frankie would get her to Edinburgh. He would know to telegraph Sally Ann.

Looking up at the sky, she shivered with cold. The temperature until now had been warmer than usual for June. From the east, she could see the storm's fury moving toward them.

"We shall find your trunks," the driver reassured her. A few other men who had been combing the flooded area for belongings were now pulling up in carts to the walkway behind her. "Tomorrow we'll return and begin looking farther down the road."

Even if she did find her trunks, what good would they be to her? Everything inside would be ruined.

Thanking the man for his help, she shouldered through the crowd of milling people, hoping to find the innkeeper inside. The room smelled unpleasantly like wet dogs. She still wore her blue velvet traveling skirt and white blouse, minus the fitted jacket and bustle. She'd lost her hat, gloves, and all of her hairpins. Her hair hung to her hips and, though dry now, needed a good brushing. Someone had loaned her a cloak. Surprisingly, she'd not lost her reticule in the fiasco and still carried it wrapped on a string around her wrist.

The innkeeper was not behind his desk. She looked across the press of people, anxious to get to a room where she would be free of the disturbing gazes cast in her direction. A woman alone. What did she expect? The common room was crowded with people spilling over to the tables in the dining area, children running underfoot.

The inopportune flood that had closed the ford across the creek had just stranded her in the middle of nowhere with no trunks, no money and no means out of here.

Be careful what you wish for, her grandmother had often told her when she'd catch Cassie daydreaming, always wanting to be somewhere other than where she was.

She'd wanted to escape her life, but reality wasn't nearly so romantic as her imagination had painted it. She'd been destitute for four and half hours and already didn't like it. She was hungry. She wanted a hot scented bath and to sleep on satin sheets. She wanted her cello. The sight of a young maid carrying a bucket of hot water upstairs brought forth a sigh of envy.

She straightened when she saw the harried innkeeper stooped over a rag, cleaning something from the floor. With few coins left, she could eat or sleep, but not do both. She had no idea which she would choose for the night.

"My inn is full, Madam Ambrose," he said from over the spectacles on his nose.

"But I had a room here just a few hours ago."

"All beds are sold. I'm sorry, but there is no place for you to stay."

Panic began to rise within her. She was an American in a foreign country. "Where am I supposed to go? There is no other inn. The river crossing is out."

"I apologize, mum, but there is nothing I can do. And as ye can see, I'm very busy."

She breathed in and out slowly, forcing herself to calm down. Looking around her at the crowd, she clutched her reticule to her chest and found her eyes on the stairs. She *did* know one person. Perhaps not a gentleman by any stretch of the imagination, but he had helped her yesterday. Surely that counted for something.

"Is Mr. Holt upstairs?" she asked when the innkeeper brushed off his trousers and stood.

The man's brown eyes narrowed, and she rushed to reassure him, "We're acquaintances." It was not really a lie. "He is an American, is he not?" she said, as if all Americans were personally acquainted with one another by virtue of living on the same continent.

"No, I believe he might be an English lord, lassie."

"An English lord? Mr. Holt?" The notion was absurd. "You are mistaken."

"Then perhaps you would care to tell those men he is your compatriot instead. They were also asking about a woman seen with him yesterday. You?"

A shiver of alarm went down her spine. Someone bumped her elbow as the innkeeper pointed to two large men standing like granite bulwarks near the window. The men wore fur caps over wide foreheads and sported heavy dark beards. They looked as warm and cuddly as two igneous rocks spewed from a volcano. One was talking to the agent who had sold her coach tickets to Edinburgh yesterday. "Cossacks," the innkeeper muttered in contempt, and spat. "A bad lot, lassie. They are accusing his lordship of killing the son of a Russian diplomat over the man's wife."

Oh, my God! He really is a killer! She thought in alarm.

"But if Mr. Holt is the man those two want, I can assure you they will not find him with my help," the innkeeper said.

"Wait." She grabbed his arm. "If the man murdered someone . . ."

"Mr. Holt has come through here many times over the years. He orders a hot meal and a bath, treats my family with respect and pays me very well for my services. I am not one to judge his guilt or innocence in state matters, lass, or why he chooses to remain anonymous. If he killed a man, he probably had good reason."

"They aren't the law?" Cassie looked back at the men just as the agent pointed at her.

"No, lass. They are not. And if they are looking for you, I suggest you leave."

She sidled closer to a pillar. This was the world balancing itself, reminding her that her mother had been right to try to protect her. This predicament was her own fault for thinking she could manage on her own. She had practically been social with Mr. Holt last night, as he sat across from her while she was playing cards. Would they think she was some accomplice by virtue of association? But more than the fact that she found Mr. Holt unpleasant to be around, she disliked the uniformed men walking with purposeful strides in her direction.

When she returned her attention to the innkeeper, the words she'd been about to say stopped. He had moved away and disappeared behind an archway. The name of the public house and a picture of a swan etched into a wooden sign above her head indicated the division between the inn and the public taproom. She caught him in the next room. The pandemonium nearly made her shout. "Where is Mr. Holt now?"

"Perhaps he is already gone."

"But he *can't* be gone."

"I am sorry, lassie. But I can't help ye."

A girl came through the door, balancing a tray heavy with tankards. The innkeeper moved to let the server pass, then wove his way to the back of the room.

Cassie was suddenly alone in the crowded room. She felt dizzy with something akin to real fear. Would someone stop a Cossack from dragging her out of the inn?

Smoke and noise rose in drafts to surround her. She turned her attention back to the doorway and saw the uniformed men pushing through the crush in her direction. Clutching her reticule, Cassie wound her way to a back stairway. She asked a passing chambermaid where Mr. Holt was staying, then rushed up the stairs.

Nothing made sense, and right now she was too frightened to care. What kind of a fool knocked on a stranger's hotel door anyway? The desperate kind, that was who.

The door opened, swinging ajar as if pulled by a ghost. She peered around it. "Mr Holt?"

The bed showed signs of having been slept in. A soapy masculine scent lingered in the air like a tangible presence, as if the room's occupant had recently washed. Even beneath the unkempt image surrounding him yesterday, she'd smelled that scent.

There was no other hint of anyone's presence. A damp towel lay over a hip tub near the window. Something that looked like blood stained the pale fabric. She glimpsed bandages in a porcelain bowl on the dresser and an empty whiskey bottle next to it. Yesterday, she had not sensed he'd been wounded or hurt.

Setting down the towel, she looked outside. The rain had momentarily diminished to a drizzle and created a halo of mist around the nearest street lamp. She could see nothing in the stygian blackness beyond the sphere of light. Panicked, she flew to the second window. A tall man disappeared into an alley down the street. If she had looked away for an instant, she would not have seen him. Recognizing the familiar form, she felt her heart leap. She dropped the corner of the curtain and hurried from the room.

Devlyn sensed the steps behind him before he heard their fall on the wet walkway separating the alley from the main street.

Bloody hell.

Someone had been tracking him since he left the hotel. He was sure of that now. Ivanov's men must have seen him leave. Jogging across the street, he sidestepped a hack drawn by a single horse as he continued down the walk. But for the sound of a tinkling piano coming from the establishment at the end of the block, most of the street seemed deserted. He ducked around the corner of the nearest building and slid beneath the overhang in the alley. There he crouched. His breath came harder than it should have and pain stabbed his shoulder. No one would be following him unless he or she considered Devlyn an easy mark or worked for Nicholas Ivanov, and by the swish of petticoats, he knew this particular individual to be female.

A breeze added to the increasingly frigid air. Lightning blinked across the sky. It was dark enough that he was not afraid of discovery, but a street lamp provided enough light that he could watch the walk.

A moment later he was rewarded as a cloaked figure ran past.

Separating from the shadows, he stepped out onto the walk and with silent tread became the pursuer. Then Devlyn noted something familiar about the woman's height and recognized his quarry. The Bedlamite cello player from the inn had not made it across the river. The part of him that did not come to attention in her presence considered that this particular female could not possibly be working for Ivanov. He'd witnessed the exchange between the ticket seller and Mrs. Ambrose when she'd first arrived in town.

Still, sometimes things were not as they seemed.

"Why?" He asked the despairing question of the discordant sky. "Why does this have to happen to me?"

Her cloak billowed around her. He had to admire her speed, all trussed up in a corset the way she was, as she forced him into a jog.

The distant slap of approaching horses turned Devlyn's head. Two riders galloped up the street in his direction. Recognizing the red and gold uniform of one, he quietly swore and in three steps was upon the girl. He grabbed her mouth with his hand, muffling her scream, and pulled her into the alley.

"Mrs. Ambrose." Without removing his hand from her mouth, he pressed his lips to her ear. "If you value your life, do not make a sound."

They waited in the darkness out of the rain, his breath falling softly against her temple. Her heart pounded against his forearm, but to her credit, she made no sound.

A woman on the streets alone was prime fodder for trouble. What he didn't understand was her reason for following him from the inn. Holding her against him, he leaned around her to look down the street. The men were no longer in sight. She emitted a small mew of frustration when he still hadn't released her mouth.

Devlyn frog-marched her to the brick wall. Her breath came in a hoarse grunt. "What are you doing?"

"I should ask you that."

"I saw you from the hotel window."

He slipped his hands beneath her heavy cloak to her warm, soft body. She stiffened as if shocked by an electrical current that seemed to travel through her body and back to him. His own pulse kicked up a notch. "If you wanted to rob me, you would have taken my money yesterday," she rasped.

"Lest I find a toad-stabber between my ribs, Mrs. Ambrose."

He didn't care if she was Mother Superior herself. He frisked her bodily, running his hands over her waist and under her breasts, along the length of her arms to test her reticule. The soft sides of the reticule allowed him to feel what was inside. Then he stepped back and she spun to face him, her action swirling her cloak against his calves.

"Do you intimately acquaint yourself with every woman you meet on the street, sir?"

"If I can, love." The breeze brought with it an exotic breath of ginger he'd smelled earlier on her hair, and the sound of her furious gasp. But he was in no mood for coy games. "No man lives long who trusts a woman walking the streets at night. And lady, you better have a damn good reason for being out here tonight. Why are you following me?"

She peered around the voluminous hood of her cloak over her shoulder as if debating to flee or stay. He wanted her to flee, even as he found himself wanting to pull her toward him. He cursed himself for letting her have any effect on him.

"I know you're hiding from those men who just passed us," she said. "The innkeeper does not believe what they are saying about you."

"And what might that be?"

"That you murdered a man over a woman."

"You heard that?"

"They were at the inn looking for you tonight. I also know you are injured. I saw the bandages in your room."

His patience with her vanished. "And you came to warn me? Or blackmail me, Mrs. Ambrose?"

"You are going to Edinburgh. Please, take me with you."

Wary of more requests by damsels in distress, he only knew that whatever it was she was running from, he wanted no part of it.

"Did you really kill a man?" she asked.

"Go back to the inn, Mrs. Ambrose."

"Wait!" She blocked his path. "Frankie and Mary made it across the river. I haven't anyplace else to go. The innkeeper said you had supplies sent over to the livery. If you could just get me to Edinburgh, I could pay you."

Lightning provided a brief reprieve from the shadows. "A joke, Mrs. Ambrose?"

"Truly, I have money—"

"The part about you going with me."

"You . . . don't understand."

"I understand that you want a way out of here. But it won't be with me. Now go back to the inn."

The livery was the last structure at the edge of town and visible as a dark shape at the edge of the village. Devlyn left her and dashed across the street in hopes of escaping her, hoping that if he ignored her she would tire of her quest and go away. He knew he was being obnoxious. But he did not intend to allow her to talk him into taking her with him. If Ivanov's guard had followed him here, then it wouldn't take long for Ivanov to figure where he was going. The trip would be dangerous enough for him without having to pamper some helpless debutante who probably didn't know the front end of a horse from the back.

The hostler was in the tack room kept warm by an old woodstove. A stooped-over man with corncob hair, he looked like a wizened gnome as he turned from the woodstove to greet Devlyn.

"You've na' chosen a good night to travel, Mr. Holt." The hostler took him to the stall where his horse waited saddled and ready to ride. "He's a fine Irish thoroughbred. Won't let too many people near him, though."

"I hope the packhorse can keep up," he said. Once given his head, the stallion would fly, and he didn't want a laggard mount holding him back.

The man cackled as if he'd made a joke. "She's a sprightly mare named after me wife, Rose. Thorn be the horse's name."

"Temperamental, is she?"

"If ye give her a chance, she'll head right into the woods. She's got a particular favorite patch of grass what grows at that old white farmstead what used to be her home."

"I'll keep that in mind."

With a rasping chuckle, the hostler waddled out of the stall. Devlyn tied the haversack on the back of the saddle, checked the cinch and the bit, then took the reins.

The sorrel stallion had been with him since he was foaled twelve years ago. The stallion stood seventeen hands high. His light reddish brown coat glistened with the polish only a good hand with a curry comb could give it. If he'd taken the coach, the horse would have been well cared for here until his return in a few weeks.

He turned to step out of the stall, only to find Mrs. Ambrose awaiting him. "I'll give you a thousand dollars when you get me to where I need to go."

Jesus, he wanted to shout at her, and was preparing to dress her down for making such an outlandish offer, only to stop in his tracks as his eyes fell on her in the full light, standing so close to him he could smell her French perfume.

Her hood had fallen from her head and lay billowed against her shoulders. He had not seen her face since last night, and even in the shadows of the common room she had not been forgettable by any stretch of the imagination. But the golden halo of light cast from the lantern on the wall would forever frame her in his memory. Without the wide-brimmed hat she'd worn yesterday, her appearance was as dramatic as snowfall on a bright sunlit day. The cold weather along with the brisk walk to the livery had heightened the pink in her cheeks. The slant of her verdant eyes gave her the exotic look of an expensive courtesan. He'd never seen hair the color of moonlight. It fell in lush waves down her back, and it was all he could do not to lift a strand and see if it was real.

The girl was beautiful.

But she had yet to learn her own power, for the patently deliberate gaze holding his was not that of a woman who had incorporated such assets into her arsenal of attack.

Indeed, she regarded him with something between

distrust and uncertainty, and every instinct honed by nine years of survival told him her foray into the world had yet to include sleeping with a man. "Do you actually *have* a thousand dollars?" he finally asked, mentally exploring the incongruity of that last thought.

She fidgeted. "Well . . . not exactly with me."

"Of course you don't." His gaze dropped to her bosom, then down the length of her. "Where would you put it, after all? A carriage for hire costs ten guineas, Mrs. Ambrose."

He took the bridle and led the horse down the row of stalls, the clip-clop of hooves muffled against the straw.

Mrs. Ambrose stepped around him, apparently a habit of hers. "I swear, I can pay you anything you want," she said. "Just not at this moment. Name your price, Mr. Holt. Just take me with you, please. I can't stay here."

Still holding the bridle, he slid his gaze down her blushing cheeks and throat to rest briefly on her blouse, the uplift of her breasts. He looked at what remained of an obviously expensive traveling garment, the white lace bow of her décolletage tied prettily just above her bosom, and thought of a price.

But something told him she was trouble. Nothing that beautiful ever came free. It was a lesson forever ingrained in his psyche from the first time he'd jumped out of a second-story window to escape an irate husband and broken his leg—the same lesson served to him yet again a week ago.

"Are you married, Mrs. Ambrose?"

She gazed at him blankly, an expression she'd clearly perfected through practice, he thought with growing amusement.

"What does that have to do with anything?"

"It is a simple enough question."

"I will be wed by summer's end."

For the second time that night, he sidestepped her. "Then I can't afford your offer and you couldn't afford my price."

Mrs. Ambrose remained stubbornly attached to his heels as he brought the sorrel around to mount. The little packhorse stood at the ready beside the door. He and Mrs. Ambrose had been speaking in rushed whispers, and the old hostler, unaware of the content of their conversation, held the reins.

"The agent who sold me the coach seats told those men following you that I was talking to you yesterday. They are looking for me, too." She lowered her voice still more. "I panicked and ran. I can't go back. What would I say to them?"

"Go back to the inn. Find the sheriff if you have to. Unless you have a reason for running from a Russian crime consortium."

Her eyes snapped wide. "A Russian crime consortium?" Then she shook her head. "Did you truly kill someone?"

He walked around the side of the horse to check the other stirrup. Much of his life was shrouded in secrecy, but that fact obviously wasn't one of them anymore.

"I killed the son of one Nicholas Ivanov. The patriarch of said consortium." He raised his head and peered at her from over the back of the horse. "Twenty people heard him call me out but will all testify that I murdered him in cold blood."

"Did you?"

"I did if one counts that he ran into the end of a very sharp blade." Bracing both arms on the saddle, his senses still flirting with that bow at her neck, he rested his gaze on hers. "*Now* do you still want to travel with me across Scotland?"

"Why were you dueling with him?"

"Because another woman like you came to me for help." Gathering the reins in his gloved hand, Devlyn stepped into the stirrup and mounted.

Whatever humor had briefly touched his mood vanished when he reined the high-stepping horse around. He took the lead of the packhorse from the hostler.

He hesitated, reluctant to leave her alone in the stable. Yanking his hat lower, he ignored the shot of pain through his arm. "Whatever your problems are, I can't help you, Mrs. Ambrose. As you have guessed, I've problems enough of my own."

"Because you are in love with another man's wife?"

Without answering, he flipped a coin to the hostler, who had dragged open the stable door leading outside to the back of the livery. The smell of rain touched his nostrils. "See that she gets back to the inn," he told the man. "I have a room there."

Then he rode out of the livery.

The drizzle hit his face, welcoming him into the night. He turned the sorrel left, down the narrow backstreet, and spurred him into a trot.

Maybe he was in love with Maria Ivanov. He had first met her while in St. Petersburg three years ago, the consequences of which had brought him to this point. It was enough that he'd arranged some sort of sanctuary for her outside England.

But love?

He didn't know what that meant exactly. He didn't know how to define his relationship with Maria.

Maybe she had merely weakened him enough to help

her kill her husband for her. He'd wondered about that all week as well. Though he hadn't needed much push. Killing Stefan had been personal.

The sound of fast-approaching horses snapped his senses back to alert. Skirting a fence, he reined his mount around to face the livery. Lightning flashed close, revealing a half dozen uniformed guards dismounting in front of the livery.

Ivanov's men.

Devlyn's attention shot to the back doorway as the hostler became aware that he was about to be invaded by Russia's finest assassins and fled the livery on foot.

The horse shifted beneath him. Pulling tighter on the reins, he studied the darkness with a hunter's eyes. Eyes that had already gone cold as the night. His chest pulled tight at the thought of the girl still inside, knowing that even if she'd heard the riders, she hadn't had enough time to hide. She'd earned their attention by running, but surely they would grasp her mistake and realize she had no connection to him.

Bloody hell, a thousand times over, she wasn't his concern. He was not a man prone to self-sacrifice. If he wanted to reach Lord Ware alive, he had to leave.

Devlyn watched the Cossacks go inside and waited for them to give chase. He was certain she would give him up to them. But no one came outside.

Then, realizing she held some absurd loyalty toward his person, he somehow knew she would protect him despite what he'd told her.

She had no idea what kind of men she was dealing with and, as misguided as his gallantry was, that realization defeated him.

He was about to do something else stupid, he could feel it building inside. Except he knew Nicholas Ivanov wanted him alive. His guards wouldn't kill him. That fact was at least in his favor.

"Merda," he mumbled, already kicking the horse into a gallop, and, with a strange sense of inevitability, he rode toward the livery.

Chapter 4

The wide livery doors burst open and slammed against the walls. Cassie jerked her gaze toward the gaping maw just as a procession of uniformed men strode into the stable. She swiped her sleeve across her face, her tears no longer of import. If she had not been distracted by her distress, she might have heard their approach. But she had not heard them and now they swarmed into the stable.

A frantic glance around told her the hostler had vanished. The shorter man in front of the others stopped upon seeing her. She stepped backward and lifted her chin a brave notch. Better that she face them. Where would she run anyway, wearing a long skirt and petticoats? She couldn't climb into the loft.

"*Allez.* Go." He motioned for his men to search the stable, his eyes a blue blaze. "Find his lordship."

Bringing his attention back around to her, the man stood poised for a moment, his curly black hair and mustache beaded with drops of rain. She did not recognize him from the inn, but she did recognize the two men she'd seen earlier, who said something about her from over his shoulder. Her stomach went hollow. Did this man consider her an accomplice to murder?

He approached her, slapping a quirt against his gloved palm. His unpleasant eyes did not bother with the vagaries of courtesy as they moved over her hair. "You are the one with the cello."

She didn't understand what that meant, or why he would know that about her. But the fact that he did scared her.

"It isn't that difficult to follow a cello from Hexham, Miss Sheridan. I do believe that is where you caught the public conveyance that was detoured to this place. Is it not? We've been following your trail. Where is the Englishman you came here to meet?"

"I don't understand," she whispered.

"You were seen with him twice yesterday." He yanked her reticule from her wrist and she watched him loosen the strings. Crashing noises came from the back room, as if someone was ravaging the place. Cassie wished she'd had the foresight to pull her hood over her head or remain at the inn, anything except chase after Mr. Holt.

Except she'd done nothing wrong to deserve this manner of treatment. Cassie didn't cause people problems— at least not on purpose. It was against her nature to break rules. She would tell this man what he wanted to know if she knew the answers herself or if she didn't fear that anything she said would be turned into a rope and knotted around her neck. "I'm an American, on my way to see the ambassador," she stated with all the authority one used when speaking to a servant, though the weight of her voice lessened as the captain took a step toward her. "He is visiting in Scotland," she whispered. "You have no right to detain me or go through my personal things. You aren't even British."

"The ambassador is in Scotland? Then Lord Ware is here as well?"

"I don't know who that is," she replied, feeling as if she'd said something wrong.

"Lord Hampstead is a dangerous spy. He is wanted for murder, and you would serve yourself and your American ambassador well if you cooperated with us."

"Lord Hampstead?" Despite her unwillingness to show emotion in front of this barbaric captain, she stared at him in shock. "I don't know what you're talking about."

"No?" He held up the miniature portrait in her reticule. "Then who is this?"

Her eyes moved to the photograph. "You are telling me you did not meet this man yesterday?" he asked.

Surely this was fate going one step too far. She did not understand the implication or what a photograph of her betrothed had to do with anything. "The man I met with was no Englishman. I mean, I thought the man I was speaking with was an American—"

The officer placed the quirt's grip under her chin and pressed upward. "We will do more than detain you, *dyé voosh ka*. Where is Lord Hampstead?"

"I don't know." Cassie looked into his brutal eyes and realized he was about to strike her. "I don't know! I have never met him!"

"I will ask you only one more time. Where is Hampstead?"

"Behind you, Captain Valerik."

On a quick breath, Cassie shot a look toward the familiar voice.

Mr. Holt stood in the doorway, a pistol in one hand pointed at the officer. He swung a second revolver around on the sergeant to his right as that one stepped into the lantern light. The sound of pistols cocking resounded in the stable's confines as every firearm came to bear at once on Lord Hampstead. Cassie could scarcely breathe, didn't dare, as the tableau froze into a standoff.

They would all die in a hail of bullets, of that she was sure.

Then in a perfectly cultured British English, he said, "Now step away from the lady before I do something rash that *you* more than I will regret."

"You're late, Hampstead," the officer remarked casually.

"I hope you don't hold that against me, Valerik."

But standing in shock, her eyes on him, Cassie held everything against him.

He'd lied about his identity. That Mr. Holt and the Earl of Hampstead were the same stole her breath. It could not be! She would have known him.

But how could she have imagined that the Earl of Hampstead could be a crazed British spy with no sense of self-preservation or qualms about pulling a gun on six armed Cossacks and getting her killed in a gunfight? Her betrothed was a madman!

She would have pounded his chest in anger had she not realized that his noblesse oblige would probably get him killed before she got the chance.

"I see we have a problem," Valerik said in an arctic voice.

"Standoffs are never healthy." Lord Hampstead stepped back, keeping his two pistols pointed, one at a spot between the captain's eyes and the second at the sergeant.

His comment had sounded both light and conversational, but something in his voice chilled Cassie.

"Mrs. Ambrose," he said without looking at her. "Step over here."

Cassie sidestepped the bullish officer, ran to Lord Hampstead and stopped just behind him, her heart still racing, her mind in confusion.

"You look weary, Your Lordship," Valerik said. "I was told you were seriously injured."

"My horse is outside," Lord Hampstead said to her. "I suggest you go now."

"What about you?"

"I don't intend to die, Mrs. Ambrose, unless you stall me longer."

Cassie lifted her skirts and turned . . . directly into the barrel of another gun. A uniformed man stood in the wide doorway.

Devlyn heard the click of another revolver hammer. His eyes remained on Valerik and he raised the revolver in his own hand ready to shoot the bastard between the eyes.

"You will kill her, too," Valerik warned.

He heard Mrs. Ambrose's small gasp of pain. "You're a son of a bitch. Let her go."

"If I warn you again, the next sound you hear will not be a pleasant one."

Dropping his guns, Devlyn held out his arms and turned, a picture of surrender as he faced the man behind him. Mrs. Ambrose stood with her back to the door, restrained by one of Valerik's men, a gun to her head, her eyes wet and bright in the amber light. Devlyn shifted the full force of his gaze on the man's scarred face.

"Release her," Devlyn ordered.

Scarface shoved her into his arms. Devlyn caught her waist as she fell against the length of his body to gain her footing. He looked down into her tilted face. Her pale hair framed the delicate lines of her jaw and sent a wave of protectiveness through him. "As entertained as I've been, you've quickly proven to be a lot of trouble to me, Mrs. Ambrose."

"Why did you come back?" her voice rasped.

"I'll let you know when I figure that out myself, love."

"I want four men outside." The order was not given in English, but Devlyn understood Valerik all the same. "Find his horse and anything else in his possession. Bring everything to me." A gloat of satisfaction thinned the barbarian's lips. "Search him, Sergeant."

Devlyn stared coldly at Valerik. Two men patted him down.

"You don't have the authority to do this, Valerik."

Devlyn's shoulder sheath was empty, so they left it strapped to him. The tip of the quirt traced the holster. "Now tell me which arm you did *not* injure. Hmmm?" Valerik struck his left shoulder with his fist.

Pain exploded in Devlyn's body. He'd seen it coming but not in time to evade the shattering blow. "Did you think Ivanov was not aware of your government's little investigation into his affairs? Did you think he hasn't known your true purpose for months?"

Valerik's fist smashed his midsection as someone kicked him in the back of the knees. He fell to the ground on all fours, gasping for breath.

"Before this night is out, I promise you'll be eager to tell us where you took Maria," Valerik taunted.

"Stop it! You'll kill him!" Mrs. Ambrose dropped beside him.

The sergeant clapped manacles on his wrists and jerked him to his feet. The bastards. Devlyn couldn't have fought if he'd tried. His head was ringing.

"Nicholas Ivanov wants what you stole from him, including his daughter-in-law. Or he will present your government with depositions that claim you murdered his son in cold blood."

"With his usual Machiavellian zeal for justice, no doubt." Devlyn pushed out the words. "Except my arrest will only force him to reveal all of his dirty secrets in a public tribunal." Bracing his palms on his thighs, he dropped back to his knees. "You and I both know justice is not what he has in mind. Let the girl go. She has nothing to do with any of this."

"She has everything to do with this. In fact, she led us directly to you tonight."

Beside him, he heard her gasp. "Apparently she is also on her way to see the American ambassador currently in residence in Scotland. Isn't that a coincidence, that you should both meet here? Does that mean your Minister of Foreign Affairs is also there? Unless you work for the Americans now."

Devlyn felt something cold wash over him. "I don't know what the hell you are talking about. She and I don't know one another."

Holding the dainty pink and pearl-encrusted reticule in one hand, Valerik presented him with a small photograph in the other. "It's hardly a current rendition of you, is it?" He presented Devlyn with a look. "But it does somewhat resemble you."

The man in the photograph was not him. Most people would not know that, though. He and his brother looked enough alike when they were younger that people once confused them.

Dominick had sat for the photograph while attending Eaton; it was probably the only likeness ever taken of him as an adult. But the full implication of the picture being in Mrs. Ambrose's possession was startling. He turned his head and looked at her. She was shaking her head, her eyes jewel-bright in the lantern light. Who did she work for? The Americans? *Christ!* Why would she tell Valerik that?

"It isn't what you think," she whispered.

"And what pray tell is that?"

"You really do not know who she is, do you?" Valerik asked.

Devlyn shifted his focus, aware that he'd somehow missed something of import. Something beneath Valerik's baiting humor that was now watchful and alert in his eyes. "Lord Hampstead, meet Miss Adelaide Sheridan. Maybe you've heard of Magnus Steel and Shipping, my lord."

Devlyn laughed outright. The pronouncement was so far from what he'd concluded that it was ludicrous. The entire civilized world had heard of Magnus Steel and Shipping. "Is that what you told Valerik?"

He took back everything he was thinking about her. She wasn't a spy for anyone. She was certifiably mad. She didn't know Valerik as he did. She didn't understand the ramifications or the danger to her own life. "You have no idea what you're doing telling anyone that cockeyed story."

"It doesn't matter if you believe me or not."

Her pale hair framed the delicate lines of her face. Despite his anger, despite every antagonistic thing he should have felt, he softened. His gaze dropped over her, kneeling beside him. "You're right. It doesn't. Does it?"

But his voice lacked conviction and, caught by an irritation he could not explain, he fought the tempest brewing within him. Too many coincidences usually meant a hill of lies beneath. She was either the most accomplished actress in the world and putting on a show for Valerik's benefit, or this was no act at all.

"Let her go," Devlyn said. "I don't care who she is or what she's told you. She's not part of the equation between me and Ivanov."

Valerik slapped him on the arm with the quirt. "Then you will tell me where Maria Ivanov is? One life for another?"

Devlyn's anger swept through him in a fury. He would have launched himself if two guards were not holding him down.

"We have a list of your people who have been working on this case," Valerik said. "Those who are still alive. You will be credited with giving us those names."

A boot slammed into Devlyn's ribs and he swore he'd break Valerik's leg just before he crushed his neck, if it was the last thing he ever did.

Outside, the storm grew worse. Wind and rain buffeted the livery. Above him, the timbers creaked. He was vaguely aware that he hovered on the fringe of consciousness. He felt the clasp of manacles being snapped on his ankles.

"It cannot be so hard to find his horse . . ." he heard Valerik shout in answer to another voice. "Go around to the front. Check the alley surrounding this livery."

A pair of muddy boots appeared in his line of sight and Devlyn turned on his back. "Do you think I'm stupid enough to leave anything important on my horse?" He laughed, then he told Valerik in fluent Russian what he could do with himself just before another boot smashed him in the ribs.

Two pairs of hands clasped Devlyn's arms and yanked him back to his feet. Devlyn fell against the one who had just shackled his ankles, only to be yanked back, but not before he'd stuck his hand in the other's pocket and taken the key.

Mrs. Ambrose stepped between them. Her back to him, she faced Valerik. "Please, he is injured enough. Can't you see he is bleeding?"

"Lock them in the cellar." Valerik tossed Mrs. Ambrose the reticule. "I hope you will both be happy together in the short time you have left." To someone else, he said, "If he escapes, I'll kill the lot of you."

"But Capitaine . . . there is no lock on the door."

Valerik swung around on the unfortunate sergeant. "There are four of you here. He is chained hand and foot. Surely three of you can drag him to the back while one of you finds a lock!"

Devlyn turned to face the guard who had shoved him down the stairs. "I hope you plan to provide us water?"

His hat hit him in the chest. He caught it with both of his shackled hands just as the door slammed in his face. "Or a hot meal would be nice!"

A flash of lightning illuminated the room and he caught a glimpse of his surroundings. They'd put him in some sort of storeroom or cellar. The air was musty, filled with the scent of straw and oiled leather. The chains on his ankles dragged against the dirt floor. Manacles weighed heavily on his wrists and feet. He swore as he dropped to a stave barrel and bent over to release the leg shackles with the key he'd taken from the guard. He wondered how long it would take the idiot sergeant to realize he was missing the key.

"Bastard," he muttered.

The wrist manacles wouldn't be as simple to remove as the ankle shackles. Valerik held the key to those. His gaze finally fell on Miss Sheridan, or Mrs. Ambrose, or whomever she was, standing beside him. Another flash of lightning threw her face into relief. He saw the sparkling brilliance in her eyes and had an urge to choke the life from her.

"You're bleeding," she said. She held a handkerchief balled up in her hand.

He caught her wrist before she touched him. She had courage; he'd give her that. She hadn't screamed or broken down and wept.

Opening his shirt, he pressed the kerchief against his shoulder and looked up the rickety wooden stairs at the door. Damn right, he was bleeding. Who wouldn't be, with such a boot kick to the shoulder? He couldn't tell how many of his stitches were torn.

"Will they bring us water?" the girl asked.

"I hope so."

He walked up the stairs and tested the door but found it wedged shut. With an oath, he scanned the room.

Thunder exploded and vibrated the thick timbers overhead. A small window ten feet above the ground provided scant light and little means of escape. He tried to reach it, but a body would have to be skeletal to climb through it. He could see shadows passing across the light seeping beneath the door. He kicked at the stairway support. The first time in fury. The second for good measure, because the attack tore the moorings from the wall. Finally, he returned to attending his wound. There was nothing he could do until someone opened the damn door and brought water.

"Why did you come back for me?" the girl asked when he'd calmed down enough to sit. "You don't even like me."

Devlyn raised his head and looked at her as if for the first time. "You give me too much credit for thinking your rescue through. I don't know you enough to like or dislike you. And you don't know me at all or you wouldn't have to ask that question."

"I didn't know who you were when I met you at the inn," she said. "I thought you were a criminal in dire need of a bath. I thought you were an American. I mean, I didn't think you were an American because you needed a bath—"

"Your countrymen will appreciate the honest sentiment, I'm sure."

"You don't trust anyone, do you?"

He stood. The shackles stretched across both wrists rattled with his movement. Again, he cursed Valerik. "Not when it comes to protecting something I value."

"And what might that be?"

"My life?"

"I have a right to know who and what you are."

Devlyn braced his palm against the stone wall at her back. He'd had enough of her deception. He didn't care if she was innocent of any connection to Nicholas Ivanov. She'd lied about who she was. "Do tell, love. Where did you get that photograph?"

Her chin came up, and whatever self-control she had vanished. "Are you always this rude, Lord Hampstead? Or do you merely reserve your kindness for your *mistress*?"

The brazen comment, completely out of order in the scheme of things, made him laugh aloud. "Are you offering to replace the one I currently have?"

Her fist clinched. "I can think of nothing less appealing, my lord. You have convinced me to become a nun."

It was the fact that she was not being disingenuous that gave him pause. He realized then, with some degree of shock, that he'd been in perfect control of his faculties, he'd been sane up until the velvet woman and her Stradivarius walked into his life. He'd jeopardized this case. And for what?

"Give me your reticule," he said.

"No."

He raised a brow. She knew well and good he could take it. That he would, with no compunction to conscience or propriety, search her bodily if he had to.

She tried to dash around him. He grabbed a handful of her cloak. Instinctively evading her hands, he swept her legs from beneath her and landed with her on a pile of straw. He pinned her arms, his breath hard and fast. His weight rested on her hands positioned on either side of her head as far as his chains would allow. He did not have to touch her. Not with the very devil in his eyes.

"Have you lost your mind?" she panted.

"Aye. Completely." His gaze passed over her mouth before rising. She lay on her back beneath him, merging his senses in a hot rush between his legs. "More than likely, it fled the moment I gave up my seat on that mail coach. No, wait. My sanity abandoned me when you walked into the inn with that cello, like God's scourge to humankind."

"How *dare* you insult Lady Rose." She pushed against his hands. "I did nothing wrong except make the single mistake of . . . of wanting your seat on that mail coach for something that was precious to me. That does not make me guilty of espionage."

He sat back on his calves. "The reticule, Mrs. Ambrose or Miss Sheridan, or shall I call you Adelaide or something else entirely?"

"You think I'm lying about who I am? Oh, indeed. As if you don't have enough problems without getting a head full of notions about your vainglorious deeds. Do not discuss lying and secrets to me. Your mother ran off with an actor? You didn't know your father? Please spare me your indignity, sir. You've been lying to me since we met."

"And I want to know how someone with your supposed pedigree turned up in a mail coach, penniless, in a remote village in the middle of nowhere, with no footmen, no guards, and no chaperone. Your reticule, love."

Her chin came up like a Nordic warrior, her lily-blond hair a beacon in the shadows. Then she dug a hand into her pocket and threw her purse at him. "You are abominable, Lord Hampstead, a morally bankrupt misogynist with no allegiance to anyone but yourself."

He laughed at the truth of her words. "I thought my actions tonight swayed you otherwise," he said, as he remained straddled across her thighs.

"I'm sure you've shocked yourself in that regard."

Spreading the contents of the reticule over the straw with one hand, he glimpsed a small vial of perfume, hairpins, a compass, and seven coins.

His first thought was to try to free the cuffs on his wrists with the hairpins, but that trick never worked despite what storybook tales claimed. He glanced at the compass, then wedged three fingers inside the purse. The photograph fell out and he turned it over in his hand. His mother's flowery script marked the date on back and the initials *DSC*.

The photograph definitely belonged in his mother's collection. But below the date someone had drawn two hearts with his initials inside and connecting to another heart with the letters *ACS* inside. Adelaide Cassandra Sheridan. He paused. As far as he could recall, no one had ever drawn a heart around his initials.

Except the three letters weren't his initials. They were his brother's.

Devlyn had agreed to the betrothal arrangement soon after he'd come home from Marseille and buried his brother not quite a year ago. In the end, he'd consented to procure the needed fortune and heir for the family, if only to make peace with the St. Clair legacy and his own father.

If Dominick hadn't died, his brother would have been the one at the betrothal ball he'd missed, and Devlyn wouldn't be here now.

"You look nothing like that photograph," he heard her whisper. "Certainly you are not who I thought you were."

His gaze dropped to her mouth before sliding back to her eyes, nearly black in the shadows covering her face. He didn't blame her for hating him. "How do you know Ambassador Maxwell?"

"His daughter is my friend. We've known each other since we were children."

He gently tilted her chin and looked into her eyes now filling with tears she did not want to shed in his presence. "Why did you follow me from the hotel?"

"You were the only person I knew to go to for help."

"Did it ever occur to you that you would be compromised? Or that your life would be in a great deal of danger?"

A flash of lightning cast a silver pall over the room. The light briefly swam in her liquid eyes to reveal the depths of her vulnerability. Few men—certainly not he—could resist the hurt he saw there. Something shifted inside him, something primal and possessive that caught him.

He knew she was exactly who she claimed to be, and his indifference to her plight vanished. No spy worth anyone's attention would be carrying around a well-frayed ten-year-old portraiture of someone she thought was him.

But it wasn't him.

She was moonstruck over his brother.

He sat back on his heels, still straddling her hips, throwing another impatient glance at the door. He was not normally a man who waited for fate to find him, but there was nothing he could do until someone came to open that door. "If I'd known who you were from the beginning, we could have avoided this particular misunderstanding, Miss Sheridan." He reached across her for his hat and slapped it on his head.

"Then I expect we can remain amicable until we dissolve the contract between us. We need to escape here first. Then you and I will part ways and we'll forget we ever met."

He couldn't have framed the sentiment more eloquently, though he did like the feel of her beneath him and would prolong the moment. At least until he heard the guards returning. "Are we already negotiating the terms of the dissolution of our betrothal, Miss Sheridan?"

"There is no negotiation. We no longer have business between us, Lord Hampstead."

"And here I thought we were getting along so well."

"Get off me this instant. I wouldn't wed you if you were the last man on earth."

And Cassie was appalled at her own terrible words. She felt nothing but shame that the shackles that draped his wrists were proof of what he'd endured tonight because of her. Yet, she could not apologize even if she knew how to frame it in her mind.

"No?" He leaned low over her. "Do you want me to prove what a hypocrite you are, Miss Sheridan?"

"Do not speak to me of duplicity. At least I am honest."

He observed her with an arch smile. Then rose to his feet, scattering straw in his wake. He dropped to the stairs so he could better watch the light seeping from beneath the door. "I forgot. You don't steal or cheat, either," he said, drawing his knee to his chest and turning his attention to her as she scooped up the spilled contents of her reticule.

"Or kill," she said.

"But someone has to be able to take care of the unpleasant, dirty business, so people like you can sleep safely at night."

"Circumstances should not govern one's morality," she whispered, fearing the high road was no longer within her reach and that, for some reason, he was mocking her, marking time, and that he really didn't care a whit about her moral bias.

"Indeed." He laughed and nodded to the garnet-encrusted fob she held in her hand. "Where did you get that compass?"

Cassie folded her hand protectively around the compass. "You know from whom I purchased it. You were standing at the window watching."

"That Gypsy peddler is a thief."

"And who are you but the pot calling the kettle black, Lord Hampstead?"

"Yet you purchased something that was stolen. Worse, you probably suspected it was stolen and bought it anyway. What does that make you?"

"I . . . didn't *know* for sure it was stolen."

"Then you admit circumstances can dictate right from wrong."

"No circumstances justify stealing or lying."

"It depends on what you believe, *Mrs*. Ambrose. Neither my nor old Hector's beliefs amount to one black and white answer. And just because the answers differ from what you believe does not make one right or wrong. Hector is what you call a garbage collector. He finds things along the roads, in the hills. He scavenges abandoned cottages, and might even rob a grave or two, where I suspect that compass came from. He does it to survive and, in doing it, makes the world a little cleaner for someone else. You just benefited from his efforts. So do not judge what you do not understand."

Feeling the reproach in his voice, Cassie looked at the compass for which she had traded her fur muff and knew he spoke the truth to some degree. But moral shades of gray did not take away from right and wrong.

Suddenly he was beside her, pushing her against the wall. "Someone is coming."

She strained her hearing for the noise that had alerted him, but no sound rose above the hammer-beat of their hearts. His mouth touched the soft shell of her ear. "Listen to me well, Princess. Unless you want to get yourself handed over to one of the most brutal men you'll ever have the displeasure of knowing, you won't leave my side again until we reach Edinburgh. Do you understand?"

Her eyes wide, she nodded. He retrieved his leg irons, wrapping one end around his wrist, his motion so fluid she wondered how many times he'd done this before.

"What are you going to do?" Scraping the hair from her eyes, she peered up through the darkness at his bearded face.

Despite everything else she knew about him, she trusted that he would get them out of this alive.

"A chance not taken is an opportunity lost, Miss Sheridan." The door latch moved, and he pushed her to the wall. "If you don't like violence, shut your eyes."

Chapter 5

Pressed against the wall, Cassie squeezed her eyes shut.

But only until the door squeaked opened. One uniformed man stepped through onto the wooden platform to hold the door for another carrying a bucket of water. Even before they could order him to move away from the wall, Lord Hampstead kicked out at the rotten stair post and sent the contraption crumbling to the ground. The third guard appeared in the doorway, bringing his rifle up as Lord Hampstead swung the leg shackles. Like a snake, the chains wrapped around the steel barrel. He jerked forward, yanking the guard atop the first two with a bone-crunching thud. In thirty seconds, Lord Hampstead had cleared the doorway and already retrieved a gun from the groaning rifle-toting guard.

"Time to leave, Miss Sheridan," he said.

Using the men on the ground as leverage, he bounded

up into the doorway, turned and pulled her up. No one else was in the stable.

"Run!"

Lord Hampstead pushed her out into the night and slammed the stable doors shut behind them. Rain pelted her face. Cassie could see nothing in the night. Lightning stabbed the sky, flashing twice, revealing an empty corral and an overflowing field. Her half boots stuck in smelly muck. She wiped the water from her eyes and yanked her feet out of the mire. Only desperation kept her from falling forward, face first.

"Where are the horses?"

Lord Hampstead grabbed her upper arm. "Just run!"

She was too terrified not to and followed him blindly. She valiantly tried to match his stride, but her corset was not laced to endure a marathon and her skirts were a heavy weight against her legs. The yard leveled off and then she was no longer running but was on her knees behind a lean-to trying to catch her breath. Rain slanted in a blinding sheet across her vision and she could see nothing, but Lord Hampstead seemed to have the eyes of a cat.

She heard shouts, but the rain distorted the direction from where they came.

Lord Hampstead pulled her beneath an eave and pressed her against a wooden wall. "They left two men outside the livery," he rasped near her ear, looking toward the yard, taking a rough sighting of the direction they needed to go.

Taller than she, he stepped in front of her, his body and heavy cloak blunting the force of the rain. Her breath came in heaves. She held on to him because she didn't know where else to hold. For a second, she thought she smelled him. Soap and rain and warm flesh against her chilled skin. Startled by the quickening sensation in her belly, she let go of his arm. The movement pulled his gaze around.

"You can't run in those skirts," he said.

Well, she certainly wasn't going to strip naked. Her voice came out raspy and chilled. "I can run fast enough."

"The hell you can."

A blade flashed in his manacled hands. *Where did he get a knife?* He dropped to one knee in front of her. Cassie caught herself on his shoulder. She felt the heat of his body and the power of his muscles beneath her palms. His palm brushed her calf and the intimacy of the touch nearly made her jump. The gown tugged and tore. Her petticoat did not suffer the same fate, as it reached only to her ankles.

He stood and his attention paused on her face. Lightning flashed and briefly revealed his dark eyes. The wind whipped her cloak around him. She felt strange, as if the storm had moved from the sky and into her veins. Her pulse danced in her throat. Something was happening between them and she knew he felt it, too. Right there next to the shed, with danger exploding all around them, something elemental was taking root. And worse, she had the uncanny horror that he knew what she was feeling despite her dislike of him, despite the fact that she'd called him an abominable, morally bankrupt misogynist with no allegiance to anyone but himself.

These feelings were absurd. This tall, arresting stranger was the worst kind of rogue, autocratic and atrociously overconfident in everything he did.

His gloved hand wrapped around her arm. "I have a feeling I know where the horses went."

She had no idea where he was leading her. They dashed across the empty field toward a white farmhouse barely visible in the woods. She saw the horses in front of her huddled beneath a tree and nearly cried out with relief. She reached the sorrel stallion. Somehow, in garments that did not allow her to stretch upward, she got one foot into the stirrup, felt a hand boldly at her backside, then landed astride the saddle, her skirts crumpled against her thighs. Lord Hampstead pulled himself up behind her and, with chains stretching between his wrists, brought both his arms over her head. He reached around her and grabbed the reins. The horse, unused to the extra weight, sidestepped.

"We'll break our necks," she shouted over the rain.

One of his hands was splayed on her waist and pressed her to him, not out of any need to draw her close, but instead to anchor her to the saddle. "In case you don't know it yet, love, I just saved your life."

In that split second, she heard the call to arms behind her.

A shot shattered a limb above their heads.

Checked by Lord Hampstead's strength, the sorrel stallion turned in a circle, leading the packhorse around, and suddenly shot forward, throwing her backward against his chest.

A cold spray of water leapt to life all around them, then they were galloping across a meadow away from town. Lord Hampstead's manacled hand stretched over her right rib cage just beneath her breast. And for a nightmarish moment, she felt safe in his arms, a contradiction of circumstance to be sure. His embrace was the least safe place for her to be.

For an hour, Devlyn saw nothing in the darkness as they moved at a dangerous pace over terrain set with ditches and gullies. Dawn, briefly jarring itself free from the millrace of darkened clouds, made a skittish appearance over the treetops and revealed the ravaged countryside. A dilapidated farmhouse painted a gloomy picture of past floods along this route. The nearby meadow had turned into a miniature lake and, keeping to the trees on higher ground, Devlyn skirted the rim past a single brown cow that had found shelter beside a felled oak.

Twice during the day, he stopped so they could eat and rest the mounts, too cold for conversation. He did everything he could think of to get the shackles off his wrists. The hairpins in Miss Sheridan's reticule didn't work. He beat the bloody chains with a rock until it was all he could do to mount a horse and ride. By late afternoon, he quit looking over his shoulder, concentrating only on staying in the saddle. The afternoon remained a montage of wind-whipped trees and, as he came up over a hill, reining in the horse to an abrupt stop, he stared down at the raging river.

It was a scene from hell, with raging floodwaters and broken branches caught in the rapids. He closed his eyes. An acute sense of the inevitable gripped his gut, amplified by the roar of the crushing cataracts. His options were rapidly fading. With the daylight, he'd lost his advantage against those hunting him.

The Cossacks were like wolves. Once they were on his scent, no spring storm, not even one that had flooded the countryside, would keep them from their task.

Devlyn pulled the field glasses from the haversack and looked south, then east behind him. It worried him that he'd lost a lot of blood and would not be strong enough to fight should Valerik find him again. The land lay empty and quiet, covered in moss, a beautiful river valley spreading west like fingers.

He felt Miss Sheridan's eyes on his profile, the warm

whisper of her breath on his cheek, and he lowered the glasses. She had not spoken and he was glad for her silence.

A fresh gust of wind whipped against them. "We need to find another way," he said.

This time, he looked south. And as the daylight hours passed into another wind-driven night, he worried about the sorrel taking on so much weight for as long as he had. Despite an increasingly slower pace, the terrain was proving as dangerous as the river. Then, just as the moon broke free of the clouds, an eerie howl echoed through the trees. Something ran across the narrow path under the hooves of the tired horse. The stallion shied and reared, nearly throwing them from the saddle.

Bringing both horses to a stop, he swore, but Miss Sheridan had clearly had enough. Devlyn knew he would kill the horses if he didn't stop. Somewhere ahead of him, he could hear the sound of a waterfall. Hell, he thought, looking up at the sky, he wasn't anywhere near where he should be.

"I have to get off this horse now," Miss Sheridan said.

"The devil you are—" But she had already started to slide off the saddle. "Calm down. I'll help you dismount."

"W-worry about yourself, Lord Hampstead. I know you've been f-favoring your shoulder. I prefer to d-dismount on my own."

He caught her arm, but the effort only slowed Cassie's descent. What little feeling she had left in her legs and hands helped to rouse her back to life, but it hurt to move. She didn't think she could feel more despondent until she hit the ground like a novice equestrian and sprawled flat on her backside.

The tears she had managed to hold back all day burned just beneath the surface, and two days without sleep did nothing to bolster her stamina. Lord Hampstead crossed one shackled wrist over the other and looked down at her as if she'd lost her mind.

Maybe she had. She'd already convinced him that she was not normal and was certainly doing nothing to persuade him otherwise. He didn't want her with him and she didn't particularly want to stay with him. He'd made his feelings clear to her from the moment she'd met him, but as he remained on the horse looking down the path where she knew he wanted to go, it came as a shock that she felt safe with him and feared his abandonment.

"Are you all right?" he finally asked.

Struggling to stand, she brushed off her stinging backside. "I am fine."

"Watch where you are standing around the horses," he said, dismounting as he spoke. "The horses are skittish enough as it is. If either one runs, you aren't going to like it if we have to walk out of here."

She stepped away from both. The big horse was limping, and Lord Hampstead dropped to one knee beside its left front leg. "This is as good a place as any to camp." He ran one gloved hand along the foreleg. "We'll remain."

She hated seeing the shackles on his wrists. Nothing he had tried that day could get them off. She hated seeing that his horse was hurt. "Do you know where we are?"

"Not where I need to be." He peered up at the sky. "Too far south, maybe. I don't know."

Cassie looked down at the shackles on his wrists as a sudden dawning struck her. He was wearing iron manacles.

Why hadn't she realized that before? On her father's

ships, anything made of iron was restricted from the main bridge away from all navigational equipment. It was one of the first things an officer learned. "The manacles are made of iron," she said. "A compass will give a false reading when set too close to an iron field. We could be anywhere from four to twenty degrees off your intended course."

The moment she'd mentioned the shackles, the same thought clearly struck him, and it was not a pleasant one as he swore, an indiscreet word that she'd never heard spoken in her life.

"At least knowing that should give you an idea where we are," she offered. "It will be easy to find ourselves on the chart."

"And what will that tell us? That we are in the hills?"

"I know a little of navigation. I could help."

Shaking his head, he stalked to the other side of the horse. "I have an idea where we are," he said. "And in some bloody thieves' hidey-hole isn't a place we want to be, Miss Sheridan."

"Cassie," she said quietly. Her teeth had started to chatter with the cold. "M-my name is C-Cassie."

He looked at her shivering. An eerie mist clung to the ground. He stood and faced her, watching as her gaze chased up to his. "We need to build a fire and take what warmth we can. Gather wood."

The moon shone faintly overhead through a weave of branches and she looked around her as if seeing the darkness for the first time. Then she heard the not-so distant howl of another wolf. "What . . . sort of w-wood?"

"The kind that burns would be a great place to start." He scraped his hand over his jaw. "Stay away from green wood."

It wasn't fair that he expected her to know everything

he did and discarded anything she might contribute as unimportant. Clutching her sodden cloak, she looked at the woods.

She had once read about a roving pack of man-eating dogs devouring an entire settlement in the Northwest Territory. Sally Ann had told her such stories were fiction people wrote to sell newspapers, but here in the untamed wilds of Scotland, she believed them to be true. She had no desire to venture alone into the forest, and it came as a shock to feel how afraid she was. She didn't want to need Lord Hampstead any more than she wanted to be afraid of the darkness, wolves, or any of the other sundry of dangers surrounding her.

"The wood, Miss Sheridan."

A fluttering sounded in the tree branches above her. This time, she watched his gaze shift to the shadows as if something were wrong. "What is it?" she asked alarmed.

"I'm not sure. Picts, barbarians from the north, maybe." A trace of amusement laced his reply.

"Picts."

"Leprechauns," he added over his shoulder as he pulled blankets and another bundle from the packhorse. "Hairy ogres."

She frowned at his back, irritated by the fact that he was familiar with this countryside with its subtle nuance of danger. He must think her childish fears inane and her navigational skills laughable.

But knowing that anyone they met in the wilds of these woods was as much likely to be foe as friend, she hiked through the bushes and underbrush after him. It would serve him right if there really were ancient Picts over the hill with arrows drawn back in bows ready to launch into his heart.

"Will the sheriff know what has happened to us?" she

asked, no longer able to control her shivering. Her sodden clothes clung to her with a chill she'd never experienced in her life. "Surely he would arrest C-C-Captain Valerik for what he did to you."

He did not reply to her statement. Instead he said dismissively, "We both need sleep. There's nothing more we can do tonight."

"You're not immune to d-death, my lord."

"We all die," he said with equal impatience in his voice. "Some of us sooner than others."

She found her own ire rising. "Yes, we do. But somehow I don't believe you are as cavalier toward the care of your mortal soul as you want me to believe."

A slow grin, one that did not entirely reach his eyes, turned his beautiful mouth into an invitation to sin. "It isn't my mortal soul that concerns me."

"Aren't you af-fraid of anything?"

"Let me tell you the future as I see it, Miss Sheridan." He dropped the haversack along with everything else he carried at his feet. "Valerik doesn't have to be behind us. He already knows our destination. My only hope was that I can beat him across the river. Obviously, I won't now, which means you and I will have to work a little harder together to stay alive. I need you out of every stitch of wet clothes you are wearing before you get sick. I need you healthy. And I need you productive. *Capisci*, love?"

"*Perché sì, signore.* Of course," she said, folding her arms tightly about her torso.

A thrill went through her at having shocked him. She'd studied the language every day for the past year, in a pathetic endeavor to make an impression on his beautiful Italian mother.

But if he found wit in her statement or respect for her

proficiency, she'd never have guessed by the dark look in his eyes. And suddenly pride deserted her. She wanted to throw something at him, a childish and uncharacteristic reaction that shocked her as completely as if someone had tossed a frozen snowball in her face. Cassie didn't lose her temper. She didn't allow her emotions to run amok like some screaming fishwife. But this was too much. She knew she suffered from a case of self-pity as much as the trauma of the day. Until now, she'd never realized how truly boring her life was. She liked boring. Boring was safe.

He had hurt her in a way he'd never understand because she'd never tell him, but despite her best intentions, she couldn't contain the wobble in her voice.

"I hate seeing those shackles on your wrists," she said. "What happened at the livery was terrifying for me. And I'm sorry that I do not know the difference between colored and noncolored wood! But I've met roustabouts with better manners than you. In *fact*"—she raised her chin—"you are an arrogant ass. A-S-S, the hind end of a donkey, which in proper American English m-means you are a nincompoop of the first water." Her voice caught on a sob.

"Is that right?"

"Two weeks ago, I was preparing for my wedding. My life was perfectly structured, tedious, and safe." She wiped the back of her hand across her cheek. "Now I'm running from the Cossack guard of some Russian consortium that thinks I am your accomplice and wants to kill me. Had someone asked me yesterday if I would be standing nearly soaked to the flesh in front of a lunatic today, I would have been scandalized at the word *flesh*."

He peered at her from beneath his hat brim and laughed. "Lunatic?"

"I dislike you, Lord Hampstead. And you can do with that information what you will."

Cassie dragged up the weight of her skirts and walked with as much dignity as her aching muscles could afford. The damp fabric of her skirt rubbed against her legs with every step. But she trudged through the underbrush, gathering pieces of wood that didn't look green and that felt as dry as possible to the touch. Lord Hampstead had dropped the blankets in a clearing near an earthen overhang, and she managed to build a substantial pile. Ignoring her, he dug a hole in the ground, divided the wood, and pulled out a tinderbox from his haversack. The flames spread and soon a crackling fire destroyed the comfort of concealment she'd found in the darkness.

Cassie turned and walked into the woods. She didn't go so far that she couldn't see the fire. Only far enough to get away from Lord Hampstead. She didn't think she could be more despondent as she worked the ties on her skirt and petticoats. Finally, she peeled away her blouse and draped everything she could remove over some bushes. She could not get to the laces on her corset. The rest of her clothes were rags, unsalvageable, and she thought irrationally of her parents' horror if they should see her in this state. She didn't want to fall apart. She certainly didn't want to collapse in front of Lord Hampstead.

The tears came despite everything she did to stop them. Huddled beneath her cloak, she opened her reticule and withdrew the photograph. Cassie held the picture in both hands barely visible in the flickering firelight behind her. She no longer saw the carefree youthful man of her dreams, but a dark, predatory hunter that only a charitable person would call a gentleman. She saw his Italian mother in his dark eyes and, looking at the portraiture now, didn't know how she'd missed that resemblance when she'd first met him at the inn. He'd been wearing a hat low over his face and he had a close-cropped beard, not counting the ten years that had honed his features. But still, Cassie possessed a remarkable memory—photographic, as her grandfather used to say—which made her an excellent navigator when they went sailing off Cape Cod in the summers. She'd come to England with such lofty hopes and dreams, schoolgirl and childish. She'd been a fool!

Cassie ripped the photograph into tiny pieces and let them flutter to the mud. She blinked when Lord Hampstead knelt in front of her, her thoughts unfocused as she attempted to peer at his features partially hidden beneath the hat brim.

"You understand, love, this is an intractable blow to my heart."

She pressed her hand against her nose and sniffled. "Perhaps I would believe that if I thought you had a heart."

"Drink." He handed her a silver flask. "It will help alleviate some of the chill."

She poked her fingers from beneath her cloak and reached for the flask. He took each of her ice-cold hands and turned them over in his. "You've gone the entire day with no gloves?"

Puzzled by the concern she sensed beneath the callused exterior surrounding those words, she raised her gaze and found his. He was as wet to the bone as she. She tried to withdraw her hand. "I lost them in the flood. You must be freezing, too."

"I wasn't sitting on the front of the horse through the brunt of that storm," he said, urging the flask to her lips. "Drink."

With shaking hands, she sniffed the contents. Her eyes watered. She would not have him think her inept or afraid of her own shadow even if she was. Holding her breath, she swigged. Though she coughed and choked, she managed to swallow an entire mouthful. *Lord in heaven, the stuff was vile.*

"What is this?" she rasped.

The corner of his mouth slanted. "It's Royal Lochnagar." He affected a Scott's burr as easily as he'd spoken American English. "The queen's favorite. It's an acquired taste."

She swigged two more times.

"For such a cream puff, you drink whiskey well," he said dryly, and watched as she drank another swallow. "Are you going to get drunk on me?"

She burped delicately into her hand. After the initial burn and gasp, she felt the mellow warmth expand from her stomach. "I m-might, if I thought it would k-keep me warm," she said, handing back the flask.

She felt his intense scrutiny, and watched in incredulity as he pulled a wicked-looking knife from the sheath inside his boot. Devlyn St. Clair was not a man overburdened by a conscience, and clearly found nothing wrong with murdering her in a fit of rage. His manacles did not help her image of him.

"Let go of the cloak," he said in an almost gentle voice.

"I most certainly will not— What are you d-doing?"

Turning her around, he pressed his lips against the shell of her ear. "Getting you warm." He sliced through the wet knots on her corset. "You're soaked to your bones."

She possessed no strength to prevent him from doing whatever he wanted, and caught the corset as it fell. His movements impersonal, he peeled her cloak from her body and she was suddenly standing in front of him wearing only her underclothes. He briskly rubbed her hair with a blanket. Breathing in his redolence, she felt his strength overwhelming all other impressions she had of him, and she found herself leaning nearer to him for warmth.

His woolen cloak was black with rain. He wore a black shirt, a revolver he'd taken from one of the Cossacks sitting in a sheath beneath his arm, he looked no more than a shadow in the darkness of the forest. A lock of hair had fallen across his brow, and she looked away. She'd been wrong in town to assume that the attire he wore was shabby; everything he owned was first-rate. "I don't know if you'll dry out before we leave." The rubbing stopped and he gave her one of his woolen shirts. "But this is better than sleeping in wet clothes."

She took his shirt, the fabric fine and clean in her hands. She lifted her chin, nervously aware of the implied intimacy in accepting that garment. "Thank you."

Lord Hampstead's eyes dropped to her mouth and let loose the butterflies in her stomach. She didn't understand the physical anomalies that occurred in her body when he was near. Tomorrow when she was stronger and warmer, and not so exhausted, she would delve into the darker corners of her mind and examine her confusion. But for now, the heat from his body warmed her like a sunbeam separating her from the chill and the men hunting them. She felt an acute sense of comfort in his presence.

A comfort she did not desire when nothing else about him was calming to a young woman alone for the first time in her life. Perhaps because he had killed a man over another woman, and had done so with no remorse. His dangerousness shimmered around him now.

She told herself to step back and take a deep breath. She told herself to look away. And then a blaze started to burn. She felt it spark deep within her and knew he felt it, too, in the same way she had when they'd stood by that shed with lightning exploding all around them. But even as her mind sought to analyze and crush her reaction, her heart urged her onward to explore.

His hands were suddenly behind her, the manacles dragging against her hips. "Cassandra?" he whispered, his upper-crust accent more evident than she'd heard before.

Was he asking her for a kiss?

Or telling her that he was going to kiss her, giving her no choice in the matter? He was standing toe to toe with her, and now more than a curious longing moved her to lift her chin. No man had ever kissed her. Though no challenge had been issued, his words lingered over her lips like a soft erotic whisper, the brush of his breath a curious tickling against her tender flesh an instant before his mouth slanted seamlessly across hers.

He tasted heady like whiskey, and the constriction in her chest spread to her abdomen before she could rein it back. She let her eyes drift closed. A desperate part of her wanted him to take note of her as a woman, wanted to make him remember her always, and so she kissed him back harder, concentrating on the contour of his lips and trying to follow his every movement.

His thumb traced her jawline. And as if to confirm her consent, he pulled away and, for an instant, they each seemed caught by the other's gaze. The gentle pressure of his thumbs on her chin nudged her lips. "Open your mouth, Cassie."

Then he melded his lips to hers.

She made a startled sound. The heat was unexpected.

Burning. It surged into her veins, transforming the beat of her heart into something explosive in her chest. For several long seconds she could not breathe, and started to raise her palms to his chest to push him away, only to find they were clutching the fabric of his shirt. He growled the same way a wolf might upon discovering that he does not want to devour the lamb all in one sitting, yet finding himself too ravenous to stop. The warm hands cradling the back of her head threaded her hair, the pad of each gloved finger a point of heat on her scalp. And any misconceptions she'd ever held about merging lips and seducing a rogue vanished in a hot haze of passion as he thrust his tongue into her mouth.

Clinging to the sensations pouring through her, her response was entirely unbidden, borne of instinct and something more.

He was the antithesis of everything anodyne that she was. Her life was structured. Predictable. She was disciplined and educated in the gentler arts that shaped her into a proper lady. She'd eaten chicken on Mondays, beef on Wednesdays, and sherbet every Friday for as long as she could remember. Her entire life had been run by someone else's schedule, or rules, or the fear that she would disappoint those she loved.

Their slow sensual meeting of tongues became a dance, a sybaritic waltz of the senses, the devil's dance for its wicked touch on her soul. Biting back a soft moan, Cassie opened her fists and pressed her hands against his chest. The beat of his heart thumped against her palms. He was hot and smoothly contoured. She felt the bulk of the dressing he'd put on his shoulder and the first spark of reality intruded. His arms tightened around her, the sound of chains pulling her from her bliss. She felt his mouth move across her cheek to her temple, sending tremors down her body.

But with the pleasure, there also came pain and fear. Why else would she hesitate when her body clearly wanted more?

Because Devlyn St. Clair was not safe. He was dark and dangerous. Everything she could never be. He promised seduction and heartache and lies to explain away his life.

He hesitated for the slightest fraction. Then he pulled back and his finger traced the curve of her throat, his dark eyes on hers assessing as he tilted her face. She knew then that his mask had slipped, if only a bit. If only for a breath, she'd seen something else beneath the amused cynicism that was as much a part of him as the cloak of darkness he wore like a mantle over his body.

Her hand trembled. It was all she could do not to touch her fingertips to her lips. Suddenly drained of the will to stand, she snatched up the blanket and the woolen shirt he'd given her where both had fallen at his feet.

"Bloody hell," she heard him murmur, and could not have voiced the sentiment more eloquently as she dropped to a tree stump, though she didn't understand that his frustration with the situation could possibly equal hers.

"How old are you, Cassie?" he suddenly asked, his eyes surprisingly gentle.

"Nearly twenty," she said, tentatively. "How old are you?"

"Twenty-nine."

After a moment, he sat beside her, his elbows braced on his knees, his boots planted on the ground. They remained thus while the fire continued to crackle behind him. At last he spoke, forcing her to look at him. "Have you ever really *met* a roustabout?"

She didn't like that he so easily roused her deepest emotions. Nor could she help the mist that formed in her eyes. "My grandfather loved the docks," she said, knowing an English aristocrat would have no fondness for someone as completely anomalous as her grandfather had been. Someone like her. "He was my father's father. He had his beginnings designing ships, but he was *common*, as the Knickerbocker regime would say. And I say common in an affectionate way. There was never anyone like my grandfather. I'm sure you wouldn't have liked him. He certainly would not have liked you or your family."

He pondered the iron manacle on one hand. At last he spoke, forcing her to look at him. "I wish I could explain everything to you, but I can't," he finally said. "My father was apprised of the possibility that I would not be in Hampshire for the ball. But he elected to proceed as planned because in his supreme arrogance and in his opinion of me, he could not fathom that I might be involved in a larger cause. One that affects him more than he knows."

"He does not know what you do?"

"No, he does not. And it probably wouldn't matter if he did. My father sees his world through his own tinted glasses. I see mine through an entirely different pair, and my vision never involved the plans he had for me. But that doesn't mean I had never intended to fulfill them. The contracts are signed and come summer's end, you and I will wed."

She looked into the flames before pulling her gaze from the fire. "You make it all sound like sordid business."

"It is sordid. You and I both know why you are in England, don't we? The whole of the ton understands the intricacies of this particularly arranged marriage. My family needs something you have, and yours wants something I have. Since when do marriages ever have to do with the two people actually taking their vows because of love?"

Cassie lowered her eyes, then brought the full import of her gaze on Lord Hampstead. "I don't want this marriage any more than you do."

"But we are rather stuck with each other for now. Aren't we?"

She supposed they were. A companionable silence ensued. His thigh pressed against hers and she became aware of its warmth.

He held his gloved hand beneath her chin and tilted her face. "Am I your first?"

"Marriage?"

"Kiss."

She saw the crook of his mouth, and it was in that moment that Cassie understood even minimal physical contact was enough for her to feel off balance.

She came to her feet. "Is this conversation truly necessary?"

He followed her up. "You're avoiding the topic."

Of course she was avoiding the topic. "I'm quite aware of what goes on between a man and a woman, if that is what you are asking, though I do not see my knowledge as pertinent to our current situation."

"How aware?"

She squirmed beneath his scrutiny. "Sally Ann and I once saw her brother in the gardens at the ambassador's Yuletide Ball two years ago," she related, remembering that day as one of the worst in her life. "Braeden probably thought he was being discreet."

"Braeden? Ambassador Maxwell's son?"

Surprise touched her voice. "You know him?"

Something in Lord Hampstead's expression told her

that he knew Braeden, if not well, then at least well enough to form a sizable opinion. "We've met," he said without inflection. "A few times, in fact, over the years."

"He's a former naval officer," she said. "Did you meet across the bow of his ship?"

"Nothing so heroic. He would be the first to tell you that. You saw him kissing?"

Her tone was cool. "They were doing a lot more than kissing."

And Cassie had been heartbroken to see her childhood crush in the arms of another woman. Braeden Maxwell had been all things truly heroic to her from the first time she had seen him standing at one of the ambassador's functions in full uniformed regalia, principled and valiant. Cassie had never forgotten.

"And you were not enthralled," Lord Hampstead said, "because you wanted to be that woman?"

"Yes, I wanted to be that woman more than anything. But I wasn't. And I think you should not kiss me anymore. It isn't something I enjoyed."

His face remained in the shadows beneath his hat, his expression guarded. She faced him like a captain on her own sinking ship, clutching the blanket to her shoulders, watching as he took a step nearer, until they were toe to toe. Then he reached around her and lifted his haversack.

"Clearly, Nicholas Ivanov is afraid of you," she whispered. "Will he see you arrested when we get to Edinburgh?"

Only his eyes lit by the firelight showed the patience the rest of him lacked. "Ivanov is a man who prefers to handle his own internal affairs. He will never allow this case to go to a tribunal."

"You seem to know his family well."

"I once served in a diplomatic capacity in St. Petersburg where I had the misfortune of meeting Nicholas Ivanov."

"And were you working in a diplomatic capacity when you killed Ivanov's son to steal his wife?"

His eyes held hers, and she stopped herself from flinching at the cold hatred she saw there. But it was not hatred aimed at her.

He was two people, she realized. The one she saw now—an extension of the man she'd known in town—and the man he'd been when he'd taken away her tears, the man who had kissed her.

"Let me tell you a little bit about Nicholas Ivanov and his son, Stefan," he said. "Stefan was the number two man in his father's growing empire that has found a cozy little foothold on British soil under the guise of diplomacy. No one can touch him because nothing can be linked directly back to him. He imports opium from the Orient, which funds his weapons trade in which he supplies other nationals to undermine British interests across the globe. Nicholas Ivanov watched as Stefan killed the last man Nicholas thought was snooping in his affairs. Then they dumped him bloody and naked on a public Paris street."

"He will do the same to you." Her voice was low.

"I intend to bring the consortium down. But Nicholas Ivanov I will kill myself." The words sent an icy chill down her spine.

He slung the haversack over his shoulder. "Never weigh a man's character on his giving up a seat for your cello, Miss Sheridan."

Then he was gone to tend to the horses. His manner might be brash, but she had glimpsed something of his vulnerability when he'd come face to face with that river today, and last night with Valerik. She'd seen it a few moments ago when he spoke of the man Ivanov murdered. Devlyn St. Clair might have survived a dangerous life, one she would never begin to understand, but she suspected he wasn't as defiant in the face of death as he seemed to want the world to believe.

She did not awaken when Devlyn walked into camp later and dropped his gear.

He found her curled with the only two blankets asleep beneath a frothy overspread of low-hanging branches, protected from the sounds of the forest and nearby wolves. She wore his shirt.

The silver whiskey flask still lay beside the fire. Uncapping the lid, he sat back on one knee and glanced at the horizon. The storm may have moved west, but he felt another brewing inside him. He was tired and edgy and didn't know what was happening to him.

He looked down at the shackles still on his wrists. He would give his left ballock to get his hands around Valerik's bloody neck and break it. Braced on one knee, he struggled to remove the shoulder sheath that held his revolver, finally cutting it off, as he couldn't pull it over the chains. He felt a weakness go through his muscles and began to worry his body would fail him.

Now he felt exposed in another way. Raising the flask to his lips, he looked over at the sleeping Cassie, who was unaware of his dire thoughts concerning her. The cold analytical part of him was caught by the sudden realization that he'd gone soft . . . or suicidal. Both characteristics represented the same end to him, and he didn't like the lack of control implied.

There it was, and the idea both amused and bothered him, for though he had always planned to honor the promise he'd made to his father after his brother's death, he had not anticipated Cassandra Sheridan. The marriage agreement had been and always would be a business arrangement between both of their families. Nothing more. Devlyn couldn't afford her idealism, any more than he could afford resentment, grief or self-doubt to cloud his judgment. So he simply willed the emotions away and let his gaze travel over her where it was wont to stray anyway.

Absently, his eyes tracked across her shoulder. She had her back to the fire, the sinful length of her hair fanning around her. His gaze slid down the deep curve of her waist, the bewildering sexual pull he felt toward her seeping into his body, a warming fire he knew would be difficult to douse if he allowed it to burn hotter.

And he was reminded that for one wild and insane moment beneath the moonlight, he had kissed her. Planted both palms on either side of her head and kissed her as if no tomorrow chased him. Bloody Christ, what was that?

It had been an incongruous act. One that came amid the chaos of his emotions and the rush at the end of a chase. But one he took stock of now as the whiskey began to ease the pain in his ribs and shoulder.

He could not have anticipated meeting her the way he had. Nor have anticipated the complication she was suddenly proving to be.

He only knew his opinion of Cassie Sheridan had changed. Maybe it was the moment he'd realized who she was. And even as he'd congratulated himself on finding the chink in her armor when he'd kissed her, he'd felt like a bully. He took no pleasure in challenging her honor to compensate for his lack of any.

He looked toward the sky. He had to get them both to Edinburgh. Then he would deal with his own bloody demons, a reluctant bride, and a future that, until now, he hadn't been sure he wanted.

Chapter 6

⟨ornament⟩

Cassie sat up.

She groaned and pressed her hand to the small of her back. But with movement came pain. Her muscles hurt in places she hadn't known muscles existed. Even her fingernails ached.

She flexed her hand and watched the pattern of light change, realizing it was daylight already. She looked up. A canvas tarp draped the branches around her and lay in folds on the ground. She did not remember building a shelter. She wore Lord Hampstead's woolen shirt. She brought her forearm to her nose, inhaling the familiar spicy scent of his soap. She liked the way he smelled, and she realized she was clearly attracted to him.

Cassie leaned over and lifted the edge of canvas.

A soupy fog had formed during the night. She couldn't see anything but indistinguishable shapes, and a hush had fallen over the glade.

"Lord Hampstead?"

No answer came above the distant sound of a waterfall, a lonely, inviting noise against the silence.

She tucked the blanket over her breasts and beneath her arms as she peered around the glade, but her efforts at modesty were wasted, for Lord Hampstead was nowhere in sight. She called his name again. Silence.

Cassie crawled out of the shelter, and her racing heartbeat slowed. No other sound came to her.

Coffee boiled in a tin pot over a small fire some feet away. A plate of bacon cooked to a crisp sat next to the coffeepot. Cassie dropped to her knees beside the food. She could find no eating utensils anywhere. Finally, she gave up looking and burned herself reaching across the coffeepot for a slice of bacon. No five-course meal served on silver had ever tasted this wonderful. She savored every delectable morsel. Even the coffee smelled good. Licking her fingers, she poured a cup and, as she drank, tried not to gag on the substance.

Her hunger sated, she took mental stock of herself and her surroundings. She'd slept surprisingly well. The morning temperature was comfortable despite the fog. But nothing else about her had fared well. Her clothes were in tatters. And her hair . . . she reached up to pat it. Lord, her hair needed a comb.

She wondered where they were. Looking around the campsite for something that might contain a map, she paused, surprised to see the haversack lying behind a rock. Lord Hampstead usually kept the pack within reach. In fact, she'd wondered more than once what could be in it that was so important to him.

She picked it up and peeked inside. She found a tin of matches, ammunition for the revolver he carried, a chart—which she pulled out—and sundry other objects, including an odd-looking leather casing. But no comb or soap or anything with which to clean her teeth. After emptying the haversack, she looked at the bottom. It was empty, yet it still felt as if something were inside. She looked again but couldn't see anything more.

Giving up on it, Cassie spread out the chart and studied the markings. She understood topographical maps, which were much like the charts used by the captains of her father's shipping vessels when negotiating shoals and narrow shorelines. Last night they'd ridden west out of town, yet sometime before dark they'd veered south. Rivers veined the entire area. Clearly, they weren't going to be able to go anywhere until the fog dissipated.

As she repacked the haversack, her attention paused on the leather casing. A red serpent with the head of some creature had been carved into the soft leather.

She flipped open the leather strap and gasped to find it filled with papers, old broadsheet clippings, and a bundle of currency notes an inch thick.

Sitting back on her calves, she thumbed through the banknotes and guessed he carried a thousand pounds along with false identification papers, since his name wasn't Holt. She skimmed the papers, unable to read the strange-looking backward script, and speculated that it was some form of Russian lettering, considering who was after him. There were other letters as well, written on flowery stationery in French, everything addressed to *D* and signed only with *M*.

Cassie didn't understand all the foreign syntax. Speaking French was far different from writing it fluently, but she knew enough to recognize these letters were clearly written by a woman deeply in love.

Her hands trembling slightly, she unfolded the first broadsheet article that had been slipped in the fold beneath the banknotes. It was his betrothal announcement to her, written before she'd arrived in England two months ago. The write-up beneath the announcement was a patronizing riposte about the very popular British marriage mart and the newfangled craze that drove wealthy American fathers to Great Britain to purchase aristocratic grooms for their daughters.

She felt a tide of color wash over her cheeks. The article was insulting and demeaning to both her and Lord Hampstead. It seemed strange that even a family as powerful as his was not protected from public ridicule.

A bird thrashing in the tree branches startled her. She didn't know how long she had been on her knees going through his things. Carefully refolding the items, she placed everything back into the leather casing and returned it to the haversack, then stood. Not because she had lost the sudden desire to forage through Lord Hampstead's belongings, but because nothing seemed right any longer. The haversack shouldn't even be here.

"Lord Hampstead?" she quietly called again, more than a little alarmed now that she'd been awake for at least an hour and he still had not returned.

Her clothes remained wet. She cringed as she pulled her shift over her head and stepped into her drawers, then slipped on her petticoat. She hadn't realized just how badly her thighs were chafed from the long ride last night until she put on her stockings. After lacing up her half boots, she grabbed the blanket before turning and searching for her reticule. She dumped out the compass, took her bearings and left the glade.

She made her way on a faint path through the woods toward the sound of the waterfall. She couldn't see twenty feet in front of her. She found the packhorse chomping obliviously on a patch of long grass. The beautiful stallion was farther down the slope lying on his side. He lifted his head and tried to stand when she approached, but after a moment gave up the struggle.

Cassie knelt and touched his neck. She understood now why they had not left despite the fog. "Last night hurt you, didn't it, boy?" Her extra weight may have killed Lord Hampstead's horse.

Clutching the blanket around her shoulders, she stared around her in an attempt to get a feel for the area. For all she knew, a cliff could be in front of her. Then her gaze caught something dark and damp on the rocks at her feet. Cassie touched the spot and held her finger to the light. Blood.

Alarmed, she followed the trail away from the waterfall. The crash of rushing water began to fade, and in its place she heard the faint clink of rock hitting metal. The sound stopped, then started with more force. The eerie fog distorted the noise, making it sound like someone pounding at an anvil in the sky. Cassie continued cautiously until her path merged with a rushing stream, probably a tributary to a bigger river.

She turned left, following a recent boot print in the softer earth until the woods opened into an alluvial clearing.

She saw Lord Hampstead sitting on a felled tree, one hand pressed against his temple. His shirt, half unbuttoned, hung from his trousers as if he'd tried to bathe with only partial success. She could see white cloth wrapped around his shoulder and part of his chest. His floppy felt hat shadowed most of his face.

Watching him, she tried to tell herself that his current fix was his own fault, but her mind fashioned the fatuous idea that he would not be in this position if he had not come back for her at the stable. She wished now he had not.

A twig snapped beneath her foot. Too late, Cassie realized her mistake in trying to avoid being seen. She saw his hand move, and he was suddenly staring at her with pitch-dark eyes, looking dangerous and purposeful with a revolver in his hand.

"It's only me!" Cassie held up shaky arms.

Quickly learning just how cautious he could be, she watched his gaze snap past her as if he expected someone to be following her. He had shaven, she noticed. Without his beard, he looked surprisingly younger, though still not quite civil.

With an oath, he set the revolver on the flat shelf of stone at his hip. A knife lay beside a shredded cloth that used to be her blouse. His hand trembled slightly. "What are you doing down here?" His other hand held the canteen and he brought it to his lips.

"It seems somewhat odd that a man with your perceptive powers should ask such a question."

His eyes took in her laced boots beneath her petticoats, and she could tell he wondered what else she wasn't wearing. Indeed, she wasn't dressed beneath the blanket, at least not in anything remotely ladylike. But surely, in all this wretchedness, she should not have felt her body respond to the touch of those eyes. Familiar eyes. The ones from the photograph . . . almost.

"I saw your horse," she said. "Will he be all right?"

"I don't know." He leaned his elbows on his knees. "Maybe he'll find some of his strength before this fog clears."

"And if he isn't back on his feet?" But she already knew by the harsh look in his eyes what he would have to do. Her grandfather had ordered his prize stallion put down after a jump severed a tendon. She had loved that magnificent black horse. The hearty red stallion deserved more. Then she remembered Lord Hampstead's fondness for the horse.

"I'm sorry."

Despite that terrible hat and hair that was too long, the look in his nearly black eyes transformed him. His expression softened. He'd probably expected her to cry out about the inhumanity of shooting a crippled horse. She'd given him little reason to think she would react in any other way.

"He's an Irish thoroughbred," he said. "Tough. I want to give him a few more hours."

"What is his name?"

"Picaro."

The slightest smile edged his mouth. "So which is he? An adventurous rogue or a vagabond, my lord?"

"Maybe a little of both." She was surprised he still had the wherewithal to find humor in anything she could say. "My mother named him."

He'd said the words fondly, and, her eyes on him, Cassie became aware of nothing so much as an ache of wanting, something she did not quite understand but that coiled in her chest, expanded and grew. Pulling her attention away, she bent down and found a rock with a sharp edge that fit perfectly in her hand. "What will you give me if I break those chains, my lord?"

"And what sin is at the top of your list, love?"

He was so completely crass about life that she had difficulty believing he'd ever been raised an aristocrat. She held tight to the blanket with one hand and the rock with the other. "A brush to clean my teeth? And a comb?"

He came to his feet. "Everything is on the rocks. As

long as you know you're sharing. Unless you find it distasteful to use my toothbrush."

"You do that on purpose, don't you?" she said, her voice surprisingly steady. "You're always testing what I will say or do."

His dark eyes no longer guarded, he laid the shackles over the sharp edge of a large rock. "You're welcome to give it a go, Cassie."

He doubted her ability to break the chains, which only increased her determination. Riveting her attention to the small dent in the iron links, she smashed the stone down on the chain. Pain slammed into her palm and jolted her. She could feel his eyes on her face. The stone had slipped and she'd scraped the knuckle on her little finger. But she was as much determined to ignore him as she was to concentrate on this task.

"Have you thought about just shooting the chains?" she asked.

"Every passing moment."

She whacked the link. "But a gun makes a lot of noise."

"The bullet is lead," he said, clearly to placate her curiosity when she glanced up. "Small-caliber. Softer than these iron links. I'd have to brace the chains against the corner of this rock. Because of that, whoever pressed the muzzle of the gun to the link would risk the gun backfiring into her hand."

"You know a lot about guns."

"Most Englishmen do."

Perhaps, but he knew more.

Cassie smashed the rock down. She wanted to ask him if most Englishmen knew about mistresses, too, but she did not. Her curiosity made her feel more vulnerable to him and she wished that she had not found those letters in his haversack. That he would save them meant they were valuable to him. She sensed something inherently honorable in the way he seemed to care for the woman who had written them.

It was a notion that she'd strangely equated with him from the moment she'd met him at the inn and he'd slid her coins back across the table. He was a rogue much of the time, and was obviously in a dangerous mood now, but she knew instinctively that he was a man of conviction and would get her to Edinburgh or die trying.

"I'd appreciate it if you would not stare at me," she said.

"Is that what I'm doing?"

Cassie started to respond, then realized any response on her part would only serve to amuse him. But she wasn't able to check her heart from knocking. She was sure that if she looked at him she would want to kiss him, so she denied herself his gaze.

With each strike, she hit the chain link harder. Learning came easy to her. Usually, it took only one try and she could master a task. Her hand, unused to such labor, would be blistered after this. She didn't care. She wanted to be the one to break the link for him. For once, she wanted her actions to count for something important.

"You're going to hurt yourself," he said after a moment. "Slow down."

"We need a bigger rock," she said in frustration.

His hand caught her wrist and stopped her momentum. Her eyes shot up to his. "You need to take a rest," he said.

"No."

"Yes." The blunt ends of his fingertips brushed her palm and eased the rock from her hand. "Let me have another crack at it."

"You do not have three hands that I can see. You *need* me."

"I'll do it," he insisted.

Her gaze traveled from the tensile grip on the shackles to the black woolen shirt she'd seen him wearing when she first met him, the cloth defining the ridge of muscle in his upper arms. "You were bleeding today," she said.

He leaned against his palms and peered at her from beneath his hat. There was humor in his dark eyes. "Isn't that a redundant observation?" He laughed softly. "I've been bleeding for two days."

She lifted her chin, feeling as if it were always her fate to sound young and unworldly next to him.

"Take off your hat," she said.

He raised a brow.

"You've seen me without my hat and veil," she reasoned. He'd seen her in a lot less. Certainly, her current attire was scandalous if one considered that she wore his shirt over her petticoat and little else. "I wish to see you without your hat."

He surprised her by reaching a hand to the brim and removing the hat. Water dampened his wavy black hair, which was longer than she'd first thought. A few drier strands brushed his brow. His eyes were nearly as black as his lashes.

She was so engrossed with her study that her instinct for fixing things almost took over. But even as she started to reach up and brush the hair from his brow, she froze.

"Would you care to inspect my teeth as well?" He observed her with the same lazy grace displayed when she'd met him at the inn.

She already knew he had perfect teeth, but was tempted to ask him to open his mouth anyway. Her request would serve him right.

Finally, he slapped the hat back on his head and tugged it low over his brow. The gesture dismissed her as plainly as if she were a bothersome puff of smoke to be ignored. He grabbed the rock and returned to the chains.

He didn't think much of her as a person. He thought her pretty, she could tell that easily enough, but he didn't find her worthy of any other consideration. It wasn't an uncommon reaction. The few men of her acquaintance didn't like her much and no matter how she tried to understand what it was about her they found disagreeable, she could not.

Clenching her fingers into her palms, she told herself she couldn't care less what he thought about her, but she would not have him dismissing her. They were in this together whether he wanted to recognize that fact or not. More than that, he would never break those chains without help.

Cassie looked around her feet before walking away. She found a large rock in the water and hefted it, knowing it weighed at least fifteen pounds. She knew a little about physics, having seen what rocks did to the metal-rimmed wheels on carriages. The bigger the rock and force of the strike, the more chance of a fracture.

Lord Hampstead looked up as she walked over to him, saw the stone and swore just as she slammed it down on the chain.

The link shattered.

"Goddammit, Cassie—" Beyond coherent speech, he tore off his hat and scraped a now-freed hand through his hair, his dark eyes stormy. "You could have broken my bloody hand."

Cassie peered into his furious face. She didn't smile, but she *was* satisfied. "Sometimes a chance not taken is an opportunity lost," she stated, echoing the very words he'd spoken to her at the livery just before he hit the guard over the head with his shackles. "And now you are free. Maybe you can bribe another morally bereft soul in the next town to get you out of those bracelets still on your wrists."

"Lord." He raised his gaze heavenward. "Save me from American women."

Cassie's eyes narrowed, and in that moment of further enlightenment, she realized she was no longer incapable of violence. "I imagine you don't know me very well, my lord, but I am a quick study. All you have to do is teach me."

A corner of his mouth tilted and he startled her by coming around to her side of the rock. Her heart began to thunder. "I am not stupid, my lord."

His face remained in the shadows beneath his hat, and she was conscious of the now-familiar restless stir inside of her as she wondered if he would kiss her now. "I would never accuse you of that."

Then his palms were pressed on either side of her hips against the rock. The chafing of the chain was pleasantly abrasive against her thighs. For years, she had stood at the ragged edges of her life and thought herself incapable of feeling any manner of passion, whether it be anger or great happiness or the racing of her heart from the promise of a man's touch. To have such a thing roused inside her and to have it be so different from the romantic fantasy of him she'd boxed around her emotions stunned her.

"I admire your restraint," he said, and his breath smelled like peaches. Where had he gotten a tin of peaches?

"I pride myself . . . on my restraint, my lord."

"You're a very beautiful woman, Cassie. You're forthright, outspoken and direct. A man can stand only so much temptation all wrapped up like a warm crepe. And trust me when I tell you I'm no gentleman."

Having never been compared to a warm crepe, she was momentarily left speechless.

"I'm also a lot older than you, out of your realm of experience. What you are feeling right now isn't something you want to explore with me."

She flushed, but whatever he might do to her would not be against her will. "I see."

His gaze settled on her lips. "I believe it is important you do."

"You think me missish?"

"No, I do not."

She wanted to touch him. But was afraid. His hands were at her hips and she could feel them imprinted on her flesh, warm and inviting. "Do you find me odd? You would hardly be the first."

"I find you . . . not boring. You're also young. And our future is anything but settled."

"I understand perfectly. You have someone else."

When he pulled away, she thought he was going to walk past her, but he didn't. "No doubt you prowled through my haversack before venturing down here. But despite what you may have heard to the contrary or what you read in those letters, Maria Ivanov is not my lover. I'll clear that up with you now."

"I don't understand." What was she to him, then?

"I don't expect that anyone does understand. The fog is thinning," he said after a moment.

"Where are you going?" she asked when he turned away.

He reached behind his back to shove the revolver in his waistband and grimaced at the pain in his shoulder. "To do a little reconnoitering," he said. "To find a way out of these hills without backtracking the way we came in. I don't want to end up trapped against a cliff."

She watched him turn away and felt the heat go out of the air. Just like that, it evaporated, leaving only the chill of the fog and the question he had yet to answer. But before she could debate the matter of his heart, the howl of a wolf sent a chill down her spine.

"Wait!" she blurted, and caught up to him just as he reached the horses.

He tipped the hat off his face and she was suddenly looking into his eyes. The man was maddening, but he had eyes like hot Turkish coffee, as masculine in the warm way they made her feel as the rest of him. Sally Ann might know what to do with a man like Devlyn St. Clair who looked at her with eyes that could melt the clothes from her body, but Cassie, cowardly soul that she was, panicked.

"You wouldn't ride away, would you?" She stepped around him. "I mean, if you decided to ride away, you would tell me first. . . ."

The hat no longer shadowed his face. "I give you my word. I will inform you first."

"And you are baiting me," she whispered.

He didn't deny it.

"Do wolves hunt day or night?"

"They hunt when they are hungry," he said, without taking his eyes from hers. "Clearly, they are hungry today."

The stallion had climbed to his feet. Placing both hands on the bridle, careful not to allow the chains dangling from his wrists to further agitate the stallion, Devlyn seemed to calm the horse, his hat shielding part of his profile as he softly spoke the animal.

Cassie lifted her gaze from the soothing hands that

moved over the horse with such gentle reassurance to the face of this man who had confronted five Cossacks, incapacitating three without batting an eyelash and ridden out with her into the dark of the night through a terrible thunderstorm.

"Do you love her?" she forced herself to ask. "Maria Ivanov, I mean?"

His hands paused in their movements, but he did not look at her. Cassie felt the warmth leave her face. She folded her arms, pulling the blanket tighter across her shoulders. When she looked up again, she found him watching her curiously, and it was difficult to swallow. "Do you still?"

His amusement showed in the faint lift of his mouth. "You ask a lot of questions, for someone who isn't interested in my personal life. Nor will it do you any good to go back to the camp and snoop through my belongings— again."

"I didn't deserve that."

"Yes, you did. You snooped."

Cassie did not pursue the matter of Maria Ivanov, though she suspected he'd left much unsaid. "I truly do not understand you," she said, but the statement could have been more easily aimed at herself, for she did not understand her response to him.

"Likewise," he replied.

Did he mean in reference to her or to himself?

Then he was leading the horses away to a new patch of grass, and she heard his gentle reassurance to the stallion, his voice fading as he disappeared into the fog. Cassie looked up at the shadowy trees. Yet, even as the sounds of the forest seemed to underline the danger surrounding her, she understood the real threat did not come from the woods. It came from what Devlyn St. Clair's presence did to her.

Cassie returned to camp after she retrieved the comb and toothbrush at the river. It took her a half hour to find the trail up the rocky incline. Lord Hampstead had picked their campsite well last night. She almost missed seeing the small path that took her to the secluded glade. An hour later, he still hadn't returned, and she silently told herself that wherever he went, he would be back for her.

After putting more wood on the fire, she laid out her velvet skirt and tried in vain to level the hem where it had been cut, but the more she pulled at the frayed edges, the more her skirt unraveled. Finally, she put it on anyway.

Sitting on the ground beside the fire, she didn't allow herself to think about the kiss last night that was now indelibly imprinted in her thoughts. Or her desire to kiss him again.

But not thinking about him proved impossible.

After she worked the ties on her skirt, she combed her hair and tied it back with a piece of lace from her petticoat. She drank the last of the black coffee and rinsed the grounds off the bottom with some water from the canteen. Then she fell asleep.

When she awakened hours later, she discovered she'd slept away the afternoon. Most of the fog had dissipated. The sun hung low in the sky less than an hour before sunset—and still he'd not returned. Uneasiness prickled through her.

Grabbing the burlap sack holding the food, Cassie decided to return to the riverbed where she'd found him that morning. Even if he was avoiding her, he still needed to eat. But when she walked out of the glade and down the incline, her gaze passed over the place where he'd pick-eted the packhorse. She came to an abrupt stop.

The mare was no longer there.

Cassie dropped her load. From the ravine below, she heard the shriek of a horse. Her first thought was that Lord Hampstead was killing his precious stallion. Her second thought came within a heartbeat of the first as she looked down at the scene below.

The stallion had reared on his hind legs, fending off the trio of men attempting to rope him into submission. The horse crashed his front forelegs down, his mane fly-ing, his hooves striking blue sparks on the rocks. Every shriek tore into her. A man struck him with a whip and something cold gripped her heart. They were killing Lord Hampstead's horse.

Cassie cried out and brought her fist to her mouth. Even as the stallion snorted and tossed his head, it was a moment before she realized the hands subduing the magnificent beast had stilled and five pairs of eyes were watching her on the hill. Her breath halted.

Slowly backing away, she lifted her skirts, then turned and raced up the hill, her footfall soundless on the soft ground. She kept running. Above the noise from the falls, she could no longer hear her breath gasping in and out of her lungs. She stopped and leaned flat against a tree, drew in deep breaths and glanced around her shoul-der. The saddlebag and burlap sacks remained where she'd dropped them at the entrance to their camp.

But it was too late to retrieve them. Someone was com-ing up over the hill.

Chapter 7

"I'm tellin' ye, she ain't here, Angus."

"And I'm telling ye, I seen her go this way. Fleet as a deer, she was."

Two men were picking their way through the underbrush below where Cassie pressed behind a tree. She picked up her skirts and ran deeper into the forest, her steps muffled by the soft, fecund soil as she sought somewhere more substantial to hide.

Then the waterfall was in front of her, a monolithic cascade of crushing water that tumbled a hundred feet to the boulders below. The river was fed from a dozen creeks and smaller tributaries that snaked these hills and made the slope too slippery to descend. Heart pounding, she dropped behind the rocks and threw her cloak over her body. She huddled in a ball, listening frantically as two men continued to climb the incline looking for her.

Breathe. Just breathe, she told herself.

"Ey, girlie," one called out as if he were coaxing a cat

down from a tree. "We're not here to hurt ye none, lass. Tell 'er, Sam," the man rasped. "Tell 'er we're no' going te hurt her."

"I don't like none of this, Pete." The voice came to her from just below where she'd dropped. "Why does O'Donnell want the girl so badly? We should just take the horses and get."

"Then take the horses, Sam. No one's stoppin' ye."

A distant shout startled her. "They got somethin'."

The men made a tangent to the left as they scrabbled clumsily back down the hill. Her every sense followed the retreating footsteps as they moved farther and farther away. Squeezing her eyes shut, Cassie willed her pulse to slow before she passed out.

Lord Hampstead was out there. Possibly dead. Was that why she'd not seen him all day?

These men did not belong to Captain Valerik. Clearly, they were cattle and horse thieves, some of the many who frequented the hidey-holes in this area that old Gypsy trader, Hector, had told her about in town.

She couldn't hear anything else except the falls. How long before those two came back to resume their search? A gust of wind sighed through the trees. Heart hammering, Cassie eased the cloak off her face and breathed deeply of the cool humid air.

She sat up. Twigs snapped with each slow movement. Cassie froze.

But nothing jumped out of the forest shadows to grab her. She eased from the underbrush. The waterfall muffled any sound she made as she found a trail. Thick trees kept the forest darkened. To the left, the slope fell away abruptly toward the falls. She moved right and worked her way back down until she reached the place on the hill where the mare had been grazing. Dropping to her stomach, she looked over the hill at the scene in the glade below.

A fire cast light over three shadowy figures rummaging through her and Lord Hampstead's supplies like cockroaches. What remained of their provisions lay scattered over the ground. Cassie could see the haversack behind the saddle of a second horse. She searched the glade for Lord Hampstead, but didn't see him anywhere. A sick feeling ate at her stomach. And fear.

Heart racing in her throat, she crawled backward into the sphagnum beneath the protruding root of a large oak. Making her way through the shadows down the backside of the hill, she dropped and pressed her back against the hard, damp surface of a large boulder. The coffeepot hit the ground with a metallic clink. She drew her knees to her chest, then, pulling in a breath, peered around the rock. She had to know if he was there.

The two men who had been chasing her stood bent over items littered on the ground, tossing what they didn't want into the fire. Sparks exploded high into the sky. Another sat hunched on a rock, sharpening a knife, while yet a fourth rummaged through the haversack on the back of the mare. The smoke billowing from the fire burned her eyes.

"Christ, Pete. There must be a thousand quid in this pack."

Pete walked over to the mare. A tussle ensued. "Let me see."

"Bloody hell, no. I found it first."

"You'll share, O'Donnell."

A scrappy beard framed O'Donnell's heavy jowls. He was big enough to hold his own against all three men. "You'll get yer fair cut just like the others. Later."

Pete tipped back his floppy felt hat. "Anything else in that bag we should know about?"

"There's nothing else." O'Donnell shoved the money back into the haversack and looked up at the sky barely visible through the smoke and the treetops. You and Sam take the horses. Angus and Robert should be back by now. How long does it take to deal with one Brit?"

The red-haired man sitting on the rock sheathed his knife. He looked no older than eighteen or nineteen. "Ye shoulda let me do it, O'Donnell. Robert doesna have the stomach to butcher a barnyard cow."

"If Red thinks he can do it better, then send him," Pete said. "And have him find that bloody chit while 'e's at it. She's worth a lot to us."

O'Donnell nodded his head at Red, and the man strode off toward the river.

Cassie pulled back. Barely breathing, her muscles tensed, she squeezed her eyes shut. She hated the helplessness. Pressing her forehead against her fists, she prayed that Devlyn was not dead. She prayed for the courage to do something. She had to know which direction the man named Red was headed. Then what? Follow him?

Cassie peered around the rock and through the smoke toward where the other men had left the glade, taking the horses, including the sorrel stallion. There was no other movement.

She rose from her crouch and started to move when a gloved hand suddenly yanked her down. Her mouth flew open on a gasp only to find a hand pressed against her lips. "You little fool." Lord Hampstead was kneeling beside her. "What do you think you're doing?"

Dear Lord. He was alive!

She couldn't answer because she had sagged against

him, her mind and her heart hopelessly entangled with more than relief.

He loosened his hand on her mouth. His eyes on hers were concerned. "Are you all right?"

She stared at the play of light and shadows on his face, the ruthless expression framing his lips. "They took your haversack. And your horse—"

"I know."

He paused in the middle of opening the chamber of the revolver he'd pulled from his waistband. "You're going after those men?" she asked.

Spinning the cylinder, he started forward, then hesitated. "Do you know which way is north? Point."

She pointed north.

"An hour from here, there is an animal trail that will take you into the valley. Wait for me. If I'm not there by nightfall, keep walking."

"But—"

"I mean it," he rasped, halting her protest.

Then he kissed her.

Her eyes flew wide. The tip of his gloved finger brushed her chin. When next she caught her racing breath, she was alone in the shadows.

Devlyn heard the sound of footsteps long before he acted. Hell, even above the din of the waterfall, the man made enough noise to give him a week's warning to prepare. The growing darkness remained in his favor. The bloody bastard was looking for the pair who had tried to cut Devlyn up into tiny slices and feed him to the fishes. Christ, they were as bad as the Cossacks. At least the Russians had a certain code when they tortured a man to death. Valerik's misguided principles were entrenched in loyalty, revenge and punishment, part of some medieval standard of justice. These men killed for pleasure. He'd counted six. Three had taken his horses and left. Seeing Cassie sitting next to the boulder not thirty feet from where they had been arguing still made his stomach lurch.

The rocky riverbank broke away to his right. He caught himself on the tree for balance a second before he stepped out into the path of the approaching target. He raised his good arm, aware that the other one wasn't working well, and poleaxed the man in the throat with his forearm, sending him feet up and straight onto his back. In one movement, Devlyn reached behind himself, pulled the gun from his waistband, his thumb on the hammer, and put his boot across the gasping man's bruised windpipe.

Fear and rage twisted the young man's face as he looked up. "You'll do one thing and one thing only if you want to live," Devlyn said, aware that he was also suddenly dizzy. "And that is to lie there and answer my questions."

"Where's Angus and Robert?" the younger man gasped. "Where's my brother?"

"That depends on who your brother is." With an effort, Devlyn cocked the hammer back on the gun.

Devlyn studied the man, a mere kid with bright red hair and freckles. He eased the hammer back on the gun. "Where is the bastard going who took my horse?"

"I donna' know, fer sure." Red's eyes widened. "Maybe camp, maybe back to town. If they don't shoot that ornery stallion first. That's where Pete takes the horses we . . ."

"Steal? How many men are you?"

Red hastily cooperated. "Six. We found your trail this morning. We'd have just robbed ye quiet nice if we hadn't seen the girl. If she's the Yank heiress everyone is after, someone put a bounty on her."

A chill went down Devlyn's spine. "Where did you hear that?"

"Here and there. Someone wants 'er real bad and they don't care what kind of shape she's in when they get her."

"Are you working with Valerik?"

"Valerik? I don't know any Valerik. But O'Donnell will be back for me when I don't show up in camp with the girl."

Devlyn doubted that. The other man had the mare with the haversack. "Are you sure *O'Donnell* cares about any of you? Him, with all that money?"

Devlyn stepped away. His back to the river, he slid the gun into the waistband at his back. A cold numbing dread had swept upon him.

Devlyn knew who had put out the bounty on Cassie's head. Nicholas Ivanov had to know that she was in England. Valerik had been following her. Maybe long before she'd even reached the hotel, which meant it was purely by chance that the captain had found him at all. Christ, they weren't after only him. They would use Cassie to force him to turn over Maria. One woman's life for the other's.

Red then did something Devlyn anticipated, only his reflexes lagged and he did not respond quickly enough. The man's foot shot out and clipped Devlyn's thigh. In a stream of motion, Red pulled a knife from a sheath somewhere on his hip. Then Red—God bless his amateurish predictability!—charged him. Devlyn stepped aside to allow the man to sail past. There was nothing behind him but a long drop to the river. Devlyn never even heard the splash. He was already walking away.

Cassie walked for over an hour before she found a place at the top of the ridge that looked down into the valley. In the distance, silhouetted against the setting sun, she glimpsed the steeple of a parish church through the high-waving grass that ran the length of the meadow. Some of her terror of the approaching darkness and the strange night noises abated in the wake of her worry that she would never see Lord Hampstead again, that she would be wandering the Scottish lowland for the rest of her life. Recognizing the direction of the sunset, she had managed a northerly trek without consulting her compass.

Finally, worn out, she sank to the ground. Braced with her back against a tree and her legs drawn to her chest, she leaned her forehead on her knees and told herself she would not cry. She would go to the next town, find the sheriff and tell him who she was.

Still, as she watched the sun dip behind the distant hills, she waited. Waited until the moon touched the treetops above her head, until she could wait no longer. Cassie tied a knot around the blanket where she'd stowed some items and food she'd been able to salvage from their provisions and made her way down the slope, slipping half the way and sending rocks sliding. She was exhausted by the time she reached bottom. After washing her hands and face in the creek, she walked north again.

Surprisingly, the farther she walked, the less frightened of the night she grew. And the longer she walked, the more she realized she was not helpless.

Sometime later, she found a grove of trees beside a slow-moving river and ate what remained of the food she'd salvaged. No longer able to hold her eyes open, she let herself drift to sleep. She came awake to the radiance of moonlight spread over the ground. She lay on her side in the dewy grass with one hand tucked beneath her cheek.

As reality penetrated, she opened her eyes to find Lord Hampstead hunched beside her. His face stamped with moonlight and shadows, he wore his cloak and gloves. He smelled like the morning mists that gathered over the fields when the temperature dropped.

"You had me worried." His voice was quiet.

Startled into awareness of her surroundings, she sat up and looked around her before returning her attention to him. The haversack and two saddlebags sat next to him.

"You walked nearly five miles. I was beginning to think I'd lost you someplace."

A jarring rush of emotions betrayed her. She took a shuddering breath. He was safe. "I couldn't walk any longer."

Clearly fatigued, he dropped next to her, and she was suddenly in the crook of his arm as he sat with his back against the tree trunk. She leaned her head against his uninjured shoulder if only for a little while, and took reassurance from the steady beat of his heart. For the moment, it seemed the most natural place to be. She did not attempt to fill the silence with questions. Not yet. They sat in communal silence, saying nothing as he drank from a canteen, then offered it to her.

"Are you hurt?" he asked.

She shook her head. "Are you?"

She didn't want to know what had happened to the brigands. She didn't want to know because she didn't want to be happy to learn that they may be dead.

Holding the canteen with both hands, she swallowed greedily. Rivulets of water dripped down her chin. She plugged the canteen. It was then that she noted the mare and another horse hobbled nearby. The stallion was not there.

"They stole your horse," she said. "They were terrible and cruel."

He set the canteen aside. "They won't get far, Cassie."

"I wish I could have stopped them. Or struck the man who'd wielded the whip myself. And they stole your haversack—"

"Which I've recovered." He glanced over at the item in question. "Had you considered it, you would have realized that stepping into that camp would have been only the beginning of your problems. I was never in danger of losing anything of vital importance."

She pulled back to peer at his face, irritated that he would reprimand her when she had only been there to aid him. Whatever he carried to Lord Ware, he obviously carried it on himself. "How did you manage to keep that hat on your head, my lord?"

His dark eyes softened and, at once, he did things to her insides that made her will go to honey. "I need to know something, Cassie. When you said that Valerik followed you from the hotel, what did you mean?"

"He found me at the hotel," she said, uncertain about the reasons behind the question. "But he'd been following me since England. Somehow, he knew who I was. Did those men belong to Valerik?"

"Those men knew who you were."

She drew in a shallow breath and looked away not sure what that meant. "I don't hold you responsible for someone else's actions," she said. "If Captain Valerik was following me hoping I would lead him to you, then I am doubly sorry to have done so. As for yesterday, I know you weren't in camp because you were trying to find a trail out of the hills. I would only have held you back again."

He leaned his head against the tree. She could not see his eyes. For a moment, neither spoke.

"From now on, you go where I go. And the first rule of your survival and mine: you'll cover your hair at all times." He reached across her, dragging one of the saddlebags into her lap. "In the morning, change your clothes."

She sat forward and peered inside. She found a tin of peaches, coffee, woolen socks and . . . "But . . . these are trousers. Do they belong to a dead person?"

He tipped the floppy hat over his eyes. "The man to whom those clothes belong is very much alive for now," he said from beneath his hat, his words clipped and his usual amusement gone from their tone. "They belong to me."

Twisting around, she gave him her full attention. His face was strategically covered, thus depriving her of his response. All she could see of his face was his mouth.

She found herself staring. He had sensual lips for a man, perfectly shaped. Lips that made a woman remember his kiss and want to return for more. Stubble marked his jaw. He wore his dark cloak. His gloved hands of the same color as his cloak rested one atop the other on his lap. Everything about him was dark. And she took the full measure of his legs to his feet. He'd crossed his ankles. The tips of his boots were muddy.

He was exhausted. Already his body was relaxing, the tension draining from his muscles. He was drifting to sleep.

No matter how much she'd convinced herself otherwise, she wondered if it was possible to care about a man and still disagree with everything he was. Surely there was a civil way to manage their future. Maybe she didn't even know what she wanted or did not want anymore. Suddenly anonymity felt less appealing.

Her fingertips went to her bottom lip. Even as she became aware that her leg was resting intimately against his, she was aware that some of the tension had returned to him.

When she returned her attention to his face, she found that he'd tipped the hat off his eyes and was watching her, his gaze partially hooded, almost as if he were giving her the freedom to look, unless one noticed that his lips had tightened.

His eyes so darkly intent on hers, she could scarcely temper her breath. It was too easy in the moonlight to stare at his face. Too hard to look away.

Her feelings ran counter to everything she knew about him and herself. She wished the moon was not so bright so he could not so easily read her thoughts. She did not want him to learn what was in her mind, but she found that once he did, she wanted him to know more.

She let him slide his hand across her nape into her hair. The subtle pressure of his palm tightened. And he pulled her into him for a kiss.

Chapter 8

 $\sim\!\!\circ\!\!\heartsuit\!\!\circ\!\!\sim$

Cassie caught the hint of whiskey on his breath. His lips were warm and dry and gently exploring. He raised his head and looked at her inquiringly.

It seemed that she should protest, that he was waiting for her to do so, but that proper reaction eluded her. She touched his arm, but not to push him away. When he dipped his head again, he raked her into a melding kiss, no longer teasing or asking permission but taking her mouth in a possessive sweep of her lips. And this time, she kissed him back.

His tongue pressed against hers, making it impossible to remember her own name as he pressed her to the ground. She caught the sound of her voice, a small sound at the back of her throat. Her fingers slipped past the pulse beat at his throat and into his hair, dislodging his hat. It tumbled unheeded to the ground.

Braced on his elbow, he lifted his head, but she surged upward for more.

His gaze locked on her mouth, and she was unsure if the turbulent wave flowing over them came from him or her. She was breathing hard. He was barely breathing at all. The fabric of her shift proved no hindrance to his stare, and the rapid rise and fall of her breasts pressed her nipples against the thin cloth. Slowly he raised his gaze to hers and she raised her arms and linked them around his neck, pulling him into a kiss.

There was no sound outside the circle of warmth surrounding her. She could hear her own heartbeat. This was nothing like she'd ever experienced, nothing like she'd ever glimpsed. She didn't want the feeling to go away. She knew not what was happening to her, except she'd grown wings and could suddenly fly.

Devlyn twisted so that he was partially on top of her, his thigh pressing over hers, the intensity of his need overcoming the pain in his shoulder. Her long soft body defined his drive, focused the momentum of his desire and shaped the force of the hunger sweeping through his veins. Where fatigue had grabbed him only moments ago, his entire body now thrummed. The fullness of his sex pressed against the confines of his suddenly too-tight trousers. She moaned, restless, careless of her virtue. And yet, he couldn't bring himself to care.

His breath thickened over the kind of thoughts that burned him to the quick. He wanted to be rid of his gloves so he could touch her completely. Feel the soft, perfect flesh of her in his palms. He bit down on the tips of his glove and yanked it from his hand. His shirtsleeves covered the manacle bracelet, but the chains jerked and rattled with the abrupt movement. His eyes followed his hand as he shaped it to the curve of her ribs, passed his palm over the peak of her other breast, then moved higher to brush his thumb over her bottom lip.

But, pulling away, as he watched her expression shift and change in the moonlight, Devlyn understood that the growing attentiveness in her eyes was not as much born from invitation as it was hesitation.

"Is it your wish to consummate our budding courtship, Cassie?" he said against her mouth, looking into her face, at the moonlight in her wide eyes, and not bothering to rein back the reality in which he found himself ensnared, or the familiar primal instinct he felt when around her. Instinct that was quickly slipping its tight leash as he became subtly aware of the odd feeling at the base of his stomach.

He had one thing on his mind. And the barest suggestion that he would do exactly that touched his eyes. In every way, he was sure that she would let him.

The fingers of his left hand shimmered through her hair, exploring its silky depth, and he dipped his head to catch the tiny moan of pleasure from her lips. A shiver seized her and went over him. Her hand slipped into the coarse thickness of his hair, leaving him well on his way to forgetting he might ever have been a gentleman.

Still fully dressed, he pushed up her skirts to her waist, his tongue sweeping hard into her mouth as he slid his hand up her thigh between the slit in her drawers. His breathing became hers. She did not twist away when his body moved over her, her kiss all but consuming him.

"Sweet Jesus—" he whispered against her lips, his upper-crust accent more evident than before. He needed suddenly to understand her, to know her thoughts and the way of her mind. Did she really understand what she was doing? "What is it you want from me?"

She opened her eyes and looked up at him. "I want to feel."

"Feel? Feel what, Cassie?" One hand fell to her shoulder to keep her from pulling him back into another kiss. The darkness allowed him only to discern what he'd heard in her voice. "I am not your fantasy. I'm not the man in your photograph—"

"How could you be?" Her palms tightened on his scalp. He resisted being drawn to her again and her hold loosened. "Neither of us is who we were ten years ago," she said. "Think about it, my lord. Ten years ago, I was nine."

He made a strangled sound. Strands of moonlight hair lightened her temple. He brushed a knuckle down the line of her throat and over the fullness of one breast to curl over her beating heart. "Do you want to feel here, Cassie?" he asked over the sudden rise of her chest, then splayed his palm over the concave curve of her abdomen to the juncture between her thighs. She burned wet beneath his touch. "Or here?" he boldly challenged when he saw her eyes widen, and he was suddenly touching her in a most intimate way. Flesh to heat.

"Can true physical pleasure exist without the emotional?" Her words touched his lips with something like a promise. "Would not the lack of one affect the pleasure found in the other?"

He didn't know her, he realized. She was foreign to him still.

In truth, he was a poor study from whom to draw any opinion. He'd had one or the other at various times in his life, but never both together, never one in harmonious conjunction with the other. A bemused smile touched his lips. "Perhaps."

Suddenly, finding himself lying with Cassie, minutes from carnal intimacy, no longer seemed right. Something idiotic was happening to him, and the discomfitting notion that she was the cause pulled his hand away from her hot center.

"It is why I find refuge in music," she said after a pause.

"Why?"

"Music is man's gift to his soul. It is melody and harmony together, the emotional and the physical, like the ebb and flow of the sea against your legs. You hear it and you feel it at once. I want to know life in that way."

"Life is not tandem with music, Cassie."

"Then I want to know what it is like to live without tandem and without restraint."

His mouth tightened. "We all have restraints."

"You don't."

Bloody hell. "I do." He turned to his back and stared up at the velvet sky and a thousand stars visible through the tree branches. "In any event, you cannot be like me."

He put his forearm over his eyes and felt the cold band of iron around his wrist beneath the shirtsleeve. She rose on one elbow, spilling the wealth of her hair over her shoulder. "Why not?"

"Because you are nineteen years old, Cassie," was all he could think to say.

She had been playing with dolls while he'd been serving in China.

"Do you believe someone could fall in love with another person from a photograph?" she asked.

"Be done with it, Cassie," he said wearily.

She sat straight up and faced him in the darkness. In the stillness that followed, the rasp of her movement was loud and congruent with his mood. He had hurt her, but clearly, she needed a fuller measure of reality to deter the direction of this conversation. There could never be emotional intimacy between them. And using her only to beget an heir suddenly seemed cruel and ruthless, like plucking the wings from a butterfly.

"What you feel has nothing to do with love or emotions," he said flatly. "It isn't comparable to music or the harmony and melody of an ebbing tide. It is plain old-fashioned lust."

"Your cynicism is not well done of you, Lord Hampstead," she said after a moment.

He turned his head and narrowed his eyes on her. "Do you fancy yourself in love with me?"

Her chin lifted. "I did not say that."

He heard the quiet defiance in her words. "I am relieved to hear that," he said. "I would hate to have you suffer that afflicted state."

"Oh, please, spare me your sarcasm. I find lightning beautiful, too, but only a fool would touch it. I only meant . . . I meant that I think you are more than that photograph portrayed."

He pulled the haversack beneath his head and turned on his side, facing her. She'd pulled her legs to her chest and set her chin on her knees. She tightened her arms around her legs. "Which could explain why I didn't recognize you when I first met you at the inn. You see, I have perfect recollection. I don't make mistakes."

"Of course," he said facetiously, amused by her confidence. "Then again, maybe your memory is only slightly more perfect than your judge of character. You should consider reassessing both."

She did not respond but pressed a hand to her temple, and his mood was not immune to the pain he saw evident in that gesture. "We have a few hours before dawn," he said, unwilling to allow himself to feel sentiment. Unwilling to allow himself to feel at all. Tightening his jaw, he lifted the blanket. "It's cold," he said. "You need the warmth as much as I, Cassie."

She reclined and turned on her side away from him. Both of them lay in silence. No part of her body touched his, yet he could not escape her warmth or the rasp of her skirts against his thigh. He could not escape himself.

"Why haven't you asked me if those men who attacked our camp are still alive?"

When she didn't answer . . . or couldn't seem to answer . . . she shut her eyes. "Because I don't care," she whispered on a thread of sound.

"Yes, you do," he said. "And that is the difference between you and me, Cassie. I *don't* care."

She remained on her side looking up at the moon as it peeked from behind a layer of clouds, accepting that he was right about this, too.

Quiet did not come to her easily.

It *was* cold, and she did care.

"That stallion came in last night," the man working the livery told Devlyn the next morning when he and Cassie finally made it to the village nestled at the edge of the expansive vale. "He's a spirited beaut. Not seen the like in this area."

"No, I imagine you haven't."

Devlyn stood at the paddock, one arm hanging over the fence. The stallion pranced up to nuzzle his hand. A wooden rail separated Picaro from the other horses present.

The sorrel's presence in plain view of the town only told him that the men who had stolen him did not worry overmuch if Devlyn had survived their attack. "Where are the men who brought him in?" he asked.

The hostler scratched his head. "Might be at the public house down the street. Likely sleeping off a drunk."

Devlyn soothed the stallion. "I'll take grain for the two horses behind me," he told the hostler. "As well as this one."

The old man scrubbed his hand across his bewhiskered chin. "That stallion belong to you, does he?"

"He does."

The hostler looked past him to Cassie standing beside him, her cloak open to reveal the baggy trousers she wore. She could be wearing a bucket over her head and no one would mistake her for a man. Underneath the tatty clothes, there was a very feminine, soft, round body. "All I have are oats. Will that do?"

"Oats will do." Devlyn reached inside his cloak and withdrew a gold sovereign. "That is for your expenses, sir. I'll be riding out as soon as we get supplies. Unless you have an objection."

The hostler held the sovereign to the sunlight and grinned a toothless smile. "Not me, guv'nor."

Keeping Cassie next to him as the man hurried away, he knelt beside his horse and ran his hand up and down the left foreleg, but his gaze went around the town.

Next to the alley between the livery and the hitching post, a dog scavenged in the refuse. Shaded by a wide-spreading tree, the stone-and-thatched-roof building in front of him belonged to a row of similar structures that abutted the empty market area. A bootmaker's cottage stood abandoned across from a church at the end of the street. Three men congregated in front of the general store and, just past them, tethered on a line were a half dozen horses.

His instincts were already screaming at him to leave, but he needed supplies or they wouldn't last the day. "It's still tender, is it, boy?" He felt above the fetlock and was relieved that the swelling had diminished. At least the stallion was well enough to travel. Devlyn came to his feet.

Cassie sidled beside him. "What are we going to do?"

He returned to where he'd left the mare and the gelding he'd taken last night from O'Donnell. Dragging the haversack off the mare, he scanned over her shoulder. "Keep the hood on your head," he said.

He made her check the shackle bracelets he wore tucked beneath his sleeves, acutely aware the she was wearing his trousers and his shirt and had bathed using his soap this morning. His physical reaction was not as unexpected as its depth was a revelation to him. Her touch sent a current through him like the static he sometimes felt before an electrical storm. And for a moment, as their eyes caught and held in the wavering light filtered by the old tree, he felt her pull, as he had last night. As he had since he'd first seen her at the inn.

Strangely, *he* seemed fixated by the desire to kiss her again and finish what she had started last night. He'd felt that way the entire bloody night, lying next to her. For even as he'd been the first to turn away, it had been she who had thoroughly dismissed him in the end. This morning, she'd awakened before him, washed in the slow-crawling river and changed her clothes, managing to figure out the mechanizations of the male attire on her own. They'd eaten breakfast in silence. She had not complained when he had set her astride the mare and driven her for hours at an exhausting pace. Exhausting to him, anyway. But then, he was not at his best, he realized. It was past time he found a doctor. This morning, he'd been close to passing out.

"You are warm." She smoothed his cuff with her palms, caring over the minutest detail.

He looked down at the top of her hood bent over his hands. "Thank you, love. I believe that is the nicest thing you've told me since we met."

He felt her stiffen and she dropped her hands from his sleeve. "It wasn't meant as a compliment, Your Lordship."

"Look at me, Cassie."

He waited, aware that she might decide not to oblige him. He wondered what he would do if she chose not to look at him. But years under Lord Ware's directive had taught Devlyn to choose his battles carefully. And he was not ready to engage in this one, yet.

Without another word, he handed her the canteen. She tucked a length of her hair behind her ear and accepted a drink.

"Are ye folks from around these parts?" a man asked, stepping out of the store in front of them. He wore neatly pressed trousers held up with braces and a brown woolen shirt beneath. A pair of reading spectacles sat on the bump of his nose, and pale blue eyes quickened with interest behind them. "Seems we've had a lot of strangers traveling through here these past few days."

"Are you the shopkeeper?" Devlyn asked, taking the canteen from Cassie and tying it to the saddle.

"I am."

A dozen goats tethered on a wooden rail in front of the shop bleated at him as he turned back to the shop.

"They don't look happy," Cassie said, reaching out her hand to pet one.

"Ye don't want to be touchin' them goats, lass," the shopkeeper replied, his hand on the door. "They look harmless enough until the billy decides ye be a threat to his harem." He peered at her. "It be a male matter, lass." He chuckled at that. "The male gender doesna' like strangers around his women."

Cassie looked at Devlyn as if to confirm the veracity of the statement. "Do you think he knows that about goats because he is male or because he has the mentality of a goat?" she whispered.

Smiling, Devlyn stepped around her, his hand still on her arm. "Some basic male instincts transcend species, love."

He saw her color and smiled to himself because he could do that to her. A fast-moving dray thundered past and sprayed water over a couple standing at the corner of the walk. Her laughter caught on a gasp; she jumped backward out of the splash, jolting when he prevented her from stepping into his arms. His shoulder could barely tolerate the contact. "Get what you need inside, Cassie." His cloak swirling against her calves, he leaned around her to open the door. "We won't be here long."

A bell cheerfully tinkled as he opened the door. The scent of cedar and tobacco filled their senses. Wooden buckets of every color hung from the ceiling. Medicine bottles lined the wall behind the countertop where a group of men stood talking over a pouch of tobacco. As he entered, two looked up, pausing in their conversation as he stopped at the counter. But their eyes weren't on him.

"I wish to purchase hand cream," Cassie told the shopkeeper, her voice like a golden beacon in a room full of thieves.

The storekeeper returned with a jar of something that smelled like lowland wildflowers. Cassie brought it to her nose. "This is wonderful."

Devlyn took the blue jar from her palm, caught her hand and found the blister she'd attempted to conceal. His eyes narrowed on hers. "You should have told me," he said.

"I want the cream." She eased her hand from his. "I'll pay you back."

"And deprive me of the pleasure of putting you in my debt?" he said for her ears alone. "I think not. Just use it sparingly or you'll attract a multitude of native wildlife."

"Does that amuse you?" she managed politely. "To have me in your debt?"

He leaned a little closer and in a devilish voice whispered, "Come, now. I thought having spent the entire night together changed everything between us."

"That's true." She smiled behind a whisper, leaning nearer until her lips touched his ear. "But the last man I spent the entire night with, Daddy shot."

"Is that right?"

Clearly pleased with herself, she rested her case like a barrister in his prime, smiling primly at the shopkeeper, who was watching them both oddly, his hands poised as he awaited the rest of the order. "Add the hand cream," Devlyn said as Cassie walked around him to explore two crates.

Devlyn gave his order, adding whiskey, iodine, needle and thread. "And soap," he said, leaning on his elbow as he faced the men down the counter. They quickly diverted their eyes and went back to bickering over the tobacco. Devlyn's attention focused on Cassie. A lock of her hair had fallen from the hood and gleamed like a pearl in the dim shadows of the store.

"Don't have the whiskey or iodine," the shopkeeper said, returning with a handful of goods. "Ye can find needle and thread at O'Malley's Boutique near the edge of town. Soap, I have."

"Is there a doctor in town?"

"Simon Macgruder and his daughter-in-law are the closest one you'll find, which doesna' say much considerin' how far away he is. Old Simon owns the apothecary in Glentress."

The shopkeeper packed the other sundry items Devlyn needed in burlap sacks. After the supplies were tabulated, he asked about riding gloves for Cassie, bought arecanut tooth powder in a flat tin, peppermint and a ready-made flannel shirt to replace the bloodstained one he wore beneath his cloak. He was hungry and knew Cassie was as well. A public house at the end of the street served hot food if he wanted to risk getting poisoned, but the fleeting thought of eating a hot meal passed the moment the door swung open.

Two more men walked into the store, their laughter fading to something else entirely as their eyes fell first on him, then on Cassie. She returned to his side and, keeping her head low, peered in the glass case at the row of glass buttons on velvet.

Both men approached the counter. The older had stark blue eyes beneath his felt hat brim, and wore a dirty woolen vest over a gray shirt. A whip hung like a curled snake at his hip. Devlyn didn't know if he was armed with anything else. He'd seen the whip striations on the stallion.

The two took up positions around him. "That's a lot of supplies, mister." Blue eyes slouched against the counter beside Cassie. He smelled of stale sweat. "Maybe ye should be lookin' into buying a dress for this lady to go with those fancy buttons she likes." He smirked. " 'Less you want us to buy her one. Why don't you remove the hood so we can see what you have beneath?"

Ignoring the man, Cassie stepped around Devlyn to his other side. "I'll help with these," she quietly said, sliding one of the burlap sacks off the counter.

The shopkeeper looked over the top of his nose at the man who had spoken. "Pete, Sam, you lads best not be causin' trouble."

"Who's causin' trouble?" The one name Pete laughed. "Maybe we just want to get a better look at the girl. Ye canna' deny she's a comely lass."

Devlyn laid down the necessary coin for the provisions. "That's a nice stallion locked in that paddock outside," he said casually to no one in particular, but the statement had the effect of silencing the room.

The shopkeeper's hands froze. The two men watching Cassie returned their attention to him. "He is," Pete said, "and he isn't fer sale."

"I wasn't asking."

For a moment, the meaning didn't register. When it did, two red flags rose in Pete's cheeks. His eyes snapped to Cassie. He stepped around Devlyn. "Why don't I be takin' off the hood, Yank, so I can 'ave a better look at ye?"

Devlyn's gloved hand caught the interloper's in a painful grip. "Do you think you will miss your hand if I break it . . . *Pete*?" His icy soft voice left no doubt that he would do exactly that if the younger man did not stand down.

"Leave off, lads," the harried shopkeeper warned. "He isna' any kind of cove to take yer lip."

Pete yanked his hand from Devlyn's grip. "Mayhap we like it here, old man, and we ain't afraid of any—"

Cassie smashed Blue Eyes over the head with a wooden

stave bucket. He stumbled forward and fell headlong into the candy jars, spilling horehound over the floor. "If his hand doesn't deserve to be broken, then his head does," she snapped, clearly fighting to keep her voice even. "They attacked us yesterday and stole all of our belongings. They are naught but horse thieves."

She would have smashed him again had Devlyn not caught her wrist. "Cassie—"

"Do not say one word to demoralize me." She grabbed his shirtfront in a tight fist and brought her nose nearer to his. "I swear I will hit you over the head as well, sir."

Devlyn looked down at the white-knuckled hand bunching the material of his shirt and found himself responding to more than the physical pull of her fist. He was acutely conscious of wanting to shake the life out of her and then kiss her senseless if he did not laugh outright first. "Far be it from me to criticize you, love." He brought his forearm around her and rested his jaw against her temple. "Desist, Cassie. You've knocked him out."

She faced the shopkeeper with no apology in her eyes or her voice. "If I had my reticule, I would pay you for the damages, sir. But those miscreants stole that as well."

Devlyn dropped a handful of coins on the countertop. "Half of that is for the damages," he told the shopkeeper, then turned the force of his attention on Sam, who only stared at him with wide brown eyes. "The rest is for the horse and saddle I took from O'Donnell last night after you left with my horse."

"Yes, sir," Sam murmured.

Pulling the second burlap sack with him, Devlyn wrapped long fingers around Cassie's upper arm as if he owned her or had a right to bully her, when he would have cracked that bastard's skull himself. He faced the remaining men standing slack-jawed behind their felled comrade.

"O'Donnell won't be back unless he manages to free himself," he said. "You can ride to where he is camped and trussed like a hog to spit, or you can ride somewhere else. But if any of you follow when I leave here with what belongs to me, you won't like what I will do to you. Do you understand?"

Slowly the men nodded. Recognizing that his temper was at a flash point warned him, and he turned with Cassie. The shopkeeper ran to open the door for him, setting off the melodious bell. "You best be riding fast, folks," he quietly offered.

Cassie strode out of the store. She swept past the tethered goats, raising a bleating chorus in her wake, and reached the mare before Devlyn caught her arm. "We're not finished," he warned.

She snatched her arm away. "I am," she said, and turned her back on him. "And I'm not sorry."

Narrowing his eyes, Devlyn glared at her back. But she seemed to understand the need for haste, for in the time he'd retrieved Picaro, she'd tied the sack she carried to the back of the saddle with a knot that only an old salt could negotiate, then stepped a foot into the tread and mounted without his help.

They thundered out of town a few moments later, Picaro in tow carrying oats enough to feed the horses for three days. Cassie rode the mare, having overcome any problems riding astride earlier that day. Her hood billowed and slid off her head. How many bloody people in town saw her and could give a description of her should someone inquire? Hell, who would not remember a woman with hair the color of lilies?

Only when the streets faded into an unplowed field and

they'd put another two miles behind them did Devlyn lean over and grab the mare's bridle, pulling the horse to a stop. Cassie did not avert her eyes; indeed, her reaction was quite the opposite of what he'd expected. Nor was he so much furious with her as stunned by her continued ability to shock him. Eventually, when the roar in his veins receded, he released his grip on her pommel.

"Are you all right?" he asked.

"Those men would have hurt you."

"No, Cassie." He pulled the field glasses out of the haversack and studied his back trail. "They would not have."

"Will they follow us?" she asked after a moment.

Wind surged through the trees. "They might."

"That man beat your horse. If I could have struck him with his whip, I would have. Tell me that you truly disapprove."

He lowered the glasses, hard-pressed to take her to task for anything. "You swung that bucket like a born milkmaid." The corner of his mouth tilted. "I was relieved that you did not smash me instead."

Her sudden smile was like the sunlight in a summer sky. Shifting in the saddle, he found his gaze drawn to her lips. It had not been his intent to reward her and he frowned slightly, though his first inclination was to kiss her. He might have if he wasn't worried about being followed. "Do you still have your compass?" he asked, returning the glasses to the haversack.

She dug into a pocket and retrieved the fob. Because he still wore the iron wristbands from the shackles, he didn't take the fob. "Point northwest."

"But Edinburgh is that way."

Devlyn watched her calmly point in the opposite direction without consulting the compass. Rather than waste his breath arguing, he gave her a sober look. "How the deuce do you know that?"

"Because I saw the chart yesterday." She returned the compass to her pocket. "Ettrickbridge is our closest crossing. Once we cross, there is a fork in the road that could work to our advantage. One leads north to Yarrow, then to Glentress, the other east to Selkirk. Captain Valerik, if he is waiting for us, cannot be on both roads at once. Let us hope he is not on the road that will take us to Glentress." She peered at him, a slight crease between her brows when he failed to reply. "That *is* where you wish to go, is it not? To see the doctor?"

"Yes," he managed to answer.

She licked her finger and held it to the wind. "The breeze is coming from the east." Her eyes searched the sky. "We could be in for rain by tomorrow. We should be off."

Devlyn was still looking at the stark dome of blue sky overhead when she wheeled the mare around and trotted off.

Very few women managed to shock him more than once and, as Devlyn stared at her back, his hands folded across his pommel, the compilation of seventeen years' worth of experience managing women and the other affairs in his life seemed to take flight. His insight about Miss Adelaide Sheridan was no longer so neatly parsed in his head, for the pieces no longer fit to make the whole. He was just pleased that he had managed to remain so composed.

Chapter 9

⟳

The rain hit late the next day, dousing the beautiful colors of late spring. Cassie took refuge with Devlyn beneath the spreading branches of a huge oak to eat and wait out the weather before continuing into the hills.

The subject of their mutual passion never came up, even when they'd shared the same blankets away from the storm. On the third morning, he paid the toll and they completed the second river crossing at Yarrow, along with a crowd of people. To eyes other than her own, he looked no different from any other traveler. But she had watched him grow increasingly weaker. She worried about him, about the blood on his shirt. He had gotten progressively worse during the last few days.

As they approached Glentress, a small village less than a day from Edinburgh, the forest thickened. Careful to remain hidden within the shelter of trees, Cassie raised the field glasses to her eyes and panned the valley below. Elk grazed among the wild bluebonnets that grew in the valley. She had never seen such wild, lonely country. She saw no sign that they had been followed after their unfortunate encounter with horse thieves.

A half-moon was already visible above the trees as the sun threatened to soon dip beneath the horizon. She turned her head toward where Lord Hampstead rested beneath a tree. He was still asleep.

They'd only stopped to rest the horses a few hours ago. It looked as if they'd be spending the night. He was running a fever. A high fever, from the heat of him.

She dined alone on cheese, fruit, jerked beef, and the last of their bread. She'd been afraid to make a fire at first, but the descending night had stolen the warming sunlight from the sky. Having seen Lord Hampstead build a fire many times, she'd found the tinderbox in his haversack and dug a shallow hole behind a screen of bushes, yet far enough from them not to send the forest up in flames. After she ate, she retrieved the coffeepot from the fire and walked to the creek, where she laid out a comb and soap beside the toothbrush. She sank to her knees next to the bracing water and vigorously washed her hands and face.

She thought of Lord Hampstead and his worsening condition. She had little experience dealing with sickness. With the exception of an occasional tummy ache, which her grandmother treated with special teas, she had never been ill. But she knew the dangers of disease. Her older brother had died at age sixteen of an infection after scraping his arm on a rusty nail at their grandparents' estate in the country. Cassie, twelve at the time, remembered his horrible week of agony with an ache in her heart. Her father had held his parents responsible for the death of his only son and never forgiven them. After that awful summer, Cassie had never seen Papa or

Mama Sheridan again, except to attend their funerals two years ago.

Once she finished washing, she combed and plaited her hair as her grandmother used to do for her when she was a child and tied off the end with one of many strips of cloth she'd ripped from her petticoat that afternoon. She'd grown to like her atrocious costume. There was something liberating about breaking her own mold and doing something outrageous. Cassie wet another of the cloth strips, filled the coffeepot and approached the camp—only to stop.

Lord Hampstead was sitting with his back against the tree, one leg drawn to his chest, the whiskey flask dangling between his fingers as he watched her approach. All her reserve fled in the wake of her quickened heartbeat. With a hunger she understood, Cassie let her eyes go over him—his strength, his hands, the way his shirt clung to his shoulders. She knew he was studying her as well. But his gaze held no lazy aura of charm. Indeed, it reflected more than the firelight, a fire that Cassie was beginning to realize lay deep within him as well.

She had promised herself that she would keep her emotional distance. She knew how to do that well enough—she wasn't called the Ice Princess back home for nothing. But she did not know how to stop wanting him to kiss her again or how to keep him from affecting new feelings over which she had no control.

"How long have I been asleep?" he asked.

Ignoring her rapidly beating heart, she knelt beside him with the remaining strips of petticoat and the coffeepot and tried to force calm into her voice. "Most of the day."

He swore. "Why didn't you awaken me sooner?"

Even without touching him, she could feel an appalling heat from his body. "My grandmother used to give me tea," she offered. "I only know that it tasted wretched."

Devlyn pressed a palm against his forehead and shook his head. "That is the least helpful advice I've ever been given."

"A physician, I am not."

Devlyn leaned his head against the aged tree trunk and gave her his full regard. "You're inebriated, my lord," she said none too gently, pressing the cold wet cloth against his forehead.

He winced. "Dammit, Cassie. Your bedside manner rots."

"You're burning with fever. Don't you care?"

"Will ye be missin' me, then, if I should perish, lass?"

She sat back on her heels, crossed her arms over her chest and affected her own impressive Scottish lilt. "Not i'tall, my laird of nowhere. But I canna' be liftin' your dead weight to your horse to bring you back to your dear auld family. Do you na' think they could bear to lose their only heir?"

Devlyn swigged, eyeing her over the flask. He watched as she twisted around and carefully arranged the cut strips from her petticoat beside him, sliding his gaze down the baggy trousers and shirt belonging to him. A folded strip of her petticoat served as a belt. Because of her height, she hadn't needed to roll up much of the legs. It was the most ridiculous garment anyone could ever have contrived of wearing and he was surprised that she had. As she stretched to grab the last strip of cloth, the trousers pulled taut across the round globes of her backside, and he rolled his eyes upward.

"Saints alive, I'm in mortal fear of expiring," he murmured, his voice so somber, she lurched around to face him. He laughed at her look, until the movement caused his shoulder grief and sobered him a fraction, before the hunger of his passion steered his mood into something more carnal. "I need you to save me from those clothes, Cassie."

But before she could respond, he lifted a hand to her wet braid. "You've bathed. I'm sorry I didn't awaken sooner."

He brought her hair to his nose. He liked the scent of it. Of her. His gaze lingered on the tiny woven knot that held the braid before raising his eyes to find her watching him.

He drew his brows together and let her hair drop.

She'd already built a fire, he realized after a moment. She'd done everything correctly. The flames were hidden from the valley, and close enough to them to give out warmth.

"I'm only an incapable cook, my lord," she replied with more poignancy than rebuke, and he remembered the conversation the first night after the storm. She might have been incapable of many things that night, but he doubted the same truth held now.

"You'll need to boil water," he said after a moment, taking the coffeepot and rinsing out his mouth. He sat forward and rested his elbows against his knees, scraping his hands through his hair. His face was rough and unshaven. He needed a hot bath. "Have you checked on the horses?"

"Yes. An hour ago. I gave them oats. I don't know what else to do for them. I heard wolves earlier. I wasn't sure—"

"Cassie . . ." He took her chin gently into his palm and forced her to look at him, her name on his lips somehow tempering his escalating emotions, and hopefully hers.

"I need this wound cleaned with soap and hot water. All right?"

She nodded.

He attempted to unfasten his shirt and failed. Cassie moved nearer to him. Brushing aside his hands, she efficiently worked the buttons. His senses closed in on her slim fingers and the long curve of her neck as she helped ease the shirt from his shoulders.

Before she could intervene, he peeled the soiled bandage away from the wound. Blood seeped to the surface, as if he hadn't already lost enough. Thanks to Captain Valerik's tender care, the swelling purplish flesh had burst most of the stitches the physician in Carlisle had so artfully sewn. The wound showed signs of infection.

"I need hot compresses on my shoulder."

"You *need* a surgeon," she whispered, having only been able to get his shirt to his forearms, which was fine with him, as it would help keep his hands restrained.

"It should have healed. Would have healed if Valerik . . ."

He briefly shut his eyes, his greater strength rendered useless by weakness. Maybe if Picaro hadn't gone lame, maybe if the thieves hadn't attacked the camp, he might have reached Edinburgh before the fever took hold. But now he couldn't even stand. He was afraid he would pass out, leaving her alone with few provisions and people hunting them both. He leaned his head back against the tree, knowing that if the wound had already gone septic on him, he'd be dead inside a week.

A half hour later, she had the water boiling. "You must think me an incompetent ninny," she whispered, settling beside him.

Because she had meant the words as a reassurance

that she was not, Devlyn was loath to doubt her. He'd stopped thinking her incompetent days ago.

He detected the tremble in her fingers as she dipped a piece of cloth in the hot water. Leaning over him, she worked to clean the ragged flesh with soap. The pain momentarily blinded him.

"I'm sorry," she rasped. "I'm trying to be gentle."

Despite the pain, he felt the corner of his mouth lift. "You aren't going to faint on me, are you?" he asked.

The possibility that she considered he might think her weak-kneed did much to embolden her. Drawing in a shaky breath, she looked with determination at the wound and continued to work.

He trained his eyes on her temple. "Talk to me." He knew she was scared. Hell, this wasn't a turn around the dance floor for him, either. "Tell me something about yourself that I don't know."

"You don't know anything about me," she said without looking at him, her voice unsteady and barely audible.

"You're wrong, Cassie." Her head rose and her eyes found his. He knew a lot about her. Beneath her icy soft exterior—which wasn't so icy when he kissed her—she possessed passion, backbone and honor.

For someone who had spent her entire life in a world filled with privilege and security, the veracity of her courage was apparent. "I know that you cherish a cello named Lady Rose." That made her smile. "You can predict weather." He closed his eyes. "You swing a deadly bucket. You don't cheat at cards, which means you are inherently honorable despite my desire to prove you otherwise." A grin touched his mouth. "You have a fancy for Gypsies, and you could plot a course before you were twelve."

"How would you know—?"

He opened his eyes and saw hers narrowed with dawning. "That first afternoon in town. You spoke to Hector afterward."

He didn't deny he'd been spying on her.

"Mr. Devlyn be a 'oly terror to anyone what be gettin' on his bad side." She mimicked the ne'er-do-well's very words. "Be careful wit' yerself, mum. It's rumored he's a Gypsy." Folding her arms, she peered at him down her slim nose. "Tell me you two don't know one another rather well."

He swigged from the flask and let his gaze go over her face, humor in his eyes.

"What else do you know?" she asked.

He knew he was thoroughly beguiled or drunk. Probably a combination of both.

He knew that when he made love to her the first time, it wouldn't be on the ground with the dirt at her back. He wouldn't be wearing shackles on his wrists and he'd be washed and shaved. He knew that he was demented with fever, to be thinking all that.

He also knew he'd been a complete ass. He'd missed their betrothal ball. Without so much as a personal note or by-your-leave to her, he'd allowed Cassandra Sheridan to face his elitist family and scores of his peers alone. Not because he considered his crown affairs more noble than any social event, but for a reason far more nefarious and selfish. The reason waited for him to come to her in Whitehaven.

So why had his future suddenly become ambiguous? His goals less defined?

"I regret that my actions have brought harm to you," he said, finding little clarity in his thoughts, certainly finding no reprieve for what lay hidden there. He fought to remain conscious. His hand brushed aside her hair. "If something happens to me . . . go north . . ." he rasped. "North to Glentress. Find Eve Macgruder. Her father-in-law . . . owns . . . apothecary. Tell her . . . contact . . . Rory Jameson. I . . . m-missed our rendezvous three days ago. He'll know what to do—"

"I don't care about your mission, Devlyn St. Clair! Do you understand me?"

One corner of his mouth lifted. "You have a temper, love." He drew in a breath, then another. "But I haven't spent the last three years in the dregs of hell to lose everything now." He shut his eyes. "Do *you* understand me?"

Cassie wrapped her arms around him as he started shaking.

She worked through the night to keep hot rags on his shoulder, drawing out the poison, the world becoming a nightmare of feverish agony for them both. She covered Lord Hampstead with his cloak and blankets. She made him drink water and fed him watered rice. Then she smoothed away his hair, bathed his face, his neck, his chest. She must have dozed, for when she next looked up at the sky, she saw a hint of dawn in the sky.

Something had awakened her.

Blinking away sleep, she straightened.

The stallion was making noise. Beside her, Lord Hampstead was unmoving, his dark lashes like shadows on his stubble-roughened cheeks. "Lord Hampstead?" Her touch failed to stir a response. "Devlyn?"

Snatching up the field glasses, she ran to the berm near the creek and peered over the earthen lip. But the glasses only revealed the stark emptiness spread out before her. Yet, she could feel something out there.

They weren't alone.

Cassie dumped the contents of the haversack on the ground. She couldn't find the revolver. She knew Lord Hampstead kept it near him, but a desperate search turned up nothing. Coming to her feet, she turned in a circle, her glance taking in every corner of the glade. She finally found the pistol lying beneath the blanket where Lord Hampstead had fallen asleep.

The worn bone stock was cold in her hand and felt awkwardly big for her grip. In the stables, she had seen Lord Hampstead pull back the hammer with his thumb as he aimed the gun at Captain Valerik. Was it that simple to kill a man? Just aim and fire?

Cassie shoved her hair beneath his floppy hat, hesitated and removed it from her head, turning it over in her hands. But she was too apprehensive to ponder what had made her pause. She slapped the hat back on her head and hurried away from the campsite, careful to remain in the trees as she approached the horses. Lord Hampstead had picketed them down the hill. Thank God the stallion was no longer limping. As she approached, the wind tugged at her hat and pushed a cloud across the sky. The horse paced the length of his rope in a high-stepping gait, agitated enough to make her nervous. He was a powerful horse with sleek lines and a beautiful pale mane, rather like his master in bearing. Was the horse just restless?

The mare continued to graze. The gelding had lifted his head when she'd appeared, but otherwise seemed uninterested in her presence. Some of the tension left her body.

She walked over to the stallion and held out her hand. "Be a good boy, won't you, please? I'm going to ride you to Glentress and you're going to let me. Do you understand?"

Lord Hampstead would surely die if she could not bring help. Glentress was less than ten miles, she was sure. On a fast horse, she could be there and back before nightfall. She looked around for the saddle. If she was going to leave, she had to go now.

Relaxing her grip on the revolver, she turned . . .

Directly into a strange man.

Cassie screamed just as a leather-encased hand grasped her wrist in an attempt to subdue her or protect himself from being shot, she couldn't tell, and they nearly went to the ground. "Bloody Christ!" he said.

He spun her around and locked an arm around her. "I'm not your enemy, Miss Sheridan. I swear I'm not here to hurt you."

The blue wool of his shirt on the arm that held her was all she could see. But she'd glimpsed a hat and had the impression of quicksilver eyes beneath the brim. "If I let you go, am I assured you won't scream?"

Cassie nodded. It would be foolish not to agree. She would scream in a heartbeat. His hand eased from her mouth. She put distance between them and whirled.

"How do you know my name?" she demanded.

One hand on his hip, he tipped his hat back with one finger. "If I'd bloody well known who you were in town, you wouldn't be out here now. Half the countryside is looking for you."

She knew that voice, recognized the man's eyes from her encounter with him at the trader wagon. He was no longer a stooped-over old man with red bushy hair and an accent. "Hector?"

"Jameson," he corrected. "Rory, to be exact, if you're

not indisposed to using me Christian name, Miss Sheridan." The words were carefully enunciated and very British. "Where the hell is St. Clair?"

Devlyn tried to open his eyes, but the effort was too much. There were voices around him. Hands lifting him. The creak of a wagon. Heat. The softness of a woman's lap. Then he was walking, attempting to stand upright, and he thought he might be sick on the ground. Jameson supported him on one side, Cassie on the other. They bore him through a door and into a room smelling faintly of carbolic soap. Ahead of them, Eve Macgruder pulled back the covers on a narrow bed.

"Sit him down here. We'll need to get his boots."

"You're safe," Cassie said, brushing the hair from his face. She stood above him. "We've made it to Glentress."

He looked at the man and the woman standing beside the bed, her dark hair bound by a red kerchief. "Jameson," he said drunkenly. "How are you, Eve?"

The woman rent a white cloth in two. "I've been better, Hampstead." Her voice hinted at familiarity. "So have you."

His gaze focused on Jameson. "Get Miss Sheridan to Edinburgh," he said, his voice slurred. "Away from here."

"I won't go."

"At any rate, not tonight." The physician stepped around Cassie and gave her the scissors. "Cut his shirt off. And Jameson, do something about those bloody manacles on his wrists."

Cassie stepped forward to remove his soiled shirt. His wound had opened up again during the wagon ride. She could feel her stomach sinking as the doctor injected Devlyn with morphine.

Not just sinking like a ship caught in turbulent seas,

but like an anchor slamming against the sea bed. Her gaze chased to his. The breath left her lungs.

"If you are going to faint, Miss Sheridan, I suggest you do it someplace else."

"Leave her alone, Evie," the doctor told his daughter-in-law. "She stays. I need all of you here. Hold him down, Jameson."

"Will the morphine work?" Cassie asked the doctor, whose rheumy blue eyes hinted that he had just been awakened.

"Let us hope so," he replied, setting the syringe on a wooden tray beside the bed. "He won't like surgery without it."

Jameson pressed his hand against Devlyn's other shoulder. "We don't have enough people to do the job, Macgruder. Don't you bloody have any ether?"

Cassie climbed onto the bed and straddled Devlyn's thighs. "Do what has to be done," she told the doctor.

"Aye, Macgruder," Devlyn murmured, looking at Cassie with a faint smile on his lips. "If you don't do it now, you may find me doing something else instead."

She looked into his half-lidded gaze. He was awake and appeared almost lucid. She gently scraped the hair from his brow. "I believe you will *not*, my lord." At least not in public, her eyes told him.

"The wound on your shoulder must be lanced, my lord," the doctor said.

"Just do it," he said without taking his eyes from Cassie.

The doctor placed a leather sheath between Devlyn's teeth.

Fresh tears burned in her eyes. "I'm sorry," she whispered at the first cut.

He jerked and bit down hard on the sheath, his pain a

palatable thing that arced from him and into her. She did not deflect her gaze from his. "Look at me, Devlyn," she pleaded, aware that every movement of the blade was a measure of his concentration not to stir or jerk. But he finally did cry out, his voice muted behind the leather. Fresh blood welled with the gore and helped cleanse the poison from the wound.

Cassie didn't know how long the doctor and his daughter-in-law worked, cutting through each stitch, opening the site where the infection lay. It took all of her strength to keep Devlyn still, not to watch.

But finally the surgery was completed, the wound lanced and draining and new stitches applied. Devlyn had long since lost consciousness when she felt Jameson lifting her off the bed.

She felt him put a blanket around her shoulders. "Let him sleep."

"I won't leave him."

"He isn't going anywhere, Miss Sheridan."

Cassie let him take her out of the room. "Have you eaten anything?"

She hadn't. Not since last night. Jameson sat her down at the table and dished stew from a kettle hanging on a tripod in the hearth. "I should have been suspicious of you in town when you knew *Mr. Holt*," she said when Jameson slid the bowl in front of her. Savory carrots and potatoes were covered in a thick lamb broth.

He took his place across the table from her. "Eat, Miss Sheridan."

Cassie did as she was told. After the first bite, she realized she was starved. Even the thought of displaying poor manners in front of this man could not diminish the speed in which she consumed the meal. When she was finished, she burped delicately against a napkin, looking up to see Mr. Jameson watching her with amusement in his silver eyes.

"I won't tell," he said.

Cassie set down the napkin. "That is nice to hear," she replied. "Nor will I tell anyone you aren't really a Gypsy."

"Ah." He smiled. "But my mother was indeed a real Gypsy." His gaze sobered. "What happened to Hampstead?"

Cassie told him about Captain Valerik and everything that had taken place with the horse thieves. Mr. Jameson pulled the leather casing from inside his shirt pocket. "Do you know if he had anything else on him besides this?"

Knowing the love letters he must have read that were inside the casing, she folded her hands in her lap. "No, I do not."

With a frown, he set down the casing. "Hampstead asked me to get you to Edinburgh, Miss Sheridan. Is there someone I need to contact?"

That was it? she wondered. Devlyn would send her away? Wasn't that what she had once wanted? "Braeden Maxwell," she quietly said. "You can contact him at his residence in Stirling."

"Ambassador Maxwell's son?"

"He is my friend's brother."

Cassie wondered what she'd seen in Rory Jameson's eyes. Then she stood when Dr. Macgruder entered the room. "Is Lord Hampstead all right?"

Dr. Macgruder walked to the sink and pumped water into a bucket. He cleaned his hands. "He's washed and resting," he told Cassie. "You may go in and see him."

Eve was leaving the room when Cassie entered. Her arms filled with soiled bandages and linens, Eve stopped. "He should sleep through the night."

Wearing her old trousers and her hair uncombed, Cassie imagined what she must look like to this woman. "If I need anything I will ask," she said.

"Rory is staying in the room next to this one. I will make a bed for you upstairs."

After Eve departed, Cassie shut the door and sat in the chair next to the bed.

Devlyn lay on clean sheets, a white bandage across his shoulder and anchored around his chest, the contrast to his darker skin more apparent in the lamp light. The iron manacles were gone. She did not want to cry but the tears came anyway and she wept quietly against the mattress. She awoke at dawn, her head resting on the blankets. Devlyn was sleeping soundly.

Taking his hand, she turned it over in hers, bringing it to her cheek. His skin was no longer dry and hot. She felt his fingers move and raised her head.

"I must be addled"—his voice was a rough whisper— "or I'm dead and in heaven."

Cassie smiled. "You aren't even close to dead."

"You smell like wildflowers."

By the light of the lamp, his eyes grew lambent, regarding her with bemusement and sending her senses stumbling. "I should have made love to you when I had the chance," he said.

It should have been impossible for him to be so injured and appear so strong to her at once. But he was awake, and in the dim light, his eyes were a striking deep brown. "You are remarkably unprejudiced in your desires while in a drugged state, my lord," she said, realizing he still must have morphine in his system.

Their hands twined, he fell asleep.

Cassie remained beside him for two more days. The doctor kept him sedated, but it was obvious when his fever broke by the end of the week, he would be all right and was on a quick road to recovery. Later, Cassie moved to the room upstairs for there was no more reason to keep a twenty-four-hour vigil in his room. Someone was always in the chambers with him, and more and more, Cassie felt like a third wheel on the apple cart.

She didn't understand the relationship he had with Rory Jameson and Eve Macgruder, so she spent less time in the room when they were present and continued to stay away from his room for the next few days.

Not because she didn't want to be near him. She did.

More than anything in the world, she wondered what it would be like to awaken next to him, to feel his arms around her in passion.

Maybe that was the crux of her problem. Devlyn St. Clair made her feel wild and wicked, and more alive than even her music made her feel. She could not think when she was around him, and more than anything she needed room to think. So she kept to herself, helping in the kitchen, befriending Eve's little girl, and learning how to boil her own water for a hot bath.

After spending over an hour filling the tub, Cassie bathed that night in hot lavender-scented water and washed in the soap she'd purchased from town. She dried off on a sun-dried towel and stepped into one of Eve's borrowed red skirts and a white blouse. Looking at herself, Cassie felt like a Gypsy. She'd never looked like a Gypsy. The thought made her smile as she sat down on a warm bench and began brushing out her hair until it crackled in a shine.

It was late when she heard footsteps in the hallway. Cassie stood when Eve entered the kitchen and stopped. Her black hair, tightly restrained at her nape, gave Eve Macgruder an exotic appearance little handicapped by the spectacles on her nose. Cassie thought she was beautiful in the Romney fashion of a true Gypsy woman. But for the color of her eyes, she and Rory Jameson could have been brother and sister.

Eve carried a dinner tray to a bucket of water in the sink. "Devlyn has eaten and bathed, and just threatened my father-in-law with imminent harm if he gave him another shot of morphine. I believe his lordship is quite recovered."

"I imagine he'll want to leave here soon," Cassie said, self-consciously running a hand through her hair, surprised to find that she did not want to leave.

"I imagine, he will. He is a terrible patient." Cassie sensed the other woman's awareness increase. "Rory said you kept Devlyn alive when he was ill."

"I would not credit my efforts with that feat, Mrs. Macgruder. He was very sick when Mr. Jameson arrived."

"We haven't really been formally introduced," she said, offering her hand. "Please call me Eve."

Cassie shook the proffered hand and saw it was horribly scarred. Her first startled reaction had been to withdraw her own hand. "I usually wear a glove when I'm around strangers," Eve said in apology, her fingers curling into her palm, a reaction to Cassie's rudeness.

Cassie never felt more mortified for her discourtesy. "Please, don't apologize. It was impolite of me to do that. I'm sorry."

A merchantman who had worked in the engineering room on one of her father's ships had been horribly disfigured in a boiler mishap and made a virtual pariah. Cassie had visited him twice at the infirmary before her father had not allowed her to go there again, but she had seen the cruelty directed toward him when he'd been well enough to walk the streets, and Cassie had sworn she would never thereafter be unkind to anyone.

Cassie set down the brush in her other hand. "When Lord Hampstead was ill, he asked me to find you and Mr. Jameson. You are all friends?"

"Devlyn and I have known one another for ten years," Eve said. "He was best man at my wedding. My seven-year-old is quite in love with him." She smiled whimsically. "She never plans to outgrow the pony he gave her last year. But her grandfather is sure she'll have the lads knockin' at our door before too many more years pass."

Eve returned her attention to the tray and set the dishes in the water. "Her father died a little over a year ago in St. Petersburg."

"St. Petersburg?"

"My husband and I were Devlyn's partners. I was burned trying to get my husband out of the warehouse when it caught fire. Nicholas Ivanov likes to burn things." She placed both palms on the countertop. "This business killed my husband, Miss Sheridan."

"I'm sorry for your loss."

"Are you in love with Devlyn?"

Caught off balance by the query, Cassie felt oddly dizzy, as if she'd just consumed a dram of his whiskey. Her gaze shifted sideways, not in avoidance of the question, but because she knew the answer.

"Then perhaps he is worth the fight, Miss Sheridan. Or I would tell you to walk away."

Cassie turned her head. "Knowing what you do now of your husband, would *you* have walked away?"

Eve considered the question, her gaze focused on the flames in the hearth, and smiled faintly, answering Cassie's question without saying anything at all. "Devlyn has been asking about you all day," Eve said after a moment.

"He has?"

"I believe he's still awake." Eve dried her hands on a dish towel and set it aside. "I'll see you in the morning, Miss Sheridan."

Devlyn was sitting up in bed when Cassie entered his room a few minutes later. His hair was still damp from his bath, his skin bathed in warm shade by the fine lamp glow. He'd been looking out the window but turned his head when she shut the door behind her. His gaze touched her standing in the shadows, the aquiline planes of his face sharpened by light and shadow. She smiled.

She didn't know what had happened between them since she'd first met him that she could be so sure of how she felt. Yet, something had changed inside her, and that knowledge was part of an inner realization that he was the man she wanted, despite what her father might have told Devlyn's father behind closed doors, despite any decision they might have made about her future.

Her father would not be forgiving of her more recent actions, she suspected.

Yet somehow she couldn't gather the momentum to regret what she'd done or what she was about to do. Being with Devlyn, she felt some of his wildness infuse her with a passion. And once rooted within the fertile ground of her heart, that passion had begun to grow and expand. She would be twenty in a few months. A grown woman by the standards of her peers. Old enough to make her own decisions. She was no longer a silent participant in her own future. So, must her pride worry that Devlyn's heart might not yet come with the bargain he had once asked of her?

"What are you wearing?" he asked.

"Gypsy clothes, sir." She smoothed her skirts with nervous hands. "They belong to Eve. How are you feeling?"

His gaze followed her to his side. She was conscious of his bare chest and the wrap of the bandage around his shoulder and upper arm, something that did not seem to hamper his mobility for he had been in and out of bed all day. She brought cooling fingers to his brow, only to find that his hand wrapped around her wrist. The faint smile that had curved his lips was gone. She met his gaze and suddenly knew what it felt like to feel passion in a cause.

"Why are you still here, Cassie?" he quietly asked. "I told Jameson to take you to Edinburgh."

She drew in a shallow breath. "I know. I remember."

His voice had taken on an edge. "You need to go. Not just away from this cottage. You need to leave Scotland. Go back to New York. It isn't safe for you here."

She wouldn't leave, of course.

For the first time in her life, she knew what she wanted.

"What are you doing?" he asked in a cautious voice as she hiked her skirts high enough to climb into the bed.

"It is only because it's cold, my lord." She stretched out beside him, on her side, and arranged the quilt over them. "I've been told you will fully recover in no time at all." After a moment she said, "I've missed you, Devlyn."

"Is that why you've been avoiding me?"

"Then you've missed me as well? I'm glad."

"Cassie?" His voice was an unsteady rasp, and something else far more carnal. "I don't want you in this bed—"

His inarticulate groan was muffled by the press of her mouth on his. She didn't kiss him long. Just long enough. "You are in a surly mood," she replied.

His hand went beneath the spill of her hair to her nape

and pulled her back into a kiss. "And you're taking advantage of me," he said when he let her breathe again.

"I hope I am, my lord," she whispered above his lips.

"You have a taste for the piquant. It's dangerous, Cassie."

"You collect that I should not want this, my lord? That there is a fine distinction between love and lust?"

The thought flickered through her mind that she was only in danger of doing or saying something to humiliate herself.

"I can't do this with you," he suddenly said against her mouth. There was strength in the hand that held her nape and yet tenderness. "Don't ask more than I can give, Cassie. I will only hurt you if you do."

His words frightened and sobered her at once, but the sentiment behind them imbued her with courage. "Then consider me warned, sir."

Her lips brushed his. A tentative whisper at first, emboldened more by trust than dimmed by uncertainty.

He was the one who changed the tenor, answering the question those lips asked. Devlyn tightened his palm around her head, and a shiver that had nothing to do with the chill went over him.

He luxuriated in the sweet softness her lips offered him, deepening the kiss until he felt her breath build and catch on a groan. A groan that fueled the heat in his blood, hot enough to make cinders of his control. The quilt slid to the floor. He wore nothing beneath the remaining sheet, and his erection tented the white muslin that covered his hips.

She was untried. A virgin. Confused between love and desire. Need and lust. Yet, she was making a royal hash of his control. He finally pushed her away, if only to breathe.

She turned her head away, only to stop as he edged his finger across her cheek. Devlyn looked into her face and felt the world shift. Or maybe it wasn't the world at all, but him. Something inside.

He had not considered she wouldn't deem him less than a hazard to her person. Or that he would doubt himself or his purpose. He had closed off his life years ago out of necessity, shut the door on his emotions. Yet she'd found a crack just wide enough to slip through. He held her gaze, felt the whisper of his name on her lips, leaving him off balance and no longer indifferent to his future. Until this moment, he'd had every intention of letting her go. He'd decided when he'd awakened last night to find her asleep that it would be in his best interest as well as hers to end their betrothal.

"I want you to go home, Cassie," he said.

"Because you think my presence is a threat to you?"

Because there would always be someone who would want to hurt her to get to him. Because he was not the person she thought he was.

"Am I so ugly, my lord, that you cannot stand my presence?"

"Ugly?" He laughed. "You put the sunrise to shame."

Tears welled in her eyes, and he felt her vulnerability.

"I desire you, Cassie. . . ."

It was the way he felt when he spoke her name that froze this moment in his mind. But it was the lengthening silence that sealed her fate to his.

Lifting his head, he rolled her over onto her back and waited for the dizzy feeling that rose in him to pass. He was unsure if the dizziness came from physical exertion or something far deeper. Her hair lay in a cascade over the pillows. He touched a silken strand. Regretting that he could no longer restrain himself, he framed the soft curvature of her jaw with his hand. Her skin was cool, yet promised warmth, her fragrance elementally pleasant to his senses.

Her green eyes, bright in the lamplight, searched his. He could not look away.

She held perfectly still beneath him, and he wondered, if he kissed her body all over, would she taste like milk and honey? Still he did not touch her. Though he found he wanted to more than anything else at that moment.

"Lock the door," he said.

Heat flared and raced between them in burning waves. "No one else is awake."

"Still . . . lock the door."

Chapter 10

Cassie peeked into the hallway, then shut the door. As she went to lock it, her hand froze. There was no key in the lock.

A hand went over her shoulder to the door. Devlyn stood behind her, all heat and fire against her back. She inhaled the scent of cloves from his damp hair. A glance over her shoulder revealed that a sheet hung loose on his lean hip, but he wore no shirt and nothing on his feet. He reached above her to the doorframe, ran his finger along the top and produced a key.

"Eve keeps the key out of the way so Amy won't lock herself into one of the rooms."

He inserted the key into the lock. A click followed. They were alone.

He braced his palm against the door, and the world faded to his physical presence surrounding her. "It's different when the reality of the moment is upon us, isn't it?" he said in a low voice.

Her stomach tangled in a knot and impaired her breathing. He was correct in his observation. Reality was not the same as fantasy. But Cassie closed her eyes, aware that this was what she'd wanted. She turned in the narrow space that separated her body from his and they were face to face. His hair lay like dark silk on his brow.

His thumb traced the sensitive edge of her lip. "What do you know about bearing children, Cassie?"

"I know that you can't get with child the first time," she said, a tremble in her voice.

Devlyn pulled back, amusement lighting his eyes. "Who told you that?"

"Sally Ann heard it from her cousin who's married."

"Is she the source of all of your sexual education?"

"You don't think I'd ask my mother. She'd—"

"Faint?"

"She'd want to know why I was curious. After she awakened from her faint."

She thought he might change his mind at her apparent naïveté, but, suddenly smothering a curse beneath the fall of her hair, he clearly lost the reins to what was left of his control. His warm breath coasted over her mouth. "You're out of your element, Cassie. For better and for worse. After tonight, there will be no going back. You understand that?"

She closed her eyes and breathed, certain there could not be this manner of passion between them without love. "We're practical people," she said, her forehead pressed against his mouth.

"Adults," he agreed. He pulled at the ties on her skirt. "I've seen you in fewer clothes."

Her skirt dropped into a soft scarlet puddle around her bare feet. She was barely aware as her blouse followed.

She wore her shift beneath, but she may as well have been wearing nothing. The dusky press of her nipples shaped the fine white fabric. It was not the room's chill that made her body react. From a space of inches, his coal-dark gaze met hers, even as his breath rasped against her lips.

"Put your hand on my neck, Cassie. Like we were about to dance."

"Your shoulder—"

His grin turned roguish. "You don't know enough about the inclinations of men to realize pain is not always a deterrent to carnal drive." He settled her palm opposite the injured shoulder. "My sole inclination is to make love to you."

Her lips parted for him on a breathy sigh that touched his mouth. He made her feel needy and weightless. He made her feel desire. He made her . . . feel.

Her breathing escalated. His body responded. His mouth opened hers wider, his tongue penetrating with melting intimacy. The hard line of his shoulders became her tactile focus. His hand slid down her back, splayed her bottom, his motives identified by the hard press of his erection against her abdomen. She could not stop herself from touching him. The coiling muscles in his arms defined his restraint, the husky rasp of his voice, his passion. She avoided his bulky bandage, but nothing else was out of bounds to her touch. She explored, every velvet touch a revelation, his body stirring her senses into a cauldron of fiery emotions. Her tongue dueled with his, and like the devil's dance he'd promised, he stepped fully into the kiss, and suddenly they were lost in each other against the door, moving to the steps of their own orchestrated melody, its score set by the rhythmic cadence of his hands and his lips on hers.

He was sin incarnate. And deep inside, Cassie knew she was doing something that would send her to hell a hundred times over, but heaven help her, she did not want to leave the flames.

She dropped her head back with a gasp. His lips moved across her cheek to the column of her throat, where he stopped kissing her. With both hands planted on the door he lowered his head, as if he too needed to catch his breath.

The sheet no longer shielded her from his body. The fabric lay discarded atop her skirt, every muscular inch of him bared to her gaze. The rigid length of his erection stretched tautly from a dark thatch of hair. Cassie had never seen a naked man, certainly never a towering one who stood unselfconsciously nude in front of her. Warmth flooded her body.

"Are you all right?" she breathed, alarmed.

"No." But his shoulders moved as if he were laughing. "I believe you have put me into a state of passing out, love. All the blood has left my brain and gone elsewhere."

Worried that she might kill him, Cassie helped deliver him to his bed. They staggered together across the room and she watched as he sat. "Is that . . . common?" she asked.

This made him shake his head and when he finally raised his eyes, she found they were laughing. "Only with you."

She didn't like that he seemed to be enjoying himself at her expense, when she wasn't even sure what the joke was. "It's because you've been ill."

"That, too, I'm sure. The mixture is a deadly combination for a man in my state."

He pulled her down with him to the bed, and she

caught her palms against the mattress, holding herself over him, her smile breathless when she realized she'd been the cause of his reaction. "How deadly?"

"Painfully deadly. Torturous," he groaned, making her forget everything she'd been lectured about temptation. "Amused now?"

"Only at your expense, my lord. But I still would not wish to see you expire tonight. How would I explain it to Lord Ware?"

He laughed, and Cassie found herself watching him in awe, loving the shape of his mouth, the complete transformation in his eyes. Surely no man was more beautiful. She kissed him, holding him with nothing but the pressure of her lips. He changed the kiss, making it more carnal as only he could do. Straddled as she was over his erection, almost nothing separated her virginity from his full penetration. His groan hummed against her mouth. Without touching her, he suckled her lower lip. Cassie sipped from his mouth, equally imbibing in sensual bliss, already drunk with new-felt passion.

"I will only expire if I do not see you naked, Cassie." He bunched the loose fabric of her shift in his fist. "Take it off."

She rose up to her knees just as he slipped the shift over her head. Beneath it, she wore nothing.

His hands on her waist held her still, his eyes on her body so physically primeval, she felt the touch to the core of her being, shattering her inhibitions, as one would crush the most delicate crystal framework. Its pieces lay in shimmering chaos around her, and God help her, she felt free. She let him look his fill, shocked by the low growl that was her name on his lips.

Devlyn slid his hand against her nape and pulled her

into another kiss, rolling her onto her back, the seductive pull in that one act coiling in his lower abdomen. Even naked, she looked absurdly virginal, with her lily hair and porcelain-smooth skin. She smelled virginal, too. Like a pristine meadow at dawn, or the orangery in the full blush of spring.

"What are you thinking?" she asked.

Her beauty robbed him of breath. His mouth went to her neck, to the pulse racing there, then to the curve of each breast. "I'm thinking I like what you are not wearing." He took one nipple into his mouth, suckled her, then moved to the other.

She made a noise like a hungry kitten. He liked the innocence of her reaction, her curiosity, and the lack of sophistication in her response. His hand fell over her hip, utterly captivated by her abandon. She was hot to his touch. "I'm thinking that I don't think at all around you, Cassie." His voice was a groan.

"And I'm thinking you are beautiful," she breathed with coquettish overtone, prompting him to reconsider her lack of experience and the wisdom of her giving herself so completely over to him. "I like the way you make my body feel." Her hips lifted. Her fingers tangled in his hair. "I'm thinking . . . I don't wish to wait any longer." Tension coiled in her body.

"Do you know what it is you feel, Cassie?" he asked against her lips, knowing exactly what it was she was feeling and how to help her.

Her hand drifted lower and she closed her fingers around the hard length of him, and Devlyn nearly jettisoned his restraint.

He turned on his back, pulling Cassie with him, their soft laughter born of mutual haste and desire. She pressed him into the mattress, and because his shoulder could not sustain his weight, he allowed her to do so. Her hair fell forward over his chest.

"I've never touched a man," she whispered.

Her fingertips were like cool rain on him. She tentatively stroked the smooth head, her explorations then taking her palm to his sac, before he could pull her wrists away. She smiled and gave a shivery sigh. Hunger lashed through him.

He inched up against the headboard, eyeing her warily.

"Does it hurt?" she asked.

"Christ . . . no."

He'd never been stared at with such interest. He pulled her against him and kissed her thoroughly. Devlyn found himself alive in her response, utterly revived in her arms. The scent of meadow flowers surrounded him, stirred him. His fingertips trailed up her back, splayed her shoulder blades, then traced the curve of her back to cup her firm bottom.

Devlyn didn't know if her body was prepared to receive him. He was going too fast. But his body didn't seem to be listening.

He moved his hand between her legs. She was hot and wet for him, her body tight.

"Press your knees alongside my hips," he said, his mouth against her ear. He lifted her bottom and, following his lead, she found her seat straddling his thighs so that they faced each other in anticipation. "It won't hurt for long, Cassie."

Cassie sucked in a lungful of air, but his mouth was on hers, breathing for her, taking her shock. He slid past her barrier. Her head fell back against her shoulders; the long curtain of her hair brushed his thighs. Devlyn tightened his arms around her, giving her time to adjust to his size.

A small cry broke from her lips. She instinctively moved against him. Breath hissed between his clenched teeth.

Christ, she was tight around him. His hands locked on her hips. "Not yet, Cassie."

"Just . . . just tell me when," she whimpered, her voice tightened on a ripple of tension.

Then he was buried to the hilt inside her. Lost in her arms.

And they remained locked until her breathing stilled, until she pulled back to look into his face. At first, he rocked her gently, holding her close, his body hot against hers.

She clung to him, her breasts crushed against his chest, the whisper of her breath rasping in his ear as she followed his lead. Soon theirs became no gentle mating. He no longer thought about moving his body, only knew that he did, the silky pleasure as intoxicating as it was unanticipated. Her nails dug into the bunched muscles of his back. His hands crushed around her hair. With a rough throttled sound, he buried his head into the salty crook of her neck. Her back arched like a bow. He drove himself into her and his heartbeat became the silken pulse of his release.

With his last inhalation, Devlyn fell with her onto her back.

Sanity returned to him in slow degrees.

For a time, there was only the soft hiss of the lamp. Lamplight glistened on Cassie's skin. Their breathing slowing, they stared at each other for a long time, the house silent around them.

He was aware of every searing sweet detail of her, the blush that was even now touching her cheeks.

What the hell was happening to him?

"Is it always like that?" she asked.

It had never been like that for him.

"That depends on the two people involved."

"Will it always be like that for us?"

Devlyn didn't understand what was happening to him. He rolled to the edge of the bed, hesitating as a bout of dizziness rose, then passed through him. He padded naked to the washbasin, wrung out a rag and cleaned the blood from him, then brought the basin to the bed. He dipped the wet rag into the water. She let him wash the evidence of their lovemaking off her body. He didn't talk. He was suddenly uncomfortable without knowing the reason why, and felt the bite of his temper without fully knowing the cause.

"Do you want your shift?"

Confused, Cassie sat up and nodded. He gave her the shift, then wrapped the sheet around his hips. He checked the bandage to make sure he hadn't torn the stitches. Devlyn returned the basin to the stand, opened the window and dumped out the water. He walked to the armoire, but when he couldn't locate his clothes or the hat, turned to find Cassie's eyes shyly on him.

"Where are my clothes?" he asked.

"Mrs. Macgruder took them and your boots into the kitchen to be cleaned. Mr. Jameson took your haversack."

Devlyn saw the leather casing on the nightstand. Cassie saw it as well. He returned to the bed, thumbed through the contents and dropped it on the stand. "Where is my hat?"

Cassie pointed to the top of the armoire. "I was wearing it when Mr. Jameson brought you in. Is something wrong?"

Devlyn sank into the chair Cassie had occupied for the last few days. "There is a lot I don't understand at the moment."

"Did I do something wrong?"

"Wrong?" Devlyn raised his head and looked at her. This was all new to him. "No, Cassie. You did nothing wrong."

"Then you are thinking about her." He watched her touch the leather casing that held the letters she had read and knew she was questioning his heart and his capricious mood. He studied his hands. He had not exaggerated when he'd told her there was much he did not understand. He had not been thinking about Maria Ivanov. But he did so now.

"Will you go to her after we are married?"

He speared a hand through his hair and stared at her in disbelief. "Leave off, Cassie. I'm still wearing your blood and you already want to know if I intend to commit adultery? Christ, Cassie. The last person I want in bed with us tonight is Maria Ivanov."

Cassie slid off the bed. "I don't want her in bed with us, either. But I feel as if she is."

"Where are you going?"

She padded across the green rope rug to the door where she fumbled into her clothes. "I should bring more peat for the stove in the corner. It's chilly in here. It gets cold at night," she said. "And you're barely out of your sickbed."

Her hands trembled. Her clothes had been a lot easier to remove than don and she struggled with the ties. Bent over her blouse, she couldn't see past the blurring in her eyes. "Or if you're hungry, there still may be lamb in the pot. It wouldn't take that long to warm."

She clicked the key in the lock and opened the door.

Devlyn's arm suddenly went around her, shutting the

door with force. He placed his hands on her shoulders and turned her into his arms. "Don't leave."

For a long time she laid her head against his shoulder, holding him to her. "I'm in love with you," she said.

"No, you aren't, Cassie."

He said the words so easily as if he expected that response of her. As if he suffered women falling in love with him and knew how to handle such a circumstance. He'd told her before such feelings had to do only with lust, but Cassie did not know how to separate the two. Perhaps he had the experience, but she did not. "I'm not sorry about what happened tonight," she said quietly.

His hands slid to either side of her face. Looking into her eyes, he scraped his thumbs across her damp cheeks. "I'm not sorry, either," he said.

But Devlyn's words proved to him only that he was a more accomplished liar than even he had imagined. For everything had changed. And he was sorry that she was young and he would end up hurting her.

Sorry that he was a coldhearted son of a bitch who'd rarely known an ounce of compassion in his bloody life. There was a reason he was good at what he did. And despite his recent blunders, he would continue to be an asset to Lord Ware.

He didn't understand Cassandra Sheridan or what it was about her that affected his judgment. But he kissed her. Settled his mouth across hers and possessed her lips.

And the kiss that began with him ended with her body arched against his and her tongue in his mouth. He sifted his hands through the silken strands of her hair, and all the logic he'd erected to explain his need for her and excuse his restlessness crumbled to his feet. He had blamed her earlier for his lack of control. Now he blamed only himself. Desire consumed him, and the last vestige of restraint ended. He wanted her, after all.

He moved her back to the bed, undressing her all over again, before following her down onto the blankets. They made love with none of their original haste. There were no words between them. No laughter. The emotion was elemental, unfiltered and uncensored by conscience. His orgasm powerful and consuming.

Later they fell asleep in a tangle of sheets and blankets. His mouth lay against her hair, and he found it odd that, even sated, he wanted her again. But the night had exacted its toll on his body and soon he succumbed to fatigue and slept.

There were no dreams of his brother to haunt him. No bitterness toward his father. Only sleep.

When Devlyn opened his eyes again, daylight filled the room in muted grays and shadows. Devlyn's hand went to the empty pillow beside him. He raised himself on one elbow. A glimpse at the small oval clock on the nightstand told him it was nearly four o'clock in the afternoon.

His mouth tasted like opium and brandy, the last vestiges of the drugs he'd been given before he'd grabbed Dr. Macgruder's wrist and nearly scared the life out of the old man. Christ, he hated opiates.

Waiting while the dizzy spell passed, he took stock of the bedroom, his mind clearer than it had been yesterday, and he looked at the room as if seeing it in color for the first time. Rain beat on the roof and sheeted against the windows. Tied back with a tassel cord, green curtains framed the casement. He collapsed back on the pillow.

The swish of skirts turned his head toward the door.

Eve entered, carrying a wooden tray of food. "Where is she?" he asked, his voice a harsh rasp against his throat.

She set the tray on the table beside the bed. Propping himself against the headboard, he waited for the room to stop spinning. Eve filled a glass with water from a pitcher on the nightstand and gave it to him. "Miss Sheridan isn't here."

"What are you talking about?"

Eve leaned over to the table and turned up the light. "At Miss Sheridan's request, Jameson took her to Edinburgh this morning. Braeden Maxwell is meeting her. It seems they know one another well. Under the circumstances, we agreed it was best someone she knew bring her back to her family. Jameson should be back late tonight."

A surge of anger tightened Devlyn's chest. He didn't know what bothered him more. That Cassie was with her childhood crush, of all bloody people? Or that she had left here without telling him?

He rubbed his temple with the heel of one hand. "I thought Maxwell was still in France. How long has he been in Scotland?"

"Do you think Maxwell would tell Jameson that? Honestly, the man is an arrogant jackanapes. I never did like him."

Devlyn shot Eve a glance from beneath his elbow. She merely cocked a shoulder against the tall bedstead and folded her arms. "Why didn't you ever pay so much attention to me when we worked together?" she asked.

He grinned. "Maybe I was concerned your husband would have planted me a facer, Eve," he said.

"Yes," she said. "I believe he would have. He was fond of you in that way."

Leaning his head against the headboard, he blinked away the last dregs of sleep and examined her more closely in the daylight. Eve wore a shiny red dress imprinted with flowers the color of her blue eyes. She sat on the mattress next to him and smoothed her skirts over her lap as she settled the tray beside him, her slim hands revealing the scars that he knew extended up her arm and across her torso. An experienced chemist, Eve had nearly died in the fire that claimed her husband, his former partner. He knew she had taken a great risk by allowing him to remain here. If he could have gone anywhere else, he would have.

"I didn't want to come here, Eve. Hell, both of us know what would happen if Ivanov suspected you were still alive."

She smoothed her skirts. "You are overdue. Knowing Ware, you will have a lot to answer for."

The leather casing from the haversack remained on the nightstand beside the bed. "I have something that will placate Ware," he said, and asked Eve to pull out one of the British currency notes inside the leather fold on the dressing table. "Tell me what you see."

She snapped the note tight and held it to the light, carefully examining every detail. "If this is counterfeit, then it's the best I have ever seen. Where did you get this?"

"Maria gave me the notes from a safe in her husband's house. None of this would be possible without her. At any rate, she is on her way out of the country by now."

Eve turned her attention to jars and vials that lined the shelves behind her. She withdrew a vial and dropper, shook it vigorously, then popped off the lid. Bending over the note, she dabbed acid on the paper, then stood back and waited.

"All government treasuries use a unique combination of rag paper and dyes," she said, holding the note to the light. "This is nearly faultless."

"Discrepancies only a test could reveal."

"Or someone with a trained eye. If enough of these are circulated, it could undermine the British financial system worldwide," she said with growing interest. She knew as well as he the significance of the find would be a coup for Ware. "The consortium already has a counterfeiting foothold in America. This is why Maxwell is here."

He knew where Ivanov procured the dyes and paper used to make the currency, and the artist who'd created the plates. He carried evidence to see Ivanov brought to a tribunal for a dozen crimes against the crown. But not for the murder of his brother or Eve's husband. In that quest, he'd failed. A failure he'd have to live with for the rest of his life.

"No man has ever lived to bring charges against the consortium," Eve said after a moment, worry in her voice. "I know you must feel this is not enough. But you've made a discovery more valuable to our government than a murder conviction. The penalty for counterfeiting is death. In the end, it doesn't matter how Nicholas Ivanov is convicted and hanged. Only that he is."

Eve was right. But in his heart, it wasn't that simple. It had never been that simple.

And yet . . . suddenly he wished that it were.

He thought of Cassie. His reaction to her last night not one he had expected or could have anticipated. Somehow everything had become personal. For the first time in his life, he thought of what it would really be like to settle down. Would his past allow him the luxury? Signing those contracts had been an easy choice when he didn't know her, when he'd had no face or body to put to the name. When his only constraint in this life was to produce an heir. He hadn't wanted anything else that went with the title, anything that tied him down to this life.

Until now.

"Miss Sheridan saw the broadsheet this morning," Eve said, as if reading the direction of his mind, and nodding her chin toward the tray. A folded newspaper was tucked behind the soup bowl. "That you were dueling with the son of a Russian diplomat over said son's beautiful wife rather than dancing in attendance to your future bride at your betrothal ball has made for scintillating gossip. The only thing missing from the account is your connection to the Foreign Office."

Devlyn frowned at the idea of his father reading such a piece, though he was probably used to it by now. Cassie's family would not be.

"You still haven't told me how you two ended up together in Scotland."

"She and her cello met me by accident in Dodburn," he said. "She got caught in my business before I learned who she was."

"Knowing you, I'm sure it wasn't that simple. She is a bit unsophisticated for your standards, is she not?"

"Eve . . ." he warned.

"That girl is in love with you. My guess is that you have some strong feelings on the matter yourself. The man with the legendary heart of granite has softened. Does she know what it is you really do? Or does she only know the good parts?"

Good old reliable Eve. Some things had not changed. Two years could pass and she still considered herself an expert at deciphering the details in his life. As if he'd ever given her leave to do so. It annoyed him that she could home in on the very bloody thing that troubled him, when he didn't even understand it himself. He was annoyed with himself for allowing his emotions to show. "Succinct and to the point as always. But you can save your breath. Cassandra Sheridan is in love with the idea of falling in love. Hell, she's in love with some bloody fantasy of my brother."

"Just like Maria Ivanov all over again. It must gall you to continuously play second fiddle to your brother even in death."

Devlyn looked away and swore.

"Do you know what I think?" Eve said, needling him. "I think something happened to you out there in those hills."

"Something did happen. I got the bloody hell beat out of me."

"She saved your life," Eve said bluntly. "When Jameson found you, you were unconscious. Your debutante was preparing to ride that hell stallion of yours in an effort to save you. Only *she* seemed to be able to calm you enough so that my father could operate on your shoulder. She didn't leave your side for days. You can't buy that manner of loyalty. Certainly not from Maria."

Her eyes remained troubled. "And if you aren't careful, that one will get you killed the same way she's gotten every man killed who has ever loved her."

Devlyn opened his eyes and found the same censure in her gaze that he'd heard in her voice. But he had no intention of discussing Maria with anyone. She damn well knew it.

Finally giving up on a response from him, Eve shoved away from the bedstead. "I'll prepare a bath for you in the kitchen beside the fire before Amy returns with her grandfather. You'll probably want to shave before you eat supper."

After Eve left, he forced himself to sit on the mattress edge. He wrapped the sheet around his hips and paused when he saw the blood. He dragged the sheet with him to the window and leaned against the glass, his intent to leave this cottage anytime within the next few days dashed by the ensuing weakness. He looked out on a neatly trimmed hedge, a white picket fence and the growing sunrise. He looked toward Edinburgh.

Out on a world different somehow, realizing it wasn't thoughts of Maria Ivanov that filled his mind. But of green eyes the color of spring and a smile that warmed him.

Chapter 11

Cassie sat on a velvet-tufted seat next to the window overlooking the flower gardens. The daffodils were barely visible in the late afternoon mists as the sun began its descent. Golden light no longer filled the private parlor where Braeden had taken her to enjoy tea. A hush surrounded her and held her captive. She drew in a steadying breath.

Her reflection in the glass came into focus. The hasty trip to the modiste upon her arrival in Edinburgh a week ago had produced the pale pink satin gown she now wore. It was her only suitable attire until the rest of her clothes arrived.

Her less-than-feminine height compounded with the problem of long legs and arms made it impossible to find anything ready-made. Once again, she was an oddity.

She'd been somewhere outside Edinburgh for nine entire days, for her safekeeping, instead of at Amber Rose, where she desperately wanted to go. Rory Jameson

had filled Braeden in at the rail depot about the events
that had led her into Lord Hampstead's care. But if she'd
known she'd be kept a prisoner, she never would have
asked her best friend's brother to meet her.

Her eyes found Braeden Maxwell outside. He stood
on the terrace dressed smartly in a dark suit and knotted black tie, holding a leather satchel, awaiting the
men who had just arrived in the shiny black carriage to
see her.

Braeden, her childhood hero.

From a long line of Scotsmen, he had roots buried
deep in this country. He had been born at Amber Rose
Castle in Stirling before traveling to America with his
father when he was an adolescent. He'd distinguished
himself as an American naval hero before he was twenty-
one. He was steady, devoted to his family, a man who
would never lie or cheat at cards, the opposite of everything Devlyn appeared to be.

Until now.

Now he was the man keeping her from leaving this
despicable place. Though he had at least sent a telegram
to her parents informing them of her whereabouts.

With a sigh, Cassie turned back into the drawing
room. She'd been relieved to learn that Mary, Frankie,
and her cello were with Sally Ann. Her staff of two had
arrived safely with Lady Rose. She only wished that
they were all together now and didn't know why she was
being kept apart from them. She suspected part of the
reason had to do with the men who had just arrived.

Raised voices outside recaptured her attention. Braeden
was speaking to a silver-haired man she didn't recognize,
but who made her uneasy. His demeanor reminded her
too much of her father when he'd just heard bad news
about the stock market. Though she couldn't understand

what was being said, she recognized the tone in which the words were exchanged.

Then, as if sensing her presence in the window, the group looked toward where she sat, their stern visages sending a quiver of alarm down her spine. Good heavens, they were talking about her! And Braeden's manner made it obvious that he didn't like what was being said. Was an interview with them imminent? She heard the back door open. Braeden wouldn't allow anyone to hurt her.

Would he?

She looked toward the archway, folded her hands in her lap and waited.

A current of cooler air preceded the three men into the room.

The silver-haired man had eyes the color of a North Atlantic ice floe. "Miss Sheridan?"

Braeden stepped past both of them, but his attention was riveted on the man with silver hair. "I'm warning you, Stratton. Miss Sheridan is a friend to my family. You *will*, by God, treat her with respect or this interview is over before it begins."

Stratton pulled his gaze from Cassie. "You are welcome to stay, Maxwell."

He turned his attention back to her. "I work for the U.S. Treasury Department, Miss Sheridan. I am Mr. Maxwell's colleague. Mr. Roth here is Pinkerton." He nodded to the shorter, brown-haired man with mutton-chop whiskers beside him. We came up from London as soon as Mr. Maxwell wired us that you were here and might be able to help us. Do you mind if we sit?"

Without looking at Braeden, she nodded. Both men slid chairs nearer to her window seat. Stratton looked up at Braeden. "Would she care for any more refreshment?"

"No," Cassie answered, not wishing Braeden to leave the room.

"You must be wondering why Mr. Maxwell has brought you here, Miss Sheridan," Mr. Stratton said.

"Clearly, he is not in Scotland on holiday."

"Yes . . . well—" Mr. Stratton cleared his throat. "Amberly House is often used by visiting American dignitaries and other guests of our government. But allow me to reassure you we are not here to accuse you of complicity in any crime that Lord Hampstead has committed. We hold him entirely accountable and know you had nothing to do with the events that conspired before your near abduction."

"Accountable for what? Lord Hampstead saved my life," Cassie said. "Captain Valerik was attempting to kill us."

"Captain Valerik is dead. Whatever threat he posed to you is no more."

"How?"

"Valerik was found dead outside Hawick. Or what was left of him, downriver and too battered to determine his identity for sure. That is all we know. That and the fact there was an altercation between Valerik and Lord Hampstead."

Cassie looked over Stratton's shoulder at Braeden. "The implication is absurd. I was with Lord Hampstead, and I guarantee Valerik was alive when he left us at that stable. No one died that night. Why is the U.S Treasury Department interested in any of this?"

"Did Lord Hampstead mention anything about the man that he killed in England? A man named Stefan Ivanov?"

Cassie disliked Mr. Stratton heartily. She had no intention of telling him anything.

"Tell them what they want to know, Cassandra." Braeden had moved from the liquor breakfront, where he'd poured a glass of brandy, to the window. He'd placed himself out of the dialogue but not so far away as to leave her alone. "It's important."

"Lord Hampstead told me that he had dueled with a man named Stefan Ivanov. Captain Valerik worked for Stefan's father. Someone named Nicholas Ivanov."

"Did Lord Hampstead mention the contents he might have taken from a safe that night at Ivanov's estate? Did he carry anything seemingly important? Journals, account books, letters or the like?"

Cassie had seen intensely personal love letters as well as other papers that were written in Russian script. But she didn't like the tone of this interrogation and didn't trust these men not to harm Devlyn. Something else was wrong here. Something she didn't understand.

"Cassandra?" Braeden dragged her gaze back to his. "If you know something, tell them."

"Why are you asking me this?" she demanded.

"I don't know who you think Hampstead is, that he needs your protection," Mr. Stratton snapped. "Maybe Mr. Maxwell can explain Hampstead's character. I don't have the time or the patience to enlighten you about the organization in which he serves. But he has a connection to Nicholas Ivanov's consortium—"

"That's nonsense, Stratton, and you know it," Braeden fired back. "She isn't going to believe that manure."

"Our people are dying, Maxwell. Someone on the inside sold out both of our governments. We need to know what he took the night he killed Stefan. We know someone has been selling secrets. A list of our operatives was sold to the highest bidder for a great deal of money. There may also be other sensitive information—"

"Things the British must want as well?" Cassie said.

"The source of the leak could only have *come* from someone high in the British government. We will have the identity of that person. If the British get the journal, it may be something we will never learn."

"If Hampstead even has the journal," Braeden said. "Have you considered that he does not?"

"She's protecting him, Maxwell." An unmistakable edge turned up the corner of Stratton's mouth. He observed more than her face. He was reading her thoughts, his gaze hard and clinical as he assessed her. "We know you are betrothed to the man. But how much do you really know about Devlyn St. Clair?"

"Why are you doing this?" Cassie demanded.

"Maybe you'll be more cooperative when you know he's been involved with another woman for years."

Braeden came around to face the man with an icy gaze. "Leave off, Stratton. She doesn't know anything."

"But you do, Maxwell. Tell her it's a lie, then. Or are you willing to allow the infatuation of a silly young girl to jeopardize the lives of our men and their families? This investigation is no longer just about counterfeiting. We need to know how many of our people have been compromised."

No naval captain worth his salt was a soft touch, retired or otherwise, and some of that brittle hardness inherent in Braeden's stance now showed in his eyes. But Cassie turned her head away, realizing suddenly that no matter how she felt about Lord Hampstead, about everything they had shared, including his bed, nothing had really changed for them.

Why had she thought for one moment after the last few weeks that life could be different?

"Is this 'other woman' you're referring to Maria Ivanov? I know that he was protecting her."

"Then you know that her husband murdered Hampstead's older twin brother last year," Mr. Stratton said.

"I don't understand." Cassie looked from Stratton to Braeden. "Lord Hampstead had a twin?"

"You didn't know?" Braeden asked.

She shook her head. "Father never told me."

"Dominick St. Clair was a highly respected English diplomat murdered in Paris last year," the Pinkerton said when the other two did not speak. "It is understandable that you were never told." He, too, looked away, as if he had overstepped some invisible line.

She suddenly remembered something Devlyn had told her about the man horrendously murdered, mistakenly killed as a spy. A sick feeling formed in her stomach and she clasped her hands in her lap. "How was his brother killed?"

"Horribly," Braeden replied, his eyes focusing on her once again. "And that's all anyone is going to say on the matter."

"St. Clair was working in Marseille at the time of Dominick's death," Stratton said. "He missed his brother's funeral by two weeks. What a bloody wretched way for a man to learn that he had just become his father's only remaining son and heir. It was a bitter reality for His Grace, the Duke of Hastings, to swallow, considering he had been estranged from his younger son for a number of years. It is well known in certain circles they hated each other."

Cassie turned her gaze outside. She had lost her brother. She could not imagine losing a twin, much less living with the horror that he had been murdered. "Were they identical twins?" she asked when she could find her voice again.

"No." Braeden sat next to her on the window bench and leaned forward with his elbows on his knees. "Though they looked enough alike at times that one could pass for the other." The sleeve of his jacket pulled up to reveal the white of his shirt cuff beneath. Everyone suddenly looked uncomfortable. "No one is questioning Hampstead's loyalty to his country, Cassandra. Certainly not I. I know him and would trust him with my life. But Stratton is correct when he says someone has passed on the names of our men."

"You believe Lord Hampstead knows who it is. Isn't that akin to treason, Braeden?"

"We're only interested in finding the source of the leak, Miss Sheridan," Stratton said. "We know you'll see Hampstead again. We need you to find that journal for us."

"You mean you want me to spy on him."

Braeden bent nearer and took her hand. "Cassandra."

She shrugged off his touch. "Don't—"

"Listen to me."

She didn't want to listen to him. She wanted to be left alone. Clearing her mind, she lifted her chin and looked directly at Braeden. "You clearly have a past acquaintance with Lord Hampstead. Did you know he was betrothed to me?"

"Not counting the fact that I have been out of the country for a year, what exactly would I have said if I had known of your betrothal before you left New York for England?"

"Will you help us?" Mr. Stratton asked.

Cassie swiped at the wetness on her cheeks. She hadn't even realized she'd been crying. "Unfortunately you have wasted your time coming to me. For you see, Lord Hampstead and I have decided not to wed. If you had merely asked me, I could have spared us all this clandestine scenario." Looking away, she swallowed over the tightness in her throat. She would run away before she'd ever spy on Devlyn. "I am returning to New York. So, you see, I can't spy for anyone."

"Does Hampstead know he's made the decision not to wed?" Braeden quietly asked.

"We've spoken about our betrothal."

"Then why is he turning over Edinburgh looking for you, Cassandra?"

Her heart gave a tiny jolt. "He's here?"

"He arrived two days ago," Braeden said. "He learned that you were not at Amber Rose."

"And you didn't think to tell me?"

"We asked that you be allowed to speak to us first, Miss Sheridan," Mr. Stratton replied. "Maxwell was following orders."

"I will not be your spy." Cassie came to her feet in a swish of pink satin, followed by all the men as decorum dictated. "Now, if you gentleman will excuse me."

Stratton stepped in front of her. "This dialogue—"

"Is now over, Stratton," Braeden said.

Cassie lay on the bed, her cheek resting on the crook of her arm. She'd locked the door. Outside, she could finally hear the carriage pulling away. They must have stayed for late tea. She flung her legs over the side of the bed and ran to the window. The trees blocked most of the view of the drive, but she glimpsed the wretched carriage roll down the hill, just before it disappeared beneath the brick archway and off the grounds.

A knock sounded on the door. She remained where she was.

"Cassandra?" Braeden's voice came through the door.

Folding her arms tightly across her chest, she ignored him.

"The interview should not have gone as far as it did," he said from his side of the door. "I regret that you were placed in the position you were."

She didn't respond.

"Cook has prepared an excellent dinner. I'd hate to eat it alone. Cassandra?"

She strode across the room and twisted the key in the lock. She flung open the door. "Just because you've known me most of my life doesn't give you the right to use my Christian name, *sir*." She was aware that she had spoken to him when she'd sworn she would not.

"Then would you rather that I called you Adelaide?" he asked lightly, his cool hazel eyes missing their customary sternness.

She disliked the simplicity of his reply as much as she despised the complexity of her emotions.

"As soon as your new clothes arrive in a few days, you will be free to leave for wherever you wish to go. But Sally Ann will be disappointed if you do not see her."

Cassie turned away and walked to the fireplace, not wanting Braeden to see her upset. One hand closed reflexively over the other. "What will happen to Lord Hampstead in the coming weeks?"

"Currently, his people don't know where Hampstead is."

"But you do."

"I do because I know where he stays when he is in Edinburgh."

"Where?"

"He keeps a flat in Edinburgh, but he sometimes stays at the old Jacobean lodge outside Bathgate his grandfather built. Some years ago, Hampstead rescued his grandparents' estate off the block. No one else in his family wanted the upkeep of an old hunting lodge that his grandfather had transformed into a house."

Devlyn had never told her about the house. "Have you ever been there?"

"It isn't much, but it could be something with a little tender care. I only know that he cares for that old rundown place as much as he does for that stallion of his. For such a hard-nosed Brit, he can be sentimental about the oddest things."

Cassie tightened her arms across her torso. "I have to know something, Braeden," she said. "A year ago, I was promised to the Hastings heir. A year ago, Dominick St. Clair was alive. Though nothing was yet signed, Father had been in the process of negotiating the contracts. Now I learn that Devlyn had an older brother. The man I was supposed to wed was Dominick St. Clair, wasn't it?"

"Devlyn was the younger son," Braeden agreed.

Why had she thought Devlyn an older son? She'd heard rumors there had been a brother and a tragedy had befallen him, but which was never discussed in the household.

She blinked away the tears welling behind her eyelids, realizing Devlyn had been as much a pawn as she. Worse, he'd suffered through the horrible death of his brother, a death he felt had been meant for him. Then he'd stepped into his brother's place—including betrothal to her. His life had been irrevocably altered by the events. He would marry Cassie while his heart sheltered another.

Maria Ivanov.

"Was she ever his lover?" Cassie looked up at Braeden. "Maria Ivanov?"

His eyes widened and he seemed ludicrously shocked at her blatant query.

"Don't behave like a prig, Braeden Maxwell." She swiped at her face, no longer aware that only a short time ago she would never have asked such a scandalous question of any person. Certainly not of Braeden, a man she'd wanted to marry since she was ten years old, until she'd seen him with another woman in the gardens of his father's house. "I know firsthand that you are not."

"You probably think you know a lot. But you don't."

Cassie refused to allow just how ignorant she truly was. Or that she'd practically prostrated herself beneath Devlyn before he'd finally taken what she'd freely offered.

Braeden led her to a high-backed chair, sat her down and knelt beside her. "You've been through much," he said.

She wanted to lean her head against his shoulder.

But she did not. It was important that she remain strong.

Yet, knowing that emotional ceremony did not come easily for Braeden, the appearance of his softer side meant that much more.

He'd always known just what to say to make her and Sally Ann smile. The special *tendre* he'd held for his sister had somehow always extended to her. Braeden had been the one who'd danced with her at her coming-out ball when her awkward height had made her an outcast. But what she'd always felt for him was a deep abiding affection akin to that of a brother. What she felt for Devlyn St. Clair grabbed at her middle and tore her in half.

She didn't want to know that Devlyn loved someone

else. That he would lie with another woman when he should only be with her. She didn't want to feel young and foolish, yet she knew she must have seemed both in Devlyn's eyes.

And her own father? What of his responsibility in all of this? He should have been more forthright with information. He must think her a ninny, to assume she would not have eventually figured out the timeline in this tragic affair.

Cassie came to her feet. The pressure in her chest tightened. "I cannot stay in Scotland, Braeden. I have to go home. Away from Lord Hampstead. Everything will be easier if I can just leave."

"Why?"

She walked to the window and looked out over the park. A deep indigo light brought the copper beech and oaks into dark relief. She leaned her head against the cooler glass. "Because it's better not to see him again, Braeden."

"Are you in love with him, Cassandra?"

She shut her eyes and shook her head, too weary to delve into her heart. "I know I am not savvy about such things," she said without turning. "But he protected me. It was my fault that Captain Valerik caught him, put him in chains and hurt him. At the very least, I owe him my loyalty. If he is guilty . . . of anything, I will not be the one who condemns him."

He moved behind her. "So you would leave Britain rather than jeopardize his honor? Shouldn't you talk to him first?"

"Talking would only lead to other things, Braeden."

"What other things?

Cassie turned and experienced a quiver of fear.

"Did Hampstead touch you?"

That Braeden dared voice such a query sent a hot wave flooding her face. But the glitter in his hazel eyes told her he not only had the nerve to ask but would demand an answer. "Did he?"

Devlyn had touched her in places no man had ever touched. But only because she'd allowed herself to be kissed, and she'd *wanted* him to touch her. He had been the one to pull away the first time. "I am not a girl, but a woman, Braeden. Do not treat me as if I am some untouchable Ice Princess whom nobody wants."

She startled when Braeden uttered an oath. "Then you could be carrying his child."

"I . . . no!"

Her denial, though, was late in coming, the consequence of her actions with Devlyn suddenly too real. She hadn't yet considered whether her menses were late. She'd not been regular enough these past months since leaving New York to take note. "I swear, Braeden." She strode past him to stand at the door, inviting him to leave her bedroom. "If I had a candlestick I would be tempted to violence." Her chin lifted at Braeden's approach. "Out!"

She stepped into the hallway as he swept past. "For your information, Lord Hampstead was quite restrained the entire time we were running for our lives across the country. I am the one who compromised him!"

And as she slammed the door, she had the satisfaction of knowing at least that much was true.

Three days later another storm pounded at the house. A chilly gust eddied through the opened windows. The draperies billowed around the canopy tester bed. But it was the faint whicker of a horse that brought Cassie fully awake.

She rose and walked to the window, her sleeping gown

flowing around her legs with each step. But she could see nothing in the predawn darkness.

She shut the draperies, hating the chill surrounding her, a chill that had nothing to do with the weather. Not too long ago, Scotland was paradise in her eyes. Now she was only convinced that it rained more here than any place on earth. She'd wanted just once in the last few days since she'd argued with Braeden to walk outside in the gardens and enjoy some much-needed sunshine. She wanted to breathe and not think about Devlyn or the wickedly capricious fate that had brought him into her life.

She would be leaving Scotland. Her new gowns had finally arrived last night. She'd left them spread out on the chairs. Now she fingered the fabrics. The gowns, though less extravagant by Worth standards, reflected a country charm that she welcomed in lieu of shiny satins. Or, that is, she would have welcomed if she were planning to remain.

"Shall I put the gowns away, mum?" Her maid stood in the doorway, breakfast tray in hand.

How had she even known Cassie was awake?

The woman, middle-aged and less than five feet tall, with curly red hair, reminded Cassie of an efficient and capable elf with a no-nonsense attitude, whose ancestors were most like Picts. Braeden had no doubt hired her as a turnkey to make sure Cassie didn't leave the estate on her own.

Cassie set down the dress, self-conscious that she had been caught admiring the clothes like someone who couldn't afford to buy a hundred such gowns. Her mother would say such displays were unseemly. "Leave them out for now."

Wrapping a shawl over her shoulders, Cassie moved nearer to the fireplace and stoked the coals. "I thought I heard a horse approaching. Is Mr. Maxwell expecting a guest at this early hour?"

"I could not say, mum." She set down the tray. "Is that all?"

She was lonely and didn't want to be alone. She stopped herself from asking the maid to stay and join her by the fire, if only to talk about mundane things like the weather.

"Thank you for breakfast," Cassie said instead.

The kindness was out of her mouth before she could pull it back. She'd been made aware her very first day in England that to thank one's servants for work they were being paid to do was a severe breach of etiquette. But here in Scotland the simpler way of life replaced the persnickety British attitude.

Cassie returned to the window. "I will ring when I am ready to dress, thank you."

"Of course, mum." The woman bobbed a curtsy.

Cassie's room overlooked the parkland and part of the drive. It was not yet dawn and the sky remained black. Cassie leaned against the cool glass and stared outside. Wind slashed at the treetops. Somewhere a loose or broken shutter banged against a window down the wing. Below her on the drive, light from the manor separated the shape of a horse from the darkness. It was the first time she'd noted its presence. Two footmen sought to calm the high-spirited mount, cooling it down after a hard ride.

Cassie suddenly straightened and leaned nearer to the glass, her heart racing.

Even in the predawn darkness, she recognized the sorrel stallion.

Chapter 12

Cassie ran down the hallway to the stairhead chamber, stopping when she heard the voices below. Masculine voices. Low. Agitated.

". . . torn up Edinburgh looking for her."

Catching only clips of conversation, Cassie peered over the polished banister. The foyer where they stood rose two stories, but most of that, including her vantage point, remained in darkness. A wedge of light from an opened door splayed across the polished marble floor below. Devlyn stood there, still wearing his coat. Drops of water glistened in his hair.

"How much haven't you told me?"

"Leave off, Maxwell. Since when has my personal life become your business? Now, where is she?"

Carefully removing each of his gloves, Devlyn let the footman take his sodden coat. Beneath it, he wore a gentleman's riding attire, tailored to his perfect form. Mud-splattered high black boots hugged his calves and would have distracted from the perfect harmony of his otherwise faultless apparel if he were not so breathtaking. Even from where she stood, she could smell the rain on his woolen coat. No more the rogue who had saved her from Captain Valerik, he looked exactly like what he was. An expensive aristocrat like his peers in England. He made it simple to remember why making love to him had never been a wise idea.

"I told you I would do this your way," Devlyn said.

"I have a lawyer here to make sure everything is in order as we agreed."

On the landing below, the tall clock struck six times. She stepped back into the shadows and remained pressed against the wall, staring at a formidable marble bust of George Washington.

Braeden was a traitor! Nothing less than a Benedict Arnold to her.

They were moving out of the foyer. She felt her chest tighten. Whatever any lawyer intended to share with him, she had a right to be present and to speak on her own behalf.

"Wait!" she called out, running down the stairs, her diaphanous gown flowing around her like a cloud.

Both men turned.

Cassie had forgotten she'd left the bedroom wearing only her nightdress and a thin robe. The shock on Braeden's face might have been cause for amusement if the equally darkening frown on Devlyn's did not force her to realize her error too late. Perhaps she might have boldly accepted her breach of modesty as the cost of doing battle had a tall vicar not stepped out of the library at that very moment and drawn her up short at the bottom of the stairs, abruptly ending her defense before it had even been launched.

* * *

Devlyn was not in one of his finest of moods that morning, but Cassie's appearance on the stairway struck him harder than he thought possible, considering he'd been angry as hell that Maxwell had taken it upon himself to play her caretaker these past two weeks, as if he had the right. Her hair hung loose and free-flowing like the gown. There was a faint wash of color in her cheeks, a blush that matched her lips. He took a step toward her, but Maxwell stepped in front of him. "Let me pass," Devlyn warned in a quiet voice, not of the temperament to bode with interference.

"I haven't told her yet."

He'd granted Maxwell more leeway than he had his own men, but a man could only be pushed so far. He thought of Cassie with Maxwell these past two weeks and then he thought of wringing Maxwell's bloody neck for hying her off—probably for some bloody interview somewhere. Devlyn knew Mr. Stratton was in Edinburgh. Just like he knew Lord Ware had returned last night from Balmoral.

The vicar's voice broke the stalemate. "Shouldn't His Grace be here as well, Mr. Maxwell?"

"My father doesn't make my decisions." Devlyn never looked away from Cassie. "He hasn't yet. And won't in the future."

The vicar moved next to Devlyn. He was not a tall man, but was wide of shoulder, with a pugilist's broken nose to darken his solemn expression. "I came here at Mr. Maxwell's behest to do what is morally right." He looked from Cassie to Devlyn. "But is it true your father has begun proceedings to disinherit you? If it is, shouldn't that fact be taken into consideration before we do something rash this morning that cannot be so easily undone?"

Devlyn turned his attention to Maxwell. "Is this what you wished to discuss with me first?"

Maxwell's reply was lost as Devlyn glanced at Cassie. He glimpsed tension running through her. "Would your father do that to you?" she asked.

"Even if my father was inclined to disinherit me, which he isn't, the estate is entailed. Isn't that what it is that interests your family, after all?"

"It isn't what interests *me*."

His gaze gentled on her troubled green eyes. "Your money doesn't interest me, either, Cassie." His voice softened. "If your father had done a more thorough study into the matter, he would have discovered that I don't need the influx of cash into my coffers. My father does."

"Then what exactly does interest you, my lord?" she asked.

He was looking at her, and if it wasn't in his eyes for all to see, then it was in his heart for him to feel. Maybe it was more than honor to fulfill his side of a fair bargain struck. Maybe it was something in the way she made him feel. Not quite respectable but not tainted, either. Clean. More alive than he'd felt in years. Whatever it was, it pulled him to her.

Then he smiled a wolf's smile and confronted Maxwell's stare. "Maybe you would like to explain to her why there is a vicar here, and why I am carrying a special license in my pocket. You were certainly willing enough to blackmail me into coming here. What was it you were threatening? You would wed her yourself?"

Cassie gasped. Her great American hero looked amusingly uncomfortable in the crosshairs of her glare. "Does someone want to explain what this is about?"

"You are about to become a countess," Maxwell said, ever the diplomat when it came to wriggling out of an international crisis, but Devlyn didn't appreciate the interference.

"I warned you there would be no wedding, Braeden," Cassie said.

"It will be done," Devlyn replied, his voice turning her around.

She remained steadfast and proud standing in the foyer wearing nothing but her flimsy gown in front of Maxwell and the others who had filtered out of the library, and whom Maxwell quickly ushered back into the drawing room before shutting the door. It was all Devlyn could do not to carry her out of the foyer himself and be done with this bloody charade.

"No, it will not be done," she said. "I'm not . . . you wouldn't *dare* force me!"

Devlyn fixed his gaze on his soon-to-be-very-wed betrothed. "I *would* dare."

And her eyes told him he didn't fight fair. "My great-grandmother was the daughter of a border laird," he said. "In her day, grooms kidnapped their brides, *then* wed them. Don't put it past me not to consider that option, Cassie." He smiled in mock apology for the lack of tact in his somewhat dubious proposal. "Especially looking as scandalous as you do. Far be it from me to point this out, but after this morning, one of us present would have to marry you."

"Oh!" She flew at him in fury. He caught her hands easily, aware of her soft, warm body and her desire to pummel him to a pulp.

His eyes amused, he easily subdued her. "Temper, temper, sweet. What will everyone think?"

"Go to hell, Hampstead!"

"For God's sake, what has gotten into you?" Maxwell demanded, but neither she nor Devlyn paid him any heed.

Devlyn's world had faded to black around her. His eyes remained on hers. He didn't give a fig what anyone thought of his *aristocratic* arrogance. She had made her bed with him. Literally. Now she would bloody well lie in it, he considered cynically, her change of heart a sore point with more than his own pride. A part of him knew there had to be a reason for her volte face.

The other part didn't care.

"Neither you nor Braeden can stop me from calling off this betrothal," she said between her teeth. "I will go all the way to the Orkney Islands and no one will ever find me again. I'll marry a shepherd before I marry you, Hampstead."

He still did not release her, but loosened his grip on her wrists, aware that she'd stopped fighting him. "You could run to the tail end of Scotland," he said against her hair. "I still would find you, Cassie."

"But I don't understand," she rasped, clearly needing desperately for him to let her go. "I know you weren't the one to whom I was originally promised. I know now that it wasn't even your picture I carried. I know about your twin brother. I could not have borne what you've been through, Devlyn."

He pulled her into his arms and held her because he couldn't help it. He held her because he needed her to understand that she did not belong in that part of his life. She didn't belong to Dominick or in any part of their respective parents' schemes. "I should have told you about the photograph," he said. "But it seemed a moot point after you shredded it, love."

She laughed and sniffled indelicately. "I don't need you to do this, Devlyn. I haven't honor enough to save."

"Maybe it isn't *your* honor I am saving, sweet." His eyes, dark and intent, bored into hers, but his voice was gentle. "Now go upstairs and change your clothes unless you want to wed me in your nightdress and robe." He could offer her a moment's privacy even if nothing else. "I'll be waiting in the library."

"But . . . you cannot wish to marry a woman who . . . who is unwilling. You cannot!"

He tilted her chin with the edge of his hand and looked into the depths of her jeweled eyes. "Shall I prove just how unwilling you really are, Cassie?" And to make it clear he uttered no idle threat, he scraped his hands into her hair and tilted her face. "This discussion is closed. It closed weeks ago. You know it as well as I do."

Cassie went rigid, appalled yet excited by the danger shining in his eyes.

"Go," he said quietly, as if no one else were in the foyer listening to every word spoken between them.

As if a man of God weren't watching their exchange with a paternal interest that surely sealed her fate. And because she blamed Sally Ann's brother for her entire misfortune, she aimed the last broadside at Maxwell. "To think I once considered you a man of integrity, *Mr.* Maxwell. I must have been mad to think I was ever infatuated by—"

"Cassie?" Devlyn warned. "If you aren't back down here in twenty minutes, the vicar and I will be knocking at your door."

Cassie was married in the breaking daylight of a new day. Her head bowed, she listened to the vicar tout the virtues of marriage, the bringing together of two families, neither of which were present to witness the union. Nor was Sally Ann, her maid of honor. She didn't even wear her beautiful wedding gown. It remained somewhere in

England packed in a trunk and she would never look at it again.

Conscious of the heat radiating through her body, she stood beside Devlyn wearing a rose-colored gown, feeling vulnerable beside his overpowering presence in a room filled with strangers and little warmed by the blazing fire in the hearth. Rain slanted against the thick crystalline panes of glass that looked out on a stark world, its shadows eclipsed by brief flashes of lightning. Appreciating the power of the storm's fury, she wondered if it was an ill omen that the heavens should always swirl with such angry passion when she was with Devlyn.

Were it not for the circumstances of this wedding, she might have found herself blissfully content. As it was, her pulse raced. Perhaps she would still find some contentment, though not of the kind she had hoped for.

And then "You may kiss your bride" finished the ceremony.

She felt the warmth of his hand against the curve of her jaw, tilting her face, and she suddenly felt painfully flustered, looking into his eyes. They were enigmatic and beautiful in the growing light. But it was the humor she glimpsed there that brought her back erect.

"Don't look so tragic, love," he murmured, lowering his lips to a warm breath from hers. "People might get the wrong impression."

"What impression is that?" she said against his mouth.

"That you are not in love with me, after all."

Before she could respond, he kissed her, warming her from the outside in. Then, lifting his head, he brought her hand to his lips before her wits returned. In too brief a time since their first meeting, she had become Lady Hampstead.

His wife.

Her mouth went dry. Hysterical laughter boiled up her throat.

"I apologize that I do not have a ring, my lady." He pressed a gentle kiss to her palm, his eyes now partially masked as he peered at her over the curve of her fingers. She sensed that he was not as outwardly composed as he seemed. "But you will not find yourself any less wed, I assure you."

He tucked her hand beneath his arm and turned with her. They received good wishes from those present. One was a barrister, an American lawyer of Braeden's acquaintance, who represented her interest in these proceedings. Two other men remained at the back of the room away from the light and did not come forward.

Her lawyer, who reassured Braeden that all was legal and in order, inspected the documents requiring signatures. Braeden penned his name as witness. Beckoned forword, Cassie accepted the quill last. Devlyn had already signed his name. The beauty of his script drew her gaze and it dawned on her that this was the signature she'd seen on their betrothal contracts.

Signing her name took all her effort. Her hand shook and her *C* was crooked. When the deed was done, she looked around the room to each man. "Now, if you will excuse me, I wish to go to my bed."

Silence followed. Horrified by the verbal blunder, especially in front of the vicar, Cassie struggled to retain her dignity. Her maid stood in the doorway and for the first time that night, she was grateful for the other woman's presence. "I mean . . . I am tired," she said. "I wish to rest. Alone. In a separate bedroom."

Devlyn rescued the quill from her hand before she accidentally injured herself. Cassie refused to meet his eyes, afraid she would weep or do something equally humiliating. She whirled on her heel, preparing to escape this madness.

Only something was wrong. She sensed the mood, like an underlying current going through the room and charging the air.

Her gaze passed over two men standing at attention beside the door before it came back again to stop. Men she recognized now as out of place. Braeden's men. She'd seen them with Mr. Stratton when he had come to interrogate her.

Slowly, she turned back into the silence of the room. "What is going on?"

"Sir," the maid said to Maxwell, "your driver has asked me to convey that he is ready. Her trunks have been loaded."

Cassie looked at Devlyn. He had hoped to bypass this part. Clearly, she would not allow it. "Where am I going?" she asked.

"Give me a few moments, Maxwell," Devlyn finally said.

"The honeymoon wasn't part of the bargain, Hampstead."

"Five minutes, Maxwell," Devlyn said.

"Wait in the corridor," Maxwell told his men. When they were gone, and Maxwell stood at the door, he faced Devlyn. "She's leaving in the carriage or she will not make the rendezvous point. My sister will be awaiting her arrival in Stirling."

"Why wasn't I informed of this?" Cassie asked.

Maxwell turned on her in exasperation. "Frankly, I didn't trust you not to run away. I still don't. And as far as anyone else is aware, you've been with Mary and Frankie since you've left England. My sister and I will vouch for that. None of us will argue the wisdom of keeping your recent adventure with Ivanov quiet. It would only bring attention to an already unpleasant situation."

Her heart racing, Cassie looked from Maxwell to Devlyn. "What is going to happen to Lord Hampstead?"

"I don't know," Maxwell replied, giving Devlyn his full regard. "What do they do with aristocrats accused of murdering one man and wanted for the death of another? I only promised I could bring him in and keep him here."

"Do you honestly think you and your men could keep me here, Maxwell, if I chose to leave?" Devlyn said.

With an oath, Braeden finally stepped around Cassie. "Five minutes," he relented.

Then he shut the door.

Cassie had not moved her eyes from his face. "You came here knowing this would happen?" she demanded. "Are you under arrest?"

"Braeden doesn't hold the power to arrest me. He and I are working on the same case. We both answer to the same man. And I've been summoned."

"Then why come here at all?"

She had wrapped her hair in a thick coronet around her head, altering the shape of her eyes. The firelight brought the warmth to her face. Did he find her beautiful? Her rose gown soft to his touch?

"I came here to see you." He leaned forward against the door at her back, bracketing her between his arms. "And I agree with Maxwell that you are safest at Amber Rose. Being here raises too many questions about the last few weeks. About me."

"But I should be with you."

Reluctant though he was to allow such sweet torment to leave, he knew their time together was limited. "You've given Maxwell your deposition. If we need it,

I'll use it. But at the moment we've agreed that your name needs to be kept out of public record. What happened in Dodburn is more easily explained to our families if they think we came to Scotland to elope."

"Does this save face for you or for me, my lord?"

"Perhaps for us both."

"I don't want you thinking you can make me a prisoner, Devlyn."

"I don't want you thinking you're free." What he wanted was to kiss her. He'd been aching to kiss her since he saw her floating down the stairs like an angry cloud.

"Will you miss me?" he asked.

"I believe I will not," she said, fingering his jacket lapel, skirting her hand gently over his shoulder. "Is your injury healed?"

"Healed enough," he said above her lips.

And when he raised his head, she followed his mouth up, pulling him into a kiss. His arm was already behind her back, dragging her full against him. Her voice hummed against his lips and he slanted his head, deepening the kiss, opening her mouth to his as he cradled her face between his palms. Devlyn kissed her deeply, his body moving against hers wanting to finish what his mouth had begun.

He'd always intended to marry Cassie. Perhaps Maxwell didn't understand that. But after Jameson had lost the trail to where Maxwell had taken her, Devlyn had turned territorial as hell. For two weeks while he'd been recovering, he'd attempted to keep her separated from the rest of his life and from his job. But her growing presence in his mind seemed to redefine those boundaries. For some reason he could not name, she had become vitally important to him.

The fragrance clinging to her skin brought his face

closer to her hair. "What happened earlier in the foyer?" he asked. "What happened to our agreement?"

She looked away, but Devlyn would not allow the partition between them. "Have you had your menses?"

Her face hot, Cassie opened her mouth to reply.

"I am your husband now, Cassie. It is a legitimate question. Are you with child?"

"Is that what Braeden told you?"

"It would please me if you were. You know that, don't you?"

Their gazes held for a heartbeat. Then two. "It would please me as well."

"What happened after you left Glentress?" he finally asked.

"Braeden asked me to spy on you."

Devlyn raised a brow. "Did he, now?" He looked down at her, suddenly amused. "And you refused?"

Her eyes snapped to his. "Of course I refused."

"So, you were planning to run away instead."

"What manner of marriage would we have if we could not trust one another? There can never be love without trust."

He pressed his mouth against the shell of her ear. "And what is Braeden Maxwell after, love?"

"A journal of some sort." She breathed the answer, then, after a passing moment, asked, "Do you have what he wants?"

Devlyn moved his lips to her temple. "No, Cassie."

She splayed her palms on his chest, careful not to touch his shoulder, which even after two weeks still bore tenderness. Her gentleness touched him. "You aren't angry at him?" she asked.

A smile framed his mouth against her temple. "I expected Maxwell might ask something of you, especially since he didn't take you to Amber Rose. Did Stratton interrogate you?" When he felt her nod, Devlyn froze. "Did he hurt you?"

"No." She raised her arms to his neck. "But Braeden is with the Secret Service. Part of our Treasury Department. Mr. Stratton said the British and the Americans have both been working the same case against Nicholas Ivanov. The case must be very important to both of our countries," she said, and he couldn't believe she was actually quizzing him for information, that she had pressed her body to his, and he was suddenly thinking about exploring what was beneath her clothes. "If you had something important in your possession, you would *share* the information. Wouldn't you?"

"You mean rather than allow the information to be seduced from me?"

She nipped at his lower lip. "That would be preferable to discovering you have lied to me, my lord."

He'd found her original frankness intriguing. Now he was only aware that he trod on hallowed ground and was disinclined to pursue this topic. "Stick to what you do well, Cassie. I like you better honest."

She dropped her arms from around his neck. "So you can stick to what you do well? Lie?"

An impatient tap on the door intruded. But Cassie held up the key. "No one is getting in here. We can fight over the key if you wish. But if you try I will only throw it in the fireplace."

No matter how much he thought he knew about her, it never ceased to amaze him he didn't know enough. Looking over his shoulder, Devlyn measured the distance to the fireplace against her threat. "You think you can hit it from this far away?"

She tested the key in her palm. "Easily." Her grin was

bold. "My brother and I used to throw rocks at mud dauber nests in my grandfather's barn. I became a very proficient shot."

A frown creased his brows. "You had a brother?"

She blinked. Lowering her gaze, she looked away. But only for a moment. "He died of an infection when I was twelve. And I became the sole heir to my father's little steel and shipping empire." Her finger traced the key. "My brother and I were very close, too."

The knock came again. Louder this time. "Dammit, Hampstead," Maxwell's muffled voice intruded from the other side of the door. "I knew I shouldn't have trusted you."

"What is it you want to know of me, Cassie?" Devlyn pressed.

"That if you had such a journal, would there be a reason you would not share its contents?"

"If I had such a journal and kept it secret . . . I would have a very good reason for doing so, Cassie."

Her gaze probed his, seeking the veracity of his statement. A moment passed. She turned and inserted the key in the door. "I don't even know where you live, Devlyn."

"For now"—he turned her in his arms—"you are safest with the ambassador's family. A guard will escort you to Amber Rose. I will join you as soon as I can. And Cassie," he said softly, tilting her chin to look into her eyes. "This will be no marriage of convenience between us."

Chapter 13

By midafternoon, a heavy fog had crept around the outskirts of Edinburgh, blurring the buildings and the large cathedral until one street was indistinguishable from another. The wheels of the hack clipped over the cobbled streets, the sound muffled by the weight of the air. The hack stopped and Devlyn stepped out onto the walk. Wearing a dark coat, he pulled the woolen collar close and moved aside as Maxwell followed him out of the conveyance. Both looked up at the townhouse with its blazing windows.

"It looks like a full house," Devlyn said, gazing at the carriages lining the street. "Are you sure we aren't late?"

Maxwell removed a silver fob attached by a silver chain to his waistcoat and flipped open the lid. "Lord Ware had a meeting earlier," he said, reading the watch. "We're early."

Devlyn didn't think so. Glancing up and down the empty street, he disliked the intrusive doubt. He disliked feeling like a supplicant attending his own inquisition.

At the door, both men surrendered their coats, gloves and hats to a liveried footman. Large gilt-framed mirrors increased the visual dimension of the waiting room.

Lord Ware's private secretary met them. "This way, my lord. Mr. Maxwell." He led Devlyn and Maxwell across the corridor and up another set of stairs into a dark paneled room. The heavy draperies were partially drawn. Cigar and pipe smoke hovered in the air. Men sat on all sides of a long rosewood conference table.

Devlyn stopped in his tracks.

Nicholas Ivanov relaxed at the end of the long rosewood table. A glass in his hand, his pale blue eyes, almost colorless like shards of ice, did not move from Devlyn's face as he sipped.

Lord Ware rose to his feet. Not as a matter of courtesy, but of command. A man in his sixties with graying temples, he still struck an imposing figure that too often paralyzed the hearts of his underlings. Devlyn had served his entire career in this man's command and, until tonight, would have trusted him with his life.

"Sit down, Hampstead," Ware said. "You and Mr. Maxwell are late as usual."

Instinct warned him to be silent. They were in fact earlier than the time requested, or so he'd been told. But Devlyn didn't note that fact aloud or that Ware had not asked about Jameson and Rockwell.

Stratton was present, as was the American Pinkerton agent, Mr. Roth. On either side of Ware sat two balding men he did not recognize, but deduced by their attire that they were from Scotland Yard. The other men, flanking Ivanov, Devlyn suspected as representing the Russian's legal interest.

Ivanov.

The bastard.

A silent fury grew within Devlyn. He turned and met Maxwell's stare.

"Don't fault Maxwell," Ware said. "He was under orders to tell you nothing."

Devlyn cocked a brow. "Since when do you take orders from the British government?"

A tic worked in Maxwell's jaw.

"Since this case falls under my jurisdiction, Hampstead," Ware said in Maxwell's stead. "Now sit, if you will?"

Devlyn was disinclined to sit, but not to do so would have brought Ware out of his chair a second time. As he sank to a chair, he kept his attention on Ware.

"Lord Hampstead," Nicholas Ivanov greeted him in flawless English. "It is good to see you again. I am sorry I missed your visit with my son. Had I been present, perhaps we could have avoided the misunderstanding that cost him his life."

"Stefan tried to kill me, Excellency."

"And it is only because he underestimated your proficiency with the sword that he did not."

"What are you doing here?" Devlyn asked, but the question was aimed as much at Ware.

"It is common knowledge in the right circles that Lord Ware is here," Ivanov replied, studying his buffed nails.

It was not common knowledge. Ware didn't give out an itinerary of his travels. Captain Valerik would have been the one to tell him that Lord Ware was in Scotland. But Valerik was dead. Penalty for his failure?

"Some days ago, Nicholas Ivanov came forward and has been cooperating fully with the authorities," Ware finally deigned to say. "It seems, in part thanks to your efforts, he has recently discovered the extent of his son's illegal activities and found Stefan responsible for an entire counterfeiting operation stretching across the Atlantic. He's naming names."

"Convenient. And you believe him?"

Ivanov leaned forward into the lamplight, a glint of silver touching his hair. "You speak most bravely for a man who lies for a living, Your Lordship."

"I wouldn't betray my colleagues, Excellency."

"So you say."

Devlyn tightened his jaw against the first retort that leapt to his mind. "Am I on trial here?" he inquired of his superior, stretching out his legs and leaning back in the chair.

"Lord Ware." Ivanov's barrister cleared his throat. "It is not Mr. Ivanov's intent to cast doubt on the character of one of your men."

"What is his intent?" Devlyn asked.

"Mr. Ivanov is dropping the murder charges against you," Ware said. "We are about to grant him immunity in exchange for his testimony. The orders come from above me."

Devlyn shook his head. Christ, the bureaucrats in Parliament were insane. Three years of his life thrown away on an investigation, only to end with a murderous bastard like Ivanov walking free?

The Americans, he'd noticed, were not their usual boisterous selves. Accepting a glass of port, he let his eyes go around the oak-paneled walls, touching briefly on the distinguished portraits of men who had served as prime ministers of England over the last hundred years. A portrait of a youthful Queen Victoria hung over the fireplace, a reminder of whom he served, whom he would still be expected to serve when he walked out of this meeting tonight.

"That's not all, Hampstead," Ware said.

The barrister leaned his elbows on the table. "He wants his daughter-in-law's safe return so he can help her rebuild the life that his son destroyed."

"Maria has been through a difficult time." Ivanov cleared his throat and looked pained. For anyone present who didn't know him, the man could look downright paternal, when he chose. "She needs her family."

"Turning her over to you is tantamount to a death sentence."

"You will give me my grandson, Lord Ware." Ivanov turned to the elderly statesman. "It is *the least* you owe me for my cooperation. Unless you are accustomed to your underling making all of your decisions."

"She remains where she is," Devlyn answered.

Ware shot Devlyn a look that could kill.

"As we said earlier, Lord Hampstead, we have witnesses who have agreed to sign depositions saying you acted in self-defense," the barrister replied. "Mr. Ivanov is here only to do what is right by you, my lord. He is also willing to drop all other complaints against you if you cooperate in this matter."

"And what charges are those?" Devlyn forced himself to ask.

"Trespassing, theft, the kidnapping of Maria Ivanov, damage to private property." The barrister withdrew a folder filled with papers. Sliding the top sheet from the stack, he looked down the table at Devlyn. "You're a British subject and as such can be dealt with under British law, no matter who protects you, my lord."

"By that, you mean summarily imprisoned."

"If it comes to that, my lord."

"But that would require a public tribunal," Devlyn said. "Aren't you afraid that some self-important member of

Parliament might take exception to your accusations without demanding a *public* investigation into your activities?"

"You mean my son's activities," Ivanov said.

The barrister settled his gaze on Devlyn. "Would you care to hear more, my lord?"

"No, he would not," Lord Ware said.

"Quite the contrary." Devlyn leaned forward on his elbow. "Please continue."

"Treason."

Devlyn held Ivanov's gaze, a slow fury beginning to burn and spread into the pit of Devlyn's stomach. He knew what the other man was doing. Ivanov knew about the journal. Devlyn was damned if he spoke, damned if he didn't. But until he read the entire journal, until he knew for sure about Dominick's involvement with the consortium, Devlyn could not destroy his family—even if it was the proof he needed to condemn Nicholas Ivanov.

"That is nonsense," Ware replied, clearly shocked. "I will not countenance that accusation."

Unruffled, the barrister slid the documents across the table to Ware. "Then ask him what he has done with the items Maria Ivanov gave him from the safe. Ask him what they were."

"This is what Maria Ivanov gave me." Devlyn slid to Ware the leather casing from his inside pocket that contained all the counterfeiting information, names of those who supplied the ink, papers and plates. Papers containing even more that Maria had pulled from her husband's safe. "None of this information I have brought to you matters now. Ivanov has already blamed the actions on his son. What I have in my possession will only corroborate what he has probably already given you."

"There was more," Ivanov replied.

Devlyn shifted his attention. "Perhaps if you would care to describe what it is exactly I am supposed to have, I could tell you if I've seen it."

Something cold flickered in Ivanov's gaze. "No matter," Ivanov said. "There is still the issue concerning the whereabouts of my daughter-in-law."

"Do you know where Maria Ivanov is?" Mr. Roth, the American Pinkerton agent, asked.

"Of course he knows where she is," Ivanov said. "She is too important to his case against the consortium. Or maybe he has a more personal reason to keep her now that my son is dead."

Devlyn stood.

"Sit down, Hampstead," Ware said.

"With all due respect—"

"You are out of line."

"—granting immunity to Mr. Ivanov does not mean I am required to share the same air he breathes."

A ruddy flush climbed into Lord Ware's cheeks. He rose to his feet. "I believe we have gleaned all we can from this meeting. I would speak to Lord Hampstead. Alone."

Devlyn remained standing as the room cleared. His hand in one pocket, his jaw clenched, he kept his attention focused on a smudge in the shiny table, anywhere but on Ivanov. Beside him, Maxwell shoved back his chair and came to his feet. He paused as if he would speak, but in the end he turned and left. When Devlyn looked up again, the room was empty, except for himself and Lord Ware, and the door behind him had been shut.

A low fire burned in the hearth, but the room was not warm. Still, Devlyn felt a need to loosen his tie. Lord Ware stood looking out the window, his hands clasped behind his back. "Where is Jameson?" he asked, facing the window, his back stiff.

Devlyn's first impulse was to say nothing. But he'd been running on impulse for the last few months, which had brought him to this fatal point. It was enough that he had not leapt across the table and wrapped his hands around Ivanov's throat. But it wasn't enough to save him from the ax Ware wielded. "He is bringing in Ian Rockwell," Devlyn said. "By now Rockwell will have followed directions and gotten Maria Ivanov out of the country."

"Then she is gone from England?"

He seemed relieved to have one volatile impediment to negotiations removed from England's jurisdiction. "Our people in Italy will see to her safety and her new identity."

"I went against instinct when I allowed you to remain in England after your brother's funeral," Ware said. "I should have sent you back to our office in Marseille, which I am about to do now. In a few months, this investigation will clear you. You will be free of scandal. People will have grown bored and moved on."

"As long as Ivanov is alive, I will never be free, my lord. And damn the consequences. I can't go back."

Lord Ware turned into the room. "There are men on the council who feel Ivanov is more useful to us as an ally than as an adversary."

"Nicholas Ivanov, not Stefan, owns the consortium. Why would he come forward now to cast aspersions on his own son? Because he knows what I have in my possession. He is selling out only those he can afford to lose to give the council just enough to appease them."

Ware harrumphed. "Don't you think I know that?"

"Three bloody years, I have done the council's bidding. I am neck-deep in the blood you've demanded I spill, all in the name of justice. Everything Nicholas Ivanov is selling to us for his immunity, we already know. And we've been slowly closing down his operations."

"I understand what we've asked of you these last few years. But this is bigger than just your want for vengeance. We could have made an example of Stefan, and through him destroyed the father."

He raised an arm when Devlyn started to protest. "No. The British government does not prosecute a diplomatic emissary representing the Russian czar without being bloody damn sure of his crimes. Even then, a tribunal would be risky. Unless you can offer me something substantial, all we have left are the accusations of one woman. A woman whose motives some call into question because of her relationship to you."

Devlyn knew if he opened his mouth again, he would say something he would regret. So, jaw clenched, he looked away, saying nothing at all.

"I know how you feel about Maria Ivanov."

"With all due respect, my lord, whatever you think I feel, you are wrong."

"How old is her child, Hampstead?"

Devlyn scraped a hand through his hair. "Thirteen months."

"You can say that without hesitation?" Lord Ware walked into the circle of lamplight, his eyes missing nothing in Devlyn's expression. "Does Ivanov have any idea that he is not the boy's grandfather? *Answer* me, Hampstead. Does Ivanov know?"

Devlyn's voice went soft. "I believe he does not, my lord."

"Nine months before that baby was born, you were still in St. Petersburg and she was in Paris." Lord Ware came around the table. "But your brother was working in the consulate in Paris. There was rumor that they became involved." Ware's voice lowered. "Am I nearing the truth yet?"

Devlyn clenched his mouth shut again.

"You knew Maria in St. Petersburg. You were in love with her while you both were living there, before she married Stefan. It must have hurt to learn she and Dominick had become involved in Paris."

"Am I dismissed yet, my lord?"

"You are protecting the child," Ware said.

He could never allow Nicholas Ivanov to have the boy. "Would you not do the same in my place, my lord? He is my father's only grandson. All that is left of my brother."

He'd been guarding Dominick's secret for two years, hoarding the anger, holding it so close to his chest that to speak of it now tore him in half.

Without ever knowing how Devlyn felt about Maria, Dominick had wanted Devlyn to come forward and claim the child as his, find a way to get Maria away from her husband. Devlyn had connections; he had land near Edinburgh. He could hide her. Dominick had pleaded, begged him as he always had when he'd gotten himself into trouble and needed Devlyn to bail him out.

Devlyn had been furious with him. So angry that he'd inadvertently left his brother helpless to Stefan's brand of justice. Dominick had never been a fighter and, in the end, had paid the ultimate price for his indiscretion with Stefan's wife. It wasn't until Devlyn had received the journal that he realized the extent of Dominick's crimes. For the first time in his life, the world had beaten Devlyn back and left him bloodied and bruised.

And then he'd met Cassie.

"You've allowed personal feelings to affect your judgment, which is a death sentence to one in our position." Ware shook his head and passed his gaze across the portraits lining the wall. The only sound in the room was a fire dying in the hearth. "You leave me no choice but to suspend your status in this organization. You'll face an internal inquiry for Stefan Ivanov's death as a matter of procedure. You can leave your revolver when you go."

Devlyn hesitated, then took off his jacket. He removed the gun and the shoulder sheath and set both on the table.

"Until such a time when a review of this case is brought up before the league council, Maxwell has offered to manage your . . . safekeeping. You aren't a prisoner and can come and go as you please. But allow me to restate." Ware leaned forward, his palms on the table. "You are no longer under the protection of the crown. You had best hope Rockwell and Jameson follow through on their instructions to get Maria Ivanov out of the country. If you go near her again, I will have you arrested for obstruction. Do I make myself clear?"

"As a bell, my lord."

Ivanov and his barrister were waiting in the corridor when Devlyn emerged, shoving his arms into his coat before he saw them and hesitated. Reining in the primal instinct to go for Ivanov's jugular, Devlyn slowed, his shoes making little sound on the parquet floor. Better to have an enemy in his face than at his back. Instead, he pulled his gloves out of his coat pocket and waited for the two men to precede him.

But they did not move. "I understand you took out a special marriage license," Ivanov said, his voice no more than a low intonation, but more menacing for its implication. "Could it be you are planning to wed your pretty cello player? Or maybe you already have. How convenient for me and for Mr. Maxwell to have her so close at hand."

Devlyn continued to apply his gloves to his hands, aware that he was very close to stepping across the corridor.

"I thought you'd have learned by now that beautiful foreign women were not your forte, Hampstead. Those you trust the most will always betray you." Ivanov smiled, his affable manner pure art, the courtier when it came to arrogance.

His menace was aimed at Cassie, the threat as real as Ivanov's attempted provocation and Devlyn's hot rush of rage.

He would see Ivanov dead before the bastard touched one hair on Cassie's head. He stepped forward, prepared to say exactly that, when Lord Ware walked out of the room, saw the three of them and stopped just beneath the archway.

"My lord." The barrister stepped forward, his weaselly lilt affected by the haste of his recovery. "Is Mr. Ivanov free to leave? He would like to be in London by the end of the month."

"Until such time as we remove to London, he stays in Edinburgh where we can summon him. That was the agreement."

"I have already consented to this, Boris," Ivanov said in a bored voice, his eyes on Devlyn as he fingered his lion-headed cane. "I will remain in Scotland. In fact, I would consider it my pleasure to do so."

Chapter 14

Cassie did not arrive in Stirling that evening as planned. The rain had muddied the roads and halted her carriage's progress, causing a detour.

She was not overwrought at first. She was settled in a quaint hostelry in a warm room and had a hot meal in her stomach. Standing at the window, she realized she had come to like the rain, which only amplified the sudden feeling of disquiet that had come over her in the last few moments.

There was no moon in the sky. Surely no cause for the shiver that cloaked her, yet . . .

She moved away from the window, as if something were out there in the darkness watching her. She turned her attention to the room. A warm fire fluttered at its hearth. Other women were present, as well as a few small children.

Except for the occasional curious glance in her direction, no one was singling out her or the men who had entered the hostelry with her. But she couldn't dislodge her disquiet.

"I wish to leave here," Cassie said to her maid sitting in the chair nearest her, a pair of lethal-looking knitting needles in her hands. "Where is our driver?"

Her Pict turnkey had not allowed Cassie from her eagle-eyed sight all day, yet looked up at her now as if Cassie had spoken Italian. "Pardon, my lady?"

It felt strange to Cassie to hear the title. The shelter of Devlyn's name felt at once of security and of danger. She could not forget that someone had already tried once to get to her new husband through her.

Let Mrs. Smythe think she was spoiled. Something did not feel right and she regretted her skimpy knowledge of the local terrain and proper safety protocol. "I wish to leave. If we hurry, we can still make our rendezvous with Miss Maxwell. Send the driver and one of the liverymen outside to prepare the coach-and-four." Cassie was already reaching for her cloak. She despised that her hands trembled. "We have been here long enough. And Mrs. Smythe—" She touched the other woman's sleeve. "You and I will leave through the back door."

The driver protested being roused from his warm place beside the fire, but he went out to check the coach. Returning, he informed Cassie that the rein terret on the lead horse was frayed enough to need replacing. When Cassie showed worry, he shrugged without concern. "It happens on occasion, mum, though I know his lordship sees his coach-and-four well cared for. Perhaps I overlooked the problem."

"This coach belongs to Lord Hampstead?"

"Yes, mum. He has an estate just outside Bathgate. He trades his time many months of the year between there and his flat in Edinburgh. Few people know that much about him."

"But you do."

"Me and me family's been with him for nigh on a decade. Since he come to Scotland, mum."

"Please see to the coach," Cassie said after a moment.

By the time the moon rose, the carriage was on the road. Cassie peered once at the road behind her, half afraid she'd see Captain Valerik, though logic told her she would not.

The coach continued to bounce and bump its way at an unsafe speed. Only when the horses were lathered did the coach finally slow. Another hour passed before the carriage finally reached the outskirts of Stirling.

Soon she would see Sally Ann. Braeden had told Cassie before she left that Sally Ann would meet her at a rendezvous point so that they could all arrive together at Amber Rose as if Sally Ann had been with Cassie the entire time she'd been in Scotland. It was that thought that energized her and helped her put aside her fear. Beside her, Mrs. Smythe slept. Cassie dimmed the lamp and pulled the curtain away from the window. She looked beyond the moonlit drive to a loch and bands of limestone hills bathed in chalky white.

The historic town of Stirling had been built around a fortress near the highland boundary fault, the division between the lowlands and highlands. Sally Ann had spoken of this place her entire life. Cassie couldn't wait to see the place her friend loved, and the friend who loved it.

Unlike Braeden, who had been born in Scotland, Sally Ann had been born an American. She was vivacious, outgoing, her Americanisms bold as brass. Amber Rose was her grandparents' home and her Scottish birthright. Cassie had wanted to come here since she was old enough to look up at the sky and recognize the constellations, knowing that explorers had used stars to travel the world from the dawn of time. There was an entire world open to her outside the walls that enclosed her life. She had come to Scotland to see Sally Ann, but had somehow found herself.

Cassie was weary of being afraid of everything. Afraid to laugh, afraid to live. She was worn down by people around her living with personal agendas and secrets. She wanted to explore this new world. Learn its secrets. She wanted to love and be loved in return.

Yet for all of her desires, Cassie was who she was. An American in Great Britain, a little eccentric and too tall. She was a musical virtuoso, more intelligent than most men, with money enough to do as she wanted. The only disparity now was she no longer saw her differences as personal burdens to endure but strengths to celebrate. The past weeks had taught her more about self-reliance, trust and risking her heart than all the past nineteen years combined. She no longer wished for the anonymity she once wanted so desperately. Not any longer. Her heart would no longer be confined.

A tap on the roof alerted Cassie they were approaching the rendezvous point with Sally Ann at the Green Loch Inn. Cassie looked up at the sky. Their earlier delay had made them late. If Sally Ann wasn't present, she didn't know what she would do.

When the coach rolled to a halt in front of the inn, Cassie flung open the door, without waiting for the step to be lowered. Heedless of the mud, she lifted her skirts, made the giant step down and scampered across the drive.

As she entered the inn's common room, she scraped the hood off her head and looked around. Only a few patrons were there, but Cassie had worried for nothing.

Sally Ann, her bright chestnut curls piled high atop her head, sat at a trestle table near the great stone hearth that radiated heat over the room. She wore a bright apple-green gown and hat with a dramatic sweeping feather that framed her generous smile upon seeing Cassie in the doorway. Beside her sat Frankie and Mary and, next to them, Lady Rose inside her polished case, leaning elegantly against the table. Only Sally Ann really knew how much that cello's presence meant!

Cassie laughed as they flew into one another's embrace.

"I didn't think I would ever make it here," she said, when they pulled back to inspect each other with a more thorough eye.

"You have grown taller, I think," Sally said with some authority on the topic, since she was quite petite.

Cassie laughed again. "And you have not grown at all."

Their public display drawing attention, Sally Ann pulled Cassie to the table where she greeted Mary and Frankie and lovingly stroked Lady Rose. "She made it all right?" Cassie asked Frankie.

He stood, kneading his hat between his hands. "Yes, ma'am."

"We're knowin' your fondness for her," Mary said. "Frankie would see me washed down the river before he let go of Lady Rose."

Of course it wasn't true. Frankie and Mary were so in love anyone could see it between them. "I'm glad that you are both safe."

Her reunion with Sally Ann and Mary and Frankie was filled with the kind of joy only good friends could share, and Cassie overimbibed on berry wine. They ate supper and later left the inn for Amber Rose Castle. The carriage ride to Sally's home seemed to last only minutes.

Amber Rose resembled a castle in every sense of the word, with stone turrets and battlements dominating the central structure from which two newer wings extended on either side, all surrounded by gardens. Upon her arrival, Cassie learned that the ambassador was currently at Balmoral for business. Cassie wondered if it was the same business that involved Devlyn. But Sally Ann made her instantly forget.

"Now tell me everything Braeden wouldn't," she said when she had escorted Cassie to her apartments and shut the bedroom door behind them, her plump face pink and breathless. "Tell me all about Lord Hampstead. And whose ingenious idea it was to come to Scotland and elope? And why wasn't I included on this plan earlier?"

Cassie removed her gloves and laid them on the dressing table. Sally Ann had left New York last year on a whirlwind tour of the continent shortly after Cassie's betrothal contracts had been signed. Everything her friend knew, Cassie had relayed in the many letters she'd sent to Scotland before she'd left New York to begin her new life in England.

Now Cassie told Sally Ann about meeting Lord Hampstead in Dodburn, skipping over as much of the truth as she could without actually lying, for as much as Sally Ann was her friend, she didn't know the truth about Devlyn. In the end, Cassie somehow made it sound as if the entire fiasco at the ball had been planned just to this end.

"You must have been terrified traveling on your own across England." Sally Ann's impish smile dimpled her cheek. "I'm proud of you for being so industrious. Who would have thought it of you?"

"I'm not a complete coward."

"You haven't a cowardly bone in your body, Cassie. Only a moral sense of right and wrong that most of the rest of us lack. I only say that because you refused to help me steal that bottle of scotch from Braeden's stores on his ship. When was that? Two years ago?"

"Three, and I was punished just the same when you were caught."

They fell laughing into one another's arms again, and talked about the teas and balls they had missed together this past year. Sally Ann was as well endowed in spirit as she was in curves, a fact her apple-green gown did nothing to conceal. Her bosom strained at the bodice and the snug fit emphasized her slender waistline. With her saucy hazel eyes and burnished curls she was a fetching sight, too confident in her charms to ever make a proper English lady, which was the very reason Cassie enjoyed being around her.

"Is he as dark and dangerous as people say?" Sally Ann asked.

"Where would you hear such a thing?"

"Lord Hampstead *is* somewhat known around here. And I'll not deny that I enjoy gossip. He and Braeden have been acquainted with each other since they were children, before Braeden's mother died and Father married my mother and emigrated to America." Sally Ann lowered her voice. "*Is* Lord Hampstead dark and dangerous?"

Devlyn was both darkness and danger. He was also the light. "He's beautiful," she quietly replied.

Sally Ann took both her hands. "I'm so glad you're here. I have missed you terribly."

And later, after she'd said goodnight to Sally Ann,

after she'd bathed, and crawled into bed, Cassie turned on her side. She missed Devlyn more than she thought possible. Especially when this time yesterday she had never dreamed that today she would be his wife. She'd almost forgotten that only a few hours ago she had been afraid. Something had not felt right to her all day, a feeling of danger that returned to her now.

She'd almost forgotten all of these things. But not quite.

For Devlyn's secret life had now become her own.

"Cassie! Wake up this moment!"

She blinked when light hit her eyelids.

Holding a lamp, Sally Ann stood beside the bed dressed in a yellow wrapper that pulled the amber from her hazel eyes. "A man is outside demanding to see you," she said. "A very handsome man. Mary is on her way down to help you dress."

Cassie sat. Shoving the hair from her eyes, she looked outside. It was still dark. "Who?"

"He claims to be your husband. He's on the drive outside the window. I fear he may be shot if he tries to get in here."

Cassie flung off the down comforter and slipped her feet into a pair of fur slippers.

"Wait!" Sally Ann grabbed her arm. "You can't go out on the balcony like that." She helped Cassie don a pale pink wrapper.

"Hurry." Cassie's heavy rope braid slid over her shoulder as her friend hastily slipped the tiny buttons into their moorings.

She opened the glass doors and stepped out onto the stone balcony overlooking the drive. Moonlight spread a chalky glow over the ground, bringing in the silhouette of four men beneath the elm and ash that lined the gravel drive.

Cassie was not prepared for the sight of Devlyn and what it did to her. They stood still and looked at each other, she standing on the balcony feeling absurdly like Shakespeare's Juliet, and he atop his beautiful horse, his hands loose on the reins. Wearing a dark coat, riding clothes and high boots that hugged his calves, he'd tilted his head and found her. She could not see his eyes beneath the hat, but she thought she'd glimpsed the white of a slow smile.

He tipped his hat. "Do I have permission to come inside, my lady?" he called. "These men seem to think I have come here to do you harm."

Cassie leaned against the stone balustrade. "Have you a wicked bent in that direction, my lord?"

"Now, that depends on what you consider wicked, love."

Then he rose in the stirrup and swung his leg over the saddle. But before he'd reached the ground, she was already hurrying to the bedroom door, her fingers working to close the last of the tiny buttons. She passed Mary in the hallway and told her to go back to bed. Following the sound of harried male voices downstairs, she picked up her pace until she reached the huge cantilevered stairway. Box mahogany, ebony and ivory formed inlaid patterns on the stair tread that slowed her and kept her from slipping. Then, drawing in a deep breath to calm her racing heart, she placed a hand on the polished rail just as Devlyn started up the stairs.

They saw each other at the same time and stopped. A hoard of servants suddenly appeared, breathless, behind him, as if they had been running to catch up to him.

Unnerved by the pulsing heat deep in her abdomen, Cassie willed her heartbeat to slow and calmly met him halfway down the grand staircase. Standing on the step above him, she was taller, though he didn't seem to mind. If he tilted his face toward her, their lips would touch. He must have read her mind, for his eyes darkened on hers.

"I've missed you," he said.

"My lord," the graying butler wheezed, "shall I take your coat for you?"

Without looking away from her, Devlyn replied, "I'll keep my coat. But I need my valise brought to my wife's room. My other things will arrive tomorrow."

A strand of dark hair brushed his brow. Stubble darkened his jaw. He looked decadent with no cravat or neckcloth to offset the white lawn of his shirt open at the throat. He wore a burgundy waistcoat beneath a black jacket and a heavier coat that reached his calves. "What are you doing here at this hour, my lord? Where is Braeden?"

He advanced a step, forcing her to back up the stairs. "Do you really care that Braeden is not with me?"

She thought she detected a faintly ominous edge to the words, then his mouth tilted at one corner, exiling the transient darkness from his eyes with the amusement that was wont to lurk there. "He is not far behind me, love. I assure you."

A footman pounded up the stairs. "My lord," he said, "I have your valise."

"Where has my horse been taken?" Devlyn asked.

"Your horse has been taken to the stable yards to be cooled down, my lord. He has been ridden hard."

Devlyn was clearly a man who had no difficulty taking matters into his own hands where he saw fit. The servants were already doing his bidding. He looked around Cassie, took her arm and walked beside her up the stairs. Sally Ann stood on the landing, carrying a lamp, a bright smile on her flushed face. "My lord." She dipped into a brief curtsy.

"You must be Miss Maxwell," he said before Cassie could properly introduce them.

"And you must be the infamous Earl of Hampstead." Sally's impish glance clipped Cassie's with a smile. "He truly is as beautiful as you claimed."

"Sally Ann," Cassie hissed.

A dimple creased Sally's cheek. "In fact, my lord, you look nothing like the photograph she used to moon over."

"Indeed, I do not," Devlyn said, edging Cassie past her friend, awareness of his hand at her back like a pin-point of fire against her skin. "I've ridden a long way, Miss Maxwell. Would you direct your footman and my valise to the correct room so that I may follow?"

"I'll have water heated for a bath," Sally Ann said when they had walked down the long corridor to Cassie's spacious bedroom. "The servants are probably already downstairs doing so."

Once inside her room, Devlyn walked to the window and looked out across the night. Remaining behind a high-backed chair, Cassie watched him. He seemed agitated. He shut the draperies and turned back into the room, an action less indicative of his current somber mood than it was of something else as his eyes found her. The four-poster bed and tester dominated the chamber, the rumpled covers bearing evidence of her recent occupancy.

Sally Ann set the lamp on a dresser beside the door. "Father isn't here. We were not expecting someone of your . . . rank, Lord Hampstead. I mean, I would have had a larger room prepared for your arrival had I known. There is one on the other side of the dressing room if you wish your own private chambers. . . ." She cleared her throat. "I am being somewhat long-winded, aren't I?"

"This room is fine, Miss Maxwell," Devlyn said, still standing at the window, his tone not quite harsh, but neither did it invite further dialogue.

"I have water in the dressing room," Cassie said to Sally Ann. "Go back to sleep. It's still a few hours before dawn. Water for the bath can be brought up later."

Sally Ann walked to the door. She looked back into the room. "This is an old castle. The walls are thick and none of the bell pulls work yet. If you want anything . . . yell, loudly."

Cassie suppressed a smile. "I'll do that."

Sally Anne looked over Cassie's shoulder at Devlyn. "Goodnight, my lord. Cassie." She departed, closing the door behind her.

At last, Cassie and Devlyn were alone.

Intimate strangers.

Cassie's fingers unfolded over the polished chair back. "What are you doing here?"

Devlyn removed his coat and set it across the window bench beside the glass doors. A shimmering pink wrapper covered his bride's nightrail, a trace of white lace peeking from beneath the hem. Her long braid draped over one shoulder. Looking at her body beneath the wrapper limned by golden firelight, Devlyn paused. He felt restless under the weight of his emotions, those few seconds of hesitation nearly a lifetime to a man who understood more than most that indecision often meant certain death in the field. What was he doing here? "I don't know."

His heart never pounded like this in the presence of a woman. A fact he'd noted the moment he'd looked up from the drive and had seen her standing on the balcony.

It was Cassie who closed the few feet separating them, bridging the chasm that had opened in his life with a calmness and execution that defied her age.

It was Cassie who took him against her, who cupped his face with her cooling palms and pulled his mouth down to hers.

It was Cassie who was the stronger one.

He didn't understand himself when he was around her, any more than he understood all the reasons that had driven him here in defiance of Ware's edict to remain with Maxwell, nearly injuring his horse again in the process. But tonight he wanted to be with his wife . . . alone.

He dipped his head, holding her face cradled securely as his mouth ravished hers. There was neither patience nor tenderness in his hands, nor in his kiss. Both were desperately physical.

Without breaking their kiss, he walked her backward. Four strides took them across the carpet. They stumbled on the edge of the thick carpet and toppled, he on top of her, topsy-turvy on the bed. Like a schoolboy, he laughed at his own clumsiness.

But she clung to him, showering kisses on his face and lips, and he ceased attempting to extricate himself from her grasp.

His mouth suckled her hot and wet through the silken wrapper. He brushed aside her robe and pulled up the hem of the gauzy gown beneath, no longer caring that they were both still dressed. He wanted to touch her, to free himself of this encumbering want coiling inside him. He pulled back only for the seconds it took to unfasten his trousers.

"No." She combed her fingers through his hair. "Please stay where you are."

"I'm not going anywhere, Cassie." At long last, his hold on her slackened. Still booted and heedless of his trousers, he braced himself on his elbows above her. "Are you afraid?" he asked, unable to keep the thickness from his voice.

With no hint of coyness, she opened her eyes. "Only that I will awaken and learn this isn't real." She smiled against his mouth, neither skilled nor artful in her movements, and he felt humbled by her innocence, her desire for him, and her unquestioning trust. "I am enjoying all the hedonistic things you are doing to me."

Realizing he was smiling as well, he reveled in her inexperience, enjoyed her awakened enthusiasm for the physical pleasures shared between man and woman. He liked a lot of things about himself when he was around her. And, in her world, far away from his past, he liked that she made him forget his own.

Tumbling her over in the blankets, he rolled her on top of him amid laughter and giggles that left him feeling ludicrously young and playful, like a young cub.

She unfastened the buttons on his waistcoat and shirt until the garments hung open. Slowly unfolding her fingers over the fleshed ridges of his chest, she moved her hands lower, watching his face in the shadows.

"You have too many clothes on." His voice rough, he crushed the feathery soft cloth in his hands and yanked the wrapper and nightrail over her head.

Her body was resplendent in the lamplight. She bent over him, spreading her palms across his chest and sending sensation skittering across his flesh. "So do you, my lord."

"Devlyn." A spike of lust speared him, so powerful

he could barely breathe his own name. "My name is Devlyn."

"Devlyn," she repeated against his lips, and kissed him.

Sexual heat flooded through him. He held her to him, having no wish to tame her desire, only to manage his. Her palms glided across his chest, careful to avoid his still-tender shoulder. But they were both eager for more than physical contact.

It wasn't enough to touch. He wanted to feel. And when he could no longer wait, he turned her onto her back and pushed inside her, turning their foreplay into something hot and carnal. Her hips arched, the movement sending a current of pleasure arcing through his veins. One hand went to the nape of her neck, forcing her head down as he raised his mouth to hers. With a throaty growl, he kissed her deeply, his mouth an assault on hers that made his own senses reel. Tumbling her again to her back, he settled himself more deeply inside her.

They made love, their pace neither fast nor slow, but together, their movements in tandem, their eyes on each other.

This was all new to him, this wanting. She raised her arms around his neck and murmured something that sounded like his name. He liked his name on her lips. His tongue touched her mouth, glided upward and inside, tasting, imbibing the sensual intoxication, as if he were the hunter and she the prey. Perhaps to some extent those had been their framing roles from the beginning, yet something far more than physical had evolved. She was the only thing truly pure in his life.

A part of him decried the deception of his presence here in her bed tonight, his want to claim her when his future was no longer certain. When he didn't even know for sure what it was he sought. And yet, he was still here, seeking release in Cassie's arms.

"Don't stop." She wound her fingers in his hair, her breath hot against his ear. "Don't ever stop."

And Devlyn St. Clair willingly indulged his young wife. Sweeping his hands downward to cup her bottom, he rode her hard.

Her head flung back, she held him to her, arching beneath him. His own release built on a suffocated breath. His mouth took hers, swallowing her cry even as she swallowed his. And he met her in a long coming, spilling himself inside her, until neither of them was moving, until, braced on his knees and elbows, breathing like a schoolboy experiencing his first climax, he wondered if it was possible to still want her as he did. Wondered if he weren't obsessed, somehow unbalanced.

When she smiled up at him, still clinging to him, he no longer cared. His slow smile answered hers.

For whatever it was between them, their lust was mutual.

"Have you ever had a favorite pet?" Cassie asked. She lay on her side, her head on her palm, as she studied Devlyn half asleep. Their clothes lay strewn over her room where they'd been hastily discarded before their bath. The sheets were still damp, most of their covers still on the floor from the last time he'd made love to her. "A dog or a cat?"

"No pet," he said.

"Everyone has had some pet as a child." Even she'd had a kitten once. "A bird?" she asked. "A guinea pig?"

Devlyn lifted his arm from his forehead, revealing one eye. "A guinea pig?"

"I held one once at a zoo exhibition in Philadelphia. I

wanted to bring it home. Truly, I was tempted. But our housekeeper would have had the vapors had I brought a rodent into the house. Incidentally, guinea pigs do not come from Guinea in West Africa but Guyana in South America."

Devlyn turned on his side. "That is information I can categorize under irrelevant but interesting." He touched a strand of her pale hair and slid it from her face, his eyes on her eyes as he surveyed the result. "My mother refused me anything with feathers or that walked on four legs and went bark or meow. So I befriended the rabbits in her gardens. Do rabbits count as pets?"

"How old were you?"

"I don't know. Six. My mother never forgave me for contributing to the ruination of her prized roses, though at the time I had no idea rabbits were so evil to gardens."

"Were you always so troublesome to your parents?"

He returned to his back and closed his eyes. Outside the window, the sun had been up for hours. "Even when I wasn't trying, it seems."

"Was your brother like you?"

"No," Devlyn said after a moment. "He managed never to get caught."

"Were you close?"

His eyes opened. Dark lashes framed the darker circle of his pupils, and she thought he would not answer. "I believed we were close."

He rose on his elbow and captured her, rolling her to her back. "Since you are not yet willing to let me sleep, maybe I can occupy your time in other ways."

"What happened in Edinburgh?"

She thought she detected a scowl on his lips, but he was an expert at hiding himself. She took a small breath. "Last night, I thought I was being followed," she said.

He pulled back. "Did you see anyone?"

"No, and the feeling went away by the time I arrived here. Perhaps I was only worried about you."

His dark eyes had become impenetrable, yielding no hint of his thoughts. She didn't tell Devlyn she knew she was in his carriage last night or that she knew it was *his* driver who had brought her to Amber Rose.

"Lord Ware put me on temporary hiatus from the case, while they determine Ivanov's fate," he said, his tone even, though the cast of his eyes was not so tolerant. "I came here last night because I wanted to see you. Alone."

She eased away from him and modestly brought the covers over her breasts. "Because our vows have not yet been properly recorded and we are vulnerable to an annulment should my father choose to exercise that option. You would see that does not happen."

"Guilty."

She widened her eyes, warmed by his lack of apology. "You admit to subterfuge?"

He confined her hands with his and eased her grip on the sheet. "That is an ironic question, is it not, Cassie, knowing what I am?" Dipping his head, he brushed her lips with his. "I allowed Maxwell to send you here until your parents arrived. And because for now, it is safest for you. That is all, Cassie. I will take you wherever it is you want to go when this ordeal is over."

"Even to your estate outside Edinburgh?"

"You spoke to my driver."

"I did."

"What does the estate look like, Devlyn? Is it beautiful?"

"Has anyone ever told you that you ask a lot of questions?" he said lightly. "Especially of a man who needs his sleep?"

But clearly as he moved between her legs and covered her with his body, sleep was not what he had in mind. His finger encircled her nipple. Closing her eyes as a delicious shiver ran through her, she didn't like that he had the ability to sidetrack her and change the topic entirely. He'd done that with her questions about his meeting in Edinburgh and he was doing it again. She was beginning to realize he could seduce a lollipop from a baby and still leave that child smiling despite its loss. "Surely Ivanov won't be allowed to go free?" she forced herself to ask.

Devlyn kissed the corner of her mouth. "Hmmm." He moved his lips to her neck, and by the time he found her breasts, she'd forgotten the question.

But if there was surrender between them, it was not because he'd seduced her, but because she welcomed his seduction. Or maybe he was so practiced at what he did he made her think she was in control, that the choice had always been hers. She demanded his mouth even as he kissed her and pulled her up, still joined to him.

His palms dug into her back. They faced each other, the breathy, husky timbre of his voice close to her lips. She met his gaze unflinchingly. He was muscle and tension, each thrust a measure of his need and a mirror of hers, a rhythm that became part of her breathing. Yet that part of her mind not drugged senseless with pleasure couldn't read beyond the shadows in his eyes as her world melted around him. She buried her face in the curve of his neck, her body rising and falling with his, and held to him tightly, knowing he held the power to exploit her weakness and hoping he wouldn't.

She did not have his skill for subtle manipulation. But she did have intuition as sharp as a paring knife and recognized that somewhere beneath the layers of deception and intrigue that shaped his identity lived the real Devlyn St. Clair.

The boy who had fed the rabbits in his mother's prized garden because he'd wanted them as pets. A man she didn't really know at all.

For it wasn't until after he had fallen asleep beside her that Cassie realized he had evaded her query about Ivanov completely.

Chapter 15

❧

Though she didn't sleep, Cassie remained in bed, lying on her back, staring at the worn green canopy. The room was bright and warm and filled with dancing motes. Beams of sunlight streamed through the window and played over the bed where she lay naked beside Devlyn. He lay on his stomach, his cheek on his arm, the pillow half across his face. He was bared to the waist, the sheet loosely covering his buttocks. She could see the definition of the muscles across his back and shoulders and the shadow of hair at his armpits. He slept like the dead, unmoving and unaware of her staring.

Turning her head, she looked toward the gray plaid valise sitting where the footman had left it last night. For a long time her mind remained frozen on the bag. Finally, easing off the bed, she recovered her nightrail and wrapper from the floor where they had been carelessly discarded hours before.

Sinking to her knees beside the bag, she hesitated, no longer sure of her purpose. She was getting ready to rummage through his private possessions, not because Braeden or Mr. Stratton had wanted her to find the journal—Devlyn had as much implied that such an item was in his possession—but because . . . because she didn't like being anyone's pawn. Because she had to know what he was protecting. She knew he wasn't capable of treason. She only knew that whatever it was, it endangered his life.

Cassie unclipped the latch. Neatly folded clothes filled the soft-sided valise. She reached her hand beneath them to the bag's stiffer underbelly, only to jump when someone pounded on the door. Hastily gathering up the spilled garments, she looked over at the bed. Devlyn was not only awake, but sitting up, watching her with lazy eyes. Hair mussed, face unshaven, he still managed to look more dangerous to her at that moment than exhausted.

"What you're looking for isn't in there, Cassie."

The pounding came again. "Open the goddamn door, Hampstead," Braeden's voice came to her from the other side.

She didn't remember locking the door. Devlyn must have when he'd gotten up to wash last night. "Why is he so furious?"

"Do you need your maid to help you dress?" Devlyn asked, getting to his feet without benefit of the sheet.

Cassie felt her gaze drawn inexorably downward and, feeling herself blush, disliked having done so. "I can manage my own stays now."

He knelt until they were eye to eye, until he was so close she could smell her soap on him. "Then do so, love." He pulled a pair of black silken bottoms out of the valise, something a Turkish pasha might wear, and she wondered vaguely where he'd found such a garment.

He stepped into the baggy trousers and, tying the string at his waist, padded out of the bedroom into the connecting parlor and shut the door behind him. Cassie heard the low murmur of male voices and, drawing in a deep breath, climbed to her feet and hurried to the door. She started to lean her ear against the door when it was flung open.

Devlyn stood there like a wrathful, all-knowing Jehovah, clearly expecting to see her. "Mary is coming through the connecting room, love." He practically hummed the obligatory courtesy for the sake of their audience. "She is preparing your bath."

"What shall I tell Mrs. Smythe, Miss Cass . . . my lady?" Mary primly corrected herself. "I will have to adjust myself to rememberin' you are married." Smiling, she held the robe out for Cassie as she stepped out of the tub. "Mrs. Smythe believes she is your lady's maid, ma'am. She was most blunt to point that out this mornin' when she brought your breakfast tray. I explained—"

"Is there no way to get along with her? She will be returning to Edinburgh shortly."

Mary's brows crinkled. "I would if she were not such a snob lookin' down her nose at me as if she had airs. And her bein' in Mr. Maxwell's employ, not yours. I suspect she has allowed herself to be in his employ because his father is of Scots blood. She has a definite bias, ma'am. All the servants here do."

Cassie pressed her ear to the door separating the dressing room from her bedroom. She could no longer hear muffled voices coming from the direction of the parlor. In fact, it had become ominously silent in the last half hour, and Cassie was growing a little worried. She'd hurried her bath the first moment she'd noticed the stillness.

Mary lowered her voice as she watched Cassie. "Miss Maxwell is still abed. Should she be awakened now that her brother is back?"

Cassie tied the belt around her waist. "No. Mr. Maxwell is not in a friendly mood. He might blame her for allowing Lord Hampstead into the house last night."

"But I thought Mr. Maxwell and Lord Hampstead were longtime friends."

"Where did you hear that?"

"The cook was all aflutter about how Lord Hampstead thinks her black pudding and Dundee cake are the best in all Scotland. And Mrs. Bryce, the housekeeper, fairly swooned with joy to learn he'd wed one of Miss Sally Ann's closest friends and had come here for his honeymoon. They all know of him, at the very least."

"You can take the breakfast tray away," Cassie said.

Mary gathered up the towels as well and left through the adjoining bedroom. Now that Cassie no longer heard voices, the silence seemed more stark. She waited until she was alone before opening the bedroom door, unaccountably nervous, but not for Devlyn. He could take care of himself. On the other hand, she was just now learning self-defense. More than that, her faux pas that morning wasn't something she could easily defend, except maybe to herself.

The room looked clear. Maybe he and Braeden were still in the parlor. The doors were not so thick that she could not press an ear to the panel and hear what they were saying.

Cassie edged the dressing room door a little wider and started across the bedroom toward the parlor. She had taken a half dozen steps when the door slammed shut behind her. Cassie whirled, nearly tripping over the carpet.

Devlyn leaned against the wall, his arms folded across his chest. He was wearing a black robe that matched the baggy silken trousers, but the garment did more to enhance his physical assets than conceal them.

"Cassie," he said, acknowledging her with a polite smile that said so much more than her name. "Did you enjoy your long bath?"

She folded her arms, unwilling to allow him to fluster her. "Did you enjoy your conversation with Braeden? You're still alive. I trust I will not find his body in the sitting room. You didn't tell me the two of you were more than business associates. As a matter of fact, when I first mentioned his name that night in the woods, you never even told me you knew him. How long have you known him?"

"Should I have voiced my curiosity knowing about your infatuation with your former beau?"

"He was *never* my beau."

"But you don't deny the infatuation."

Her eyes narrowed. "You're doing it again, Devlyn. You don't want to talk about something and you steer the topic away."

"I've known Maxwell since we were boys. I used to spend summers in Scotland. His mother was Scots. When she died, his father remarried some time later. I didn't see Maxwell again for twenty years. Not until this case."

"Why was Braeden so furious with you?"

"In earnest?"

"Honesty would be a good place to start."

"I disregarded a prime directive from my superior that involved Maxwell. He took my noncompliance personally."

"Involved how?"

"Maxwell is my appointed turnkey, love." Devlyn continued to watch her. "But we have come to a mutual accord that benefits us all," he said. "Maxwell has agreed to have the bellpull in this room repaired today. And I have agreed to remain here until the investigation is concluded."

His casual disregard of her concern for him only increased her anger. "It's a wonder you've lived to be so old," she said facetiously, furious when she thought she saw the corner of his mouth kick up. "I know that isn't all that you talked about. I want you to talk to me. And I do not want your sarcasm."

"Answer me this, Cassie." His hand went to the bedpost at her back. "Would knowing every sordid detail of my life make you trust me more, do you think? Or less? Would such knowledge allow you to wake up in the morning and look at me with love in your eyes? Or would it be better for your conscience knowing I was the paragon you think I am?"

"That isn't fair."

"Fair?" He laughed, but this time his voice held no jest. "Next time you want to go through my personal effects, just ask me."

He was standing too close. She stepped beneath his arm and away. Uncomfortable with the depth of her feelings, she confronted his instead. "I don't believe that you came here last night in defiance of any edict issued by Lord Ware. You came because you are afraid of something else. Something not even Braeden knows."

"Is that right?" he leaned his shoulder against the bedpost, folding his arms. "Maybe I'm just passionately in love with you and couldn't live another day without having you. Again."

"Another lie? If you are in love, it is not with me."

"How do you presume to know what I feel for any-one? You don't own a bloody monopoly on insight. Hell, you're nineteen years old, what do you even know about love?"

"Perhaps not as much as you do. I've never been in love." She looked at her bare toe making small circles in the carpet. He was so quick to mock his heart and hers, then excuse himself. "I believe I have a *tendre* for you," she said carefully. "I believe you are decent, whether you choose to admit it or not. Your actions speak well of you."

He snorted.

"For instance," she continued, ignoring him, "aside from the fact that you gave me your seat on the coach in Dodburn, you came back for me at the stable. You could have taken me anytime we were together on the trail. I certainly invited you to do so. Yet, you did not. I could name a dozen times you've behaved valiantly. As my grandmother would say, it's all in the details."

Shaking his head, he looked at her hard. "Your character markers make no sense to me, Cassie."

"Perhaps not," she said, feeling bolder. "But they make a great deal of sense to me. I would help you now if I knew how. You need someone on your side, Devlyn."

Cassie saw him frown slightly. But he said nothing, and she pushed onward. "I already know things about you your own family doesn't. I know about Nicholas Ivanov. I know none of what has occurred these past weeks can be easy for you. I know you came here last night when you could have gone to a hundred other places to seek solace from your anger. Including to Maria Ivanov, wherever she is. Yet, you did not. Perhaps you are still in love with her. Yet, you still came to me."

He raked his fingers through his hair.

"Talk to me."

His hand fisted against the bedpost. She could feel turmoil and frustration roiling through him. It was there in his eyes with his vulnerability. He had been terribly hurt.

He turned and slumped against the bedpost. "Ware hasn't just taken me off this case," he finally replied. "He's removed me from the service. I've become a political liability. My carelessness has cost the crown its case against Nicholas Ivanov. And there you have it, love."

"Then you no longer work for the crown."

"I am suspended."

Without hesitation, Cassie stepped nearer to him. Near him was where she needed to be. "Is that so bad?" She leaned her head against his arm. "To have a new life thrown down on you?"

She felt more than heard the forced laughter. She stepped into his arms and was glad that he held her. "I've never done anything else," he said. "I wasn't born the Hasting heir. I spent my entire youth raising hell at one boarding school or another. I've been home once since I was sixteen, if I could call Sinclair Hall my home, and that was even too late for my brother's funeral. My father and I never got along. Though I wish now I had done more over the years to dissuade his opinion of me."

"But someone must have cared for you?"

"My paternal grandparents in Scotland. I was closer to them than I ever was to my parents."

His words pulled at her heart. "I was closer to my paternal grandparents, too," she said.

"There you go, then." His hand cradled her nape. "We have something in common, after all." One corner of his mouth crooked against her temple. "Except for my brother, you know more about me than I've ever told another single soul."

"You must miss him."

"I don't know," he said. "I don't know anything anymore." His lips moved to her brow. "I do know I'm not in love with Maria. Perhaps a long time ago in St. Petersburg."

"What was it that drew you to her?"

"I'd never met anyone like her. She was beautiful and coy, a pampered member of the Russian court. A talented artist. Her father had sold her to Stefan Ivanov for enough wealth to purchase a small island in the Pacific. I knew she would never be mine."

She leaned into him, until his chin rested against her head. "What happened?"

"She was our original lead in the case against the consortium. I had a job to do. We stayed close. But a few months after she married, she moved with her husband to Paris."

For a long time, his mouth remained pressed against her damp hair, his palm splayed the small of her back and he said nothing. But every inch of his body vibrated with tension. His voice lowered but did not soften. "My brother worked as a diplomat in the consulate."

Cassie pulled back. "Your brother?"

"He and Maria became involved. She later bore his child."

Cassie searched his face, but his dark eyes yielded no more. "The leather casing in your haversack . . . those letters you carried. They were written to your brother. The *D*—"

"Dominick," Devlyn replied. "Maria wrote them. She gave me that leather casing the night I took her from Stefan. She came to me for help, knowing I was back in

England working on this case. She told me she had proof that would see Nicholas Ivanov hanged. Proof the consortium was involved in an international counterfeiting operation. But she gave me something else." He pressed his cheek against hers. "Something I wish to God I never knew existed."

"The journal? It belonged to your brother? What was in it?"

"There was a breach in security a year ago and someone got hold of names of our government agents. They were being killed. We didn't know who was leaking the information. Only that someone high up in our government was selling our secrets. I didn't know for sure who until Maria gave me Dominick's journal. It listed the several banks used to negotiate various funds paid for transactions completed. I assume Stefan acquired the journal among Dominick's belongings. I have no idea why Stefan would have kept it."

The gravity of his revelation settled like a weight in the pit of Cassie's stomach.

"Nicholas Ivanov is in Edinburgh confessing to the crown his son's sins, selling out those who are expendable to his organization to save his life," he said in growing anger. "Unless I can offer up proof that Ivanov was spying, my illustrious government is about to give him immunity. There will be investigations for the next few months while terms are negotiated and people are taken into custody. I'm to remain here until called before the council. But in the end Ware will remove me from service and Ivanov will walk free."

"Unless you give Lord Ware the journal."

"And that is the crux of my dilemma, love." Devlyn's arm dropped away from her and he walked to the window. "Condemning my brother for treason condemns everything Dominick touched. Including you and your family by mere association. If I'd known the government would grant Ivanov amnesty . . . Christ." She heard the criticism in his voice. "I would never have married you."

She saw his profile through a wash of tears.

"Ivanov trumped me and knows it," he said.

"But there must be another way," she said.

He slowly turned his head.

And she saw in his eyes that there was another option, one that she knew he would use, not as a last resort but the only resort left to him.

Turmoil filled her. "You would kill him?"

"What would you have me tell you, Cassie?" His quiet words held her eyes to his.

But it was not darkness she saw inside him as he allowed her free purview over his soul, only a man who had been inaccessible and solitary for too long. A man whose actions had already proven the true color of his character. "I would have you tell me you are not a cold-blooded killer. I will not believe it of you."

She walked to him standing at the window. She lifted his hand and pressed her lips to his palm. "You are more than the person you think you are, Devlyn."

He quietly laughed. Shaking his head, he looked up at the golden cornices in the ceiling as if seeking divine guidance. Then he looked at her and she had the sensation that the world had stopped spinning, that time had halted.

"You don't know me, my lord spy, to think I would allow you to stand alone."

"You have that correct. I do not know you. I doubt your family truly knows you, either."

They both smiled at that and Cassie suddenly felt

warmth replace the chill in her veins. Clearly, he was profoundly aware of her affection for him. His fingers closed around hers, the strength of his hand more evident for the tenderness it conveyed. His mouth, no longer flat, softened, though he did not smile. He placed his palm at the back of her head and held her against him. "You present a conundrum to my way of thinking, love."

"Likewise, sir. I've never known anyone like you."

He placed the edge of his hand beneath her chin. "And I would have you know that nothing I have done with you has been meaningless to me. No matter what, there will be no annulment between us, Cassie." He slid the fingers of both hands into her hair. "I will have you swear it."

She swore it. For marrying him had been her choice. "Tell me you will not seek out Ivanov. Tell me you will not kill him."

He did not answer at first, but neither did he make up a falsehood to throw at her. "I will not seek out Ivanov."

"Promise?"

He tilted her head back with his palms. "I promise, Cassie."

She was not worldly, but she understood enough of *his* world to recognize that his promise had been more than she'd expected to receive.

And when he sought her mouth in a kiss, she let him inside, forcing practicality aside. For what she truly wanted was in her arms. He broke the kiss. She gasped for air. Her heart was beating hard and so was his, oddly unsteady against her palm.

And her passion wanted to absorb all of him. She reached an arm around his neck, her desire for him a warning of her inexperience. But she trusted Devlyn with her tender feelings.

Compressed against him, she felt dizzy, as if she had consumed too much wine. "Has anyone ever told you how beautiful you are?"

"I believe Miss Maxwell mentioned something to that effect last night," he said against her lips.

And beneath the layers surrounding him was the man she'd glimpsed that morning, the man who had allowed her inside his soul if only for a brief time, before he hooded his gaze and produced that devil-may-care smile that made her forget their life was far from perfect and that she was afraid for him.

He teased his fingertip along her lower lip following the angle of her jaw, but his gaze was dark and penetrating, his mood deliberate as if he recognized that the feelings inside him were also inside her. He moved his hand gently between her legs and touched her through the thin fabric of her robe. "How are you feeling down here?"

In truth, she felt tender. "The bath helped."

"You are sore," he whispered against her half-parted lips.

"Not . . . so much."

"And you are being considerate of my needs."

"I wasn't thinking of *your* needs, Devlyn."

She kissed him, and something seemed to break inside him, something tightly wound that began to unravel and surround her as he uttered her name.

"Do you think anyone will notice if we don't emerge from this room all day?" she asked, hearing her feathery voice.

"I think"—he coaxed her lips open—"the residents

of this castle would notice more if we showed ourselves before the week was out."

His fingers threaded through her hair, then slid down her shoulders and splayed over her back. He pulled her against him. Her body curved into his, deepening the intimacy between them. She removed his black silk robe while he untied her belt. Her dressing gown slid from her shoulders and puddled at her feet, discarded.

With searching hands, he explored her body. Her heart and body had never been closed to him, but neither had she opened as much of herself as she did now. Her unconfined hair entangled them both. She stirred restlessly, warm tension twisting in her abdomen, their problems disappearing from her thoughts.

He cast aside the baggy silken trousers, and she shamelessly touched his hardened flesh. The groan in his chest tightened her palm around him.

But he didn't allow her to remain there long. He wrapped his hand around her wrist, his eyes on hers as he raised her hand and pressed it into the draperies at her back, then did the same with her other. Crushed by his body, she sagged against his naked thigh.

She did not know how much she needed him to kiss her until he pulled away and she rebelled. "Let go of my hands."

He held her imprisoned against the wall. "Slow down, love."

She didn't want to slow down and resented his control. But he didn't seem to care. "I want to touch you," she said.

His disheveled hair fell across his brow. The sunlight that accentuated the stubble on his face also caressed his gaze. "But you'll have to wait, won't you?"

"I insist."

"You could," he agreed, nipping her sensitive earlobe, "and you could also scream. I may yet shock you."

Her head fell back against the soft wall of draperies and she closed her eyes. "You cannot shock me."

"You still have much to learn, love."

She truly did not think he could teach her much more than he already had and told him so. "I am no longer a virgin, my lord."

"Ah, Cassie . . ." His mouth smiled against hers. "You are still very much a virgin."

His lips seized hers, until she ceased to think or complain about how his body shackled her movements. His hands dropped to the weight of her breasts, seeking and exploring, molding to her waist. Before she could fully grasp what he was doing, the floor creaked as he shifted his weight and went down on his knees in front of her. She instinctively grabbed at his hair before she realized he'd let her go.

He put his hands on her thighs. Excitement shot through her. The idea that he might put his mouth on her nether region was wicked and immoral. "What are you doing?"

He smiled his wicked smile, took her wrists from their grip and locked them behind her with one hand. "Shocking you."

The touch of his tongue was like a current of electricity. Her breathing fractured. She should have expected something like this from him. Carnal sin was his vice. He kept her standing while he teased her flesh. Tight, thrilling pleasure built from within her and expanded. He made her cry out. The curtains pressed into her back, and Cassie lost herself, melting into his mouth, and would have collapsed had he not braced her weight.

Would he always be there to catch her? The vague

unwanted thought speared her body and threatened the glow.

Cassie did not know.

She gripped the corded muscles of his arms. Then he rose and was suddenly standing in front of her, lifting her to accept him. "Put your legs around my hips, Cassie."

"Where did you learn to do things like that?" she rasped, embarrassed that she did not know more. Jealous of any woman with whom he'd given that experience. "Like what you did to me."

His eyes touched hers with gentle amusement. "I don't know any more or less than most men, Cassie."

She wanted to see inside him and know his thoughts. But he'd wrapped one hand around his erection and guided himself inside her, filling her, surrounding her with his arms as he braced his hands against the wall. She clung to his shoulders. He moved inside her, a slow rocking rhythm at first that built in momentum and forced her weight upward against the draperies. His lips brushed her hair, her temple, her mouth. And suddenly the tempo changed. As if he were not yet ready to cede control, he slowed and, locking his gaze on hers, watching as he pleasured her.

Mutual awareness intensified their pleasure and linked his emotion to hers. Yet, somewhere a part of her mind rebelled at his control. Danger whispered. She tightened her hands, refusing to heed the warning.

The velvet curtains pillowed her back, but Devlyn braced her front. His ragged breathing sharpened. Their breaths mingled. Her hair draped them both. A low sound came from deep within his throat. She grasped him hard, seeking shelter within the moist curve of his neck as release trembled through her, the sensations cascading through her body, enveloping her in their entirety. She heard the whisper of her name against her ear. And for just those moments as she absorbed his climax, he belonged solely to her.

No man should have to live so dangerously.

Chapter 16

Oblivious to the speculation about their relationship, Cassie and Devlyn remained content to enjoy one another away from the household. They slept when they wished and dined when they chose. Two and half weeks after Devlyn's arrival at Amber Rose, Sally Ann insisted on hosting a small reception attended by friends of the Maxwells from as far away as Edinburgh and Glasgow. A broadsheet article appeared announcing the nuptials and the revelation that Lord Hampstead had eloped and was currently on honeymoon in Scotland with his bride. Spirits flowed freely all weekend. Devlyn imbibed, inured to the revelry after a lifetime of parties and public affairs.

After standing hours at the head of the reception line the day before, the attentive British aristocrat to his ravishing American bride, today his usefulness had faded. He'd hardly been able to get near her this afternoon and finally accepted her popularity as the cost of this weekend.

Devlyn retired to one of the large cushioned chairs next to the salon window, content to let Cassie shine as the focus of the party. The pale blue walls diffused the afternoon light in the room and he was content to relax. A small musical performance by a pair of prettily dimpled sisters was still in progress down on the garden terrace. His legs stretched out in front of him, a brandy snifter dangling from his fingers, he let his senses roam the room, the only Englishman in a room full of Americans.

Maxwell stood at the hearth discussing politics and American-Scots trade relations with the American lawyer Devlyn had met in Edinburgh. Even Stratton and his group were present, no doubt accompanied by his entire staff. Americans were an odd lot, Devlyn decided, sipping from his glass. They were overly loud, excessively boisterous and *not* British.

Outside, the music had finished, followed by the requisite clapping. From the corner of his eye, he saw Cassie step away from a circle of ladies. Devlyn stood and moved to the open window.

Wrapping herself gracefully around the neck of the cello, his new wife readied her bow, then raised her head to find him at the window.

Their gazes held for a heartbeat, then two. A smile spread over her mouth, as if she had known all along that he was up here waiting for her to take her place. Over the glass rim, his eyes returned that smile. And the rest of the world disappeared. It was an eloquent illustration of her effect on him. A few tendrils of her pale hair curled around her cheeks. Her head bent to one side, she aligned her elbow perfectly with her shoulder. Even wearing all that sunshine, she looked as poised and cool as polished marble until she began to play.

The music she created transformed her. Or perhaps she transformed the music into something beautiful. He didn't know.

What he did know was that she was truly gifted.

And as he listened to her play, Devlyn leaned a forearm against the polished wooden casement.

His mood was light. Indeed, despite a certain tension remaining between Maxwell and himself since Edinburgh, Devlyn was mildly impressed he'd not been more disagreeable around his host since his arrival at Amber Rose.

The reason was before him.

Surrounded by blooming flowers, she wore a bright yellow muslin dress with just the right hint of bustle, her thick upswept hair pinned in a proper chignon at her nape. Only hours before he'd sifted his hands through that silky length and whispered wicked things he had yet to do to her, her uninhibited response a million miles from the velvet woman she'd been when he'd first seen her in Dodburn, yet oddly more appealing.

She was nineteen and too young for the likes of him. But he'd felt more alive since he'd met her than he had in a decade of living high and dangerous, doing someone else's dirty work, living someone else's lies, some of the time glamorous, most of the time just outright isolating.

He'd learned a lot about his young bride these past weeks. She could beat him soundly at chess, whist and any other game he'd taught her, which was why he would never seriously gamble against her. A smile touched his mouth. She had a competitive bent that had surely lain dormant until he'd awakened the beast.

Devlyn's arm paused in the act of raising the glass to his lips as he realized Maxwell stood beside him. He wasn't sure how long he'd been the subject of the other man's amused scrutiny. He looked down at the glass in his hand, realizing it was empty and that Maxwell had been watching him for quite some time.

"Does she know you have resorted to sitting at this window and ogling her?"

Devlyn didn't care to quibble over trifles like his wife's popularity. "Tell me about her life in New York," he said, without looking away from his wife.

Dressed in black formal attire much like Devlyn wore, Maxwell leaned a well-tailored shoulder against the casement and studied his glass. "You've noted the lack of response from her family."

"I'm beginning to think Magnus Sheridan is an autocratic bastard. I don't care what he thinks of me. But Cassie doesn't deserve the slight."

"I only know her brother died when she was twelve and there was a major row between her father and grandfather," Maxwell said. "I think my sister has been her only friend for as long as I remember. They met while very young at the governor's picnic, then later attended some finishing school for virtuous young ladies."

Maxwell snorted. "Obviously, the school's founders didn't have my sister in mind when they named the school. But Cassandra would not be corrupted. She stayed another year even after Sally Ann was expelled for smoking. As you might suspect, my family is not at the top of the Sheridans' social list."

"Your family must be at the top of someone's social list." Devlyn turned into the room. "Your sister put this together in a matter of weeks, and people actually came."

Maxwell considered him over the lip of his glass.

"Cassandra told me you had agreed you would not hunt down Nicholas Ivanov."

Devlyn set his empty glass on the small round table next to the draperies. "I told her that, yes."

"A lie?"

"Is this a conversation we want to have, Maxwell?" He bowed slightly at the waist. "Now, if you will excuse me."

Devlyn walked out of the room, through the corridor and down the stairs to the main floor. He was in the foyer when the door shut behind him.

"Lord Hampstead."

He stopped and pivoted on his heel.

Frankie was hurrying toward him. "Someone delivered this a few minutes ago," he said breathlessly. "I was just on my way upstairs to put this in your chambers, my lord."

Devlyn took the missive and, without popping the wax seal on the back, slid it into his pocket. "How long ago was this delivered?"

"A half hour, my lord."

He knew who had brought the missive. Had been expecting it, and would see the man tomorrow. His gaze lifted to the couple standing upstairs in seeming conversation.

Not for one moment did he consider that if he stepped outside, he wouldn't be followed. Stratton and his gossoons were here, after all, watching his every movement, and he considered leading the lot on a merry chase just because he could. As much as Devlyn and Maxwell worked on the same side, they were clearly not on the same team. Besides, this particular missive was personal.

"Thank you, Frankie."

The servant jaunted off. Devlyn could still hear strains of the Bach sonata drifting to him from the terrace. Soon Cassie would finish and people would surround her again. Suppressing his sudden impatience, he loosened his tie, continued past the drawing room that opened onto the terrace and on down the corridor.

"He received a message a few hours ago, my lady," Frankie said, when Cassie finally escaped the crowd of guests and found Frankie working on the lawns where guests had been playing croquet all afternoon. "I don't know where he went, ma'am."

"Did he say anything?"

Holding a silver tray in his hand, Frankie shook his head. A lock of goldish hair dropped into his eyes. "He didn't seem worried, my lady. He thanked me. Perhaps you can ask Mary if she's seen him. She has been working inside most of the day."

Cassie accepted another glass of champagne from the tray of a passing footman, having lost count of how much she'd already consumed or had been pressed into her hand. This was her wedding reception, after all.

The sun had set, leaving a faint luminescence against the sky. The air had grown cooler. She wondered where her new husband had hied off to for the entire afternoon.

He had not been standing at the window when she'd finished with her cello sonata. Disappointment had stolen some of the joy at having played a rare, flawless performance, only to find her dearest audience had walked away before she had even finished.

To everyone at Amber Rose who enjoyed gossip and speculation, it was obvious that Cassie was smitten with her new husband. There were odd moments these past weeks when she had been caught humming while playing Bach on her cello. It was similarly obvious to anyone who knew the former Adelaide Mary Cassandra Sheridan, sole heir to Magnus Shipping, that her behavior could be construed as uncharacteristic—for she took cello-playing seriously.

Inside, the small orchestra began to warm up, and people moved toward the music. Glimpsing Mary on the lower terrace that overlooked the loch, serving tray in hand, Cassie put her hand on the rail and hurried down the stairs. Like Frankie, Mary was dressed smartly in gray and black with polished shoes, the uniform Maxwell's staff wore tonight. She smiled as Cassie approached, meeting her halfway up the stairs. Cassie asked if Mary had seen Lord Hampstead.

"I saw him go to the croquet field an hour ago, my lady."

Cassie returned her glass to Mary's tray. "Thank you, Mary."

Except she had just been to the lawns. As Cassie continued down into the lower-level gardens, she felt her heart begin to sink. She and Devlyn would be expected to start the dancing. Suddenly visions of her betrothal ball brought back a horrible sense of déjà vu, when she'd had to face the crowd alone. What if he had gone off someplace? Or simply became bored?

A second later, she sensed more than saw the warm shadow materialize at her side. "Why are you down here by yourself, love?" Devlyn said sotto voce near her ear, and, without missing a step, pulled her into his arms, sending her heartbeat racing with relief and warmth.

Her feelings in anarchy, her cheeks flushed, she wrapped her arms around him. "Devlyn . . ."

He slid his hands to her waist. "I have been looking

everywhere for you," he said, leaning close to brush her lips with his.

His fine evening jacket opened to a white silk shirt and black and silver waistcoat. He was warm and smelled pleasant. She liked that he had no qualms about bathing with her soap. Yet even though he smelled faintly like a garden in spring, there was an underlying essence far more masculine and potent to her senses. He was completely unaware of the stunning figure he cut or that she'd been terribly jealous of the feminine eyes that seemed to follow him wherever he went.

"Where have you been all afternoon?" she asked.

He kissed the place between her brows that puckered when she frowned. "I've been in the blue salon listening to Braeden talk politics with his American compatriots. I played a game of croquet with three of Miss Maxwell's giggling friends. I ate crab with two dowager baronesses from Glasgow, whom I believe are married to some distant cousins of Ambassador Maxwell's. And I played billiards with Mr. Stratton, also an American. That is the highlight of my day."

She stifled a smile and smoothed his overlong hair that lay in refined disarray at his collar. "Tell me today has not been dreadful for you. Do you promise everything is all right?"

"I promise."

Yet, something beneath the warm words, something she might not have recognized had she not known him as she did, belied the smile flashing his even white teeth. He seemed distracted. Perhaps if she had not consumed so much champagne, she could discern his mood better. He had not mentioned the note. "You left in the middle of my cello performance. Was I so terrible?"

His hand settled at the small of her back just above her bustle. "You are the most talented virtuoso in the world," he said, backing her into the shadows of a yew for more privacy. "It is to my utmost relief that Lady Rose survived her ordeal as well as you did." He kissed her lips gently at first, then more insistently, moving his mouth to her ear and further crowding out reality. "I could listen to you play all day," he said.

"You're just saying that so I won't pout."

He tucked a strand of her hair behind her ear. "What are you doing this far from the castle?" he finally asked. "You *are* aware there is a steep trail just ahead that leads to the loch. In the darkness, you could fall and break your neck. I don't want you coming out here at night alone, Cassie."

She looked around his shoulder. "I've never been to the loch at midnight."

She hiccupped.

His quiet laughter drew her gaze. "I don't think you will last until midnight," he said, his touch oddly protective.

She looked up at a thousand tiny stars encased in a velvet sky. "I have no wish to turn into pumpkin, Devlyn. Take me swimming after we dance."

He chuckled. Looking down into her face in amusement, he smoothed strands of hair from her cheeks. "I'll take you to the water sometime, but not tonight."

He put a finger on her lips, preventing her from asking any more questions. "Look"—he nodded toward the upper terrace, where she saw Braeden standing—"the troops have been alerted to your whereabouts." And with an accomplished skill she recognized for what it was, he obliterated her worry for him and directed her toward the ballroom. "Now put on a happy face for my turnkey, lest you make him regret his decision not to lock me in his dungeon."

Cassie rolled over in bed. Her hand went to the empty pillow beside hers. Her head remained fuzzy after her overconsumption of spirits last night. She opened her eyes, then twisted around to peer through the crack in the heavy draperies drawn against a bright patch of daylight. She hadn't heard Devlyn leave.

She pushed herself up on one elbow. Her gaze fell on the clock across the room, then she threw off the covers. Two o'clock in the afternoon?

"My lady," Mary said from the doorway. She carried a tray of food. "You're awake."

Cassie rubbed her temples. "Why didn't you awaken me sooner?"

"His lordship said not to, my lady."

"Mary, please," Cassie pleaded as she slid to the side of the bed and sat on the edge of the mattress. "You don't have to call me 'my lady' every sentence you speak."

"Oh, but I do." Mary's brown eyes widened. "Your rank is very important, ma'am. Did you know that servants are seated at tables in the kitchens according to the ranks of those we serve? Frankie and I are practically at the head of the table."

Cassie somehow managed not to roll her eyes. Her head ached too much. Instead, she found herself asking, "Is my husband downstairs?"

"Lord Hampstead went to the stables this morning, my lady. He has not returned."

Devlyn had gone riding, which wasn't unusual. Sometimes Cassie rode with him. Most of the time she chose to remain behind and practice. The cello was to her what riding was to him. He liked to be physically active, while she liked mental stimulation.

Already, she was growing accustomed to their habits.

Even Cassie recognized that fact, as she carried Lady Rose to the terrace just as she did every morning while waiting for Devlyn to return. Today, however, she would have gone with him, and was troubled that he'd not awakened her to ask. It *still* troubled her that he hadn't mentioned the note Frankie had given him.

For the next hour, she attacked her scales and études. "Attack" being the operative word as she started with Beethoven in an attempt to play something happy. The white lace on her sleeve pulled at her wrist and the bow slipped.

She loved music, loved the way it was supposed to make her feel, like a cloud floating against a stark blue sky. She used to imagine herself lying on that cloud. But today there were no clouds, so she imagined herself on the ocean waves, leaning against the forecastle taffrail, gripping her hair in one hand and looking toward home.

She suddenly wanted to purchase a cabin on a ship leaving Glasgow for New York. It could be her gift to Devlyn.

And while away, he would forget Maria Ivanov, forget his brother and the wretched investigation that hung over their lives. He would belong to her. And they would be happy. Later, if he wanted, they could return to England to begin their life as Lord and Lady Hampstead.

Cassie thought of the journal somewhere upstairs.

She was sure it was there, sure he had brought it with him that first night at Amber Rose. It had probably been in his coat. She wanted to be Devlyn's strength the same way she had that first night he'd come to her. She wanted to be more important than his need for vengeance or justice, and she possessed a staggering need to keep him alive.

Cassie felt the bow slide, resulting in music so disjointed the noise startled her out of her thoughts. In horror, she lowered the bow.

Sally Ann stood in the doorway leading into the drawing room, looking pert and pretty in a green velvet morning dress. "That was interesting. What was it, exactly?"

Annoyed by her friend's ill-timed humor, Cassie glimpsed several servants beating a hasty retreat from their perches just behind windows and doors of the drawing room.

Embarrassed, she held the bow, frog end toward the light, and examined the curvature as if the fault lay totally in the bow. "My bow needs to be cleaned," she observed, studying the bow with a more thorough eye and suddenly wondering if she might have actually damaged the delicate horsehair fibers.

What on her earth was wrong with her? She'd always allowed herself to become her music, never the other way around. Her mood had made a cake of the sonata.

"I know of a place in town where Braeden takes his fiddle bow. Besides"—Sally Ann impishly smiled—"the boutique across the street from the shop has brought in the latest fabric shipment from France. I wouldn't mind visiting there, too."

Cassie straightened and returned the bow to its case. Hearing the tall clock inside bong three times, she realized Devlyn should have already been back from riding. She busied herself with laying out the case on the stone table. "How does a person know if she or he is in love and not lust?"

Sally Ann's hazel eyes widened, far too uninhibited and earthy not to have suffered from one or the other at least once in her twenty years. "God forbid that I would allow either to happen. I like my life as it is. Simple, uncomplicated and, most of all, free."

Cassie smoothed her hands across her yellow skirts and folded them in her lap. "But if you *did* love someone, you would do what it took to keep him safe?"

"Hmmm." Sally Ann folded her arms and thrummed her fingers. "Compared to what I would do if I was only in lust?"

"Please, can you be serious for once?"

"Whatever is the matter with you?" Sally Ann asked. "Oh, bother."

Dismissing her friend's less-than-helpful contribution to their dialogue, Cassie sought only to change the topic. "I am sorry," she said in embarrassment. "I drank too much last night. And . . . and I am about to start my menses."

Sally Ann sat beside Cassie on the stone bench. "Is this what your doldrums are all about?"

Cassie nodded, realizing it was simpler to discuss the reality of this disappointment than her husband's secret life. "I wanted there to be a baby, Sally Ann. I can't explain why it was important to me."

Sally Ann placed an arm around Cassie's shoulders. "I have discovered you're not quite the bluestocking you thought you were." She leaned her cheek against Cassie's shoulder and tenderly smiled. "And who could have ever imagined that the oh-so-poised Adelaide Sheridan would come to England and stir up a man like the Earl of Hampstead? A man who guards you like a hawk." With that pronouncement she stood and pulled Cassie to her feet. "So his absence today is my good fortune . . . as well as yours."

Chapter 17

"I told you this would be just the thing to do this afternoon," Sally Ann whispered as Cassie stepped into the shop and stopped.

If Cassie had any misgivings about sneaking through the castle's wine cellar into the catacombs beneath Amber Rose and escaping this afternoon, they faded the instant the shop bell tinkled on the door.

The room smelled of aged leather and linseed oil. Just like her grandmother's music room. Glass cabinets displayed finely crafted violins next to a pianoforte and a harp. Music sheets lined a dozen wooden shelves and Cassie suddenly found herself in her own version of heaven.

She walked to the cello leaning with elegant grace against the wall.

"Her name is Queen Antoinette." The old shopkeeper stepped out of the back room, a rag in his parchmentlike hands. "She came to me four years ago with a broken neck that needed extensive repairs. She is a great lover of Bach."

Upon seeing Sally Ann, he beamed. "Och, Miss Maxwell. You've returned so soon?"

"I have brought you another patient," she said, introducing the leather bow case in Cassie's hand for his inspection and then introducing Cassie as Lady Hampstead. "This bow belongs to Lady Rose," Sally Ann said. "And needs to be cleaned."

"Lady Rose?" His silver brows lifted, and as he assessed Cassie with new eyes, camaraderie instantly struck. No one cared about cellos as much as other cello players.

"I'll be across the street at the boutique," Sally Ann said some moments later.

Cassie barely heard the door shut. And as she set her case on the counter and popped the brass latch, explaining the weight and style of her bow, she scarcely registered that the door had again opened, until she realized someone else was in the shop.

The shopkeeper removed his gold-rimmed spectacles and peered around her shoulder. "Is there anything I can do for you, sir?"

A slightly accented voice replied, "I am merely intrigued by your shop."

Cassie turned her head to peer at the man, but his back was to her as he studied a Stradivarius violin sitting in a glass case. He wore no cloak. His jacket and trousers, impeccably tailored to his body, bespoke of the man's wealth. His palm gripped the head of a polished wooden cane.

"Perhaps you would care to show me what is behind this case when you have finished with the lady," he said without turning.

"I will be with you shortly, sir."

Cassie continued to watch him until the shopkeeper's voice dragged her gaze back around. "I will take this to my shop in the back room and look at it beneath the glass," he said, holding Cassie's cello bow to a stream of light coming through the window. "Perhaps it is not that it needs to be cleaned, but that it needs to replaced, my lady. It may have a crack."

She remained at the counter, aware that the man behind her had moved his attention from the glass violin case to her the instant the shopkeeper left the room. She felt his gaze on her back as if he'd physically touched her, the visceral action so sharp, she almost turned. Folding her hands around the leather bow case, she pretended interest in Queen Antoinette.

"My granddaughter plays the violin," the man said after a moment. "She is six and already a musical virtuoso at such a young age. I fear her parents do not understand her and it is up to me to nurture her talent. Perhaps that is what grandparents are for, yes?"

Cassie felt something go through her. Something warm that his words had touched and brought to life. She turned. The man had resumed perusing the glass cases. "My granddaughter will be seven next month," he said.

"You and your granddaughter are close?" she asked.

A smile warmed his eyes. "Her name is Natasha." He walked to another glass cabinet nearer to where Cassie stood. "I fear I spoil her. I am visiting here on business and saw this shop. I thought to purchase her a violin. This particular craftsman is well known for his work. And such a gift will also be something of a keepsake to take back with me."

Cassie nodded toward the violin behind the glass.

"Then if you wish to bring home something she will love, choose the Stradivarius."

He nodded graciously. "*Merci*, my lady. Your wisdom is as welcome to my ears as your beauty to my eyes."

Cassie warmed. "You are French?"

"French is the language of my court. But I am not French, *dushka*." With a formal click of his polished heels, he bowed over her hand. "I am Count Vladimir Nicholas Alexander Ivanov the Third. Russian emissary to this country and your humble servant."

An icy frisson raced through Cassie's body. A pounding started in her chest. The man felt her recognition. Clearly, he'd meant her to know his identity. Cassie's smile faded. She would have withdrawn her hand had his grip not tightened.

"Have you ever been to my country, Lady Hampstead?"

She quailed in revulsion as all of her carefully constructed bastions of courage came tumbling down. She was suddenly terrified. "No, I have not."

"Your husband has," he said, bringing her hand again to his lips. "The winters are long and they are cold. But there is a certain sensual pleasure one can take in the nights. Has he told you of our Russian winters? But of course he has not. You probably do not even know what he did while a guest in my country. Why should a man such as he resort to telling his young wife the truth, after all, especially one so innocent as yourself?"

She finally pulled her hand from his grasp, the momentum taking her backward against the counter. Nicholas Ivanov stood between her and the door. "Why are you in Stirling?" she asked.

"I want your husband to know fear, Lady Hampstead."

"He fears nothing."

"I would have him know the fear of losing something that belongs to him, as he has stolen what belongs to me. You will talk to him on my behalf, will you not, *dushka*?"

Devlyn only needed an excuse to kill him.

"He will only come after you," Cassie whispered.

Nicholas Ivanov smiled. "I am counting on it."

Ivanov would use her to get Devlyn to come after him!

The shopkeeper pushed through the velvet curtain dividing his shop from the back room. "I have brought you these." He laid out three cello bows on the counter, unaware that Cassie's hands were shaking. Nicholas Ivanov moved to a glass case. Cassie tried to focus as the shopkeeper continued to speak excitedly about his presentation. "Perhaps you will find one to your satisfaction, my lady, at least until I can repair the other."

Finally settling on the bow the shopkeeper suggested, she fumbled with her reticule for the proper coin to settle her bill.

Cassie latched her cello-bow case and turned. Nicholas Ivanov tipped his hat. "Thank you for suggesting the Stradivarius. My granddaughter will like it."

"If you really knew anything at all about music, I would not have had to suggest the Stradivarius."

His chuckle followed her out the door. "Give my regards to your husband, Lady Hampstead."

"Where is she?"

Devlyn stood in front of Maxwell's bedroom door, his woolen cloak still damp from the mist layering the lawn, his boots wearing the remnants of his midnight jaunt from the stable. He'd have changed had he not returned to find his bedroom empty at this hour and Mary unaware of Cassie's whereabouts. A search of the rooms on the first floor turned up nothing. He sent the servants combing through the second-floor rooms and came here. Devlyn was on his way to see Sally Ann when the door opened.

His hair mussed, Maxwell peered at Devlyn with one eye half closed as he shrugged into a robe. "Where is *she*?" Maxwell snapped the belt and knotted it tightly. "Where have *you* been all day, Hampstead? You told me you wouldn't be gone more than the afternoon. What happened to the surprise you were going to give your wife?"

"That isn't what delayed me," Devlyn said, in no mood for banal trivialities and explanations. "I ended up meeting him in Bathwick. My meeting with the architect took longer than expected."

"Then you are planning to rebuild your grandfather's house?"

Devlyn didn't answer at first, his mind ablaze with worry over Cassie, but the seedling planted since he'd bought the old estate almost a decade ago had sprouted and begun to grow into something he could no longer contain. "Perhaps it's time."

A servant approached, having recently risen from bed along with the others combing the castle's corridors, and Maxwell directed him to the solarium on the third floor. "Cassandra didn't come down for dinner," Maxwell said. "She and Sally Ann went into Stirling today. I don't know what happened."

Devlyn stared in angry astonishment. "You allowed her to go to Stirling? Alone?"

"I didn't *allow* anyone to do anything. Sally Ann took her to the stables via the wine cellar. The door opens onto a pathway that leads to the loch. No one saw them leave this afternoon. When they returned, Cassandra said she wasn't feeling well and went to the library to find something to read."

"I've checked the library."

"Have you checked the *other* library? She's in the solarium. Follow Bingham," he said, directing Devlyn toward the stooped man. "And Hampstead." Maxwell's voice snapped him back around. "I'll believe you're capable of settling down when you've given up your private war with Nicholas Ivanov."

"What is that supposed to mean?"

"You've never walked away from a case in your life. You may have convinced Cassie you no longer have designs on Ivanov, but I know what drives you, Hampstead."

Turning on his heel, Devlyn strode down the corridor, his cloak sweeping around him like wings of anger.

Devlyn hurried up the narrow stairs leading to the solarium, having already passed the older butler on the landing below. Stopping in the doorway, he found his wife, her hands beneath her head, asleep in front of the fireplace, the book she'd been reading lying at her side. The tranquillity of the scene touched him. The solarium felt warm, resoundingly peaceful, and the tightness coiled within him loosened.

He looked at Mary standing behind him, twisting her hands worriedly. Somewhere a clock chimed two in the morning, and he looked past her to the butler. "Tell the others she's been found." To Mary, he said, "I'll get her to bed."

Mary dipped into a brief curtsy. "Yes, my lord."

Devlyn shut the door. For a moment, as he leaned

against the door, his gaze briefly touched the gilded stucco work on the ceiling and red damask wallpaper that harkened back a hundred years. He knew the solarium often served as a gathering place for the ambassador's diplomatic affairs. No peepholes or hidden doors in the walls. Cassie had chosen the most private place in the castle.

Devlyn reached behind him and turned the key in the lock. Shoving away from the door, he removed his coat and gloves and set them on the back of the chair, then knelt beside her.

She wore a pale pink wrapper, her hair a thick braid against her face. The fire highlighted her Madonna-like profile. Braced on one knee, he brought the length of her hair to his nose, only to stop breathing as he looked into her sleepy gaze. Their eyes held, then as full reality penetrated, her eyes widened.

Cassie rose on her elbow. "Devlyn . . ."

His quiet voice counteracted her relief at seeing him. "You weren't in our room," he said. "You weren't in bed. I had to call out a full-scale search to find you."

"I came to the library to read a book. I had no idea it would rouse anyone to panic."

"I returned to find our bed empty. Then I learned that you and Miss Maxwell went into town today. Maxwell said you weren't feeling well when you returned." He gently cupped her chin with a gloved hand, but she would not be able to pull away. "I've warned you not to leave this estate. Yes, I would say I was upset. What were you doing in town?"

"My cello bow needed repairs." She snapped her back straight, for now that she knew he was safe, anger rose. "Where have *you* been, sir? You left me with no note. If anyone has a right to be upset, it is I."

"I agree," he shocked her by saying. "Now come here."

"Don't you dare agree with me. No—"

Only well-honed reflexes saved him from being smacked by an angry hand. He captured her wrist easily and pulled her to her feet. "I'm far stronger and more determined, love. Especially since I've just spent the last hour in a frantic search of the castle looking for you. I'm trying to play nice."

"You may have spent a half hour looking for me, but I've suffered an entire day worrying about you," she argued. "You have no idea how frightened I've been."

Looking into her face, he smoothed strands of her hair from her cheek, but Cassie slid her gaze from his, her visit with Ivanov still fresh in her mind, her terror for Devlyn real. She knew exactly what he would do should he ever learn Ivanov had accosted her at the shop or that he was even in Stirling.

Then Devlyn pulled her, unresisting, against him. "Come here."

She wore a frothy nightdress and wrapper and warm socks for slippers. Even in July, nights in Scotland were chilly. She burrowed her cheek against his woolen collar. "I truly have been frightened for you, Devlyn."

A corner of his mouth pressed against her hair. "Has anyone ever told you how beautiful you are when you are angry?"

"So far no one I've ever met has made that observation." She pulled away from him. "Until I met you, I never *had* a temper. Now I find all my passions aroused on a daily basis."

"There were two objectives that I set out to accomplish this morning, love." He pulled her into his lap as he sat.

"In truth"—he lifted her hand and kissed her

fingers—"I wanted to do this before Miss Maxwell's reception."

He slid a ring onto Cassie's finger.

She stared down in shock at her hand. It was a simple band inlaid with tiny emerald stones. "It's . . . beautiful."

She raised her gaze and searched his eyes, his silence revealing more than his vulnerability. It seemed important to him that she like the ring.

"The ring belonged to my grandmother," he said. "She was eighteen when she married my grandfather. I had given it to a jeweler to be properly sized, repaired and cleaned while in Edinburgh."

"Before we married?"

"Before we married. I received notice that it was ready yesterday. But I wanted to surprise you."

"You received notice . . . a note?"

"From the jeweler," he said.

Cassie wiped at her eyes, but she had started to cry and Devlyn pulled her against him. "Why are you weeping?" he said in mock offense, his voice a rasp against her cheek. "I was under the impression it was a requirement of marriage to give you a ring. Even if this one is late in coming, my intent was honorable."

She sniffled against his collar. "What was the second reason you were gone so long?"

Devlyn tilted her chin. "*That* is a surprise. Will you allow me to keep it that way for now?"

She nodded. And his lips found solace against hers, her soft warm lips a balm to his. He caressed one breast, trailed his hand around her rib cage and up her back to splay at her nape, where he held her head as he deepened the kiss. But she wrapped her arms around him with far more distress than ardor and held on to him.

"What is it, Cassie?" he breathed in her ear.

Evading his eyes, she resumed her position against his shoulder. Her thick braid fell across his arm and onto his thigh. "I am about to start my monthly courses," she said after a moment. Her dark lashes swept up. "I'm not going to have a baby."

"You are sure?"

"A woman knows when she is about to begin her menses, my lord. I am sure there will be no child."

Devlyn continued to look down at her face, and she looked up at him, listening to him breathe, her heartbeat in tune with his, wondering if he would still want her. "I'm sorry you are upset," he said.

"You aren't upset?"

"I didn't marry you because I thought you were with child."

"Why *did* you marry me?" *Because you are in love with me?* she almost said aloud without realizing the words were on her tongue, without realizing she'd nearly spoken out loud something she did not fully understand herself. And the thought suddenly flustered her. Not because either of them was incapable of love, but because love made them incapable.

"I married you because I wanted to, Cassie."

"I wanted you, too, Devlyn," she said, her fingers curling into the loose cloth of his lawn shirt. "Now . . . I want to go away. Just you and I."

His half smile appeared, as he clearly did not understand her mood. "We can't, Cassie. This is the safest place for you."

"For *me*?"

"What are you doing, Cassie?"

She cupped his face. "Let me take you home with me.

We can go to New England. My grandparents' home belongs to me, to us. You'd love it in New York in the autumn. It doesn't rain nearly as—"

"Our home is here, Cassie. In Scotland, or in England. Wherever you choose to live. But it will never be New York."

She eased her palms from his jaw. "You say that as if you will never consider going there."

"I have no desire to sail across the North Atlantic to New York, now or in the future."

"I intend for my children to know their own country, Devlyn."

"*Our* children will be British, love."

Cassie stiffened in his arms. "*Our* children will be American as well. You can't just pretend it isn't so. I won't have them growing up ignorant of their roots."

"Roots?" he laughed lightly and tucked a strand of her hair behind her ear. "I can give our children roots dating back eight hundred years, to Normandy."

"Their roots also harken back to a horse thief hanged in West Virginia just before my country declared war on yours."

They faced each other, neither speaking. He lifted her off him and stood. Her gaze slid away from his. "You would have our children solely connected to a family you don't even speak to?" she asked. "What kind of future is that? At least I'm close to my family."

"Are you?" he asked, his tone equally as clipped as his words. "Are you, Cassie?"

She peered at him with less certitude than before.

"You're so close to your father that he sold you off to benefit your mother's standing in a society that is a parody of the aristocracy your country fought a war to be rid of?"

"Naturally you would say that, Devlyn. It seems to be the stance toward American brides. Yet, I don't see our money being shunned. You British have plundered half the world for profit."

"I'm glad we're finally discussing this."

"Clearly we have much that needs to be said."

"Bloody hell, Cassie." He walked to the fireplace and leaned a palm against the heavy oaken mantel. Raking fingers through his hair, Devlyn looked over his shoulder, realizing with some degree of shock that he was angry with her. "Why are we arguing over this? Hell"—he glared at the plaster ceiling—"where is my moral high ground, anyway? The way I see it, the pall of treason hangs directly over *my* family. Not yours. But I'm not running away. It isn't that simple for me."

"It can be simple if the journal is turned over to the authorities."

"Don't count on that happening and do not bring the topic up again."

"Maybe you need to have more faith in people, Devlyn."

"Faith in people?" He laughed at her continued optimism, her Platonist approach to every damn thing and person in her life, and the impracticality of such foolish romanticism when life was neither romantic nor idealistic.

He laughed because he had the giddy desire to believe in her vision and see the world as she saw it. When was the last time he'd looked around him with fresh eyes and a desire to feel? When was the last time he'd truly lived for something more than duty?

"Do you want me to tell you about my faith in people and where it has brought me? Where shall I start? With my loving father and lying brother, who traded his honor for his seven pieces of silver and a trip to hell? Who slept with the woman I once loved, and had a child with her? Or maybe I should begin with my illustrious government?"

He took a step toward her, no longer aware of the crackle of the fire or the thousand other distractions he'd found so peaceful only moments before. "Do you want to know what it is I do for my government? People like me? We're sent to the cesspools of the earth to deal with people like Stefan and Nicholas Ivanov. Do you want to know how many ways there are to kill a man, Cassie?"

"Stop it!"

She tried to turn away, but he wouldn't let her. His feelings were suddenly in chaos. Today he'd spoken with an architect to begin plans to rebuild his house outside Bathwick. His roots weren't only in Normandy. They were also here in Scotland, where he wanted a life and a family, to create something solely his own. Yet, he was trying to ruin it all before he'd even started and was powerless to stop himself.

"It's what I do." His quiet words held her eyes, forced her to see the truth. It's what he would still do if given half the chance to get his hands on Ivanov. Maxwell suspected correctly on that score.

But what if he *did* just walk away?

"I've never denied what I was," he said, some of his temper already dissipating. "You've been the one who refused to see. You talk of faith as if each of us is born to it. I have very little faith, Cassie. Except for maybe what you've brought into my life."

"Devlyn—"

"We should return to our room." He dragged up his cloak, surprised to see a tremble in his hands.

"I shouldn't have said what I said about your family. It's only that our future is so unsettled. And I am afraid."

The bleak ache inside ripped again. He felt exposed. Not because he'd doubted her commitment to him, but because for an instant while caught in the impetus of his own ire, he'd doubted his own.

Settling his cloak across her shoulders, he gripped the fabric and pulled her nearer to him. "For better or for worse, our differences notwithstanding, we are wed," he said. "It cannot be undone."

"It's true what you said about my father." His shoulder muffled her voice as she turned her head toward his cheek. "But I didn't protest his actions. Not because I cared for some archaic need of Mother's. For the first time in my life, I was valuable to someone. My parents needed *me*."

"You don't have to say anything."

She held him closer and continued to speak. "My parents never needed me for anything. After my betrothal, our sudden prestige made us popular. It got my mother invited to parties to which she'd not been included before. People wanted to meet us. That all changed when we arrived in England and ended two days after the betrothal ball. Father was furious and was preparing us to leave England when I ran away."

"I don't understand."

"I had already decided to visit Sally Ann. But then I decided I was finished with my parents laying out my life for me. There were things I wanted to do. Places I wanted to see. I was very wealthy in my own right, though Father held control of my trust. Breaking my engagement needed to be my choice. Not theirs."

Her arms tightened around him. "Don't you see? Marrying you then became my decision alone. And when you arrived at Amber Rose, I knew that marrying me had also been yours." She laid her mouth against his shoulder, where his wound was still healing. "I don't care what you used to do for your government." The warmth of her palm pressed against his chest and he felt something inside cave to her gentleness. "I only know what you are inside here and who you are now. That is faith."

Sifting through the emotion in her eyes, he no longer cared that he was yielding this argument to her. "You'll have to forgive me if I'm having a difficult time trusting in people."

She slid the hair from his brow and pressed her mouth across his in a tentative kiss. It asked the question not if he was ready to trust her with his heart, but if she could trust him with hers.

Defenseless in his need for her—a novelty, part of him realized, for he left himself defenseless to no one— he splayed his fingers through her hair, held her to his mouth and, suspended on the perimeters of this new territory, took the kiss from her.

The need between them was mutual and she responded to the pressure of his lips, the edge of her tongue pushing against his, her fingernails lightly scoring a path down his arms to his backside. She knew his body intimately, knew his responses. And in the next moment, he was simply hers.

He sank with her to the thick throw carpet warmed by the fire. As his hands braced on either side of her head, she struggled to open his waistcoat and shirt.

Devlyn rose to his knees and brushed aside her hands.

"You need me," he whispered, reaching for the tiny, stubbornly resistant buttons.

She smiled and worked the buttons on her own clothes. "You are presumptuous, sir."

His grin beckoned. "You still need me." He slipped the buttons from their moorings.

"We need each other, my lord."

She gathered the cloth of her wrapper into her fist and drew it over her head, tossing it to the floor. He stripped out of his waistcoat and shirt. She looked at him past the sculpted perfection of his chest and shoulders. He nudged her backward with the slightest pressure, following her down. "I want you, Cassie." His hands sank into the carpet on either side of her shoulders.

Her fingers splayed over his shoulders as he held himself braced above her. His mouth closed gently on her breast, sensually laving her. She was aware of each sinew and tendon, of the fire in the hearth, the scent of wildflowers in his hair, something distinctively hers that had become him. Unable to stop herself from wanting him, Cassie opened her arms. He caught her lips and lust coiled low in her abdomen to knot with her need. She moved to refine the tactile sensation of his entry; then he filled her completely.

Her sigh touched his lips. Braced on his elbows, his breath fanning her mouth, he began to move. He said her name and pulled back to look into her face, exploring her expression with eyes no longer hooded, but a liquid embrace that held her to him.

She met his passion with her own, and his eyes were the first to close as he allowed her orgasm to drive his own, until nothing remained of his reservations, and all that was left as he collapsed against her were the gently crackling flames and the answering rhythm of her heart-beat against his.

Until her whisper melded with his and she told him that she loved him.

And as she lay beneath, looking up at him gilded by firelight, she knew he loved her, too.

Chapter 18

❦

Cassie peeked into Braeden's library and found him sitting at his desk, poring over papers. Having spent four tense days agonizing over whether to come to Braeden for help, she drew in her breath and opened the door.

Sunlight spilled over the desk from the window behind Braeden's chair. He didn't hear her or look up until she'd stopped in front of the desk. Surprise briefly sketched across his handsome face before he set the papers down.

"Why is the British government allowing Nicholas Ivanov to go free?" she asked.

If Braeden thought her question odd, he didn't show it. He merely set down his pen before replying. "There isn't enough evidence to convict him of any crime. He came forward with information that puts everything on his son and has been cooperating ever since." He flicked at the papers sitting on the corner of the desk. "In addition,

Ivanov has dropped all charges against Hampstead as a condition to any immunity offered."

Cassie sank into the high-backed leather chair in front of the desk. "Then Devlyn would be free to go about his life?"

"Is that what you believe would happen, Cassandra? Hampstead would suddenly be free to pursue a life with you in peace?"

Folding her hands in her lap, Cassie looked down at the ring on her finger. "What does Nicholas Ivanov want?"

"He wants Devlyn St. Clair dead. He's just found another way to go about the task." Braeden took hold of a glass of what looked like port. "Then he will go after Maria Ivanov." He took a sip. "Hampstead has seen that she and her son are protected. He's given her money and a place to go where she can live. But I think most of us who know her realize that may not be enough."

"Is she in love with my husband?"

Braeden clearly did not like this line of examination. "If you know anything about their relationship, then you know it was ill-fated from the beginning. They go back years, Cassandra. There is bound to be some feeling between the two."

She managed her next words without inflection. "Then unless further evidence is procured, Ivanov will be a free man."

Braeden leaned back in the chair and steepled his fingers against his chin. "The United States government is not under obligation to accept terms of any immunity offered Ivanov. But we are guests on British soil, and Stratton's hands are tied."

"If you found what you wanted . . . if you gave something to Lord Ware that could prove Nicholas Ivanov's guilt in certain matters . . . what would happen to Devlyn?

I mean, supposing . . . if proof of certain crimes could be offered before Nicholas Ivanov is granted immunity—"

"I don't know, Cassandra. I don't know what Hampstead has involved himself with or why. I only know that I will help him." He paused. "Do you know where the journal is?"

"No." She bounced back to her feet and, restless, walked to the window. "I don't know what to do, Braeden."

She was as much worried about Devlyn's safety as she was that he would do something rash that would end in tragedy for him—like kill Ivanov. He would do it, too, if he knew what had happened in town a few days before. She couldn't bear the thought.

But she suddenly balked at turning over the journal to Braeden. Other than the fact that she had not yet found it, she didn't entirely trust that Braeden would know what to do with the damning evidence condemning Dominick St. Clair and the backlash to Devlyn and to her own family.

Devlyn would never understand her betrayal. Yet, even risking his hatred, she could only allow him to go so far in protecting others before she would do what it took to protect *him*, no matter the cost to herself.

Braeden joined her at the window. He smelled of shaving soap. Familiar smells that permeated the air she breathed. Safe smells she'd always associated with him. "Have you ever wanted just to go home?" she asked, leaning her forehead against the cooling glass of the window.

"I've spent most of my life on a naval ship. Lately, I've begun to think this *is* home." Braeden looked outside at the distant waters of the loch.

"You are considering staying?"

"There's something about Scotland. . . . I know

Hampstead feels the same way since he met you." His gaze followed a flight of blackbirds, as Cassie studied him, looking for the meaning behind his revelation, hoping that making sense of his perspective could help her understand more of Devlyn.

The two men were more alike than she'd once thought. Perhaps they were both only looking for peace.

If Cassie could bring Devlyn peace . . .

"You never told me how you two know one another so well," she said.

Braeden leaned against the casement. "His grandfather used to bring him and his brother here during the May Day celebration when we were boys. We lost touch when Father married Sally Ann's mother and moved us to upper New York just before my sister was born. I must have been eleven at the time."

"Then you knew Dominick St. Clair."

Braeden expelled a small breath. "Yes. He was a mischievous lad, always doing things his brother would later be blamed for. In his father's eyes, Dominick could do no wrong. But the way his father suffocated him, I felt sorry for Dominick, especially when he was no longer allowed to come to Scotland to visit his grandparents because more pressing duties prevailed. Heirs to ducal empires are groomed early here. Your children will now be those heirs."

Cassie folded her arms over her torso. "I think I do not like being away from my home for so long as you, Braeden. I miss it already."

"Your home is no longer New England, Cassandra."

She pressed her lips together. "But it could be home if Devlyn chose it to be so." If he were not too stubborn to see what she offered him. "You are your father's heir and he left here with *his* American bride. Look at you and Sally Ann. You both turned out well. Devlyn and I could leave here and he wouldn't have to think of his brother or Nicholas Ivanov or Maria again. I can take him away from all of this. If he doesn't want to live in New York, I can buy him a house anyplace he wants to go."

Braeden folded his arms and leaned his hip against the window casement, a subtle smile on his mouth. "Not only will Hampstead not do it, you will insult him by asking. There are some things even Sheridan money can't buy."

"But I'm his wife. He's been so at peace these last few weeks. Surely I can give him that and more—"

"You *are* his wife. He isn't yours, Cassandra. You are not his caretaker or protector. And don't mistake his current disposition for complacency. He knows exactly what is going on around him. He is only here because it's safest for you."

"He should be afraid."

"He is, but not of Ivanov."

"Then of what? Captain Valerik is dead."

"Haven't you figured it out yet, Cassandra?"

Cassie studied the lace on her sleeve. She knew that deep beneath Devlyn's defiant demeanor lay a man of deep honor and loyalty to those he loved. Despite everything, he loved his brother and his father. He held to his duty and honored the crown to which he served. Still.

His brother's betrayal damned Devlyn. For in the end, he could not turn over the journal without betraying everything he held close to him. His family. His principles. His honor.

But if Nicholas Ivanov walked away free, Devlyn would never be safe again. There would be no choice but to hunt down such a man and see that he never hurt anyone again. There was no doubt in Cassie's mind that Devlyn was capable of doing the job.

"He's building a house for you," Braeden said. "He's hired a renowned Scottish architect to begin plans."

Cassie suddenly realized that was the "surprise" Devlyn had spoken about the night he'd found her in the library. She looked at the distant sheep dotting the hill, then down at her beautiful ring that belonged to his grandmother.

He loved her.

"Will you tell me exactly what my husband does for his government?"

"His government is sharing information with my employer, the U.S. Treasury Department, on this case because we are tracking the same consortium for counterfeiting. But I am not privy to knowing more about the people for whom he works, Cassandra."

She shoved away from the window. "It doesn't matter anyway. Nothing will change how I feel about him."

Braeden's voice stopped her as she turned away. "I didn't believe it of either of you until I saw you together in Edinburgh." He raised the glass to his lips and looked at her, a hint of warmth in his hazel eyes. "If he had not ravished you in Glentress and gotten himself married to you, I would have found another way to keep you from returning to New York. Be glad that I'm a gentleman."

Cassie could not believe he'd just made such an outrageous statement, especially after all the years she'd idolized him and he hadn't even noticed, or maybe he had, but he'd considered one of Sally Anne's friends forbidden. It was strange how a few months could change a person. Now they had become friends.

His statement had taken the wind out of her sails and deflated some of her fear in the situation in which she found herself. "Be glad that you are a gentleman, Braeden Maxwell." The corners of her mouth inched up. "Devlyn would have been the least of your problems if you had not been."

"I trust you will do what is right by him," Braeden said, his eyes serious. "And trust me to do what is right for you both. If you want him to have any future, you'll help me."

Cassie looked away, her heart telling her she could trust him to know what to do with the journal.

She had to trust someone. She started to tell him about her confrontation with Nicholas Ivanov while she had been in Stirling, but decided he would only tell Devlyn. Tears filling her eyes, she only knew she was desperate to do something.

"You understand he will probably hate me for the rest of my life?"

"If you'd rather go to him, he is in the conservatory."

She dashed at the corner of her eye. "There is a good reason he has not turned over the journal," she said, knowing those quiet words crystallized her purpose to save her husband even as she betrayed his trust and maybe their future together. "He is protecting his family."

"What are you talking about?"

She conveyed everything Devlyn had told her about Dominick St. Clair's duplicity, from the affair with Maria Ivanov, to the child, and to the secrets he'd sold to the consortium.

"It makes no sense that Dominick would do that," Braeden said when she had finished. Visibly upset, he paced the carpet. "Good God . . . I wouldn't believe it of him."

"But the journal would be the means to convict Nicholas Ivanov. Right?"

"I need to know exactly what is inside."

"I don't know where the journal is. But it is the size of a man's palm, or a small Bible, the kind a person can tuck in his pocket. I know he carried it with him the entire time we were on the run. It must be near him now."

"It isn't in your chambers," Braeden said, distracted.

"You looked? That's reprehensible!"

"Do you think Hampstead would actually *hide* anything in his bedroom that he doesn't think I could find, Cassandra?" Braeden said. "He goes to the conservatory. He rides every day."

"You're with him most of the time. Maybe he destroyed it."

"He wouldn't. Especially since he knows Nicholas Ivanov *knows* he has the journal."

The words froze Cassie. "But then he must know Ivanov will want it back."

"He knows, Cassie."

She folded her arms and looked away. Was Devlyn aware of that when he'd looked her in the eyes a few weeks ago and promised he would not hunt down Ivanov? But he had never promised *not* to kill the man. Had he always known Ivanov would eventually come to him? And planned for that moment accordingly?

With Ivanov gone, the journal could remain buried forever along with Dominick St. Clair and a past Devlyn was trying to lay to rest. It was a tremulous balance between love and betrayal she walked; clearly, a line Devlyn walked, too.

"Cassandra?" Braeden's quiet voice pulled her around.

"Nicholas Ivanov is in Stirling," she said.

"What?"

"He found me when Sally Ann and I went into town.

He threatened me and meant for me to tell Devlyn. He meant for Devlyn to know. But I didn't tell him, Braeden, and you have to swear you won't. Swear it!"

His hazel eyes flashed, but he did not argue. "He won't hear it from me, Cassie."

"Devlyn recently brought some things back with him from Edinburgh. Look in the stables. He spends a lot of time there. Find that journal," she said. "I want my future with him. I want the house he is planning to build for me. I want Ivanov stopped before he forces Devlyn to kill him. Devlyn will do it, Braeden. I know he will."

"Cassandra . . ."

"I'll make sure my husband stays away for the afternoon. Just find that journal."

The object of Cassie's heart stood across the conservatory's sun-splashed floor, rapier in momentary riposte. She had never come here during one of his fencing exercises. She found him in his shirtsleeves. Sweat dampened the white lawn that was tucked into a pair of dark loose-fitting trousers.

The conservatory was surrounded by windows and a bright blue sky overhead. It was filled with plants in the winter. In the summer, it was a sunny sanctuary.

As she watched, Devlyn worked his way across the room in a clockwise pattern. He lunged and retreated, crossed one foot behind the other, turned and began the routine all over again, his concentration so intense, he did not see her.

Switching the rapier to his other hand, he reversed his movements, but the movement was awkward. He rested one palm on his thighs, drawing air into his lungs. "Damn," he said.

Cassie could not escape her softer feelings. His shoulder

was not completely healed. Feeling desperately protective of him, she was more certain than ever that she had done the right thing telling Braeden about the journal.

A pair of yapping puppies suddenly sounded behind her. Devlyn raised his head and looked in her direction.

"Hello," she said.

He straightened and smiled. "What are you doing out here?"

"Is there a reason I shouldn't seek you out in the middle of the afternoon, my lord?"

Cassie knelt to the yapping rascals at her feet. She wore her blue twill, which wasn't too formal for a walk across the grounds or for admiring puppies. One hand wrapped in her shawl, she scratched the tummies of the two brown and white puppies that had apparently raced across the lawns to follow her. The rambunctious pair belonged to Braeden's purebred pointer and generally caused mischief with the resident cats and horses. But today, Cassie was glad for their distraction.

Devlyn pulled a rag from a hook on the wall and, wiping his hands, walked to where she knelt. Slowly, she stood. Day-old bristle darkened his jaw. He kissed her, then, pulling back, leaned his palm against the doorframe at her back. "Hello to you, too," he said.

He smelled salty and hot as if he'd been practicing all afternoon. "Is this what you do when you come out here every day?"

He moved his shoulder. "It helps," he said. "But I won't be dueling with anyone."

Her eyes searched his. He smiled. "Not that I would, love."

The puppies bounced around his legs and she looked down at his feet. He took hold of a loose strand of her hair. "There are four more of these furry creatures running around. We should return to the house before their siblings investigate the noise these two ruffians are making."

No! They couldn't go to the house!

She wrapped her hand around his arm. "You promised to take me to the loch. Maybe we can go swimming."

Her request stopped him momentarily. His brows nudged up.

"Unless you'd rather do something else," she offered.

His hand returned to the doorframe at her back. "Are you still having your courses?"

"It's been four days. It's not an inconvenience now."

Bending his head, he touched his lips to hers. "Have you ever *swum* in a loch?"

"Have you?" she challenged.

His eyes shone with familiar laughter. "Hell, yes." He kissed her lightly. "Not for the faint of heart, love."

"I'm not faint of heart. And if you've done it, so can I."

Devlyn tossed the rag in his hand to a small bin near the door. Taking Cassie's hand, he left the yard and they walked toward the distant terrace onto a descending trail leading through beech trees and down a rocky slope. The puppies followed, then bounded ahead down the path with ears flopping, investigating every nook and crevice and sending flocks of birds spiraling into the sky.

Then the trees cleared, and Cassie stepped onto the damp and frigid silt surrounding the water's edge. She stopped, looking to the north and west toward the magnificent mountains bathed in mists and a world untouched since time began.

A cool breeze flurried the wisps of hair that had escaped her chignon. He nestled her against his chest and draped his arms around her waist. "Impressive," he said.

She found his eyes on her face. Unrepentant for allowing

himself to get caught staring, he smiled. "Very impressive."

"You aren't even looking at the water."

He nuzzled her ear. "Maybe I'm wondering if you really have the nerve to go in."

"Ha!" She removed her shoes. "You're hoping I won't, so you don't have to follow."

She'd barely straightened, presenting him the challenge, when he gave her a playful shove and she stumbled into the water. The cold brought a gasp.

He laughed. "Now that your feet are wet, love, maybe the rest of you would like to get wet, too?"

"You are a wretch, Devlyn St. Clair!" She laughed when he tried to grab her, then hiked her skirts and ran along the shoreline with the puppies yapping after her.

Devlyn caught her easily as she reached the trees, and turned her in his arms. Devlyn found himself grinning. Her chignon had fallen. The apples in her cheeks brightened her eyes. Their breaths mingled, the tug on his senses unrelenting. They sank onto the soft earth. He caught himself above her, finally bracing himself on his elbows as he made himself comfortable atop her.

"Tell me why we are out here, love."

"You don't believe I will go into the water, do you?" she said breathlessly against his mouth.

"I'll wager your delectable self won't last one minute."

"And I'll wager the entire afternoon luxuriating beneath the trees with you that I'm far tougher than you are, my lord."

Cassie stirred in Devlyn's arms as they reached the top of the path and the moon came out from behind the hills. Her clothes damp and in disrepair, she lifted her head from his shoulder and peered up at the sky. The puppies raced ahead down the path. Crickets began to greet the moon. Lantern-sized stars peered down at them and the moon clung to the sky like a single giant eye in the sky.

"Did you know that cyclops were reputed to be giants?" she said drowsily. "The only way to kill one was to poke out its eye." She pressed her finger to the center of his forehead. "Just so."

Devlyn chuckled. "You are a font of knowledge, love." He kissed her nose. "I'll remember that if I should ever face one."

"If you are going to force me to come back when I wanted to stay on the beach, the least I should do is walk on my own two bare feet," she grumbled, as she snuggled deeper into his arms. "You're going to hurt yourself."

"You aren't that heavy," he said against her damp hair. "Especially since you're naked beneath your clothes."

She snaked her arms around his neck. She might be naked under her clothes, but what she wasn't wearing she carried, including her shoes wrapped in her shawl.

"How are you feeling?" he asked.

"Is that why you are carrying me? You think I cannot walk?"

He gave her a wolfish smile. "If you can walk, maybe I should arrange another detour."

"Are all men so conceited about such things, Devlyn?"

"You sound oddly disconsolate for having outlasted me in the water, love."

Devlyn rounded the corner and suddenly slowed his step. Both of them heard the sound of a baby crying. Light shone brightly from all the windows facing the terrace.

"Someone is here," she said, and he felt a frisson of

awareness tense her muscles. It was subtle, yet he felt it slide through him.

"Maybe you should put me down, Devlyn."

Devlyn stopped. Braeden and Ian Rockwell sat at a stone table in the shadows. Devlyn's gaze shot past them to the house. In the abrupt silence that followed, Cassie squirmed. Her bare feet were showing for all to see and his rumpled shirt lay unbuttoned to his waist.

The men rose when Devlyn lowered Cassie to the ground and edged her behind him out of the light. "What are you doing here?" Devlyn asked Rockwell.

"He arrived ten minutes ago," Braeden said.

"Partner," Rockwell said.

Devlyn looked from one man to the other, his mind now focused on the crying child. "For God's sake, tell me Maria isn't with you."

Chapter 19

❝ . . . did this for us . . ."

"Maria . . . for God's sake—"

". . . won't leave without you."

The quiet voices spilled off the terrace into the drawing room.

Cassie sat on the edge of a high-backed tufted chair, her hands tightly fisted in her lap. The breeze muffled the rest of the words as another storm brewed against the distant hills.

Her husband had been standing on the terrace with Maria Ivanov for the last ten minutes. Unable to bear the sight and sound of it, Cassie had tried to go out. Rory Jameson had politely restrained her, telling her it was best to wait.

Bastard.

If she'd been the least violent, she'd have attacked him for blocking her way.

Maria Ivanov was weeping, her long black hair falling

carelessly over pale shoulders and Devlyn's arm as he held her. A half dozen thin golden bangles dangled from her wrists.

Cassie thought of her own appearance. Sitting in the shadows of the room, she had not changed, though Sally Ann had attempted to get her upstairs. Cassie's bare feet protruded from beneath her skirts. Her hair was a tangled mess against her shoulders and still damp from her swim. She was thankful only one lamp had been lit.

She wasn't alone in the drawing room. The tall blond man Devlyn had called Rockwell stood in the shadows against one glass door. He still wore his cloak as if he'd just now arrived, rather than a half hour earlier. Also across the room, Rory Jameson, in his Gypsy garb, leaned casually against the oak-paneled wall, watching Sally Ann. Sally Ann, clearly insulted by his blatant silver-eyed regard, seemed intent on ignoring him.

Cassie didn't ignore him.

"My servants will escort Maria to her chambers," came Braeden's hushed voice as he stepped through the glass doors from the terrace near where Mr. Rockwell stood. He spoke to Rockwell. "What now?" Braeden asked.

"I warned Hampstead when we were in England this would happen," Mr. Rockwell said. "Maria wouldn't leave without seeing him. Even hog-tied and stuffed into a ship's cabin, she'd find a way back to him."

Sally Ann took Cassie's hands. "Why don't we retire to your chambers?" she quietly suggested again.

Cassie withdrew her hands. "Is Maria's child being cared for?"

"He's with your maid, Mary. Let me get you something to eat."

"Go upstairs with my sister, Cassandra," Braeden said,

suddenly standing in front of her. He interrupted her protest and gently pulled her to her feet. "I mean it. You're shivering."

Cassie looked from man to man, the tension so thick she could feel it in the air like an iron weight pressing down on her shoulders. But as her gaze fell on her bare feet, she knew Braeden's order was not some random request just to be rid of her. Though it was obvious all of them wanted her to leave.

It had seemed impossible the pain could have become worse, yet somehow the fact that these men were more interested in protecting Maria and Devlyn's privacy than in sparing her feelings broke the last bit of resistance within her. She could not assume the posture of wife, when at the moment even her husband was treating her like the "other woman."

"What is going to happen, Braeden?"

He looked at his sister. "Will you give me a minute?"

Sally Ann started to protest, but with one look at her brother's darkening expression, she nodded and left the room.

Cassie saw that Braeden was holding something in his palm.

The journal.

"It was in the stable," he said to her unspoken query. "In the stallion's stall behind a plank of wood."

Tears rushed to her eyes. "I need to be present when you speak to him. He'll never understand, Braeden." Suddenly she was in Braeden's arms, pale and shaken, her face pressed to his shoulder. "He'll never understand."

"Understand what?"

Devlyn's cryptic voice came from the doorway, and, startled, Cassie jerked her head around as his eyes settled on Braeden with a distinctly malevolent edge. "Understand *what*, Maxwell?"

"Devlyn! Wait!"

"Dammit! You have no bloody idea what you have done, Cassie."

"What have I done?" She followed on his heels through the second-floor tapestry gallery. "If you weren't so pigheaded, you would see that Braeden's people can be the answer to our problems. To your problems. But you must listen to him. Nicholas Ivanov has no political immunity with the Americans."

He flung open the door to their chambers, walked through the sitting room and strode through the bedroom directly into their dressing room. Cassie grabbed his arm, felt his muscles tense against her palm. Impassively, he turned and glared at her hand.

Though wanting to hold him, she lowered her hand. "You swore to me you would not go after Nicholas Ivanov."

"I told you I would not hunt him down. But I did not tell you I wouldn't kill him."

"You are such a bastard, Devlyn." She swiped at the tears on her face. "You play with words and twist them around to your own meaning. You never intended to let this case go. I trusted you."

He faced her, his eyes dark with fury. "Do *not* talk to me of trust when you went to that conservatory today specifically to keep me occupied while Maxwell searched for that bloody journal. Trust?" he scoffed with a humorless laugh. "Look to yourself and your charming speech about faith and see the true lie between us."

"The lie is you, Devlyn St. Clair. You're so fluent in

the art of deception you don't even know who you are.
I can't live like that."

"Neither can I."

Cassie stood frozen as he strode to the armoire. He
pulled out his valise and began filling it with clothes.
Her hand edged to her stomach. She had thought she'd
borne witness to all of his moods, but she had never
seen this one. His coldness frightened her.

"Where are you going?"

He balled his fist into the shirt he wore, yanked it
over his head and tossed it to the floor. "I'm leaving."

He snapped out another white shirt and, without
turning, shoved his arms into the sleeves. His hair, still
damp from their swim in the loch, curled at his nape.

"Where?" she asked. "How long?"

"Edinburgh." He finished the fastenings on his shirt
with meticulous ease and reached into a tiny drawer for
two silver clasps. "A few days. On business."

"What sort of business? Alone?"

He inserted a cufflink into each cuff, then worked the
tie around his neck. He removed a silver-threaded waistcoat folded on the shelf. All of this he did in silence.

He was attractive, framed by moonlight behind him,
his decadent looks as much a deadly weapon in his arsenal as any other he so skillfully wielded. To how many
bedrooms had he been allowed access? How many secrets had he gleaned because a woman could not deny
him? How many men had he truly killed in cold blood?

Watching his precise perfunctory movements, feeling
his indifference stretch across the space separating
them, she suddenly knew him capable of being everything he'd ever claimed.

"Braeden can help you, Devlyn. Why won't you believe that?"

He slid his arms into a black jacket and, walking to the looking glass, looked at her in the mirror. He adjusted his lapel, straightened, and turned. "Don't leave Amber Rose, Cassie. There are enough people here to care for your needs, your safety."

He would tuck her somewhere safe while he was not? She held her chin higher. She would not be shamed for taking the steps to save his life. "You aren't going to share with me anything else? But you are going with *her*? This is because I told Braeden about the journal? Is that why you are leaving?"

"No." He shrugged into his woolen coat, then bent to pick up the valise.

She felt light-headed, dizzy, and closed her eyes, fighting a wave of nausea. He was truly leaving her. "What about us?"

"I imagine our marriage will be no different than anyone else's, Cassie."

She followed him out of the room. He was thoroughly without scruples. "If you leave with her, Devlyn, I will never speak to you again. Ever!"

He pivoted around and she backed up, one hand fumbling for the wall. She pressed the other against her wildly pounding heart. "I will hate you forever if you do this to me!"

"Hate?" He stepped nearer. "You've learned to lie well enough, love, but you have yet to master the real meaning of hate. It's ugly and it's unforgiving. You aren't capable of it."

"But then you are an apt teacher, Devlyn. And I am the perfect pupil. I remember everything."

Devlyn leaned his palm against the wall at her back, and suddenly she was staring into his black-brown eyes, holding her breath. "Would you like me to show you how much you hate me?" he said in a dangerous tone. "Would you?"

His mouth slanted across hers and she felt the touch of his lips to the soles of her feet—scorching heat from that inner flame that burned between them. He opened her mouth and took her in a full, deep kiss with a ferocity that threatened to consume her. The fluid exploration of his tongue threatened her fragile resistance.

He could be arrested, she realized suddenly.

Or simply leave forever.

These thoughts crossed her mind as she realized she was losing him.

But it was not with lovesick passion that he kissed her now, manipulating her response, wholly without feeling.

She wouldn't allow it. Dragging in a breath, she pushed him away, her eyes wide on his. Their breaths hot and mingling, she was conscious of more than her own fury. She was aware of his.

"Hate, Cassie? I don't think so."

A vengeful wrath grabbed at her temper and she struck out. He caught her hand before it connected with his cheek, as much shocked by her act as she was. If he hadn't been so arrogant, she wouldn't have been so damnably furious.

His next words gave voice to his enormous self-control. "Touché, Cassandra. But don't ever do that again."

He reached the upper foyer before her body caught up to her mind. Swaying unsteadily, she shoved off the wall and ran down the hallway. Her hands shook as she grabbed the mahogany banister, stopping him as he started down the stairs. "Devlyn?"

He slowly turned, one foot poised above the other. A knot formed in her throat. The tears she'd been fighting blurred her vision of him, and suddenly she couldn't say anything she wanted to say. The sick feeling in her stomach spread into her heart. She loved him and he was too blind to see anything she offered him, too stubbornly sightless to recognize that she stood with him.

Mr. Rockwell, wearing a dark cloak and awaiting Devlyn in the shadowed foyer, looked up. Cassie saw his movement as he awkwardly stepped toward the door. "I'll be in the carriage," he said.

The door shut behind him, leaving the scent of rain in his wake.

"Maxwell is meeting me in Edinburgh," Devlyn said. "Rory Jameson is remaining behind. I need to get Maria and her son safely away until this is over." He retraced three steps until he was eye level with her. "And I'm not your father, Cassie. If you leave here, I *will* come after you."

Even if he came back to her, they would never again have what had been between them. "It won't matter," she murmured softly, her voice more contained than her emotions. "I'm going home."

He looked at her for a taut moment more. "Goodnight, Cassie."

Then he jogged down the stairs. Without looking back, he strode out the door.

And just that quickly, he was gone.

She listened to the sound of the carriage pulling out of the drive, then turned and ran down the corridor, past servants who had come to a stop in the hallway. She shut the door to her bedroom and leaned her back against its solid surface. For long minutes she listened to the raging silence in her mind. Then, closing her eyes, she sank to the floor. Through her open windows, she heard the puppies barking, the sound of the wind in the trees, noises of life and living.

Sometime later, Braeden's quiet voice came from the other side of the door. "Cassandra?"

"Go away, Braeden. Not now. Please."

She curled up on the rug in front of the door, her hands tucked beneath her head, and listened to the rain fall.

Even with the fast-moving carriage, the dash to the train depot took longer than Devlyn had planned. Though the weather was ultimately responsible, the delay only added fuel to his already heated temper. The last thing he wanted was to be stranded in Stirling on a dark and stormy night. They finally reached the depot, the horse's breath still billowing from exertion and the carriage still rocking when he alighted.

He carried his nephew, wrapped in a yellow blanket, the babe's dark downy hair barely visible as he slept against Devlyn's shoulder. The child's nursemaid walked behind them next to Rockwell and two servants carrying Maria's trunks.

A legion of porters—alerted by Devlyn's messenger, who'd gone before—swarmed them and conducted them toward the ramp. Maria hurried beside him, her red silk skirts swishing with her gait. He couldn't keep from observing that her appearance was everything Cassie's was not. Small in stature, with dark hair and velvet black eyes, she was the epitome of the classical Russian beauty. Reeking of patchouli, she even smelled exotic—yet he found himself thinking of wildflowers in bloom on a warm spring day. She settled herself next to him in their cabin. Rockwell sat across from them. He hadn't said a word since leaving Amber Rose, and now tipped his hat over his face and tried to sleep, dismissing all of them.

By early morning, Devlyn still had not slept. He stared unseeingly out the window, thinking only of Cassie, his initial anger at having felt betrayed by her dissipating into the final reality that something irrevocable had happened between them—something that had been his fault, not hers.

When they arrived in Edinburgh, Ian Rockwell left to report to Lord Ware, as Devlyn repaired to his flat to await Lord Ware's summons.

Maria had finally finished her tearful emotional storm, shifting to defiance when she realized he expected her to go before the council with him. She'd argued.

Who would believe her deposition when she was an adultress?

Quite frankly, Devlyn didn't give a damn.

He was finished with secrets. Especially hers. And he was no longer of a mind to protect her if she could not first take steps to protect herself. They both possessed secrets that could end this case. It was time to put vendettas aside if either one of them wanted a future. Braeden had left Amber Rose last night as well to speak to his own people.

Maria went into the bedroom, quietly shutting the door behind her, and Devlyn suddenly found himself alone with an energetic toddler for the afternoon. Dominick's son was a bright-eyed, curly-haired miniature of his father. He gurgled in strange foreign sounds and laughed for no apparent reason except that Devlyn had knelt beside him. He was a happy boy.

And for just a moment as he watched his nephew play, Devlyn felt a loss and anger that penetrated so deeply it cut inside his chest. Not only for his brother, who had so carelessly destroyed his own life, but for his own loss. He thought of the children he might never have with Cassie now.

He didn't just want children; he wanted them with Cassie. He wanted to take her to his dilapidated estate outside Bathwick that no one else but he seemed to love and hear her say she wanted to remain with him forever in Scotland.

Leaving the boy in the center of the room, he sat down at the small traveling desk in the corner to write her a letter. His thoughts were overflowing, but he could not put pen to paper.

He crushed the paper in a fist and dropped it in the small refuse receptacle filled with a dozen failed efforts. Outside, the sun had already made a trek across the late afternoon sky and he saw that it was early evening.

"She is fortunate to have you."

Maria stood in the bedroom doorway, her coronet mussed from sleep. Her gaze paused on her son asleep in the middle of the room, his chubby hand wrapped around a wooden block.

Devlyn set down the pen on the leather desktop. "She will never be convinced of that."

"Please do not be angry with me any longer." Maria swept across the room and knelt beside his chair, her red skirts billowing around her like a rose in full bloom. She took his hand in her smaller one and cradled it against her cheek. "I cannot bear it."

He stood, pulling her to her feet. She was small and barely reached his shoulder. "Don't do this, Maria." He tried to push himself away from her, but she threw her arms around his waist and held her cheek to his chest.

"Safe is being with you. Not with anyone else or in some other country alone."

"Listen to me." He wanted to shake sense into her. "When this is over, you will have an opportunity for a new life."

"We could go away, together. You are my family, too."

He framed her face with his hands and tried to force her to look at him. But she clung to him, her tears wet against his shirt. There had been a time in his life when he would have welcomed Maria's affection. A time when kissing her had been everything, and a part of him had wanted her yet again that night he had dueled with Stefan.

But now he thought only of Cassie, and realized that what he felt for his young wife, he'd never felt for Maria. What Maria wanted from him had nothing to do with love. She was lonely, desperate and terrified. Women like her needed a man to take care of them, to feed their needs and worship them. Dominick had been willing to be that man, but Devlyn never had been.

"I'm not him, Maria," he quietly said against her hair. "I'm not my brother."

Her body stiffened, the dim light on the desk casting a shadow across her face. Her fingers tightened on his shirt. He took her hands and released their grip. "I love my wife and I want to be with her. Not just for a month or a year. But forever. I'm finished with secrets and protecting everyone else when the only person I should have been thinking about and have failed to protect is my own wife. Do you understand that?"

"You're asking that I risk everything I have left."

"You risked it all when you came to me with the journal. Do you know how much courage that took? I'm the one who made the mistake with the journal. Now Nicholas Ivanov is about to receive a reprieve. Unless you and I step forward, he *will* go free. I'm going before Ware with the truth. All the truth. Dominick committed treason. He gave me up to Nicholas Ivanov. Did you know that?"

She wiped at her eyes and straightened, separating herself from him. After a moment, she raised her eyes and spoke. "The letters that my husband found, the ones I gave you that night at the house. I wrote them to you after Dominick's death. I had never intended for you to see them. That is how Stefan learned who you really were and that you were working for the crown. Dominick never gave you up to them."

His mind racing, he contemplated Maria's revelation, yet even that reality did not change the fact that Dominick had still committed treason. "It doesn't matter anymore," Devlyn said tiredly. "My brother was selling secrets before he was involved with you."

She drew in a deep breath. "But what will happen to me?"

"The better question is, what will happen if you do not go in front of Ware?"

"What will they do to you?"

Devlyn gave a sarcastic laugh. "Even if Lord Ware chooses not to have me arrested for complicity to treason, I'd say my life with the service is at an end."

And strangely, Devlyn did not care.

For a long time that night, he remained awake after everyone else had gone to bed. Drink in hand, he leaned a shoulder in the doorway to his bedroom, his gaze on Dominick's son. He thought of the austere duke, the boy's grandfather, and wondered what he would do if he knew something of Dominick still lived.

That night, just before he made his bed on the settee, Devlyn wrote out a telegram to his father.

Then he sat down and wrote a letter to Cassie. He would see both sent out tomorrow.

* * *

Three days later, Devlyn received Lord Ware's summons. As Devlyn passed with Maria, his nephew and the nursemaid through the walled courtyard of Ware's Edinburgh residence, its fountain tinkling in the silence, he felt Maria's courage falter. Her fate would soon be delivered by men who had the power to take her freedom forever. *His* fate was in an even more precarious state and would depend on her fortitude. He'd faced Captain Valerik with less trepidation than he currently felt.

Ware's secretary met them in the foyer. "Your Lordship. Everything will be in readiness for you shortly."

He was glad this would soon be at an end. He'd realized days ago that Cassie—not he—had possessed the true courage to do exactly what had to be done.

He'd wanted justice against Ivanov. Wanted it desperately enough that he'd been willing to sell his soul to obtain it. What worried him now was that he'd done exactly that.

"Has Mr. Maxwell arrived?"

"Yes, my lord."

"Thank you," Devlyn said, acquainted with procedure as he walked across the soft Anatolian carpet toward another, smaller salon used as a smoking room when a meeting spilled over into the later hours of the night. It was a warm mellow room with deep-button armchairs and a carpet for the baby to sit on. He stood aside for the nursemaid. "You and the boy can wait here."

Maria started to protest.

"Your son can't come into the meeting with us," Devlyn said gently, not intending to begin this conference with a scene.

Maria gripped her son tightly, as if she were saying

goodbye to him forever. Then, with tears in her eyes, she handed him reluctantly to the nursemaid.

Crossing her arms, she moved slowly toward the meeting room. Her white slippers, encrusted with tiny pearls, made no sound on the carpet. But the agitated swish of her petticoats hinted at her distress.

Devlyn turned and gave a barely perceptible nod, bringing Rockwell forward. "Where is Ivanov now?"

"At his townhouse near the cathedral. Kept under surveillance since your arrival in Edinburgh."

"Whatever happens in the meeting today, I will take full responsibility for everything that has occurred."

Rockwell's hand slipped into his tailored jacket pocket and pulled out the journal. "Maxwell gave this to me this morning. Who is to say it hasn't been in Maria's possession this entire time?" he said with the familiarity of friendship. "I gave my deposition this morning. We all have."

"All?" Devlyn looked toward the closed meeting room across the corridor. "Who else is here?" His mind was still reeling at what Rockwell had said, when the closed door clicked opened.

And there was Cassie.

She appeared in a rustle of yellow silk, upswept hair, the rose flush in her face vivid as she came to a stop.

He blinked, sure it was his imagination conjuring her. But then Braeden appeared behind her.

He was not prepared for it. Not prepared for her.

The door opened wider and Lord Ware's secretary materialized at once beside them. "Lord Hampstead," he said, standing aside for Cassie to exit the room, "I have been directed to bring you and Mrs. Ivanov inside."

Devlyn didn't move.

His eyes remained on his wife. "What are you doing

here? Is Jameson with you?" he asked, knowing she probably had not received his letter. Where had she stayed last
night?

"He is with her servants and my sister," Braeden said.
"I thought it best that someone remain with them."

An awkward second passed as good breeding
prompted him to formally introduce Maria.

"My lord," Ware's secretary pressed, and Devlyn was
suddenly conscious of the men sitting at the table inside
awaiting him.

To hell with it. He was finished with niceties.

He took Maria's elbow lightly in hand and edged her
toward Braeden. "Give me a minute with my wife." He
didn't give a flying fig if he was holding up the minister
of foreign affairs or the inquiry proceedings.

Cassie turned on her heel and escaped down the corridor just as Devlyn caught her arm, his convoluted feelings only amplifying his need to touch her. She whirled
to face him, her skirts tangling with his legs, and he
forced himself to loosen his grip on her arm, though he
did not let her go. "Cassie—"

"Please, we've said enough."

"Listen to me—"

"I asked you to let go of my arm, Devlyn."

He pulled her to an alcove shared by a marble bust of
Wellington. "There is nothing between Maria and me.
There never has been. You need to know that."

She shrugged in a feeble effort to remove his hand
from her sleeve. But she was no longer fighting him. "I
know."

Cassie's anger went far deeper than the events of the
past few days. It went to his entire past and to the core of
who they both were. He had hurt her, something he'd

done again and again since she'd first had the ill fortune of finding herself betrothed to him. He'd tried to tell her everything in the letter, but now he would have to find the voice to speak the words aloud.

"Why are you in Edinburgh?" he quietly asked.

"Braeden said the hearing is important to your future. So I came to give my account of what happened with Captain Valerik in Dodburn. And . . ."

"And what?" he asked. She lowered her eyes, and his finger on her chin forced her gaze back to his. "And what, Cassie?"

"Nicholas Ivanov approached me when I was in Stirling."

He remembered the night he'd found her in the library after she'd returned from Stirling. "Why didn't you tell me this before now? Did he threaten you?"

"He threatened *you*," she said in a raw voice. "I couldn't have borne it if something happened to you or if you had killed him. I couldn't have borne it, Devlyn."

And so she had turned over any information she'd had on the journal. "Did Maxwell know about Ivanov?"

"Only much later when I went to him for help." Cassie lifted her chin. "Then I figured out you wanted Nicholas Ivanov to do something, anything, to give you a reason to kill him, and I could not be that pawn. I don't understand how you live with such subterfuge in your life. I don't understand you. Or maybe I do. . . ." As her voice trailed off, she turned her face away from him. "But I had to tell Lord Ware what had happened and the threat to you."

"Where are you staying?" he finally asked.

She folded her arms. "The same place I did before."

"You mean the same house where we were married."

A light summer breeze coming from an opened window down the corridor touched the wisps of fair hair framing her cheeks, and, as Devlyn stood next to her wrapped in her fragrance, all the heated nights and days they'd spent together came rushing back.

Lord, he had missed her and wanted her with a disquieting urgency. His quick glance took in the paneled long gallery hung with portraits. There was no place secluded, no private alcove in which to escape so he could talk with her. He wanted to back her up against the wall and kiss away the hurt he saw in her eyes.

"You have to go," she said. "They're waiting."

There was much left unsaid between them. He knew he had much to answer for. But he did not want Cassie present should something go wrong today. He wanted her out of Edinburgh.

And he suddenly knew where he needed her to be when he left here today. "Wait for me at Bathgate," he said with gentle perseverance, no longer so categorical to think he could order her to do anything just because he was still her husband. "I want you at home. In *my* home. Ware's driver knows where I live. Tell him where you wish to go. I'll come to you as soon as possible."

He knew then, he would leap the moon and all the stars to get to her no matter where she went. "After today it's over here for me. I swear."

Brisk movement roused Devlyn to the fact that they were no longer alone in the corridor.

"Do you mind, Hampstead?" Lord Ware's emphatic upbraid warned Devlyn the statement was not rhetorical. "Or is it your intent to convene the inquiry in the corridor at your convenience?"

He straightened. "Duty calls, love," he uttered grimly

under his breath, his hand still on her sleeve, drawn by the warmth of her skin beneath. Then, lifting his palm to her cheek, he tipped her face, desperate to ensure that she be waiting for him tonight.

"I love you, Cassie."

Chapter 20

Despite the days of antipathy, antagonism and resentment Devlyn had provoked within Cassie, his parting words had triggered the floodgates in her soul. Her heart was still pounding.

She had not expected to open the door and see him standing in the corridor with Maria Ivanov, who was as beautiful in the light of day as she had been that night at Amber Rose when Cassie had seen her in Devlyn's arms on the terrace.

Watching him go, she now realized duty would always come first to Devlyn. Deep in her heart, she knew he'd done for Maria and his nephew what he'd had to do. For honor, though its surface be smudged, and loyalty to country. That was the kind of man he was. Even in her naïveté, she knew she would never replace those elements of his makeup. The question she had to ask herself was, knowing that about him, could she live with the brash young man who thrived on danger, who had entered the

Foreign Service for sheer adventure, and who had become a part of something bigger than himself—at least in the beginning?

Yet, there was another part of him that was like the boy who had fed the rabbits in his mother's prized rose garden, the one who had never had a pet, and seemed to be searching for something to call his own. It was that part of him she'd glimpsed just now.

He didn't know her trunks were packed. He didn't know that she hadn't planned on returning to Amber Rose. But she could not leave Scotland without first knowing he was safe. Concern for his well-being was the reason she had badgered and persuaded Braeden to bring her to Edinburgh to give her deposition in person to Lord Ware.

Cassie made a small sound in her throat and opened her eyes.

At the door, Devlyn had hesitated and turned his head.

As had happened so often since she had met him, her future and her happiness hung on her gambling on his affection. It was foolishness to think she could ever forget him, even with an ocean spreading between them. And Cassie knew then she could not allow him to go inside, not yet, when she loved him so.

She grabbed her skirt. "Devlyn!"

He stepped away from the door and she launched herself into his strong arms. "I love you, too," she said against his hair. "So much that I should die if they took you away. They cannot do that, Devlyn. I will not allow it."

"No one is going to take me away," he said, but beneath the winsome smile, his dark eyes were intense with emotion. "Does this mean you forgive me?"

She hesitated, her emotions in turmoil. "Forgive *you*?"

Tears in her eyes, she kissed him, deeply and sensually. She could feel his heart pounding against her breasts, feel Lord Ware's tolerant gaze, and sensed the others in the room straining their necks to peer out the door. At the thought of pulling away, she tightened her arms.

"God, I missed you," his voice resonated against her lips.

"I will go to Bathgate and wait for you. I want to go home, wherever your home is," she murmured against his lips. "I want to help you draw plans for our new house."

Pressing his face into her hair, he seemed astonishingly calm for being the cynosure for every pair of eyes in the meeting room. "Have I no secrets left?"

"Never again."

"You came here with an escort, correct?" When she nodded, he said, "They'll stay with you until I get there. But I don't know what is going to happen today, and I want you away from Edinburgh until this is over."

"Did you mean it when you said you were finished?"

"I did."

"Then you and I will be together."

"Until you tire of me, love."

She laughed. Finally, his fingers went to her wrists and he gently unhooked her hands, bringing them both to his lips. "I have to go, Cassie."

In the end, she relinquished her hold. Too embarrassed to face Lord Ware, she lowered her eyes to the carpet instead.

The door clicked shut, and a sigh lifted her breasts.

She was conscious of her need for him, conscious that it would take more than love to settle the greater differences between them. But at least love was a good place to begin.

Ian Rockwell was leaning against the wall in the archway down the hallway. Cassie flushed in embarrassment. She had not sensed him there, and his quiet presence did not endear him to her. He was also handsome and the amusement in his green eyes only underscored her restlessness.

Cassie raised a gloved hand and pushed aside a fallen lock of hair. "Do you have a wife, Mr. Rockwell?"

His expression didn't change, but his eyes lost their subtle laughter. His lack of reply answered Cassie's question.

She sensed in his silence a world of heartache that threatened to dampen her emotions. Whatever had befallen his life would not befall Devlyn's. She would see to that.

A red-and-white-uniformed man approached and bowed sharply. "My Lady? Shall I ready the carriage and escort to take you back?"

"I am traveling to Bathgate," she said, allowing a sense of complete joy to fill her mind before she drew the joy back and held it protectively to her heart. Once settled, she could send someone to bring a message to her servants and tell Sally Ann.

With an imperceptible shrug, Rockwell pushed away from the wall. "Make sure your men are armed, Lieutenant," he directed. "And that they remain with Lady Hampstead until otherwise dismissed."

"Stefan never cared about me," Maria said. "My husband wasn't even a real man. His father knew his preferences. Only I did not. After our wedding night, I was glad he never came to me again."

Seated on one side of Maria, Lord Ware cleared his throat and reached for a glass of water. Braeden Maxwell,

Stratton, and Roth, the Pinkerton agent, sat across from Maria.

Devlyn was seated on Maria's other side at the table's end, his chair angled toward her. A single lamp on the table spilled a sphere of light across a profusion of purple orchids at the other end of the room, a splash of color against an otherwise bleak backdrop. The journal lay at the center of the table.

Leaning forward, his forearms resting on his knees, his fingers loosely entwined, he'd listened to the questioning for the past hour, when the only place he wanted to be was outside this room. But at Maria's last statement, he lifted his head.

Ware braced an elbow against the table. "You're telling me Nicholas Ivanov knows your boy is Dominick St. Clair's son?"

Maria folded her hands over her white skirts, which spread over the chair. "He knew Dominick and I met at a consulate function shortly after my arrival in Paris."

Mr. Stratton peered at her from over the rim of his spectacles. "When did you first learn of Dominick St. Clair's involvement with the consortium?"

"When Dominick went to Nicholas one night after one of my husband's drunken rages. He demanded that I be able to leave my husband. Then he threatened to go to the authorities should Nicholas not agree. Dominick later told me he kept a record of all his transactions, as protection against the future, should anything happen to him. I warned him he could never toy with Nicholas." Maria tilted her chin higher as if in defiance of her tears. "No one threatens Nicholas Ivanov and lives."

Lord Ware offered her a handkerchief, which she politely accepted and dabbed at her eyes. "They caught Dominick halfway to Marseille on his way to you. I heard

Nicholas give the order to kill Dominick myself." Her wet gaze touched Devlyn's. "My father-in-law wanted me to know the same would happen to me if I betrayed him."

Lord Ware leaned forward on his elbows. "But why would you be more important to Ivanov than Dominick St. Clair?"

Maria stubbornly looked away.

"Tell him, Maria," Devlyn warned. "Or I will."

She looked at him, then at Lord Ware. "You would not!"

"No more secrets," he said.

The dark coronet of hair framing her heart-shaped face suddenly made her look far older than her twenty-two years. "I am the engraving artist for Nicholas Ivanov's counterfeiting enterprise. I created the plates that made Nicholas a wealthy man."

"My God," Ware whispered. "The engraving artist? You?"

Her chin lifted. "I am a fine artist. Nicholas found me in St. Petersburg. I did not know at the time what he was. Only that he gave my father, a poor nobleman, great wealth to have me for his son. What nineteen-year-old girl would not be swept away by such attention? Only later did I realize why I was so valuable."

Lord Ware shifted his focus to Devlyn. "You knew this?"

"He did," Maria answered in his stead. "But it was my condition when I went to him the first time with information that he tell no one. It was not my desire to be hanged." Her eyes narrowed on Ware. "I did not work for Stefan. I worked for his father. I know it is only my word against his, but I know where the plates are. I hid them that night when Lord Hampstead came to the house to help me escape. This is why Ivanov wants me."

"What about the journal?" Braeden asked.

"People knew of its existence but no one knew Dominick gave it to me before he left for Marseille. After he was killed, I was too terrified and didn't know what to do with it. When I discovered Lord Hampstead was in England, I went to him. Stefan found out. He beat me until I told him about the journal. That was how Nicholas discovered its existence. Before he could retrieve it, however, I recovered the journal from Stefan's safe the night he was killed. After that, I believe Nicholas did not think Lord Hampstead would turn it over."

"Indeed, we were all surprised that he did." Ware raised an eyebrow in Devlyn's direction. His comment did not borrow from the illusion that Devlyn had been the instigator of today's events. Ware knew him well enough to suspect he might never have given over the journal without duress.

But somewhere between the time Cassie had helped Braeden find the journal and now, Devlyn had moved from beneath his brother's heavy shadow.

What his brother had done was no longer his burden.

Yet without that burden, he felt not relieved, but oddly exposed. He'd always accepted the weight of that delicate balance between life and death as his due. To be relieved of it felt almost cowardly, wrong.

But then, he'd never had a wife and a future for which to fight.

Devlyn raised his head and looked at Braeden, his own display of negligence these past months giving way to acuity and a need for faith. "My wife claims you can help. How?"

Stratton leaned forward, his elbows on the table. "The American government has not granted Ivanov immunity from prosecution," he said to Ware over a pair of gold-rimmed spectacles. "We will simply take him off your hands. By the time we finish with him, his people will know he betrayed them. He will welcome custody."

Devlyn leaned back in the chair. "It is a mistake to underestimate the man."

"Perhaps," Lord Ware finally said. "But it is not your mistake, Hampstead."

Devlyn considered the entire matter disquieting, but who was he to argue the wisdom of trying to snag an international liability off the streets and spirit him out of Scotland without incurring a bloodbath? "Ivanov has a Cossack guard," he said. "They will take your men down in the light of day if they sense a threat."

"All due respect, Hampstead, but Ivanov is no longer your concern," Stratton said.

And the pompous little treasury agent was right, Devlyn realized for the first time since stepping into this meeting. Even more surprising, he no longer wanted this fight.

Ware stroked his sideburns for a moment or two, then quietly came to a decision. "Sir Ian's deposition concerning the events the night Stefan was killed is the same as yours and Mrs. Ivanov's. If you had not defended yourself, you would now be dead. Lady Hampstead's accounting of Captain Valerik's attack on her, as well as the fact that Valerik as much as said he was acting on Ivanov's orders in that attack, also tells me you responded reasonably in Dodburn, and Valerik was very much alive when you left."

The next words he spoke with gravity, his weariness showing in the set of his shoulders, which had borne many of Britain's secrets and scandals over his decades of service to the crown. "If Dominick St. Clair were still alive, he would be tried for treason. But he is not alive."

Again, he grew thoughtful, before resettling his gaze on Maria's pale face. "You are sure you can recover the plates?"

"Yes, my lord."

Ware nodded to his secretary, who then retrieved a thick folder of papers from a leather satchel at his feet and set it on the table. "I think we can agree the journal has served its purpose," Ware said. "We can also agree it is in the crown's best interest no one outside of this room ever knows of its existence."

Stratton spoke sharply. "My government has a right—"

Ware glared at Stratton, whose voice died in protest. "Your government has learned what it needs to know. The leak is no more," he said. "We will also agree that Maria Ivanov, at great risk to herself, is the individual primarily responsible for the break in this case. I make no concessions to her earlier complicity, but a public tribunal on this matter will only raise more sensitive issues. I believe she can still be a valuable source of intelligence."

Stratton persisted. "What about Ivanov? We've offered a solution to the problem at hand."

Ware's tapping fingers increased their tempo, drawing Stratton's gaze to the folder, followed by everyone else's attention. "Nicholas Ivanov is under protective custody. You understand, I could never *condone* outright kidnapping."

"Of course you could not, my lord. And we would never presume to ask," Stratton said, his manner affable now that an agreement had been broached and settled with political efficiency. "Nor do we know anything about the journal. We consider it an internal matter of the British government."

Lord Ware slid the journal off the table, and Devlyn

watched as his brother's sins and crimes vanished into the pocket of one of the most influential men in Parliament. Ware would protect those secrets as he protected the reputation of his country. A scandal within the ranks of one of England's oldest families could well reach the queen, as Devlyn's father was one of her ministers.

"I am continuing my trip to Balmoral to dine with the American ambassador," Ware told Braeden. "As you know, he felt it was in our mutual interest that he not be present for this meeting. Then I'm going home to my grandchildren, and I defy any of you to stop me."

He stood and stepped away from the table, leaving the folder. "I consider the British side of this meeting concluded."

Devlyn stood, too, not only because respect demanded such deference, but because his superior meant for him to leave the room as well, which Devlyn was eager to do.

Lord Ware paused as his secretary opened the door. "I want you miles out of Edinburgh before the sun sets, Hampstead. Mrs. Ivanov . . . ?" He hesitated as he suddenly considered what to do with Maria.

They all did.

Devlyn could no longer take her back to his apartment without remaining with her. As he stood in the doorway wanting only to go to Cassie, he felt a new restiveness invade his soul with quiet urgency.

"My lord?" Maria nervously came to her feet. Her gaze briefly touched Devlyn. "Perhaps it is best I remain here in case Nicholas should try to find me. He is not above such perverse machinations. And Lord Hampstead will want to see his wife."

"I will remain with her," Braeden said. "Rockwell can return to the apartment and get her things. And bloody take my horse." Braeden smiled as he clearly suspected

Devlyn's impatience to leave. "Perhaps you can still catch her coach."

"Hampstead." Ware stopped him in the corridor. "I am rescinding your suspension. You've proven yourself more than capable. I don't want to lose you."

Devlyn forced himself to rein back the initial surge of adrenaline. This was what he had wanted all along. Wasn't it? Redemption?

Yet, Ware's offer sank into him slowly. "Thank you, my lord."

"My felicitations on your marriage as well, Hampstead. My offer will give you something to consider, then. There is always a place for you in this organization."

Devlyn watched as Ware turned and walked away. After a moment, Devlyn turned on his heel. He went in search of Rockwell and learned that Cassie had left with Ware's personal escort over an hour ago. If he was lucky and the carriage was slowed by traffic anywhere in the city, then Devlyn would catch her before she reached Bathgate.

Maria was waiting for him at the doorway. "Lord Hampstead . . . ? Devlyn?" She stepped forward at his approach.

Already his mind had shifted past the problem Maria posed to the place best to overtake Cassie's carriage.

"Where will you go now?" Maria asked.

For the first time in days, as he shrugged into his coat, he smiled. "Home."

As Devlyn set out on the quest to reclaim his wife, he only knew he felt alive. More so an hour later, when he crested a woodland hill on the outskirts of the sprawling city. Looking west across the valley below, his hands tight on the reins, he spied the stately black-lacquered carriage belonging to Ware.

He never heard the gun fired.

Only felt an intense burn across his scalp.

His horse shied, then reared, and the low branch of an oak tree slammed against his shoulder. He lost his grip on the reins and his seat in the saddle at the same time. The ground struck with tremendous force. In that fraction of a second before blackness rolled over him, he heard the faint metallic echo of rifle fire.

Chapter 21

Cassie's first glimpse of Devlyn's estate came as her carriage rattled across a stone bridge spanning a slow-moving river. In the last five miles, the green undulating countryside had slowly given way to wooded hills.

Brick outbuildings and a stable sat farther away in the surrounding woods, their gray slate roofs and a chimney visible through the oaks and birch trees. Beyond the trees, she saw an ivy-covered manor of red stone, surrounded by a lush rhododendron garden that had burst from its boundaries years ago. She glimpsed the lateral towers and two wings of a larger structure, but the vision vanished as the carriage dipped into a ravine.

This was her new home.

Devlyn's home.

Her heart fluttered and she pressed a palm against it.

Fifteen minutes later the carriage rolled to a halt on a gravel drive. Cassie alighted from the carriage as the driver opened the door, barely able to wait for the step to be set. A man and a woman appeared on the steps leading beneath the arched entryway, followed by three footmen and two other older women who wore white aprons. The lieutenant bowed over her hand and introduced her.

One of the women beamed a bright smile and hurried forward. She had black hair and shiny blue eyes set deep in a plump face. "Good gracious, my lady." Introducing herself as Ella McBride, the housekeeper, she brought Cassie forward. "We were not told to expect ye."

"We did not have time to send word," Cassie said.

"No matter." The housekeeper beamed even more brightly.

Much to Cassie's surprise, the others had lined up behind Mrs. McBride on the stone stairs and bobbed and curtsyed as she greeted each one.

Mrs. McBride introduced her two sons, husband, aunt and cousin, all who had been employed in the St. Clair household since the old master had moved from the main house to the lodge thirty years ago. Cassie remembered the structure she'd seen in the woods. Devlyn's staff appeared to be kind, and for no other reason than that these people were Devlyn's servants, the caretakers of his home, it was important to her that they like her.

Mrs. McBride ushered Cassie into the house and up an ancient oak staircase. "When can we expect his lordship, my lady?"

"He should be here tonight." Cassie hoped the tenor of her voice conveyed certainty and not the nervousness she felt. "Perhaps by supper."

"Then we shall have a feast prepared."

But by nightfall, Devlyn still had not arrived.

Cassie was sitting in the dining room, trying to appear interested in a bowl of mushroom soup, when she heard the sound of a horse's hooves on the gravel drive. She rose and hurried outside. There, she saw the lieutenant who had been in charge of her escort from Edinburgh standing on the drive talking to a uniformed young man, his face ruddy in the dim light spilling from the house, a woolen jacket buttoned to his throat.

"You are sure this missive came from Ware's staff?" the lieutenant inquired. "I have not heard of this problem."

"Lord Ware's secretary gave me the missive personally, sir. I came straightaway to deliver it to you, sir."

"How did you know where to find me?"

"I didn't, sir. He told me."

The lieutenant turned on his heel and approached Cassie, his boots crunching in the gravel. Cassie felt the housekeeper behind her.

"My lady," the lieutenant said. "Lord Ware has requested his escort meet him in Dunfermline for the rest of his trip to Balmoral."

"Then Lord Ware is no longer in Edinburgh?" Cassie asked.

"No, mum," the other man replied. "He is in Dunfermline—"

Cassie abandoned the pretext of calm. "Then the meeting has been over for hours?"

"I don't know about a meeting, mum," the other man replied. "But Lord Ware arrived in Dunfermline this afternoon."

She was suddenly terribly afraid that something had happened to Devlyn. "Was anyone with Lord Ware?"

"His personal staff, mum," the newcomer replied. "That is all I know."

"I have to take my detail and go," the lieutenant said. "But I will leave a man until Lord Hampstead arrives."

"I will also stay until morning if that will help, sir," the young soldier said. "My horse needs the rest."

This soldier seemed to assuage the lieutenant's concerns. "Again, I apologize," the lieutenant said to her as the young man dismounted and walked with his horse toward the stables.

A few minutes later, her former escort thundered out of the drive.

The man who had brought the message stood on the other side of the carriageway, barely visible in the shadows. The soldier had not saluted the lieutenant as he'd passed out of the yard. Cassie knew enough about military protocol to find that anomalous enough to draw her brief awareness before a sense of despair filled her and threatened to pull her down. Her arms tightened around her torso.

Perhaps she should have waited in Edinburgh for Devlyn. Perhaps it had been wrong for her to leave him. He might think her safer here, but that didn't make her feel less troubled.

He should have been here by now.

"Is everything all right, mum?" Mrs. McBride asked.

"Yes, of course," Cassie said, uncertain and frightened, not knowing how much to reveal. Her eyes shifted toward the hills. "How many men do we have here, Mrs. McBride?"

"We've four men who live on these grounds."

This is insane, Cassie thought. *We aren't living in the sixteenth century. Men don't invade other men's homes.*

She backed out of the wedge of light and returned inside with Mrs. McBride.

In the parlor, Cassie glanced at the clock on the marble breakfront. As the hours passed into darkness, she dimmed the lamp and pulled aside the heavy gold damask that draped the casements. She peered out, past her reflection, into the darkness.

The tears that she'd refused to let fall, broke.

Something terrible had happened. She was sure of it now.

Attempting to prevent hysteria from grabbing hold, Cassie leaned her face against the curtains, blinded by tears and the cutting realization that she was somehow to blame.

He was walking away from the case. Because of her, he had put aside his vendetta. But she had only made him vulnerable.

She sank into the chair nearest the window—she could not have made it a step farther—buried her face in her hands and wept.

"Now, now, lass." Mrs. McBride's soothing voice arrested a gulp as the woman set down a silver tea tray. "Mint tea is in order. Ye ate nothing of your dinner."

"I'm sorry, Mrs. McBride."

Cassie didn't want to drink. But Mrs. McBride poured a cup. "Drink, my lady. It will help ye to feel better. He'll not likely wish to see ye in this state, knowin' he was the cause. Something happened and he was delayed is all."

Cassie took the cup. "What if he's injured and needs me?"

"His lordship can take care of hisself. He always has."

"I should return to Edin—"

"Of course ye willna' do such a thing, lass."

Mrs. McBride's warm hands surrounded hers as she held the cup to her lips and bade her drink. "By tomorrow you'll be yellin' at him for putting the fear of God in your soul, mum."

Cassie perused the room. Her eyes paused on the long

portrait of a young blond woman who looked no older than she was now, dressed in the fashion of the time, a fine cream silk dress and long gauze sleeves. She wore the gold and emerald wedding ring that Cassie herself now wore, a gift from Devlyn.

"That be his lordship's grandmama," Mrs McBride said with a sigh. "I suppose this room is all very old-fashioned now. But he likes it this way."

"It's a warm room, Mrs. McBride."

"I've laid out water upstairs in the dressing room and a wrapper for ye, my lady. It belongs to his lordship's mother. Tomorrow you will get your trunks and ye will be right as rain again. You'll see."

Once upstairs, Mrs. McBride helped her wash and undress, taking her traveling garment away to be aired and brushed clean. A few moments later, Cassie stood at the entrance to Devlyn's bedroom. A single lamp fluttered near the half-tester bed. The small flame wavered against the fragrant breeze, billowing the sheers beneath the opened draperies. In the silence, surrounded by his things, melancholy engulfed her. She did not walk to the bed. Instead, she moved in the shadows and sat down near the window.

The tall clock on the first stairwell landing began to bong the twelfth hour. Mrs. McBride had already retired to her room in the back of the house.

Swiping at her tears, Cassie straightened. She started to turn from the window when she spied the young soldier who had volunteered to remain behind, returning from the stables. She remembered his response, or lack of one, when the lieutenant rode away. She stood, edged to the side of the drapery and leaned nearer to the window. The man walked as if in a hurry and disappeared into the woods. Cassie couldn't see the second soldier, one of the men who had been her escort that the lieutenant had also asked to stay. Her gaze went back to the woods, and the night suddenly felt eerily more ominous, the silence more threatening.

Why had Lord Ware drawn her escort away? It made no sense.

Deciding quickly, she turned away from the window and hurried to the dressing room and found her shoes and cloak. The wrapper she wore beneath was royal blue, dark enough if she was going to follow someone in the night. She raised the hood to cover her light hair. The clock was on its last deep stroke when she reached the first-floor stairwell.

One lamp remained lit near the clock. Cassie bent to turn it off just as silence descended. A floor creaked somewhere in the parlor downstairs.

The sound felt like a gunshot in the silent house. She held her breath. Again, the creak sounded. Dear Lord, someone was in the house.

A pounding started in her chest. She extinguished the lamp, plunging the house into darkness. Afraid to move, she let her senses adjust to the sounds around her. A tree branch banged against the eaves at the side of the house. No other sound met her ears. Whoever was downstairs had ceased movement.

She could neither see nor hear the intruder, but he was there, his presence palpable in the darkness.

Could he tell she was on the first-floor landing?

The branch continued to hit the corner of the house with a staccato *clack, clack*. Still, she did not move.

"I know you are up there, *dushka*."

The voice startled a gasp out of her. It came from the

bottom of the stairs. "Now, that's a brave girl," Nicholas Ivanov said. "No screaming. I have the key to the front door in my pocket. In fact, you cannot get out of this house. And if anyone tries to help you, know I will kill him, *dushka*."

"You won't get away with this. My husband—"

"Is already dead, my lady," Nicholas Ivanov said.

Paralyzed by the words, Cassie could only rasp, "I don't believe you!"

"It's true." She heard movement, footsteps on the foyer floor, then the hiss of a match. His features briefly illuminated, Ivanov held the flame to a lamp and the wick caught, turning the crystal fixture a soft white.

"Now we have light," he said, blowing out the match. "Darkness always makes matters seem worse than they really are." He held up the lamp, and the light traveled to the landing where she stood stricken. "My apologies for involving you in something I did not wish to be your affair, my lady, especially after you were so helpful when I was choosing my granddaughter's violin."

"You really *have* a granddaughter?"

"You would like her." One hand held the lion cane as he lifted the glass lamp high in the other. "I truly would have spared you these unpleasantries. But you are close to your American friends, and I have need of you. Now come, my lady. I will not hurt you."

Cassie could not slow the pounding of her heart. *Think.*

She knew the window in Devlyn's bedroom was opened. She could surely climb out. Ivanov was walking up the stairs, confident in her fear of him. She grabbed the fabric of her cloak and, tearing it off, threw it at him. It tangled in the lamp. She heard an oath in

French and a crash. But she was already running up the stairs. She put her hands against the wall and felt her way down the dark hallway. She flung open her bedroom door, only to be yanked to a halt as a hand grabbed her arm, spinning her backward against the solid warmth of a hard chest. A palm slammed over her mouth, cutting off her scream.

"Shh," Devlyn said against her hair.

Running footsteps sounded in the hallway. He moved her behind him, then locked the door.

A sob of utter joy rose in her throat. She flung herself against him and clung to him as if he were her life-ring in the middle of an angry ocean. The ends of a tattered cloth wrapped around his head trailed down his back. She held him tightly, her voice ragged against his ear. "Ivanov said you were dead."

His arms around her, he said against her hair, "No doubt he thinks I am."

"My escort was called away," she whispered urgently. "I think there is an English soldier here who is not English and that it was all a ruse—"

Devlyn placed a finger against her lips. "I know."

The bedroom door latch jiggled and they both turned. Devlyn set his finger against his lips, warning her to silence as he pulled her away from the door.

"You disappointment me, *dushka*," said the mellifluous voice on the other side of the door. "Now be a good little countess and open the door so we can leave."

A boot smashed against the door and the frame complained on impact.

"You have to go." Devlyn mouthed the words.

In the dim light of the room, she could see he wore no jacket. His shirt was torn and bloodied. That was when she saw he held a military cutlass in his other hand and wore a pistol in his waistband. "It's a long story," he said quietly, and leaned out the window. "And we'll have an exploratory dialogue on the topic and a hundred other things when this is over."

He tore the sheets from the bed. Fighting panic, Cassie looked down on the thirty-foot drop. An old oak had spread upward and across the gravel drive. The sapling branch that had been banging against the eaves overhead was not sturdy enough to support a man's weight. "How did you get in?"

He wrapped the sheet around her waist. "The iron trellis."

Cassie could not see the trellis in the darkness and mist, which meant it was too far to reach. He would have had to walk the crumbling ledge to reach this window. Behind them, the pounding on the door increased and the wood cracked.

A voice rasped from far below the window. "Hampstead!"

He bent over the ledge. "Rockwell, what the hell is taking so long?"

"Maxwell should be in place. Something must be wrong."

Devlyn pulled back and found her watching him in confusion. "As I said, it's a long story. But right now you have to go."

She understood he had a job to do. Remaining with him or delaying her departure any longer would only put him in more jeopardy. Any moment now, the door would be breached. "I love you," she said.

He yanked the cloth in a knot. His lashes raised and she found herself looking into his eyes. "I love you, too," he said, kissed her deeply, then helped her onto the windowsill.

The mist had turned to drizzle. She held her breath as he lowered her five feet over the window ledge. Smoke drifted to her on the breeze, and she tasted it on the drizzle. *Smoke?* Their eyes met and held. He smelled something burning, too.

Fire.

She remembered the sound of shattering glass when she'd thrown the cloak at Ivanov.

"Go, Cassie."

Then he swung her to the trellis and she was suddenly latching on to the rusted bars for dear life. She could see him in the window. But soon hands were helping her to safety, and when she looked up again, he was no longer in the window.

Once Cassie disappeared, Devlyn quit the window and moved to dim the lamp. A mere flame flickered its light over the room. Cassie was safe. Now he had to concentrate on himself.

Devlyn wanted to live through this night. He was no longer drawn to the passion of a fight as he once had been. He approached the ensuing confrontation with Ivanov in silence and with a healthy caution, yet no less prepared to see it finished.

By sheer luck, perhaps fate, the bullet meant for his head had not hit him between the eyes because he had moved at the last second to watch his wife's carriage in the valley. If he had not seen the carriage and reacted, he would now be dead from a bullet in the brain.

He had been only dazed, but the fall had knocked him unconscious when he hit the ground. He remained that way for most of the day. Then he had walked halfway across the valley. When Rockwell and Braeden found him kneeling beside a stream, he'd had no knowledge how he had gotten there. Only a need to get to Cassie. His head still ached.

Tension thrummed through him now as smoke curled from beneath the doors.

He stood in the center of the room and waited, one hand gripping the sword, the other pulling the pistol from his waistband. It had been all of five minutes since Ivanov had begun beating down the door. But the door held against the beating. Finally a shot shattered the stubborn lock. A kick smashed the door against the wall, dislodging plaster from the ceiling and knocking a picture to the floor. Derringer in hand, Nicholas Ivanov filled the doorway.

If Ivanov was surprised to see Devlyn, he masked it well, turning his full attention to the larger gun in Devlyn's hand. Both of them had raised their weapons at the same time. But neither fired.

At one time, Devlyn would have fired and, without batting an eyelash, dropped a man like Ivanov where he stood. He had his reasons for staying his finger on the trigger. He only hoped Ivanov was as predictable as he'd always been. In fact, he gambled on it.

Ivanov always enjoyed the drama of a kill.

"Hampstead!"

"Ivanov." Devlyn grinned slowly and said in a controlled voice, "Does this mean you've refused immunity?"

Ivanov's gun hand shook from his fury. "Did you really believe I would not hunt you down to the ends of the earth for my son's murder?" His gaze dropped to the sword in Devlyn's hand. "You think you are so skilled with a sword."

"Your son made a mistake when he assumed otherwise, Ivanov."

"I am not my son." Ivanov tossed the derringer to the floor.

He took his cane with both hands and slid his sword from its secret anchor within, drawing it forth with a metal hiss. "And know that when I'm finished with you, I will go after Maria and that brat of hers, then your parents. But first I will find your wife. Know that mine will be the last face she will ever see, Hampstead."

His arrogance was such that he had no inkling of Devlyn's mind or that Devlyn wouldn't accept a gentleman's challenge to duel to the death. When Devlyn didn't lower his gun, Ivanov raised stunned eyes to Devlyn's.

He had made a promise to Cassie, Ware, and Maxwell that he would not seek vengeance. He'd left Edinburgh that day determined to change his life, and until thirty seconds ago, he'd been willing to do that and bring Ivanov in alive. But he'd made another promise a long time ago. He would follow his moral conscience and protect that which he held more sacred than his word or some ambiguous oath to the league code which he served. He would protect those he loved. The vow had ultimately been the reason for his joining the Foreign Service.

Smoke swirled in the air, thicker now with the door opened. He heard the crackle of burning wood, felt the heat on the floor beneath his feet from the flames downstairs. The fire had found its way into the bones of the house and it was only a matter of minutes before the entire structure went up.

"Tell me," Devlyn said in a low voice, "what would two godless souls such as you and I know of fair play?"

"I will avenge my son. If not now, then I'll burn with you in hell. Some things are worth dying for, Hampstead."

"At least we can agree on that point, *Excellency*."

Devlyn squeezed the trigger and shot him between the eyes.

By the time Devlyn escaped the house, the lodge was fully ablaze, flames shooting high against the sky. Heat scorched the air. It had stopped two carriages a hundred yards away. Fire lapped at the high chimneys but had begun to battle the downpour as the skies opened up.

The rain soaked Devlyn, washing the soot from his face and arms. He was striding across the length of the yard when his housekeeper suddenly appeared beside him. "We all got oot, my lord," she said. Then he was surrounded by his anxious staff. "But we didna' get the portrait. The blaze was so hot we couldna' reach it. I'm sorry, my lord."

"No people hurt? No pets? We'll live, Mrs. McBride."

He finally saw Cassie. Only when he saw her struggling did he realize Braeden and Rockwell were holding her immobile, but she had finally seen him. When she stopped fighting, Braeden and Rockwell saw him as well. They released her.

Cassie flew into his arms. "You're safe." She kissed him frantically. "I thought . . . oh God, Devlyn, I thought you were dead. I burned it down. It's my fault—"

He pressed a finger against her lips. "You didn't burn it down, Cassie."

And then she was sobbing her eyes out and babbling that he was alive. He let her cry, burying his face against her hair, loving the way she smelled, loving the sound of her voice, loving her. He held her tightly, marveling at the way he felt and how much he loved her. He held his face to the sky and the rain continued to wash over him in cooling rivulets that cleansed him.

He met the somber gazes of Braeden and Rockwell over Cassie's head. If they suspected what had transpired in the house, neither would ever ask.

Glass began to shatter as vast mullioned windows exploded in the heat. He turned with Cassie in his arms. The old lodge continued to put up a valiant fight. He knew another portrait of his grandmother hung in a galley at Sinclair Hall. Maybe in time he could negotiate with his father to have a copy made. In fact, he would go there himself and ask.

The heat finally drove them all backward as another burst of flames forced itself out of the smoke. The roar of falling beams followed. But soon the rain began to beat back the fire, keeping it contained to the lodge and away from the outbuildings. It soaked the trees and ground, dripped from his face and eyelashes and drenched his clothes.

By morning, only a blackened shell surrounding mud and ashes remained.

Chapter 22

After a formal hearing with the council five days later, Devlyn returned to Bathgate. He reined Picaro in at the top of a hill looking down on the small village of Bathgate. Dusk and a sailor's moon shared the same sky with a canopy of stars. Another day had set over a world immeasurably altered from a week ago when he and Cassie had started making plans to rebuild their house. They had chosen to stay at a nearby inn in Bathwick while deciding their future. Devlyn had his staff to house. Cassie had Mary, Frankie and Lady Rose.

No one on the council had questioned the incident in the house or that Ivanov did not survive. There had been one English fatality, the young soldier the lieutenant had left behind. The English soldier who had brought the phantom missive to the lieutenant from Lord Ware had not been a soldier, but an operative sent to draw away Cassie's outrider escort, and he had been talking since his capture.

Sheer luck had brought Rockwell and Braeden out to warn Devlyn that night of the fire, when they had found him in the valley. Stratton's plan to capture Ivanov had failed when they learned Ivanov had not been in his residence for over a month, but had left someone there to make it look as if he were present. It had turned out that Ivanov found out about the meeting and someone had been following Cassie all along. He was after Cassie in the misassumption that Ware would trade Maria for her. But Devlyn never told Cassie this.

There would be no tribunal. The backbone of the consortium was broken, and people like Devlyn, Rockwell, Jameson, and even Eve Macgruder could now breathe easier.

This afternoon, he'd given his notice of retirement from the service. He would not take Ware's offer to rejoin the league.

And as Devlyn rode away from his past and toward his waiting wife, for the first time in his life, he finally felt free.

Cassie was standing at the window overlooking the stable yard when Devlyn rode up and dismounted. She heard him say something to the groomsman that made him laugh. After the groomsman led the horse away, her husband leaned against the fence, his gaze on the distant hills, a restless silhouette framed by the splendor of a velvet sky. The wind tugged at his hair, almost blue-black against the moonlight, his coat a perfect match to the sky. Hugging her shawl to her shoulders, she watched him until he turned his head and found her in the window.

He smiled.

She returned his smile.

And, in her eyes, she knew he recognized her knowledge of what had occurred in the house that night. No judgment. Only a deep abiding solidarity as they continued to stand together to face the past and whatever the future might hold.

Cassie was already in bed when Devlyn climbed in beside her, his feet cold. She cuddled against him as he brought the blankets over them and wrapped her to him. "What will happen to Maria and the baby?" she asked. "She's alone."

"She isn't alone. I received a wire from my father today. He is on his way to Edinburgh."

"Then she and the baby will be cared for."

"The boy is my nephew, Cassie. I will also be there for him."

Cassie nodded. She found his hand on her cheek. "There will never be anything between Maria and I, Cassie."

She smiled gently, pleased that he was concerned for her, but she had ceased being jealous or afraid that his affection belonged to someone else. He did not love Maria and, despite everything, Maria had risked her life to bring Nicholas Ivanov to justice. And now she would have a life and a family for her son. "You are a good man, Devlyn." She smoothed the hair from his brow. "You and I will make a wonderful uncle and aunt."

But first they planned to go to New York for an extended honeymoon while the architects finalized the plans for their new house. He had agreed to do that for her, even though Braeden had told her only yesterday that Devlyn had a tragic aversion to ocean travel and an acute dislike of all things marine. He had fallen off a cousin's yacht when he was nine and, if not for Dominick's quick thinking, might have drowned.

Cassie had not talked to him about his brother, but she knew Devlyn would bring the topic up when he was ready.

She traced a fingertip over the scar running across his shoulder. She kissed the place on his chest over his heart as if she knew his soul needed hers.

"I want you to make love to me," he said, his voice rough against the back of his throat.

His hands splayed over her waist and she lifted her leg to straddle his hips. She accepted all of him inside her, and he began to move rhythmically against the fluid pull of her body, now demonstrably attentive to his needs.

She understood him, moved with him, the same need driving her. And she couldn't imagine loving anyone but him.

She'd never before had that manner of connection to another living soul and sometimes it frightened her in a way nothing had ever frightened her. She'd wake up at night at times, her eyes wide, her breathing rapid, then she would see him beside her and feel peace again. It was a strange notion to be so dependent on one person for her happiness, but she not only accepted it, she welcomed it.

In truth, it was a relief to be able to hand over her heart and her soul to him, easier than she'd imagined, and she felt every bit as liberated as a gosling must feel when it learns to fly. Every part of her knew he felt the same. He let her see what burned in his eyes, let her see that he was a man in love.

Her hair was loose around them, fanned against the pillow as he rode her slowly, filling her again and again, deeply and completely. Loving her. And she answered him hungrily, bringing them both over the world to completion.

* * *

"I have a surprise for you," Cassie said sometime later, and Devlyn peered at her from beneath his forearm.

"Braeden brought me a letter from my father while you were gone," she said.

He pushed up on his elbow and ignored the hair that slid across his eyes. "When?"

"This morning." She nervously reached beneath the pillow and withdrew a packet she had hidden there. "They've been living on their yacht in Cornwall, traveling between there and Spain. Father learned through his own sources that I had gone to Scotland to see Sally Ann, and had allowed me the freedom to find my own way until I was ready to return. He had not learned of our wedding until two weeks ago. Now he's returning. You will finally be able to meet him."

Devlyn harrumphed. "Braeden seems to be spending a lot of time here while I'm gone. Should I be cleaning my dueling pistols?"

She smiled. "I also have something for you." She handed him a packet wrapped in a red satin ribbon.

Devlyn's hand hesitated.

"Braeden has been helping me," she said when he did not take the packet. "You have been very preoccupied these past weeks, so I was not sure how much you might have noticed." She pushed the packet into his hand. "This is my belated wedding gift to you."

He took the packet, turned on his side and slipped the ribbon away. Cassie watched in anticipation as he unfolded the papers and skimmed each page. His smile faded to consternation.

"It is an exceedingly handsome, three-decked, barque-rigged, steamer, propelled by two engines," she said. "It should get us to New York without sinking at the first sign of bad weather."

Devlyn swung his eyes to her face. He felt only tenderness at her attempt to put him at ease by securing passage on what looked like a sturdy vessel. "Is that a reflection of your maritime humor or an actual opinion of the seaworthiness of one of your father's ships?"

"*Your* ship." She nervously twisted her ring. "I bought it for you. Or rather, I traded some major shares in the company."

Devlyn sat up. "You *bought* me a ship." He couldn't contain his disbelief. "Don't most brides give their husbands an embroidered handkerchief or silver cufflinks?"

"Just think," she said impishly, "we can go back and forth from Glasgow to New York all the time on our own screw-steamer."

Devlyn fell back on his pillow, laughter choking him. "That sounds bloody wicked, Cassie."

She threw a pillow at him and he wrestled her back into the bed. "You've married into a family of shipbuilders, my lord. You'll have to learn the difference between a cutter and a brig and a screw-steamer."

"Have I ever told you that I get violently seasick?"

"Have I ever told you I love you?" she said, laughter in her eyes. "Wait until you see what my father plans to bequeath us."

He sobered. "I didn't marry you for your wealth, Cassie."

"I know. But we are very wealthy anyway."

"I have no idea what that means."

"You will." She flung her arms around him. "Don't you see? You will teach me about riding horses, sleeping under the stars and about Gypsies in Scotland and making love. And I'll teach you everything you will ever need to know about cellos and ships."

And about laughter, love and living, he thought.

"Have *I* told you I love you, my lady wife?" he asked softly.

"Many times, my lord."

And as Devlyn's smile opened her heart to the wilds of new love, he was sure of one thing—any lesson she taught him would be a journey that would take them into the rest of their lives. He and his velvet lady were ready to embrace life in a new world.

AVON TRADE *Paperbacks*

978-0-06-089022-3
$13.95 ($17.50 Can.)

0-06-081588-4
$12.95 ($16.95 Can.)

0-06-087340-X
$12.95 ($16.95 Can.)

0-06-113388-4
$12.95 ($16.95 Can.)

0-06-083691-1
$12.95 ($16.95 Can.)